LOST RIVER

ALSO BY J. TODD SCOTT

The Far Empty

High White Sun

This Side of Night

J. TODD SCOTT

LOST RIVER

G. P. PUTNAM'S SONS | NEW YORK

PUTNAM
— EST. 1838 —

G. P. Putnam's Sons
Publishers Since 1838
An imprint of Penguin Random House LLC
penguinrandomhouse.com

Library of Congress Cataloging-in-Publication Data

Names: Scott, J. Todd, author.
Title: Lost river / J. Todd Scott.
Description: New York : G. P. Putnam's Sons, [2020] |
Identifiers: LCCN 2019057044 (print) | LCCN 2019057045 (ebook) |
ISBN 9780735212947 (hardcover) | ISBN 9780735212954 (ebook)
Subjects: GSAFD: Mystery fiction. | Suspense fiction.
Classification: LCC PS3619.C66536 L67 2020 (print) |
LCC PS3619.C66536 (ebook) | DDC 813/.6—dc23
LC record available at https://lccn.loc.gov/2019057044
LC ebook record available at https://lccn.loc.gov/2019057045
p.   cm.

Printed in the United States of America
1   3   5   7   9   10   8   6   4   2

BOOK DESIGN BY KATY RIEGEL

This is a work of fiction. Names, characters, places, and incidents either
are the product of the author's imagination or are used fictitiously, and
any resemblance to actual persons, living or dead, businesses,
companies, events, or locales is entirely coincidental.

For Torri Lee

They were a rough-and-tumble pack, prone to violence. Unbridled. Clannish by nature. Men and women who crossed mountains for solitude. Rumor spread that the Indian word from which their new home took its name meant "dark and bloody ground" but it did not. Kentucke. Kentacke. Kentucky. Meadowland. Grassyland. The place where I was born.

—JESSE DONALDSON,
On Homesickness

LOST RIVER

LITTLE PARIS

A few hours before . . .

Little Paris Glasser stares right into the dead man's eyes and tries to see himself in them.

Danny, or maybe slow, stupid Ricky, once told him such a thing was possible, but this dead Mexican's eyes are flat and black, reflecting nothing at all.

Truth be told, they're downright creepy, like they're painted right on the wetback's skull.

A dead doll's eyes.

Little Paris *almost* reaches out a hand to rub over one of 'em; to wipe that dead man's coal-black stare right off his skeleton smiling face, smear it on his fingers like fresh paint, like fresh blood, but thinks better of it and takes another hit instead from his little homemade pipe, a GE sixty-watt bulb, and lets that hot taste of crank and CRC Bee Blast Wasp & Hornet Killer mule-kick him hard in the chest.

He flickers and flames, blood catching chemical fire.

He holds a mouthful of acid smoke, and it's like he's done swallowed a whole nest of pissed-off yellowjackets, buzzing around now inside his heart and head and behind his own dark eyes.

Goddamn, he finally breathes out.

Goddamn.

The sun's barely up, just peeking over Crown Hill and hardly casting any shadows yet, but last night still hangs on stubbornly beneath the shingle oaks and cockspurs like a drunk not quite ready to leave the party.

Little Paris ain't sober yet either, has barely slept a wink in three days, with that crank coursing through him and Danny's ghost and all them others calling out his name and his daddy forever pissing and moaning about *this* and Jamie always whining about *that* and Hardy at his too-young-to-know-better age playing the damn fool lately and raising a ruckus.

Everyone looking for a piece of him and a taste of their own, including these here damn wetbacks.

Well, one less, anyway.

When he was older than Hardy is now, but still just a boy all the same, he used to steal a little peace of mind at the family plot beneath Lower Wolf's black cherry trees. Lay himself down on them cool, cracked gravestones, where it was quiet and calm and still, where all them old skeletons and ghosts didn't seem intent on bothering anyone, to watch the bluing sky slow to a stop between the leaves and dream about everything and nothing at all.

Not a care in the world.

But it's never quiet now and the world never stops spinning and even the dead can't seem to keep their goddamn mouths shut anymore.

They talk to him all the time.

He hears 'em calling his name.

Like the Good Book says, there just ain't no goddamn peace for the wicked.

Little Paris can't even count on his fingers the last time he slept peaceful the whole night through, and though he ain't dead yet, no gravestone pillow for him, he can't help but wonder what someone might see now if they looked hard and straight into *his* goddamn sleepless eyes.

Imagines it ain't no pretty sight anyway—

Maybe a bunch of yellowjackets, big as your thumb, circling and circling and circling.

Angry as hell.

Trying to fly free of his goddamn skull.

This wetback here sure didn't see much of anything when Little Paris blew his fucking brains out four days ago now.

Never even saw it coming.

He and Jamie drove him back here wrapped in some Cabela's camo tarp and he has a vague memory of telling Jamie afterward to toss the whole fucking mess into Rockhouse Fork or even Yatesville Lake, but Jamie's now standing by Little Paris's Mustang, staring down at the dead man like he's never seen one before.

 Like this one just fucking magically appeared here flat on its back with two bullets in its skull, turning autumn Kentucky colors and going soft, setting off a mighty righteous stink, where his amigos will soon smell him all the way down in ole *Me-hi-co* or wherever the hell it is they breed 'em.

If Jamie wasn't already Glasser blood, weak and thin as it might be on his side of the family, Little Paris might find himself inclined to shoot this sonofabitch, too.

"What'd I say?" Little Paris asks, toeing the gassy body with one of his boots, but *gently*, so it don't rip like an overripe Granny Smith and explode shit and pus everywhere.

A sweet, crisp Granny Smith is one of Hardy's favorite things.

"What the fuck did I say about *this*?"

Jamie shrugs but won't quite look at him 'cause maybe he really can see all them angry yellowjackets behind his eyes.

"I know, coz. I know. Just ain't seen to it yet." Jamie goes to light a Marlboro, that dumb-ass silver ring of his catching fire with the first of the morning sun. "It ain't like we ain't been busy. That last batch this boy brought is *moving*. I'm still cleanin' up with that."

That last batch . . . the white powder H the dead wetback brought them.

DOA, motherfucker.

Everyone around three states wants a taste of it, but no matter how pure or good it is, smack has never really been Little Paris's thing. It makes him too soft, too fuzzy at the edges. The dope sex is good and all, sweet as pure cane sugar or honey, but he likes the way crank sharpens him right up, a whetstone to a knife, and *that* sex ain't half bad, either.

Rough, angry, although sometimes just a little too much of both.

"If Danny were here—" But Jamie stops sudden, wise enough, or sober enough, anyway, not to hold Danny's name in his mouth for too long. Little Paris has already done heard it a thousand times if he's heard it once—from Daddy out loud and damn near everyone else just under their breath—how he ain't like Danny at all.

How Little Paris is gonna be the one to finally let slip through his fingers these mountains that one Glasser or another has held on to with an iron fist for a hundred years or more.

Goddamn.

No, he ain't got the business sense his older brother had, probably never will, but even Little Paris knows a silver dollar when it falls into his hands, so when Jamie told him Danny's wetbacks had started sending their mules out alone, well, then only a damn fool could let *that* slip through his fingers.

Goddamn money for free.

Jamie's since been telling this boy's compadres he got paid and moved on down the highway, like always, but it ain't clear they believe him, although Little Paris figures it might help everyone if they just spoke better fucking English.

It's possible it don't matter quite what they say or even do with the body now, since pride all but dictates his amigos gotta come looking for him anyway, but Little Paris don't put too much stock in that.

One dead or missing Mexican ain't worth anyone's trouble, and *no one* comes calling uninvited on a Glasser in these mountains.

Not in Lower Wolf.

Not for a hundred fucking years.

Although the Big Sandy Power Plant no longer burns the black rock, coal is still in Lower Wolf's bones.

The deep, rolling green of the surrounding hills are knife-cut right down to them old, dark seams. In some places, the land's been blasted away altogether, woods leveled and whole mountains beheaded, hundreds of thousands of years blown sky-high, or so they say.

Strip mining's done left everything raw and exposed, slag scabs and stitches in the hollers. Years back a slurry spill sent a whole mess of arsenic and mercury right into Coldwater Fork and damn near flooded Lower Wolf, too.

Damn near poisoned everything, but folks picked up and moved on as they do.

Eastern Kentucky bears such trials and tribulations proudly, wears her scars openly, the way Little Paris shows off all his ink: colorful tats up and down his body that Daddy hates something fierce, so he gets more of 'em, just to piss the Old Man off.

To remind him he ain't Danny and never will be.

Any day of the week Little Paris can run into a third-generation miner grabbing a cold one at the Crow Bar, men who know their way around a Caterpillar D11 or a Komatsu crawler dozer. Not *his* daddy, or even his daddy's daddy before him, but *his* people all the same.

His land too . . . all cut up and forever bleeding and downright poisonous in some places.

When it rains hard, Lower Wolf's colors come back to life.

These here surrounding hills run red and black like old blood.

Today's gonna be a real corker later, hot as hell, and somewhere through them trees, tiny bugs are already dipping and dancing off the Coldwater.

Bugs like the ones working away on this dead Mexican.

Little Paris scratches at his naked torso, his latest ink still itching him something fierce, a wolf's head all shot up with arrows.

Now he says, "Seems to me Danny's got no say in it, so you better be cleanin' this up. *Today.*"

And Jamie nods through pale cigarette smoke. "Awright, coz. I got it. I said I got it."

"Damn straight you do," Little Paris answers, as he takes another hit off the bulb, setting them yellowjackets buzzing angrily again, before realizing it's just his goddamn cellphone.

When he checks the message, he can't help but smile to himself, 'cause this shitty morning just started shining up already.

Jamie eyes the phone. "You comin' on up to the Big House? We still got rest of that shit to deal with."

They need to step on the last bit of the Mexican's H, make it last as long as possible, since they don't know when they're gonna get more in . . . a problem with Little Paris shooting the messenger the way he did. But it helps this batch is so damn strong, damn near killing folks left and right.

A little goes a long fucking way, but they always come back for more.

"Yeah," Little Paris says. "But toss me some of that new stuff, I gotta run up the way for a short bit. Just a little errand."

Jamie smiles. Knows just the sort of errand that Little Paris likes to handle on his own, the *only* kind that really gets him out of Lower Wolf anymore. He reaches into his white Escalade, then tosses a bag to Little Paris, who catches it out of the air.

Little Paris roots around in it and pulls out a glassine bindle stamped with a skeleton dancing a jig.

DOA, all right, motherfucker.

And his next tat might just be a handful of those tiny skeletons on the side of his neck . . . a whole family of 'em.

He likes that idea a lot.

"You want me to take Hardy back with me?" Jamie asks, prompting Little Paris to turn to the Mustang's backseat, where a little blond boy lies sleeping.

His own boy, Hardy.

Clutching that little toy six-shooter he's so damn fond of.

A Glasser outlaw, just like his daddy.

Someday, all this will be his. These mountains, these woods and hills—all of Lower Wolf—as long as Little Paris don't let it slip through his fingers.

And maybe someday too his boy will lay up on his daddy's gravestone beneath them black cherry trees and let Little Paris whisper to him.

Little Paris leans through the window and puts the bag on the seat next to Hardy.

"Naw, no need to wake him. He can come on up the way with me. I won't be long at all, and she'll want to see him. Always does."

Danny told him during one of his little Tamarack parties that pussy was gonna be the death of him, but Little Paris figures if that's how he's gonna go out, he's just fine with that.

Better than how Danny died, anyway.

Little Paris checks his own gun, a heavy Beretta slipped sideways in his jeans, and stares down at his boy and wonders what he's dreaming and wishes he could sleep just one more day like that.

One last day.

Quiet.

Peaceful.

And not a goddamn care in the world.

DILLON

Dillon Mackey hits his first home run ever, just as his mama, Kara, drops dead in the bleachers.

The ball stays aloft in the hot, heavy air . . . spinning, spinning, spinning . . . even as Kara's on-again, off-again boyfriend, Duane Scheel, falls out right after her.

Looking on, you might think Duane's reaching for Kara—a gentle, almost protective gesture—but you'd be wrong. There's never been anything gentle or protective about Duane Scheel. In and out of Big Sandy RDC since he was sixteen, he once beat a man senseless with a McDermott pool cue.

Once put a blue steel thirty-eight revolver against a Pakistani's jaw in a liquor store holdup when he was barely fourteen, and that was ten years ago.

Now tall, thin, wasted, he doesn't look his age but a hell of a lot older. Nothing much left of him at all, a hastily scrawled stick figure, all right angles and sharp edges.

A Punch doll, a bad joke.

So when he tumbles off the rusty bleachers it's like someone's cut all his strings. He goes slack and silly, lifeless and limp, and falls forward with hardly a sound.

———

Dillon's rounding first, heading to second, smiling and laughing and raising his arms to the sky and happy for the first time in a long time—least since his real daddy, Ronnie, ran them over to that catfish place in Catlettsburg before he went back up to the corrections for a spell—when Junior Heck's mama, Tanya, starts hollerin' loud like a big ole fire truck.

Dillon passes second, slowing down now and the game long forgotten, as mamas and daddies pull away from the bleachers, a few even runnin' low and covering their heads 'cause they think it's a shooting. Eleven-year-old Dillon knows all there is to know about *that*, what to do if someone angry or strung out or just plum crazy ever bursts into Angel Middle. How you hide when you first hear gunshots. But soon as Tanya Heck started up her hollerin', Dillon already knew it weren't caused by no crack of a hunting rifle, no shotgun blast.

Most of them mamas and daddies have figured that out too, calmly looking for their kids, rounding them up with waving arms.

But some others are just standing around, wrapped up in cigarette or vape smoke, staring down, embarrassed, at something lying on the ground.

Dillon takes one last look back over the left-field fence to see if his ball's still flying high, or maybe rolling instead all the way down to the water's edge at the Fork, but there's nothing. That ball, and so many other things the boy can't put a name to, lost forever in the deepening dusk, where fireflies pop here and there like campfire sparks, like that one time he and his daddy camped down at Yatesville Lake, and what a fire *that* was. It was summer then too and way too hot, but his daddy helped him build it up bigger anyway, feeding it every piece of hickory or black cherry they could find, sitting as close as they dared, his daddy hanging one arm over his shoulder like they were good buddies. They burned hot dogs pitch-black but ate 'em anyway, then laid side by side beneath the whited-out stars as his daddy told him stories about the mines and even further back than that, when he was only Dillon's age.

The boy can't remember much of those stories now but still remembers his daddy's hand on his, the warmth of it and the weight of things passed down to him, still gently pressing there.

Dillon never makes third.

He slows down and finally stops altogether between the bases, hands still raised like he's asking a question that's got no answer.

Then he starts up again, shuffling past the pitcher's mound to see for himself what all the damn fuss is about.

He's always been fine with Duane whuppin' up on him, but not his mama.

When it happens, and it happens way too much, he knows just how it feels to get angry or crazy enough to shoot up a school full of little kids who didn't do nothin' to no one or burn this whole damn town down.

His whole world.

Duane's no good and it's all just partyin' and fightin' now anyway that his real daddy's gone. This past winter his mama forgot to pay the electric for two whole months, and Dillon had to sleep wrapped up in one of his daddy's old coats but didn't mind so much 'cause it still smelled like him, like cigarettes and beer and aftershave, safe and familiar. He found some old oak leaves and chewing-gum foil in one pocket, two white pills he sold to Junior Heck in the other, and hidden in the lining a never-used Bluegrass Blowout ticket that he still holds on to and believes is worth a hundred or maybe even a million dollars. So much money he can't even guess what it might be, but he's afraid to scratch it off and see, 'cause if he's wrong, it's like he's done scratched away the last bit of something good in his life.

So he just carries that stupid worthless ticket around all the time. Holds it tight the same way his daddy held his hand 'round that campfire and the way he tries to hold on to his daddy's stories and the flickering, fading memories of his face.

'Cause as young as he is, he already knows just how easy it is to forget.

Like when his mama's hurtin' and hard on her medicine and she damn near forgets *him*, even though she tells him all the time he looks just like his daddy, so much so it makes her cry. But his face don't mean much to her when she's sick like that, when the hurt is so bad she can't remember anything else, whispering how she needs that medicine . . . *needs it so bad, baby* . . . 'cause that pain's like a toothache and a stomachache and a headache and a whole lotta heartache all at the same time.

It's endless.

She *needs* it something fierce . . . and that means she sometimes needs a peckerwood like Duane to get it for her. She calls Duane *Doctor* like it's a joke and they all have a good laugh at that—good ol' Doc Duane, who never even finished high school.

But other times his mama goes alone to see Little Paris.

Everyone calls him the *main man . . . a badass motherfucker . . .* and she's always cryin' after, 'cause he's worse than all the others who've ever come around. Worse than Duane and even that Jerry Dix, who wasn't all that bad, all things considered. He used to high-five Dillon and laugh this goofy cartoon *hi-yuck* and say stuff like *Call me Jere, little bear,* just like they were friends, best buddies. And sometimes when his mama was all partied out, Jere used to sit on the porch with him and share a Marlboro, watching winter stars through the trees.

Jere could even name two or three of 'em, which was more than his daddy could do, until his mama told him that Jere got sideways with Little Pairs, so Dillon figures he ain't laughin' now, not ever again.

But on the rare day when his mama's not on her medicine, when she's clear and her eyes shine bright as those stars, bright as that burning campfire, she can be so sweet and gentle it makes him cry, which ain't no grown-up thing to do, although Dillon's watched his mama cry plenty.

A day just like today, when his mama finally felt good enough to come watch him play for the first time this summer and even put on some of that Avon and brushed her hair and found herself some clean clothes and promised him *today was a new day*, just another one of a hundred or million promises that'll never come to anything but somehow still mean everything, a million more lies this boy will always and forever be willing to believe and forgive, 'cause his mama was awake and present and calling him *baby* and he was gonna get in this one good day with her.

Until Duane had showed up stinking of beer and smoke and said he'd done got his hands on some of that new Glasser medicine everyone wants, everyone's been going on about, so why don't he just come on along for the ride and share a little taste?

But at least his mama held *his* hand crossing the gravel lot before the game.

Held on to him.

With that peckerwood Duane trailing a few steps behind, wobbly and barely there, drifting sideways like his cigarette smoke.

Dillon doesn't even get to where the dirt infield turns to grass before Tanya, her own thick Avon a fresh mess, runs out onto the field, flabby arms wide—

"Oh, Dillon, honey, you don't wanna see this."

She goes to wrap him up in those arms even as he pushes past her, but she grabs at him again . . . calling him *honey, baby* . . . just like his mama does . . . *just like his mama* . . . and that's when he knows it's gonna be bad.

You don't wanna see this . . .

Real bad . . . worse than funny Jere probably takin' a bullet to the head or his daddy goin' up to the corrections or Duane whuppin' up on his mama and leavin' him with his own bruises.

Like a toothache and a stomachache and a headache and a whole lotta heartache all at the same time.

It's gonna hurt worse than all those things for a long, long time.

That's when Dillon Mackey starts running again.

Cryin' all the world for his mama.

TREY

1

Kara Grace comes back to life.

Trey used to think that was a miracle but he's not so damn sure anymore.

Dobie holds her head off the grass, hands tangled in her flaxen hair, tossing the spent Narcan aside. She needed only two hits and some oxygen to bring her back from the dead and no chest compressions at all.

Not too bad, all things considered.

Kara blinks, spits, then nearly throws up. She sucks in air slow like she's sipping out of a straw and starts breathing again with a bang and rattle, a cold truck engine turning over.

Her eyes are blown wide, but it's hard to know what they're seeing, and they shine with bright, fresh tears.

Alive.

Dobie says quietly to no one in particular—

"She's going to be all right. All right."

Trey's not so damn sure about that, either.

2

There are no miracles for Duane Scheel.

He stays dead right where he fell beneath the bleachers as Little League kids and parents gawk at him. Plenty have seen a dead body before, so it's no big deal, not really. Even straight-up funny to some, because Scheel pissed all over himself. They smell it and make little effort to pretend they don't.

A few snap pictures or run a minute of video. Trey worries how he'll look on Instagram or Facebook or Snapchat or whatever—*professional, serious*? Adult. He should have gotten his hair cut a month ago but wonders if he'll even be in focus at all.

Just another shadow lurking in the back, looking at the ground.

All anyone cares about is the body anyway.

The dead are always the real stars of the show.

Dead Duane's no loss for Angel, Kentucky.

Trey didn't know Scheel enough to say hi but knew all *about* him: a miserable piece of shit running around with the Glassers and only worth crossing the street to avoid. He was bad news, contagious like someone sick, like all the Glassers and their kin. But Trey does know

Kara Grace a little. They both went to Lawrence County High, although she's several years older. He's seen her driving around town with her son—*Dale? Dalton?*—who's now wrapped up tight in the arms of Tanya Heck, fighting to hold him back while Dobie works on his mom. Kara must have had him when she was, what, fifteen, sixteen? Trey can only guess at the boy's age, but he's already taller than her, even if he weighs only a few pounds more.

Kara is frail, made of paper. The boy is all dirty arms and legs and angry intensity, refusing to let her out of his sight.

He breathes right along with her, breathing for her, willing her to stand up and be okay.

Trey could go over and put a hand on his shoulder, lie to him that it's going to be all right, *just fine*, the way Dobie did, the way Dobie always does. But Trey thinks it's better to just tell it straight, how it's not fine and not likely to ever get any better and how the kid's probably staring at the rest of his life laid out there on the grass; how he's always going to carry his mother's burdens.

She'll forever be a heavy weight on his chest, on his heart.

Some fucking miracle that is.

But Dobie's already snapping to get Trey's attention, telling him to wait with Kara so he can take another look at Duane.

Dobie slides over, politely asking the crowd to move back and give him some room, but the circle's drifting away anyway. Phones flick off one after another, show's all over. Angel PD will roll up soon and no one wants to answer questions about what's happened here or what they saw. No one wants their name in a report and no one ever knows anything anyway and no one cares.

They all just want to get on home.

Dobie gently rolls Duane over and checks the dead man's pulse a second, even a third, time. Duane must have taken a bigger hit than Kara, maybe twice as much, although he also barely weighs more than she does. Both look like hell froze over . . . and neither are going to show up well on YouTube or the local news.

Like Kara's, Duane's eyes are open, too.

Dead but still fucking staring.

What are you seeing now?

Trey kneels next to Kara to steady her, grabbing her hand in his own, an intimate gesture with a girl he barely knows.

He runs his other hand along her bare arms, tracing the tracks beneath his gloved fingers, all the tiny lesions and the tender, delicate bruises. Those pinprick holes that run along her wasted veins and the hollow places where the flesh has fallen through, that she tried so hard to hide today with makeup, a dusty foundation even thicker than Tanya Heck's Walgreens warpaint.

The last few years of Kara Grace's life written all over her skin.

Trey scans the ground for a needle, but Kara's suddenly awake now, alert and squeezing his hand, even though there's no strength behind it. Like holding hands with a fucking ghost.

She asks if Duane's okay. If she's dead already—

Am I finally in Heaven?

And with her son looking on and staring hard at them both, Trey can't do anything *but* lie, and tells her it's going to be all right.

You're fine, Kara, just fine.

Not Heaven, he says, *but you're still alive, right here in Angel. And I guess that'll have to do.*

And although she didn't even bother to ask, he also tells her that her boy's right here waiting for her.

3

Duck Andrews, the Angel PD uniform who shows up, parks his quiet cruiser behind the van.

Zero hurry, not even bothering with lights and sirens.

Everyone calls him "Duck" because of his weird, left-leaning waddle, and although Trey's dad worked with him for a time, Trey doesn't know the man's real name, either.

"Duck" was about the nicest thing his dad ever called him.

Now he walks over with a spit cup in hand—looks like he had DQ for dinner—and stands over Trey and Dobie, watching intently but not offering any help.

He blinks at Trey once, sizing him up, then ignores him.

"What we got, Dob?"

Dobie gets off his knees, rubbing his gloved hands on his pants. The purple nitrile dusts him with powder like Kara's makeup.

"One cold, the other lukewarm." That's nothing like the way Dobie normally talks, but he's playing tough for Duck, and Trey wonders why he even bothers. Duck is never going to think he's tough, is never going to think anything nice about him at all. "I gave her the usual. She'll be okay in a bit."

The usual is four milligrams of Narcan per hit, enough to bring an OD back from the edge, but not so much that it kicks their high completely out from under them. Dobie's taught him that if you pull them back too hard, too fast, they wake up pissed and already in withdrawal, eager to fight.

Dobie turns to Trey, permanent charcoal circles under pale blue eyes. He's tired, always tired. Unmarried, no kids, Dobie stays up alone late watching shitty satellite TV or reading weird books, history no one cares about anymore. Dobie believes in aliens and ghosts and Bigfoot and admitted to Trey he's had serious trouble sleeping ever since he was twelve, when hooded men burst into his family's trailer in Fallsburg. The whole thing made the papers across three states then, big news before Trey was even born, and it's still possible to find those black-and-white photos of a young Dobie, the only survivor, sitting in the back of an Angel PD cruiser, his scared face caught in a sudden flash.

Dobie asks Trey, "What did you say her name was?"

"Kara. Kara Grace."

Tanya Heck, hearing the name, calls over—

"Kara was married to that Ronnie Mackey. You know Ronnie, Delia's boy from down the way? He's up at Big Sandy RDC for a spell again. This here is his boy, Dillon."

She pushes Dillon Mackey forward like she's presenting him for some grand award, and Duck considers the boy before looking past him, out past the bridge, past the gathering night.

Park lights are coming up now, bats circling. It's humid, still pushing eighty, and damp circles are already widening under Duck's armpits. The uncertain sky is low and close, holding its breath, threatening rain, and maybe Duck is searching somewhere out there for distant lightning.

Or maybe, like Trey, he's just wishing he was anywhere but here.

Duck watches as the knots of other parents and kids make their way to their trucks, heading home. He doesn't even bother trying to call them back over.

"Yeah, I know her some, and this one, too." Duck points at Duane's quietly cooling body. "A real piece of work."

But Duck says it like he doesn't know anything about Duane Scheel or Little Paris or any of the Glassers. Like they don't all buy him beers at the Crowbar.

"That's one way to put it," Dobie agrees.

Duck ignores Duane and Kara and Dillon, turning instead to check out the recent paint job on Dobie's van. Dobie had it done over in Ashland and Trey thinks it looks pretty sharp, all things considered. At least professional.

But when Duck turns back, he's not smiling, lips drawn like a white line across his ruddy face. He has one of those faces that's always red and splotchy, forever sunburned.

"I like what you did here, Dob. The new name's nice. The way you put *extreme* on the bumper there with that big ole *X*. Even painted *police* on the left panel."

Duck looks closer, really leaning in to it. "Does that say *tactical*, right there?

Dobie, embarrassed, just shrugs.

Duck spits in the DQ cup again and then steps real fucking close to make sure Dobie really hears him—

"Just 'cause you're gettin' some fat check from the county, got yourself fancy new lights and sirens, don't make you the law now. Got that?"

Trey figures the same can be said about all the remaining cops that make up Angel PD, but Duck is suddenly some kind of goddamn mind reader, because he turns and eyes Trey hard.

"Boy, just what the fuck are *you* looking at?"

And like always, Trey keeps his mouth shut.

4

Angelcare Rescue Service started out as American Med, a one-man, one-van band.

A private ambulance service Dobie Timmons got up and running after he cleared his EMS certifications.

For years, he contracted with several of the hospitals around Lawrence, Martin, and Boyd Counties, shuttling nonemergency patients between Our Lady of Bellefonte and Three Rivers and the VA. He also ran bodies around for the county coroner and lent an occasional hand on bigger callouts, like that six-car pileup on I-64 in '15, and the gas fire two summers ago at the Marathon on Joshua Branch.

But last year, when things got bad around Angel and the ODs started piling up faster than even county E-911 could manage—far more than the city police department or the county sheriffs seemed to care about—both Lawrence and Martin County hired Dobie to triage some of those calls, a way to stem the bleeding. For some reason, Duck and the other Angel cops took that personally.

They've *made* it personal . . . and Dobie makes for an easy target.

It's not just the goofy name change and that gaudy new paint job on his old van or even the silly all-black tactical jumpsuit he wears. Everyone knows just how bad Dobie always wanted to be a real cop, until his eyes proved even worse. But Dobie sees well enough and a hell of a lot better than most: all of Angel's problems and the way it's slowly dying around them. How the whole place is sick, contagious, like Duane Scheel, gray and hollowed out and wasting away. Lung cancer's always been bad in Angel anyway—the cigarettes and coal mines— but this is somehow different, a straight-up biblical plague. Trey's got only thirty hours of his first-responder course, still working his way to his EMT-B certification, and doesn't really have a clue yet *what* he's doing when they get called out, but Dobie takes their shared responsibility seriously enough for them both.

He's saved dozens of lives alone since Trey started riding with him. Like Kara Grace, for at least one more day.

But Dobie carries around every one of those lives he *doesn't* save too, every one that doesn't make it. *He makes it personal.* Dobie can't, or won't, let one go, even a piece of shit like Duane, who probably never said a decent word to him or ever gave him a second thought.

The dead drag Dobie down. They pile up like the extra pounds he seems to put on every day.

He weighs three-fifty if he weighs three hundred, and for something you can't see, something you can't touch or hold or that might not even exist at all, Angel's lost souls add immeasurable weight to Dobie Timmons.

He's always going to carry *their* burdens.

Just like it's written all over Duck Andrews's face with biblical certainty that all those souls or lives aren't worth an extra minute or hour or day.

Not worth *his* time or effort at all.

"I'll transport Duane," Dobie says, ignoring Duck's look as the other man spits thick into his cup again. "You want to search him first? Take a second to talk to Ms. Grace?"

There's also the issue of the boy, Dillon, but Dobie doesn't even get a chance to ask about that, since Duck's already shaking his head—

"Same old nonsense, same old bullshit," Duck says and sighs, heavy and exaggerated. "And it's all the fucking same to me." He pulls at his gun belt, way too tight beneath the half-moon of his stomach. He's moving into Dobie's weight class faster than he'd ever be willing to admit. "Hey, you hear about that mess down at Lower Wolf?"

"Yeah," Dobie answers, wary for the first time. Lower Wolf is the name of both a road and a creek in Tomahawk about thirty-five miles south of Angel, way down in Martin County, but it's a lot more than that. A local legend. A *curse*, an implied threat. Lower Wolf is Glasser stomping ground, family land that goes back generations, larger than life and hardly defined by a few marks on a map or contained by some fence line. The Glassers have multiple homes and trailers spread across a hundred acres or more down there, including weed fields hidden along the creek and old barns and shacks for Saturday-night illegal cock- and dogfighting.

The sort of secrets everyone knows.

"Some, not much," Dobie adds. "A shooting of some sort, so they say."

Duck nods. "A whole lotta shooting earlier today. The FB and I, the DEA, all of 'em down there right now, trying to sort the hell of it out. Everyone dead, the whole lot of them."

"Everyone?" Trey asks, suddenly forgetting where he is and who he's talking to. But everyone is a lot, almost unimaginable, when it comes to the Glassers.

Duck stares and blinks at him again, slow and heavy, like he's finally waking up and seeing Trey for the first time.

"Hey, you seen that worthless daddy of yours lately? How's he doing?"

Dobie starts up and steps in. "Now, Duck, you know there's no call for that . . ."

But Duck rolls on. "I'll call it whatever the fuck I want. How about *your* mama, boy, how's she gettin' on, too?"

Trey goes still, clenching his fists. His dad taught him to box and he knows how to take a punch, how to throw one. How to shift his weight and lead with his shoulder and turn hard into his hips.

Stronger than his slight frame suggests, he's a southpaw and most never see it coming.

But Duck's dumb, not stupid, and his pretend-bored eyes are already locked on Trey's tense, whitened knuckles.

"Christ on a cross. You do that, son. *Please* do that," Duck says, still eye-fucking Trey, before casually turning back to Dobie and spitting in his cup. "Anyway, maybe not quite everyone . . . Don't know about Little Paris."

Little Paris is the youngest Glasser, not much older than Trey. Danny was the oldest, but he's been dead a couple of years already. Then there's Ricky, the middle one, and Old Man Glasser himself. Also, a distant cousin—Jamie Renfro—who's a Glasser in all the worst ways but name.

Trey knows all about them, and his dad crossed paths with most of them more than once.

In Angel, everyone crosses paths with the Glassers eventually.

Duck hooks a thumb at Duane's body. "Might have something to do with everything going on 'round here lately. No one's talking much about it, though."

Everything going on 'round here lately is Duck's shorthand for the latest firestorm of fatal ODs over the last seventy-two hours. Bad ones, worse than normal, and normal for Angel isn't good by any stretch. A hot batch of heroin spreading around the county and dropping folks like flies, but hardcore users like Kara and Duane are searching it out anyway, risking it all, because it's supposed to be that good. Trey and Dobie have been running ragged on little sleep—Dobie even less than usual—trying to keep up, and they can't. Not even close.

But Duck Andrews looks well rested and unbothered.

"Well, I don't know anything about it," Dobie says.

"'Course you don't. *But . . .* they might just need you down there to haul all them dead bodies out, right?" Duck presses.

"Might," Dobie concedes. "Anything's possible."

"If you do, you call me too, hear?" Duck braces Dobie, just to make sure he does hear him loud and clear. "Straightaway now. I need to know what the fuck's going on down there. Ask some questions, take some pictures or something."

Since Lower Wolf is out in Martin County, Sheriff Dunn and his deputies are probably working it, leaving Lawrence County and city police like Duck on the outside looking in. But if the recent whispers about Duck and the Glassers are true, all those long-standing rumors about Dunn too, a lot of folks are about to be damn desperate to find out what happened down there. Everyone on edge.

The sort of secrets everyone knows.

"Jesus, just make yourself fucking useful for once," Duck continues, then rolls his eyes over to Kara, who's finally sitting up. Still weak. Still out of it. But come tomorrow, she'll be right back at it, chasing that high again even if it kills her.

And it will, despite what Dobie's done here for her tonight, because most days it doesn't matter what Dobie does. Duck's made his point.

"Sure, Duck, whatever you say," Dobie agrees. Always trying to be agreeable.

Satisfied his work here is done, Duck takes one long last look at Kara and Duane. Then shakes his head and starts back to the cruiser.

"Now get these two outta my fucking park. It's embarrassing."

5

Whenever Dobie's out of the van, like now, raiding the Marathon for 5-Hour Energy shots, Mountain Dews, hot dogs, bear claws, and a big bag of Takis, Trey slips in his earbuds and listens to his latest beats.

This is how he sees the world now, how he *hears* the world. His recording setup's not much, just enough to get him off the ground, but when he's mixing and looping, it really does feel like he's flying.

Can easily get lost up there in his own head.

His current favorite group is American Vampires, out of Texas. Their music is nearly impossible to find, scattered like clues, so underground no one even knows who they are.

The band members' names are mysteries too, little puzzles to solve—

Anthem X Cross. Master the World. My Beautiful Disaster.

It's possible there's no band at all, just some kid in some other shitty little town like Angel, another Trey with a laptop.

Every few weeks he goes over to the Ten-Thirty Club in Charleston to listen to whatever band's come through, but most of the time he's content to just mix his own tracks in his bedroom. It keeps him close to home anyway, so he can keep an eye on his mom. He can later download them to his phone, forever revising and reimagining them, like the one he's listening to now, little more than drones and glitches and a downtuned sample of Ben E. King singing *the land is dark* again and again. But he thinks it has promise.

"Stand by Me" was once his mom's favorite song, and he's only just started searching for the beating heart of it. It takes a lot of work remixing something new out of something old, out of things long forgotten.

Trey figures everything you could ever want to know about him is exposed in the music he makes—*verse, chorus, verse*—his whole goddamn life nothing more than that most basic of song structures, forever stuck on repeat. *Rewind, replay.* And although he's flying high when he's mixing his beats, high enough to almost imagine he might escape this place, it never feels he's going far or fast enough to truly get him the hell out of Angel for good.

The land really is fucking dark . . .

Now Trey fishes around in his pocket for the glassine stamp bag he pulled out of Kara's hand, that intimate moment when her fingers grasped for his, too afraid to let go. He risks a single glance toward the Marathon, checking for Dobie's return, before holding the bag up to the parking lot lights, their sodium glow playing tricks on his eyes, shooting the milky powder inside with purple streaks. It's pretty, like one of those bottles of colored sand you might win at a county fair, but the color's far from right, unnatural, and Trey's got a pretty good eye for these things now.

That lavender dusting, the color of wildflowers along Old U.S. 23, shouldn't be there.

If Kara had been paying attention, she might have seen it, too. And maybe at the last moment she did, because unlike Scheel, she didn't snort or shoot the whole bag. Some small part of her held back just enough, knew better.

There's a warning stamped on that bag that's far easier to see, to understand, than the adulterated color.

A tiny dancing skeleton and three letters underneath that—

DOA.

As Dobie and Duck were talking, Trey had searched her for more DOA stamp bags. Bindles, pills, anything.

Furtive movements, practiced gestures, as the boy Dillon watched him mute the whole time.

Trey did the same again when they loaded Duane into the back of the van, giving the dead man a good once-over. Since he's been riding with Dobie, Trey's raided kitchens and bathrooms and bedside drawers, shoeboxes in closets and inside-out pockets and kicked-aside shoes. Patted down shirts and run quick fingers into bras. He always leaves the money and the credit cards, the rings and watches, so he can tell himself later he's not some goddamn thief, robbing the dead and dying. All he cares about are the pills and powder, the little bags like the one in his hand. Which is so fucking funny, because if the ODs do regain consciousness, that's all they ever care about, too.

Take it all, they say . . . just not that next hit, their next fix. Even if the last one almost killed them.

Maybe Trey's not a thief, but somehow, he feels fucking worse.

Dobie finally trudges out of the Marathon, a thick shadow in the overhead lights, a plastic bag swinging in an invisible hand.

He makes a key-turning motion with the other, signaling Trey to start her up.

Already another call.

6

Trey recognizes the car parked sideways in the middle of the street.

Like it rolled to a stop there and just gave up.

It's Mark Crosby's old metallic-blue Firebird, the one with mismatched whitewalls and the University of Kentucky license plate.

Trey also recognizes the hysterical girl standing next to it, waving her arms around in weird circles as they approach.

Anna Bishop, trying hard to take flight. Working her arms so hard, so furiously, Trey half expects her to really rise off the ground. They went out once in high school, got burgers over in Catlettsburg and fooled around in the back of his mom's borrowed car, and Anna wore this perfume then that had smelled like sugar and smoke, rich and exotic and expensive. Maybe she'd borrowed that from *her* mom. She's since changed her hair color and lost weight, more than a few pounds, just like Kara, but the girl she used to be—that Trey remembers—is still there somewhere.

An afterimage, superimposed over whoever she is now.

Her eyes are wide in the van's bright headlights—halos of harsh, unforgiving light—and she's like the proverbial deer, trapped there, with nowhere to run. She has her cellphone in one hand and the

Firebird's driver's door is open, where all six-foot-three of Mark Crosby is sitting still and unmoving, folded in on himself.

His head slumped forward, touching the wheel.

Mark Crosby was once a hell of a basketball player.

Had a solid jab step and a fadeaway jumper smooth as butter. Wanted to play at UK, but as good as he was, and he was good, he wasn't *that* good. He got a scholarship instead to Eastern Kentucky University.

Trey had a couple of scholarship offers too, at both EKU and Centre, over in Danville, but not for sports. He really wanted to major in music, but since his dad left, he doesn't ever bother to think about that anymore.

Last he heard, Mark had blown out a knee, or maybe it was a shoulder. Dropped first the scholarship, then college altogether, and supposedly got on with Brown's Food Service. Several of Trey's old classmates have jobs there too, or at Woodland Oil or AK Steel in Ashland. Ten years ago, they might have all worked Licking River mine, but no longer. There's still some good work to be had at the Big Sandy Power Plant (although it converted over to natural gas a few years ago) and even the Catlettsburg Refinery, and when the refinery's lit up by a thousand lights, Trey can still imagine, like he did when he was a little kid, that it's some sort of spaceship come down to Earth, something that could take him far from Angel.

On most days, you can still smell it—sulfur, steel, oil—miles away.

But Trey can't remember when he last saw Mark Crosby alive. Never knew Mark and Anna were dating or even knew each other.

And he doesn't know the *other* body in the car—a young girl. Younger than Anna, pretty, delicate, with lots of dark hair. She has tiny bird tattoos winging their way up her neck, taking flight over the gentle curve of her shoulder.

Swallows or sparrows gracing her slim throat.

In the glow of Dobie's flashlight, they look like pencil sketches on her bluing skin.

Feathers, maybe.

Or fingerprints.

Her eyes are open, but she's been gone long enough. Longer, even, than Mark.

Too long to save.

She finally got to fly away, another tiny bird.

Mark and Anna were driving around Angel with a dead girl.

7

Anna's edgy, nervous. She picks at her ragged, bitten nails and they're bloody moons.

She shuffles the sleeves of an EKU sweatshirt up, down, up, down, like she's shuffling a deck of cards.

She swears over and over she doesn't know the girl's real name and barely remembers anything about her at all. *She was Mark's friend,* she says. He called her *Daisy, Ruby, Trudy,* depending on his mood, and his moods were worse and wilder than bad weather.

Changing all the goddamn time.

Anna finally settles on *Ruby.*

Ruby's too far gone even for Dobie—dead two hours or more at least—but he tries hard to save Mark Crosby. Four Narcan shots, full chest compressions. Trey hands Dobie whatever he asks for, trying not to stare back into Ruby's open, empty eyes, although they follow him wherever he moves. Dobie finally beats on Mark's chest, trying to punch some life back into him, as Anna stands by and cries dry tears. Like Trey, she knows it's too late.

The only one who still doesn't seem to know it, who won't accept it, is Dobie, who keeps hammering away at Mark's chest, until Trey's own chest hurts.

Anna made the call *after* Mark passed out at the wheel, after she couldn't shake him or beat him awake either, and then only because he's the one who usually scored for them.

The one who always held their money.

Now she's in full withdrawal, already dope sick. Her body rattles and rolls and it's not close to cold outside, still only this constant, damp August hot that leaves Trey feeling like he's got a wet towel over his face.

When Dobie finally gives up, he takes a moment to himself, pacing around the Firebird. Circling the car again and again as he lights up a Marlboro.

The stoplight above him drops red to green with a loud, lonely click, like a coin in a slot, but the street remains empty. No one is going anywhere. This part of Angel is vacant and unused all the time now, with most of the shops long boarded up or shut down.

The street runs heavy with deserted shadows. Dozens and dozens of dead windows, like Duane's eyes from before.

Like Ruby's eyes now, reflecting the van's emergency lights and not much else.

Trey stands with Anna in front of all the empty stores, trying to strike up a conversation with her while Dobie circles and smokes.

She remembers him. They remember each other. But she only half listens, shaking off his questions, her whole body still trembling.

"I don't know anything about anything," she keeps saying, wiping at sunken cheeks, and there are words written in faded Magic Marker on her hand.

"No one ever does," Trey says. "I don't know shit either, Anna, but here we are."

He fakes a smile. They're just old friends catching up, standing in the street with two dead bodies in a car next to them, like it's the most natural thing in the world.

He keeps one eye on Dobie, trying to read whatever's written on Anna's hand.

"So how long were you and Mark a thing?"

"*A thing*," Anna repeats—an empty echo—like the whole idea is strange that anyone would think of them as anything at all.

Trey knows she's calculating, buying time she doesn't have with a cigarette of her own now, shaking one free from a soft pack of Newports and lighting it with practiced efficiency.

The end burns cherry as she inhales. She tilts back and forth . . . *foundering* . . . that's the word Trey reaches for, remembers. She's like an old boat at sea, shipwrecked, hoping the Newport steadies her.

"A year or two. I was taking online courses. Didn't work out."

And Trey doesn't know if she's referring to the courses, to dead Mark in the seat near her, or both. But she breathes deep again and lets the cigarette burn brighter until it makes her face younger, prettier.

It finally lights the words scrawled unevenly on her hand—
Don't forget.

"Mark got hurt," she says. "Had all those surgeries on his knee. He was driving a truck for Brown, a good job, but after a long day, that goddamn knee would just start *screaming* at him, least that's how he described it. He was taking the endos for it, then the roxys and oxys, all legal and everything . . . forties right on up to eighties. But when those got fuck-all expensive and stopped helping, and Brown let him go and there wasn't hardly any money comin' in anymore . . . and, well, you know how *that* story goes."

Trey does. Has read the book cover to cover. It starts with a perfectly legal scrip—Endodan, Roxicet, OxyContin—until the habit really takes hold, until it gets its claws in deep and all the local doctors and stolen pads are burned through and the trips to Lexington or Charleston get too risky, and it ends with whatever's cheap and easy to get now.

It always ends with the Glassers . . . and the stuff in the stamp bag he lifted off Kara Grace.

"See, it was all about his knee, Trey. Just tryin' to work, you know? Keep working. Bills gotta get paid, always another one due." And she's right, someone always owes something, and maybe that's a good enough explanation for why she's standing here in the street, thin and wasted, with two dead people in her boyfriend's car.

"How about the girl, Ruby?"

"Just a party friend, that's all."

"What did she take, Anna? What did you all take tonight?"

Anna waves away smoke in the hot night. Sweat's now beaded on her face, in the hollows of her throat.

Trey steps close, too close. He hates this and the way it makes him feel.

Lowers his voice. "Tiny skeleton. DOA?" Then imagines he catches a bit of that old perfume, a nice memory on the wind. But her skin only smells like tinfoil; like chemicals and pencil shavings.

Anna blinks. "Sure, maybe. Everyone all over is talkin' about it."

"Where did you get it? The Glassers? Little Paris?"

Now she studies him, suspicious, as her addict brain shifts into high gear at the thought of her connection, her supply . . . *her lifeline* . . . being threatened.

"Why do you care, Trey? What's it matter to you? You don't mess with this stuff."

But there's a question there too, hanging by a thread at the end of her words—

She really, really *hopes* she's wrong. Hopes maybe *he* can hook her up, now that Mark is gone.

"I didn't think you did, either," he says.

She shrugs. "I was taking benzos for my anxiety, then I hurt my back and . . ."

And as she talks, falling down a rabbit hole of excuses and reasons, Trey realizes just how little he knows about her now, how he never really spared another thought for Anna Bishop back then, after they fumbled around in his mom's car that one autumn night and she dumped him a week later for someone else. Sure, he's seen her around some, like Kara, like Mark, like so many others, but he stopped really looking for her long ago, and it really hasn't been all that long at all.

Just a couple of years.

Somehow, like most everything and everyone in his life, she became little more than background noise, just some static and hum, that two-second space of emptiness between songs on any album.

All these people he once knew now all lost, all boarded up and vacant or moved on too, like the whole town itself.

Two seconds . . . two years . . . is *nothing* . . . but in Angel it's a lifetime.

He finally stops her. "That's fine, whatever. But look, that new stuff, it's bad, Anna. Real bad. It's killing folks."

She sighs, smiles. "But it works, right? Fucking unbelievable, best there is right now. And that might just be worth it."

But Dobie's pacing is slowing down now, and Trey knows his time with Anna is running short.

"You still have any on you? How about Mark or Ruby? Somewhere in the car?"

He knows she doesn't, otherwise she wouldn't have called 911. But Anna's eyes still narrow, as those wheels in her head turn faster.

"No."

"Duck, the other cops, they're going to be here soon," Trey says. "Damn near any second now. They're going to search you, the car, everything. You've got two dead people here, Anna, and if you're still holding on to the shit that killed them, well, that pretty much makes you an accessory." Trey doesn't know if this is literally true, has no idea what the law on it really is, but it sounds good. It sounds *official*, like something his dad would have said if he were still here. "Let me hold on to whatever you have, keep it safe, until they're done with you."

She barks out a laugh. "Sure, sure. I get it. You're doing *me* a favor. Just being a friend. So where were you a year ago, when I really could have used your fucking help?"

She's about to add *before all this*, but instead flicks her cigarette into the street, trailing sparks. Straightens her hair with a shaking hand, trying to look respectable.

"Hey, you still into music, Trey? That was your thing in high school, right? The band or something."

"Yeah," he says, frustrated Anna won't focus. She probably can't walk or think in a straight line. "I played clarinet in the orchestra, drums during marching season. We went out that one time, but it didn't last. Guess I wasn't cool enough."

She laughs again. But this time it's *almost* real, just natural enough that it steals a small smile from him, too.

"Oh, sure, but you know, almost nothing lasts around here." Now she smiles more. "What, you don't think I remember? I do. Of course I do. You were so sweet, so nice. I didn't want to break your heart. What the hell did I know back then?" She risks a glance at the Firebird, at Mark's cooling body and Ruby, or whoever she truly is, huddled there next to him. They don't look real, but they are. "Your daddy left Angel, right? That's what I heard. And your mama . . . I mean, I've heard Little Paris talk . . ."

Trey's smile disappears as quick as it appeared. He's not talking about *his* own shipwreck of a life, not standing here in the middle of the street with Anna Bishop. "Little Paris is a lying sack of shit."

"Oh, I know. Trust me, I know that as well as anyone," Anna says, in a suddenly gentle, sad way that both embarrasses him and somehow makes him feel fucking worse.

"Jesus, Trey, we're really not in high school anymore, are we?"

Just as an Angel PD cruiser finally turns down the street, slow and deliberate, pinning them in its headlights.

"No. No, we're not," he says. Followed by a long, awkward silence, until Trey finally points at her hand. At the words written there.

"Hey, what's that mean? What're you trying not to forget?"

Anna looks down as if seeing the letters scrawled there for the first time, reads them aloud to herself silently, her lips moving wordlessly.

"I don't know. Got no idea. I think Ruby wrote them." She rubs at the words, trying to scrub them off, but after a second she gives up and waits for the police to take her away.

"I don't ever want to remember anything anymore, Trey. Not a goddamn thing."

8

Later, he drives the van in silence, windows rolled down, running the AC cold at the same time.

Waiting for their next call.

This stupid van and this goddamn town.

Driving around it in endless circles, waiting for someone else to die.

Full-on dark now, the moon curves over sugar maples; sterling light shining on Angel, where it sits in the crook of Levisa and Tug Forks, the arms of the Big Sandy River.

Dobie thinks Angel might have been named by English colonial settlers, the Cherokee, or even Spanish explorers, but no one's really sure. All the old maps just bear that one mysterious word, even those dating back to the Civil War, when union troops huddled in the town in the winter of 1861.

About the only thing Angel is famous for is the tri-bridge, a quarter-mile of concrete that crosses both forks, connecting Kentucky to West Virginia. The bridge has a unique turn about halfway across, the main access to Angel's Point Section neighborhood: the nicest homes, with old wood trees and big, sweeping lawns that with enough water stay emerald green even during the hot, humid Appalachia summers.

The bridge is one of maybe a couple dozen like it in the world, and sometimes visitors come to town just to take pictures of it to add to some obscure collection, but they never stay long.

They pass the Best Western and the Super 8 on the south side of town, neither of which get much more business—even with bridge sightseers—than the old Tamarack Inn way out on Torchlight Road used to during its heyday, when local kids rented out rooms to smoke weed and drink and get laid.

Like most of Angel, the Tamarack is a ruin now, too. Little Paris Glasser used to hold court there outside Lower Wolf, a prince and his kingdom, until things got bad after that young girl was found dead in the tall weeds behind it.

That girl's death haunted Trey's dad, like so many others now haunt Dobie, because even then his dad knew better than most that Glasser hands were dirty . . . *bloody* . . . with everything awful around Angel.

The sort of secrets everyone knows.

Trey rolls them on by the Save-A-Lot and the animal clinic and the Grinnell Gun and Pawn and the Super X Liquor Stop, and that barbershop where his dad used to take him. There was a group of old-timers who drank beer and ate boiled peanuts there all day, every day, talking basketball and God and the weather and the mines.

But it's closed up now and has been for a year and Jon Dorado has been gone almost as long.

They next swing by the crushed gravel lot of the Crow Bar, already starting to fill up for another Thursday night. Neon windows glow hard and unforgiving, the low-slung roof gleaming pyrite under sodium lights. Last winter Trey and Dobie ran a call here when Betsy Joyce's boyfriend, spun up on Glasser meth, stabbed her three times with a Buck Knife—once in the face, taking an eye; the second across her slim throat; and the third straight to her heart. When some of the regulars tried to pull him off Betsy, he stabbed them too, cutting a couple pretty bad. Trey handled six stitches for one of them, who was still high as a goddamn kite himself when Angel PD carted him off.

All the usual suspects were circling that night: Little Paris and Jamie Renfro, Ray Ray Sitton and Jerry Dix and Duane Scheel.

Betsy's best friend, Holly Dix, who was crying, *screaming*, although there wasn't a scratch on her.

And Duck Andrews too, although he was off-duty and claimed he was inside taking a piss when it all happened.

Betsy Joyce never had to deal with her lost eye and ruined face. She died right where she fell in a white dress way too sheer for the weather, something she'd picked up that same day with Holly at the Forever 21 in Ashland. It too was ruined, all black with blood. Dobie cut it off her with his surgical scissors to get at Betsy's chest to stop that bleeding, somehow stop all the damn blood, but it didn't matter because her heart had stopped long before they even pulled into the lot.

It had been cold that night, snow flurries gently falling all around her, caught up in her hair, where she steamed on the gravel beneath the floodlights and the headlights of the surrounding cars.

That blood, her blood, still warm to the touch.

As the Crow Bar disappears in the van's rearview, Trey can see a man outside lighting a cigarette, leaning casually against a Ford truck, looking down at the ground, and Trey wonders if that shadowed figure was there that night, too. Wonders if *he's* also remembering Betsy Joyce, lying just about where his truck is parked now, her body laced in blood and snow.

Wonders if anyone really wants to remember her and all those like her now lost and gone.

I don't ever want to remember anything anymore, Trey.

Not a goddamn thing . . .

9

They stop at DQ and sit outside at a metal table, the van's still-warm engine ticking like a clock.

Dobie's already finished off his cold hot dogs from the gas station and half the package of Takis. He's considering the Peanut Buster Parfait he ordered, way more quiet than usual; the three losses—Duane and Mark, the girl, Ruby—hitting him hard.

Hard enough they've stolen some of his appetite, leaving most of the parfait to melt in the heat. He watches instead the occasional car roll by, heading up to Old U.S. 23. It runs from Florida all the way to Michigan, but it's easier, faster, to take the newer, wider U.S. 23 loop that bypasses Angel altogether.

Trey's downed the 5-Hour Energy shot Dobie bought him but passed on the ice cream. Instead, he topped off his Mountain Dew with a little of the Bacardi Dragon Berry he's got secreted in his backpack.

Now he chews some wintergreen Certs so Dobie won't smell the alcohol.

Rhoda Nova and her six kids are all ordering up at the window. Age thirteen down to six, and only two or three have the same daddy, and the man who's been shacking up with her for the last few months isn't one of them. That's Bobby Ray Sitton, same one from the Crow Bar the night Betsy Joyce was killed, who everyone calls Ray Ray, so as not to confuse him with the *other* Bobby Ray who lives over in Ulysses. Ray Ray's got this lazy eye, always looks like he's staring at you sideways, a gift from a pissed-off horse. He tried to rob the van a month or so back when Trey was gassing it up alone, but Trey made out that weird eye through Ray Ray's homemade mask and called him out by name.

It wasn't even clear who was more scared, Trey or Ray Ray, holding a tape-wrapped gun in his shaking hand.

Ray Ray's just another fly circling shit, constantly in orbit around Angel and the Glassers, and Trey tries hard to steer clear of them all, knowing Little Paris Glasser wouldn't think twice about pulling the trigger that Ray Ray couldn't.

Although Little Paris is only a couple of years older than Trey, he's a notoriously violent, hardcore meth addict (and, some say, already a daddy), and it's hard to imagine a world where he's truly dead.

Any world that doesn't include a Glasser.

Dobie says they claim blood rights back to the McCoys of the infamous Hatfield–McCoy feud; Ole Ran'l McCoy and Devil Anse Hatfield, who it was said *was six feet of the Devil and a hundred eighty pounds of hell*. The West Virginia Hatfields were the more prosperous of the two clans, making a fortune from timbering, while the Kentucky McCoys—Angel itself only about seventy miles, give or take, from the original homestead—survived mainly off hogging, ferrying, and moonshining.

For ten years, their little war claimed more than a dozen lives on both sides of the river.

But last year alone in Lawrence and Martin and neighboring Boyd County there were more than thirty fatal drug overdoses. Add in those from the bordering counties on the West Virginia side, as well as nearby Ohio, and that number soars even higher.

Now, on *any* given Saturday night in Angel and Catlettsburg and Ashland, probably more people OD than ever fired a shot, or died from one, in that famously bloody feud.

Trey's dad once told him the Glassers moved way beyond moonshining a long time ago. Got into dogfighting and gambling and pimping, then selling weed from their fields on Lower Wolf, before expanding the family business to meth and coke and pills and heroin.

Nowadays, they're the largest suppliers of heroin in eastern Kentucky, maybe in all of Appalachia, and far more notorious than those old legends they've laid claim to.

Little Paris most of all.

Five feet of the Devil, if that, even standing in his favorite cowboy boots.

And every fucking inch of him hell.

A Martin County sheriff's cruiser flies by, sirens and lights blazing, strobing the night, and Rhoda's kids whoop and holler at it, the oldest giving it the finger.

"What was that Duck was going on about with the Glassers?" Trey asks, careful not to act *too* interested. You never want anyone to think you care all that much about the Glassers.

Dobie pokes at his melting parfait with a bloodred spoon. "I spoke with Marv, he's out there now. It's a mess." Marvin Jay Watkins is Lawrence County's coroner but handles Martin County, too. "Couldn't tell you how many are dead. They were still finding them this afternoon."

"The Glassers, really?"

"Bodies. But yeah, really."

"All of them?" Trey stresses, unable to wrap his head around this idea that Little Paris and Ricky and the rest are dead. Most everyone's always figured Old Man Glasser would never die, just get older and

meaner forever, rooted in place in his wheelchair, like the ancient oaks down at Lower Wolf.

Dobie nods. "Near about. Spread across the whole property." Dobie expands thick arms, spoon in one hand, parfait in the other, to make his point. Trey's never been down there and knows only what others have said about it and what his dad occasionally let slip: the sprawling Big House, expanded again and again since the 1800s, a handful of trailers the younger boys kept for partying. An uncle of some sort—set ablaze while he slept off a whiskey drunk in '98 or '99—allegedly had an A-frame of his own down by the water for torturing dogs and skinning folks who crossed the clan, and local kids swear to one another it still stands untouched and haunted. Renfroe too has an RV tucked somewhere up in the woods, and there is all manner of other scrap-wood meth shacks deep in the trees.

Whispers too, about a family cemetery, headstones taken out of the mines, where all that will dare grow among the graves is English ivy and black cherry.

The cemetery is real. Trey's dad told him he once saw it.

With all the girlfriends and ex-girlfriends and random kids and distant third or fourth cousins, you might fill a couple of buses with one kind of Glasser kin or associate or another. Kara even ran around with Little Paris for a while, before she hooked up with Ronnie Mackey and had her boy, and Trey can remember three girls—Love Faith, Paislee, and Willow, all from grades above and below him—who were somehow, in some way, related to the Glassers.

He wonders now if they're lying dead too at Lower Wolf.

In Angel, most everyone is tied together by blood or birth or marriage or bad luck. *Family* can be an all-encompassing word, broadly applied, loosely defined. And although the Glassers have always defined it a hell of a lot tighter than most, they're still everywhere, involved in everything.

Were.

"Duck's right, though, about the FBI and DEA being there," Dobie says. "Marv told me there's some lady Fed who's already got Sheriff Dunn fit to be tied." Dobie shakes his head. "Look, I'm not saying a woman is supposed to stay home and cook or whatever . . . but . . . it's just . . . well . . . I don't know." Dobie finally scoops at his ice cream, takes a bite. Just can't fucking help himself. "Anyway, they've practically set up camp. Probably be there for days, maybe even weeks. But they'll start moving the bodies out tonight."

"Jesus," Trey says.

"Has got nothing to do with it," Dobie offers, taking two more big bites before pushing the parfait away for good. He waves and smiles at Rhoda Nova, whispering beneath his breath soft enough that only Trey can hear, "Those are some damn ugly kids."

And that's about as mean a thing as Dobie Timmons can say, and even says it now with a gentle, good-natured smile.

"Some people just don't know when to quit," Trey says, grinning to make light, taking a long drink of his spiked Mountain Dew. "What happened?"

"Chose the wrong suitor *again*, I guess. And again. And again. And again." Dobie laughs along with him.

Only Dobie would use a word like *suitor*.

"No, dummy, not Rhoda. *The goddamn Glassers.*"

Dobie falls silent, serious. "I'd say their poor choices caught up with them, too. But you know, Trey, every saint has a past, every sinner has a future."

No, Trey doesn't know that. And until tonight, Trey would've bet nothing would ever catch up to the Glassers, just like there's never been a saint among them, either.

"We going down there?" he asks.

"Maybe . . . but you don't have to. It'll be bad."

Trey stands and takes Dobie's abandoned parfait, tossing it into the trash.

"Sorry, can't let you do it on your own. Last I heard, Ricky Glasser was up around four twenty-five, maybe more. You'll give yourself a heart attack dragging his dead, fat ass around, and I'm not ready to take over Angelcare Extreme Rescue, or whatever the hell you're calling it now. Honestly, Dobie, much as I like and respect you, there's no fucking way I'm *ever* wearing one of those silly jumpsuits."

Dobie looks down at his black outfit, straightening his crumpled shirt and brushing at a fresh stain.

Trey then waves at the parfait he just threw out and the empty hot dog packages and the Takis. "Speaking of poor fucking choices," he hints, but leaves the rest unsaid.

This would be where someone else—someone other than Dobie—might fire back a quick joke or tell Trey to go fuck himself, to stop acting like his goddamn mama. But Dobie's mama had her throat cut right in front of him, and the men who did it tied him to a chair with a floral bedsheet and made him watch the whole bloody, horrible, unforgivable, unimaginable thing.

It was rumored Old Man Glasser himself ordered it, but nothing was ever proven, no charges ever filed, and now it's just another Angel whisper; one more rumor, one more unsolved mystery.

One more secret everyone knows . . . and no one's been playing mama to or taking care of Dobie Timmons for a long time.

Trey will never understand how Dobie can be so fucked up and so forgiving at the same time.

Dobie's cell buzzes and he grabs it, listening intently. Then nods to himself before nodding to Trey that it's time to go again.

"Lower Wolf?" Trey asks, both excited and terrified by the idea.

"No," Dobie says quietly, fumbling with his phone. It's clear he doesn't want to come out with it. Finally, "the Point."

And that stops Trey dead. He knows what it means but has to ask anyway.

"Is it . . . ?"

"Yes," Dobie says. "It's *her.*" Dobie puts a hand out to him. "It's not good, Trey."

For Trey, it's a hell of a lot worse than Lower Wolf. But he shrugs, says, "Okay, let's go," before Dobie can offer to let him off the hook for this one, too. He probably will anyway, two or three or maybe a dozen times on the drive over the tri-bridge, until Trey finally tells him to shut the fuck up.

Trey opens the van door and jumps behind the wheel, firing up the engine.

Flips on the lights and sirens before they even get rolling, blasting the DQ parking lot with furious light and sound.

Anything to keep Dobie quiet.

And as they pull away, Rhoda Nova's kids are already whooping and hollering again, waving at them and watching them go.

10

They don't go straight to the house, but down to the Big Sandy instead.

They're not the first on-scene this time, with two Angel PD cruisers already parked by the water's edge.

Emergency lights paint the river red and blue, and one of them has its high-beam spot trained at a point just offshore.

A man out there, fully clothed, waist-deep in water.

And a woman, too.

She's naked.

Floating facedown.

11

Not long before he left, Trey's dad threatened to kill him.

It was right before the start of Trey's senior year, and things had been bad for a while, his dad gone a lot and his mom a mess and getting worse month by month; the Dorado family falling apart, piece by piece.

His dad claimed it was the job . . . *that it was the Glassers* . . . always the Glassers . . . but it wasn't.

It was *her*.

Trey found him standing in the spare bedroom at the Willow house with a gun in his hand.

Trey was used to his dad's guns, the mere presence of a loaded handgun itself no big deal. But this wasn't his duty gun, instead a SIG Sauer he'd bought maybe a year before over at the Fire Power Gun Show in Charleston.

Little used and still smelling of fresh grease.

And the bedroom at Willow already smelled of paint thinner and acrylic and wax. His mom loved to paint, a hobby from before Trey was ever born, and the room was her makeshift studio. She had a distinctive style, a lot of shading and shadow, everything darker than it was in real life, so it made the few colors in her work stand out and catch your eye. Every year she sold at least a few canvases at the Berea Craft Festival.

But when Trey walked in that afternoon, his dad was ignoring his wife's paintings, looking instead out the spare bedroom window into late-afternoon sunlight, staring straight into the sun, as Trey had this sudden horrible image of his dad firing that brand-new SIG either right through the glass or into his own temple. It was less the gun in his hand and more the look on his face, confused and angry and possibly even drunk. Stunned. Like he didn't quite understand who he was or what he was looking at.

Didn't recognize his own reflection.

Everyone always said Trey and his dad looked alike: same lean, whiplike frame and dark hair. Dark eyes. But Trey didn't recognize him that day, either.

His dad turned that disquieting stare on him and didn't bother to say a word about the unholstered gun in his hand.

Instead, he asked Trey about the Tamarack.

"You ever go out there, boy, out to that damn place?"

This was well after he'd investigated the dead girl behind it, so by then it was only a shell of its former self. But Trey knew what . . . and who . . . his dad was really talking about.

"'Cause if you ever get tied up with Little Paris or any of those Glassers and the things they do, ever start running around with them, I'll kill you, boy. You hear me?"

His dad then aimed the SIG at him to make his point. The room suddenly hot, closed in, smelling of old paint, and that sun burnishing the window at his shoulder a pure, blazing gold, almost too bright to look at.

But it didn't matter, all Trey could see was that gun.

"As sure as I'm standing here, boy, that's what I'll do. Because I love you, Trey. Because I love you, and I'm not going to let that happen to you."

And Trey wasn't scared, just curiously calm, even with his dad pointing a gun at him, because he really wanted to believe it was love making him do it.

Even told himself—given how shitty things had been, how distant and distracted his dad had become—that gun aimed at his heart was somehow the closest they'd been in months.

Much later, when dope-sick Ray Ray Sitton with his stupid make-shift mask and lazy eye tried to rob the Angelcare van, Trey flashed that same eerie calm again, never knowing if it was only because he recognized Ray Ray right off or because he fucking *dared* Ray Ray to do it, told him to just fucking *Do it, you piece of shit,* prompting the other man to say *Fuck it, you're crazy* and run off.

What Ray Ray really said was—

Kid, you're fucking worse off than me . . . and that's saying a lot.

But that day at Willow, Trey's dad just ordered him out of the room, so Trey left him there alone at the window, surrounded by his wife's half-finished paintings. They never talked about it again and things went on and on until his parents' fights went from bad to worse and then his dad stopped coming home altogether.

Right around the time Trey finally found out about *her.*

The woman they'd been living with all along, who Jon Dorado *really* loved more than them.

Marissa Mayfield.

Those first few months after his dad up and left, Trey often thought—too often—back to that hot, sunny afternoon, wondering how much love it takes for a father to threaten to kill his only son to save him, only to find out it wasn't near enough to make him stay.

Fuck him. He talked a good game, that's all.

And maybe that was because he wasn't talking about Trey at all.

12

Duck Andrews stops them before they get too close.

Waves them back, tells them it's a goddamn mistake they even got the call and that *real* EMS will handle it.

But Fire/EMS isn't here yet, so Trey and Dobie stand by anyway, just in case there's something they can do.

They watch Paul Mayfield pull his dead wife out of the water.

There's a mineral smell coming off the river, like a buried fortune of old pennies or nickels; wet rocks, chalk, dead fish scales.

She left her clothes neatly folded on the bank, as if she planned to come back for them when she was done with her night swim, and Trey can't keep his eyes off them.

Pale T-shirt, dark jeans.

Her once-expensive running shoes on top of it all, holding every-thing in place.

Up on the bridge, a fire truck is making its way to them. Even more Angel PD cruisers, the whole department. They're all responding be-cause Paul Mayfield is one of their own or at least used to be. He was Angel's police chief forever—and Jon Dorado's boss before his dad left—until suddenly stepping down himself a few months ago.

A hundred different reasons were given for Mayfield's retirement, all of them accepted, even if the one and only reason floats just off-shore.

Mayfield now has his wife in his arms, holding her out of the black water as best he can, carrying her gently back to her clothes. His movements slow, considered, thoughtful.

He's in a trance, lost, like Trey's dad at that window.

Mayfield's wife taught English at Lawrence County High for a while and Trey had her for a class, but she left school even before Mayfield left the department.

Her face is against Mayfield's chest, long blond hair hanging down around them both.

Everyone can see her smooth, exposed body. The curve of small breasts.

A dark tattoo on one shoulder, another on her hip.

"Goddamn it, turn off that spot," Duck orders, and the same man who didn't look twice at Kara Grace and Duane Scheel lying dead in the park suddenly wants privacy, some sort of dignity, for his former chief and his dead, naked wife.

The big white light snaps off, followed shortly by all the swirling emergency lights.

The land really is fucking dark.

But Trey can still hear the water lapping against the rocks as Paul Mayfield carries Marissa Mayfield to the rocky shore.

Before tonight, she suffered two overdoses, both at the house she and Paul Mayfield share just up from the water's edge.

A pretty place, a sprawling redbrick home shaded by trees; most of the Point families are old Angel money, lots of it, but not former chief Mayfield.

The first OD was about two or three in the morning and Mayfield found her in the living room, curled up on the couch, as if she'd gone to sleep there.

The second, he discovered her on the kitchen floor in a spilled mess of Malibu and Diet Coke when she was supposed to be up in front of her third-period English lit class. Trey's class. Apparently, she'd been baking a fancy cake, some recipe cut out of *Better Homes & Gardens*, and the kitchen was a train wreck of mixing bowls and flour and eggs and an open bottle of rum and crushed pills.

Oxy thirties and ungraded papers.

Trey didn't respond to those calls—he hadn't even graduated yet—but heard all about them anyway. *The secrets everyone knows.* That disastrous cake led to Marissa leaving teaching and Mayfield eventually retiring from the police department.

Marissa was twenty-six. Paul sixty, pushing sixty-one. He was her only marriage and she was his second, after his first wife succumbed to cancer.

Until now, things have been quiet at the Mayfield home, the couple mostly out of sight. Mayfield supposedly sent her to a fancy residential treatment center in Louisville, near where she grew up, although there were good ones much closer.

It didn't matter; she didn't stay for long.

It's no surprise to Trey they've finally found her here like this. Not to any of the gathered Angel PD officers either, trying hard not to stare (except for Duck Andrews, who's stealing glances whenever he can); not to Dobie, who's long been friends with Mayfield.

Not to the folks around town, although tomorrow they'll say it's a shame all the same.

Come morning, when the news gets out, no one's going to be shocked. And behind closed doors, those who never warmed up to Mayfield's much younger second wife will probably even say it's for the best.

———

Duck Andrews and the other officers still call Paul Mayfield *Chief,* although he hasn't officially carried that title in a while.

They stand back as Mayfield carries his wife out of the water and gently lays her down next to her clothes. Give him plenty of room and some measure of privacy as he struggles alone to dress her, even though this is technically a crime scene, and probably should be treated as such. Everyone knows better but defers to the former chief anyway, as if he still outranks them.

He's on his knees next to her, barely holding her hand. Afraid to touch her, afraid to let her go.

"What do you think, suicide or OD?" Trey whispers to Dobie, although no one is listening to them anyway.

Dobie shrugs, looking down at some useless Narcan in his hands.

"Both," he says.

Marissa Mayfield was always going to end up like this.

Everyone knew it, maybe her husband most of all.

13

She's still beautiful.

It's as if the river itself has washed her clean. Skin pale, white, mostly unblemished.

Like the girl, Ruby, Marissa's eyes are still open. Still green. Staring.

Water dries on her face like tears.

There's a thin silver necklace around her neck and a slim wedding band on her left hand.

Trey can't make out any tracks on her arms, not like those he saw on Kara Grace. But Marissa could've been snorting or injecting between her toes or her fingers to mask the scars.

Or maybe she really did just take off her clothes and go for a summer-night swim, losing her way in the wide river, letting the hidden current take her under.

Trey hasn't swum in the Big Sandy in years. Last time he did, it was cold, so fucking cold. Pitch black. Even in the shallows, that awful water felt like snakeskin, rubbing against his own.

Marissa's paper-thin, thinner even than Kara and far thinner than Trey remembers the last time he saw her alive. She barely weighs a hundred pounds, and even though she was floating in a quiet stretch of water carved out by sandbars, it still seems the river should have swept her away.

But maybe even the water was feeling merciful tonight, couldn't bear to take her for good and instead gave her back, at least for a little while.

Mayfield is a big man, but he's lost weight, too. A few years' worth of worry and stress gnawing at him. He's still solid, though, far more real than his ghostly wife.

Searching the other spectral faces gathered in the gloom, Mayfield finally calls for Dobie to come over and help him, and when he does, Trey follows, too. Duck glares but lets him go, barking instead at one of the other officers to get a goddamn blanket or something out of the cruisers, but there are all those blue sterile sheets in the back of the van, so Trey instead runs and grabs an armload, returning to join Dobie and Mayfield next to the body.

He breaks through the circled men and no one stops him.

Mayfield dries Marissa off with one of the sheets Trey hands him. One arm, one leg, at a time. He keeps wiping at her face, brushing her hair back, again and again. He doesn't look up and doesn't seem to recognize Trey standing so close by, although that's impossible.

Paul Mayfield has known Trey his whole life.

But he's too busy talking to his wife, whispering to her, and despite Trey's best efforts to catch them, the words wing away.

Trey used to scour her Facebook feed and Instagram before they were shut down and blocked. She was an open book then, her life both before Paul and after. All on display . . . *but not quite* . . . because there were never any pictures of Jon Dorado, not a single one of them together. Trey desperately searched again and again, hoping for at least one blurry profile, a phantasmal image of his dad haunting a background, some damning evidence to say *See, I was right all along.*

It seems awful now all the ways he hated her and imagined he knew everything about her and didn't really know her at all.

Trey's ashamed, staring down on her, naked, exposed, vulnerable.

He doesn't give a shit about Paul Mayfield, but it's still painful to watch him try to hold his life together, holding this dead woman in his arms.

The tattoo on her shoulder is a rearing unicorn.

The one on her hip is a tiny gold star, with the words *wish upon a star* . . .

As much as he blamed Marissa Mayfield for what happened to his family, he never fucking wished this on her.

They finally get her dressed and one of Trey's sheets pulled over her body.

Dobie is ready to turn Marissa and the entire scene over to Fire/ EMS, but Mayfield makes it clear he wants Dobie to transport her to Sacred Rest, the local funeral home. After Marv Watkins finishes down at Lower Wolf, he'll still need to conduct a postmortem to certify the exact cause of Marissa's death: most likely drowning, probably with acute drug toxicity as a contributing factor.

But he doesn't have to do that over at one of the hospitals, since Sacred Rest has the facilities and is a lot closer. Trey has seen the silver dissection table with the drains. The harsh lights. The hoses for all the blood.

Now Mayfield and Duck and Dobie talk among themselves, and Angel's current police chief, Oscar Floyd, arrives and joins the discussion. He shakes Mayfield's hand, a weirdly casual gesture, given what's just happened, and Trey wonders if Oscar even realizes that Mayfield was just touching his dead wife.

Trey stays by the van, earbuds in, listening to one of the latest tracks from American Vampires, until Dobie finally makes his way over, checking his phone the whole way.

"We're going to take Mrs. Mayfield over to Sacred Rest," Dobie says, low, but not quite a whisper. "But Paul doesn't want an autopsy, cut up like that, and I'm sure Marv will agree."

"Marv doesn't work for him," Trey says. "No one works for him anymore."

Dobie shrugs. "It's not like that."

Although that's exactly what it is.

"He's a good man, Trey, and this is horrible. Just horrible. Losing another wife so soon, so young . . ." But Dobie stops, because river or not, he understands the deep water he's wading into defending Paul and Marissa Mayfield. Dobie knows Trey doesn't want to hear anyone making excuses for either of them.

Not even now.

"He and Marv go way back," Dobie finishes with a shrug.

"*Everyone* goes way back around here, Dobie. He doesn't get to decide things like that anymore."

Dobie shrugs again, more uncomfortable. "She was clean and sober going on a month but, you know, still really struggling." Dobie pauses, and they both know he's only repeating some version of whatever Mayfield's told him. "Took a couple of sleeping pills and went swimming and drowned and the river took her."

No, Trey thinks, *the river didn't take her, because she's still right fucking here, lying beneath the blue sheet I gave her.*

Trey can still see her pale hand and the wedding ring on it.

"So that's it?"

"No, that's *all,*" Dobie says, and that's as close to a warning as Dobie can give. "I know this is hard for you. Your daddy . . . Mrs. Mayfield . . . whatever you think happened." Dobie puts a hand on

Trey's shoulder. "But let's do what we can for her. We need to get the gurney."

But a few moments later, as they're working together to get it out, Dobie says again, as much as to himself as to Trey—

"Clean a whole month. A month. And all it took was a bad day or two, and here we are."

Because he just *can't* let them go. Never can, never will.

And if a month in Angel sometimes feels like a fucking lifetime to Trey, there's no doubt one or two "bad" days in row probably do feel like forever to an addict: an hour of withdrawal, a truly endless purgatory.

But to an addict already in recovery, someone like Marissa Mayfield, a month is weirdly *nothing*, hardly time to celebrate at all, not when she's still counting the threat of relapse in *minutes*.

Just long enough, though, that the risk of overdose and death is actually higher, because she can't judge her tolerance anymore or properly dose herself.

The new DOA heroin is so lethal even those who haven't been clean for years, those with almost bulletproof tolerance like Duane and Mark and Kara, are still dropping dead. If Marissa really had a month sober but got her hands on one of Little Paris's dancing-skeleton bags, there's no way her weakened system could have handled it.

When it hit her veins, it would've been like getting hit by a fucking train, like putting a loaded gun to her head and pulling the trigger.

But up close, there weren't any fresh tracks. No needles by her clothes. No foil, no pipe.

No stamp bag like the one he lifted from Kara.

No horrible dancing skeleton, either.

So Trey won't argue with Dobie about it, because she's gone now and maybe the *how* of it doesn't matter; it doesn't matter if Mayfield lies to himself and everyone else about it, or that Dobie keeps trying to convince himself it doesn't bother him even as he too can still see her pale hand and the wedding ring on it.

Even though *how* that poor little girl ended up dead behind the Tamarack bothered Trey's dad for a long, long time, and Jon Dorado once believed the *how* and the *why* and the *who* mattered almost more than anything.

"Just wait here, Trey," Dobie says. "I can do this with Paul or Oscar, even Duck."

"Mayfield's not going to want Duck Andrews's hands near her. I still have a job to do."

"Trey," Dobie says, with that almost-whisper again, "Paul won't leave her. He's going to ride all the way over to Sacred Rest."

Trey pauses, but for only a second. "It's okay, Dobie. Really, it is. I appreciate it, I do, but fucking let it go. *Please.* I'm good."

"Sure?" Dobie asks, face still twisted in concern.

"Yeah," Trey says, even though he's not sure if he'll ever be good again.

He'll ride up front with Dobie and try not to think about Mayfield and Marissa in the back.

It doesn't matter.

None of it matters.

But it does, because Trey wonders now if he's supposed to track down his dad and tell him that Marissa is dead.

How she died.

His dad fell in love in with another man's wife: a young, beautiful addict. He lost his way and then lost his own wife and son even though he had to know he was always going to lose her too, because she was never really his to begin with.

"All right, let's get on with it," Dobie says. "And then we've got another call."

That's why Dobie was messing with his phone a few moments ago.

"Another?" Trey asks.

"Yeah, but it's nonemergency," Dobie says. "No one we can help."

And Trey gets it. And Dobie's already shaking his head—

"They're all already dead."

CASEY

14

The baby is covered in blood.

Casey's not sure she'll ever forget it. A beautiful baby girl wrapped in a Cincinnati Bengals T-shirt. Bawling her lungs out, waving stubby arms in the air.

Covered in blood.

The thing of it is, they don't know whose blood it is, and might not for days. There are two bodies in the room with her, male and female, both dead from multiple shotgun blasts, faces gone. Mostly gone. Sprayed all over the walls, the windows. All over the baby.

The room stinks like someone's struck a book of matches. Cordite. Everyone always associates the smell of blood with copper . . . *that coppery smell of blood* . . . like holding a handful of pennies. It's such a cliché now, so instead all that stinking blood on the walls reminds Casey of smoldering ashes. A basement furnace. A campfire.

The high, dry heat of Arizona, where she lived for a time; for far too fucking long.

The room breathes hot like an open mouth ready to swallow Casey whole.

And it isn't even the worst.

Not by a long shot.

———

The man is naked.

His ribs are a scroll of tattoos, black and blue prison ink. They photograph him in situ, arms spread above his head like he's trying to crawl backward off the bed, the tats nearly neon against his skin.

The woman is wearing a T-shirt, evidently a fan of Jason Aldean. Casey has to look him up on her phone.

The dead woman with no face probably has raven-dark hair, but since everything is covered in drying blood, all of it going black, it's hard to say. One of the local deputies jokes about her coloring it, but after Casey's look, the laughter dies out.

Gallows humor.

The woman is on the floor, between the bed and a makeshift bassinet, and Casey will always want to believe she was crawling to protect her baby. She's thin, though, likely too thin to have given birth so soon, but who knows about such things anymore? She's scrawled with tattoos too, a heart here, a lucky rainbow there. Initials in some hard-to-read script on her wrist, all loops and cursives. A faded, six-rayed sun sporting a sly smile at the nape of her neck. But they're nothing compared to her whole lower back, which has been transformed into a beautiful garden of wildflowers. Recently completed, the colors are still so new and bright and vibrant—*alive*—those ink flowers look real enough to touch and gather up and put in a vase.

And right above that garden, right between her shoulder blades, is a bloody boot print.

As she was struggling to get to the baby, someone put a boot on her back and blew the top of her head off.

That print glows neon too under all the photo flashes.

Casey's arrived about an hour after the first deputies came on the property, but no one's thought to pick up the crying baby. Maybe she wasn't wailing yet or they hadn't seen her and didn't even know she was there. But now that Casey's here and the baby's really going full blast, it's as if those dozens of men are just going to stand around with their hands in their pockets or resting on their holstered guns and wait for the one woman to deal with it, although Casey has no more maternal instincts than they do. She doesn't have kids, doesn't want any and probably never will, but also isn't about to let that little girl lie there alone and exposed with everyone watching.

Everyone expecting her to do it anyway.

So she slips the badge on the chain around her neck inside her own T-shirt and steps over the dead woman and pulls the baby out of the bassinet.

Pulling her close, holding her tight.

That little body is shaking all over, trembling, and despite all the blood everywhere and the muzzle blast still reeking in the air, up close and safe against Casey's chest, she smells of lavender and cream.

And as if on cue, wrapped now in Casey's arms, the bloody baby girl stops crying.

15

It's a crime scene unlike anything DEA special agent Casey Alexander has ever experienced.

Bodies blasted to pieces all over this remote, rural property; strewn inside and among the houses and trailers. Sprawled in the ivy, gunned down in mid-run, or trying to hide beneath beds. Men and women. Teenagers. *Fucking kids*. At least three dogs, too. They've been at it all afternoon, and with night falling and the last good light fading, they're still finding bodies. In one of the trailers, an active meth lab, too. Anhydrous tanks, empty bottles of Heet and Red Devil Lye and Drano and Klean-Strip paint thinner. Lithium batteries and hot plates and old Pepsi two-liters and a turkey-basting wand and some real Pyrex that looks like it was lifted from a high school chemistry class.

But other than spent shotgun cartridges and that bloody boot print, not much in the way of real clues.

The scene's already a tangled mess of competing jurisdictions and interests. Martin County Sheriff's Office. Franklin County SO. Inez PD. Kentucky State Police.

The FBI, because someone always calls the fucking FBI.

One lone ATF agent, Roderick Bell, who Casey's worked with

before and even went on one date with, claiming he owns a piece of this because he once bought or sold guns to the Glassers.

And the DEA, because Casey and her partner, Van Dorn, and their enforcement group have been targeting the Glassers forever. On her way over from Charleston, she pulled the link chart off the wall that was hanging in her office, complete with headshots and whatever intel they've accumulated about the Glassers and all their far-flung associates. When she and Van Dorn got to Lower Wolf, she spread it over the still-ticking hood of their Ford Explorer, holding it down with some rocks, and as bodies were found, she referred to it, trying to match what faces are left to the DMV and surveillance photos that populate the chart. Casey also brought hard copies of her files, including NCIC printouts and other booking info related to the Glassers that catalog whatever scars, marks, and tattoos were noted and photographed when they were arrested, because those things can also be used to identify their bodies.

Most of the Glassers have been arrested more than once.

The Martin County deputies who routinely work this area know many of the Glassers on a first-name basis, so all afternoon Casey's been watching them kneel next to the bodies, staring at them as if they can't quite believe what they're seeing, whispering among themselves.

Surreptitiously snapping pix on their phones.

Casey understands. Even in the relatively short time she's followed the Glassers and all the stories surrounding them, she never thought she would be here, either. Not like this. Lower Wolf has always been sacred ground, forbidden to outsiders.

If you had a warrant for a Glasser, wanted to risk questioning one of them, you always waited until you could catch them in Tomahawk or Kermit or Angel. Even then, it wasn't easy or safe. They have . . . *they had* . . . eyes and ears everywhere.

A lot of competing . . . conflicting . . . interests.

Casey's pretty sure not all these deputies are disinterested by-standers. Corruption has been an endemic problem in this area for-ever, so widespread, so deep-rooted, it's practically comical. The bad joke everyone is fucking in on. She's already pissed off Sheriff Dunn more than once today, and he's quickly realizing he's losing control of his crime scene. Word is already out about what happened down here, and locals are sneaking through the woods surrounding the property, trying to get a good look for themselves or make off with whatever money and valuables or dope they suspect the Glassers still have hid-den around.

The blood . . . the bodies . . . the sudden and awful savagery of what's happened . . . has left everyone on a hair trigger, and someone's likely to get shot if they're not careful. If some sort of chain of com-mand, some sort of order, isn't established here, and soon.

Top to bottom, it's a fucking mess, and Casey's glad she's not in charge of it. The homicides will take precedence over whatever drug connection there is that led to this massacre, and Casey is one hundred percent sure she will find a drug connection, eventually.

Drugs or money . . . or both.

You might kill one person because they pissed you off; said the wrong thing to you in the heat of the moment or cut you off in traffic.

You might kill two, even three, in a fit of jealousy. Infidelity. All that angst, the hurt, driving you to shoot the illicit lovers and then yourself, the classic murder-suicide.   ·

But the only reason you'd kill a whole fucking family, right down to their dogs, is because they crossed you over drugs or money or both. When Casey was working out west . . . Juárez, Nogales, Nuevo Laredo . . . she saw it all the time: the cartels fighting all along the border, cleaning up outstanding debts and sending messages.

They just fucking killed everyone.

It didn't look to be so different in Kentucky anymore.

Whoever came to Lower Wolf and butchered the Glassers here in their home, on their sacred ground where even the cops were afraid to tread, wanted to send one hell of a message.

Message received.

16

The sun's barely down and it's still hot, the portable Nomad lights the KSP and FBI evidence techs brought out helping heat up the surrounding night.

Moths wing back and forth in front of the lights, bat against them, casting their own shadows and trying to fly too close to the makeshift suns.

Van Dorn brings Casey a bottle of water where she's standing alone by their Explorer. He also found a spare T-shirt somewhere for her, a Martin County deputy's shirt complete with a gold star, so she changes in the air-conditioned SUV while he leans against the driver's-side window, giving her a little privacy as she lets the cold air blow over her sweat-slicked skin.

She sits for a long time, looking at the bloody shirt she just took off, those places where she held the baby close to her, the tiny hands grasping at her hair.

Casey's own hair is short now. Chopped way, way, down, colored red instead of her natural blond. She cut it two weeks ago and Van Dorn doesn't like it, can't grasp the sudden change, the sort of change she's prone to make on a whim or in a fit of anger or frustration or one of those storm-black moods she's always struggled with.

He told her it makes her look perpetually pissed off, which is kind of a shitty thing to say.

True, maybe, but shitty all the same.

She and Van Dorn have a complicated relationship. They've worked together for more than a year, since she first transferred into DEA's Charleston office, and his old partner before her was just that—*old*. Mitchell retired a month before Casey showed up, and although Van Dorn's eligible too, he won't follow Mitchell out the door. He warns Casey at least three times a day he's going to pull the pin and leave her all their unfinished paperwork, but so far, they've all proven to be idle threats. She still finds him every morning sitting at his desk, drinking a large black coffee from the place up the street. He goes there bright and early for breakfast and the paper before coming into the office, and he always brings her whatever paper he's finished, *The Wall Street Journal* or *The New York Times* or *The Washington Post*, depending on his mood. And her own cup of coffee.

For months now, she's been telling him she barely reads the paper and doesn't even *like* coffee, but like clockwork, he brings them to her anyway. The same harsh black he drinks without cream or sugar in the same cheap foam cup with a plastic lid. It's a fucking ritual or a rite of passage or a test of wills and he never says a word about it, even as she lets cup after cup go cold and stale on the corner of her desk.

Mitchell used to like those coffees, so maybe that's part of it, each cup a testament or memorial to the man she's replaced, a not-so-subtle way to remind her of the man she's not. But it's not that simple with Van Dorn. It never is. The big redheaded Irishman—claims to be Irish, but *Van Dorn* is actually Dutch; Casey looked it up—seems to delight in quietly tormenting her and pushing her buttons, needling her, driving her batshit crazy. He does it because it's so easy to do, because he knows she can get worked up like those moths banging against the portables, always circling, always frustrated by the light they can't reach, not realizing that the glass is the only thing saving them from themselves. And although he irritates the ever-living fuck out of her, Van Dorn is also *her* glass, protective in his own way. Saves her from herself. If she calls, anytime, day or night, he's there, and he listens. He never dismisses her wilder ideas out of hand, never complains *about* her, only *to* her, and when they're out on the street, never treats her as anything other than his equal.

He's got at least three ex-wives and maybe a son and has spent his whole career up and down the East Coast; Boston, Detroit, D.C. He asked for Charleston for reasons he won't share and no one else seems to know, although maybe Mitchell did, once upon a time. Van Dorn knows everything that happened to her back in Arizona but never talks about that either, never even *asks*, and won't let anyone else in the office ask or spread it around.

It's okay for him to fuck with her, but he draws a hard, bright line with any fellow agent or cop fucking with her. And no one wants to fuck with Van Dorn.

He's truly got her back, which is about the best thing you can say about your partner.

Like now, with his own wide shoulders pressed against the Explorer's window, his antique Dirty Harry revolver hanging in a leather Galco shoulder rig that was out of style before she was ever born. Sporting one of those short-sleeved dress shirts he always wears that are also so out-of-date, so fucking old-fashioned, his bare arms folded across his chest, watching the night and the moths circling the lights.

He's his own walking, talking cliché, too.

The water's gone warm in the bottle he brought her, but at least it's not a goddamn cup of coffee.

And there's the T-shirt. He was thoughtful enough to do that.

He was the one who took the bloody baby from her arms after they walked out of that room. Must have caught that frantic look in her eyes, sensed she was trying to hold it together, trying not to cry or scream or both.

But he waited until they were out of the room, well away from the other Feds and the Martin County deputies.

Waited until they were all alone to gently pull the baby from her.

Saw her trying to wipe away the blood left behind with her hand, smearing it, making it worse.

They both knew she really was going to scream then.

All that fucking blood and what it meant to her.

That was when he told her to head back to the Explorer, take a couple of minutes to herself, and then walked off alone, cradling the baby.

17

She stands now over at the chart she brought. It's hard to read under the portables.

Whites are too white, blacks too black.

Her fucking head hurts trying to decipher the tiny print, make out the faces in the low-res photos.

Some of the faces in those photos are dead now, sprawled somewhere in the dark around her.

Maybe all of them.

And not too dark . . . since numerous red and blue emergency lights still spin on top of parked cruisers. They're everywhere, circling her. Here and there she can make out the back-and-forth shimmer of flashlights moving between the rambling old house that anchors the property and the woods surrounding it.

She guesses the former owner of her new T-shirt is out there. It's way too large, hanging off her small, slight frame. *Birdlike* is what Van Dorn's called her in the past, and he didn't mean it as a compliment.

She gets it. He's broad and blocky, all heavy angles, not built for speed, every decision slowly considered and calculated. Calibrated. Casey's not quite built for speed either, not anymore, not with the slight limp she brought with her from Arizona, an injury she'll never fully recover from in ways that have nothing to do with the additional physical therapy she refuses to schedule.

She's seen a picture of at least one of Van Dorn's exes to get a pretty good feel for his type. A nurse in D.C., both pretty and plain, solid, just like him. He supposedly has that college-age son who lives with the ex, but he never goes up there to see either of them, even though it's only about a five-hour drive. Casey harps on him all the time about it, but he always acts like they're too busy for him, or he's too busy for them.

Casey can't imagine what he does with his free time. How many newspapers can one lonely man fucking read?

The news is the same everywhere anyway. Always shitty.

But right now he's doing his best imitation of being bored, like he really does have something better to do. He was ready to pack it in an hour ago and has been idle long enough to finally decide there's nothing for them to do. It's going to take hours or days to ID all the victims, another couple of weeks to reconstruct how it all went down, and maybe months or years—or never—to track down the men who did it. Van Dorn told her that the FBI or KSP will probably move the trailers that can be moved completely off-site, just haul them all away. They'll store them in a warehouse, where later evidence techs and future investigators can go over them again and again.

Someone is going to teach *this* investigation at a law enforcement academy a few years from now. All the things to do and not to do.

"What do you think?" Casey asks, turning her back on her chart.

Van Dorn motions at it. "I don't need *that* to know Ricky Glasser is lying dead in the living room up in the main house. That big sonofabitch was easy to pick out, even with most of his head gone. In his case, it probably won't affect the scale any."

Van Dorn once interviewed Ricky about a drug-related shooting in Catlettsburg. Ricky was never all that bright, not like his older brother, Danny, or even the younger, craftier one, Little Paris, but he was a stone-cold killer. Over the years, the bigger he got, the more violent he became. There was an anger, a growing fury inside him, that he couldn't contain and didn't even try.

Van Dorn's worked the area long enough to know as much about the Glassers as anyone. He opened one of the original cases on the oldest, Danny, and doggedly pursued it until Danny was shot dead in the parking lot of an Econo Lodge in Huntington, just over the river. The circumstances still remain unclear, the reasons unknown, and although everyone assumes it was drug-related, Van Dorn's never committed one way or another. Not officially, not in any written report.

Casey figures even after all this time, he's still considering, still calculating.

All that was before Casey arrived, and she's since helped pick up the pieces of Van Dorn's original investigation and set her own sights on the remaining Glassers. Not *just* the Glassers, but also all the local cops and deputies who've been helping and protecting them all these years.

It's a sore spot with Van Dorn, who's known many of these same men, who's worked shoulder to shoulder with most of them at one time or another.

Van Dorn continues, "Let's be honest, the world is better off without him. All of 'em."

"There were kids here, too."

Van Dorn nods, noncommittal. *Still considering.* "Well, you asked me what I think, so here it is. Someone just saved us a fuck-ton of paperwork and wasted hours. They closed all our Glasser-related cases in one afternoon. Ricky and Little Paris and all the rest of them had it coming, so I'm going to call it finally fucking karma and leave it at that."

"You don't believe that karma nonsense."

Van Dorn nods again, even though he's not agreeing with her.

"Okay, maybe I don't, but I do believe in divine retribution." He looks back toward the sagging house, the whole front lit up with more portable lights, the old Caddy where Danny Glasser died still parked like a boat in dry dock in knee-high weeds near the rotted front porch. It's visible from every window, like some weird, awful lawn ornament. A *monument* . . . as if the rest of the family wanted to be reminded first thing every morning of what they'd lost. Danny was always the Old Man's favorite, his handpicked successor, right up to when he was shot dead in his daddy's favorite red Coupe de Ville, before he even turned thirty-five.

Old Man Paris had it towed from Huntington back here, but it was never driven again, not after Danny's body was found in the front seat, his brains all over the windshield.

"And that's what happened here tonight," Van Dorn says. "Wrath of God."

She studies the house, too. It's two hundred years old if it's a day, and it's got a thousand memories of its own, not all of them bloody. They can't be. God's wrath didn't see fit to pull it down.

But she can't forget that room they were just in, either. The bodies. The tattooed garden on the dead woman and the scarlet boot stain on her back. The baby. She wants to ask Van Dorn where he took the baby, where she is now. *How are they ever going to know her name?* She's got a name, and someone knows it.

Someone still living.

"I don't want to believe in a God like that," she says, and she's not even sure Van Dorn does either, no matter how he's acting about it now. He's a nominal Catholic, with a wooden Rosary tucked away in his desk.

"Fine," he says, pushing away from the Explorer. Sweat makes his cheap shirt cling to him. "You're right, Casey, God didn't do this." He pulls the rocks away from her chart and tosses them aside, rolling it up. "But I sure don't want to meet the motherfuckers who did."

18

They'll need to get a cleanup crew to deal with the meth lab, but no one's going to be able to do a damn thing until the bodies are moved.

It isn't just the lab. One of the other trailers, an older model Lance parked about two hundred yards from the main house, looks to be where the Glassers were cutting and packaging their heroin.

There are two dead in there.

One of the Martin County deputies walks them out to it. They weave through trees, his SureFire leading the way, and it has an unreal quality. Surreal. The woods hover close, holding in the night's heat, as other men and their lights move in the distance. There's the occasional crackle of a portable radio and silent lightning suggesting rain, and everything's vague, muted.

The whole world beneath the trees is wrapped in soft gauze as hazy as a faraway memory, and the brume and dark conjure an old one for Casey—

Playing flashlight tag as a kid.

Another long, humid summer night just like this.

Lawn sprinklers and box fans.

When she was about ten or twelve, the family dog went missing, an Irish setter named Royal. There was a wooded run right behind their house in Bowling Green, a wild, untended strip of oaks and maples separating two suburban neighborhoods, where younger kids goofed off and the older ones smoked or drank or fucked, and young Casey became convinced that Royal was laid up there, that he'd been hurt and crawled into the shadows and undergrowth to wait for help. Waiting for her. After she posted up some flyers, she and her daddy spent nearly a week combing through those woods together, dodging snakes and one fat, pissed-off raccoon. Simon Alexander was already interested in Lost River by then, so he approached their efforts with the same care and thoroughness he'd learned from his exploration of that infamous local cave system. A classics and history professor, he found ways to make everything a lesson, and their search for Royal became a kind of archaeology dig all its own, where they found all sorts of stuff, the bits and pieces of lives that often get lost or forgotten or tossed out or left behind.

Old tennis shoes, a pair of cutoff jeans. Dozens of beer cans and bottles and moldy magazines and books. A twisted, rusted bike that looked as if it had been run over twice by a car.

A car door, even a whole plastic Christmas tree still decked out with pearly tinsel and a few broken ornaments.

They also found a few of those things that are sometimes purposefully hidden away—

A backpack full of girls' panties, all colors and shapes and sizes.

A kitchen steak knife wrapped in an old Bob Seger T-shirt.

A revolver that her daddy carefully put in a plastic bag and later took to the local police.

But no dog.

They never found Royal, and her daddy decided not to get a second dog. Casey was getting older then, anyway, just starting to exhibit the anger . . . *the storm-black moodiness . . . the darkness . . .* that she'd inherited from him and that would define so much of her adolescence and the Alexander household. And he was traveling more, and his attention when he was home focused on mapping and reopening Lost River. He'd become fascinated by its history, all the old stories the cave could tell. Her mom really made the decision for all of them, but secretly, Casey was glad. She never wanted to have to search for another dog like that, never wanted to again find things like those she found that first time. Unlike her daddy, she didn't want to know or tell herself stories about them, dwell on the memories and sorrows and mistakes they represented.

Or, worse, imagine the fate of those things never found.

Those things—like family dogs, like people—that are forever lost.

Sometimes stories just don't have happy endings.

The deputy's a big, beefy kid, hair cut down to stubble, and he keeps glancing around, nervous.

Looks to be in his early twenties, barely old enough to drink, yet he's got a gun on his hip that he probably really wishes was in his hand instead of his flashlight. His name tag says his name is "Buechel," but he's said only a few words, and only to Van Dorn, who knows a lot of the older deputies by name and has known Sheriff Dunn forever.

Young deputy Buechel ignores Casey, like he's afraid to look at her. She's used to it, this magical aura around her, this weird effect she has on other cops, even some of her fellow agents. They either pretend to ignore her or can't keep their eyes off her. But it's more than that now. This kid is truly scared, haunted, afraid the shadows are going to jump at them. He's probably never seen anything like this and Casey almost wants to put a hand on his flashlight arm—steady it, because it's visibly shaking—and tell him *It's okay.*

Really, it's okay. This thing is going to haunt us all.

And then, like another magic trick, his SureFire suddenly sweeps over the trailer, revealing it propped up on concrete blocks, swaybacked beneath a massive furred oak. There's camouflage netting draped haphazardly over the top of it, and deep in the leafy shadows, it's almost invisible.

Another hidden thing.

The door is open, and framed right there in the deputy's light, there's a *fucking arm*.

Hanging motionless, fingertips grazing the top step.

The body attached to it must have died crawling out, trying to escape. Didn't get far enough, didn't make it.

There are several long streaks of blood down the door, all over the steps.

Spatter. Spray.

And a ring on that hand, silver and heavy.

And as Casey pushes past the stricken, silent deputy, as she steps closer and kneels over the body, that ring is a laughing skull, staring back up at her.

Tiny ruby eyes.

She's seen it before.

She fucking knows this ring.

She knows the dead man who wears it.

19

The ring, the hand, the arm, all belong to Jamison "Jamie" Renfro, cousin to Ricky and Little Paris and the rest.

Casey and Van Dorn know all about Jamie Renfro. He used to run around with Jerry Dix, another Glasser mule and wannabe, and for a couple of months last summer Dix was their prized snitch into the whole Glasser clan.

Jamie and Jerry went to school together and were sort of tight, at least as tight as any Glasser could be with nonblood—that is, until Renfro hooked up with Dix's girl.

In fact, that girl—Jerry Dix's *wife*, Holly—left Jerry and shacked up with Jamie for a time at Lower Wolf.

Jamie Renfro had no more sense around a pretty girl than did his cousin Little Paris, who allegedly had a real problem staying away from one. Where other men collected guns or cars, Little Paris collected those men's girlfriends, wives, daughters.

In fact, if there was one thing Little Paris liked in the world *more* than drugs and money, it was pussy, and Renfro was quick to follow the lead of his younger, favorite cousin.

All small-town, small-time problems, and eventually, as so often happens in a small town, Renfro tossed Holly out and she ran back to

Dix, who took her in again with welcome arms. Everything pretty much forgiven and forgotten, until Holly turned up pregnant shortly after, and paternity turned into speculation and then a *big* fucking problem.

Renfro told everyone it wasn't his—*it wasn't fucking gonna be his, no matter what*—and left it at that. Leaving his old buddy Dix maybe, possibly, raising another man's child, while still relying on that man for the work and money to do it.

That's because throughout the whole Jerry Springer mess, Dix was a part-time addict and full-time fuckup and *still* neck-deep in the Glasser dope business and had no other choice.

By then, the Glassers didn't have much of a choice, either. After Danny died, Little Paris started calling all the shots for the family business, but as he got increasingly into meth (his drug of choice), he got even more paranoid and even less willing to leave the safety of Lower Wolf and Martin County. He was a shadow, a ghost, always on the move, forced to rely more and more on distant blood relatives like Renfro and sketchy wannabes like Dix to hold his little empire together.

Little Paris sure in hell wasn't going to end up with a bullet in the head in the front seat of a car in fucking Huntington.

But someone still had to meet the Mexican connections, still had to broker deals to keep the dope flowing, still had to make the regular payments and pick up the loads that Danny had once so carefully arranged. At first that was Renfro, but when he smartened up too, following the lead again of his favorite cousin, he put it all on Dix.

Someone who wasn't family, who wasn't any kind of blood at all.

Necessary, maybe, but absolutely expendable.

Because damned if Jamie Renfro was going to let some wetback or gangbanger get the drop on him, either.

So when Dix was stopped on I-64 outside of Teays Valley with three kilos of coke and two pounds of uncut heroin, all headed back across the river to Kentucky and Lower Wolf, he was facing his second Possession with Intent to Distribute charge in five years, and probably the better part of the next three decades in jail. That's when Dix decided once and for all he couldn't swallow that much time for the man who'd fucked, and maybe impregnated, his wife, even if that man was supposed to be his friend *and* a Glasser to boot.

He begged for a fucking deal.

He wasn't happy about it, but he had no other choice.

Again.

20

Casey and Van Dorn met with Dix a half-dozen times over that summer.

A small, rabbity man, with a thinning mullet and thick glasses. Bad teeth. Tattoos on his hands.

Lost spelled out across his left fingers, *hope* on the right.

An anchor on his neck underscored by the words *won't sink.*

Despite that sentiment, his whole life had been weighed down by a hundred invisible anchors, each one another choice he didn't have, a lifeline he was never going to take. Jerry Dix was never going to leave eastern Kentucky. He wasn't going off to college in the Northeast and was never going to wear a collared shirt in a nice office. He wasn't going to kick the Pall Mall Reds or the midmorning Budweiser tallboys or the oxys just like everyone else he knew.

Not today, not tomorrow. Not ever.

And Van Dorn *really* disliked him from the get-go, but it's hard to like most snitches. Even the good ones are desperate and untrustworthy, and the weakest of them, a man like Dix, can be downright dangerous in the right or wrong circumstances.

A rabid dog backed into a corner.

Casey had to explain to Dix again and again that *yes*, he would have to wear a wire, even though they didn't tape them to your skin anymore like they did on TV; nowadays the tiny, sophisticated transmitters could be hidden in cellphones and water bottles and the brims of John Deere hats. Even something nice and fashionable like a TAG Heuer watch, although that was the sort of watch a man like Dix would never own.

And yes, he also had to "dirty up" calls to both Renfro and Little Paris so they could spin up on Title III intercepts, another kind of wire. Dix swore up and down both men dumped their cellphones regularly and were too smart (or too drunk or too high) to say anything damning on them, but Casey figured Dix was their best shot at it anyway.

And Dix had to be prepared to testify in open court. She would do everything in her power to keep him off the stand, but when all was said and done, he had to go all in on *everyone*, every single fucking Glasser. Jamie. Ricky. Little Paris. Even the Old Man.

All of them.

All the associates and sources too, the men he was picking up their dope from.

And most important, all the fucking cops who'd been shielding them all these years.

Dix tried negotiating with a whole lot of nothing. Wheedling, almost begging, until Van Dorn lost even his legendary patience. But Casey stuck with him anyway. For once, she was the deliberate one. Considered. Fucking calibrated. She sat patiently as Dix chased one Pall Mall after another, his teary eyes lost in cigarette smoke, always searching for a new way out, always angling for a better deal or choice they both knew he didn't have. Dealing with him was its own special kind of hell, but eventually, little by little, he did give up useful intel about the silent Hispanics he'd been meeting at rest stops between both Louisville and Charleston. The Glassers were apparently getting sourced by Mexican gangs out of Detroit and D.C., and Dix was able to cough up a handful of contact numbers for them, although he claimed those changed even faster than the Glassers' cellphones, mostly just used to coordinate meet locations and times and then thrown away after.

But even those brief exchanges were risky business, he said, because the money Renfro and Little Paris gave him was forever short, everyone suspecting everyone else was angle-shooting or stealing from one another anyway.

The dope *always* shitty, the money *always* light.

Those Mexicans always made Dix nervous too, the way they stared at him with their dark eyes as they counted the money they all knew wasn't enough, the way they casually kept their shirts high enough for him to see the guns in their chinos and talked around one another in a language he didn't understand.

The way the threats they never quite made were somehow still clear enough.

He understood those just fine.

He said Renfro and Little Paris blew it off, telling him it was no big deal. They'd somehow handle it, if it ever needed handling. But Danny Glasser had been the steadying hand, the smart one, and he'd still ended up dead dealing with these Mexicans.

Those other two didn't inspire jack shit for confidence.

And it was Dix the Mexicans knew, up close and personal. He was the one they met face-to-face. Not Renfro. Not Little Paris.

Not anymore.

Dix was the one they'd put their hands on first when and if they decided it *was* a big deal.

Dix also revealed a few things about the local business itself, like the Glassers' little homemade meth labs—none of them good enough cooks to keep up with demand, though; they just didn't have the patience for it—and how they endlessly stepped on their Mexican coke and heroin to double or triple a month's supply to stretch it as far they could, just to eke out a little more. Customers complained quietly that Glasser dope wasn't shit anymore, wasn't any stronger than aspirin (at least until the heroin started hitting Angel), but where else were they going to go?

Who else were they going to go to?

Over his cigarettes and Van Dorn's black coffee—Dix always drank his free cups—Dix complained how dumb and dangerous Ricky was, how cunning Little Paris could be (despite his meth habit and fraying judgment), and just how far away the Old Man had stepped from any day-to-day decisions.

Dix liked to wax a little *too* poetic about the young girls Little Paris always had around Lower Wolf. Some who stayed on for weeks or months, others who disappeared as quickly as they appeared. In his slow drawl, Dix could describe their tits and their tattoos and their hair color and the music they liked (while staring at Casey in a way that made her skin crawl), but nothing ever important or real, no way to go back and ever identify them.

He said Little Paris even had a bastard boy by one of them, then a couple of years old, that he was already calling his *little outlaw* . . . real name Harmon Glasser, although everyone just called him Hardy.

Hardy would strut around in a little cowboy hat pulled low over his blond hair and a toy six-gun in his hand and he was more like a mascot, cooed over and looked after by all those girls.

Dix was downright eloquent about the pussy and the parties and payoffs and the constant flow of traffic in and out of Lower Wolf, including cops on the Glasser payroll—KSP troopers and Lawrence and Martin County deputies and even Angel and Tomahawk officers— but he was forever sketchy on their actual names, next to impossible to pin down with dates.

All his details oddly specific and completely useless at the same time.

He might talk about a day in July and in the same breath describe snow dusting the ground. Or mention a certain deputy running by to pick up a fat envelope during a UK basketball game one January after- noon, only for Casey to find out there wasn't a game that day at all. There was always someone else who knew more than he did, even when he was the only witness. There was no way for Casey to cor- roborate anything that came out of his mouth, everything vague, weightless, like his endless cigarette smoke.

In fact, about the only thing he was damn certain of was that he was *never* wearing a fucking wire. He accepted he was a snitch, a fuck- ing rat, but he was never going to look one of the Glassers in the eye while he was secretly recording them.

They'd fucking know.

He couldn't say exactly how or why, just that they would. *Knowing* was their real power, the true secret of their success and survival. Call it a primal instinct. They had eyes and ears everywhere and could smell fucking betrayal like a fish stink.

Little Paris most of all.

In the end, Casey didn't like using Dix any more than Van Dorn did, but she went all in on him anyway. She cut deals with her Fed prosecutor to keep him out of jail (pending his significant cooperation and as long as he didn't turn around and lie his ass off on the stand) and got approval from Assistant Special Agent in Charge Dubois to keep him on the street.

She even got him set up with a little spending money.

She ignored it whenever he was using.

And then, just like that, he was fucking gone.

Just as fast, just as completely, as all the nameless and faceless girls he'd talked about.

21

Dix was gone so fast they were never able to get up on their wires. Far too fast to testify to anything, and of course, he never set up a meet with anyone.

Leaving Casey with nothing but the dope he'd been caught with and his uncorroborated confession. The rest of his debriefings, all those wasted cups of coffee and cigarettes, equally useless, no better than fairy tales or ghost stories.

But neither Casey nor Van Dorn made him for a runner. The Jerry Dixes of the world usually didn't run, even when it was the smart move, even when it was the *only* move.

Maybe he'd been right all along, and the Glassers really did know he was talking from the start.

They'd fucking know.

Those eyes and ears everywhere he was so worried about.

Worse, within a week of his disappearance, Casey was getting angry calls at all hours of the night from Dix's twin sister, Janelle, whom she'd never met. She lived over in Nitro and wasn't particularly tight then with any of the Glassers (or even Dix's wife, for that matter, whom she clearly hated), but she knew all about her brother's involvement with them. Casey had warned him over and over not to tell anyone he was talking to the Feds, the same way they weren't telling any of the local cops he was working with them, but he ratted himself out to Janelle anyway, proving that old adage—

Once a fucking snitch, always a fucking snitch.

He spilled to her all about Van Dorn and Casey and even gave her the number Casey had given him for emergencies.

Casey had almost expected those calls from the wife, Holly, but either Dix really had held his tongue with her or she never cared that he was gone. Maybe she was even relieved. Van Dorn assumed *she* was the one who fingered him to the Glassers, but whatever the truth of it, Janelle was the only one frantic at Jerry's disappearance, demanding Casey do something . . . *anything.*

Every new call she was cussing a longer blue streak, blaming Casey personally—

Wasn't it your goddamn job to protect him?

You made my brother do these things. He didn't know no damn better. He trusted you.

You know them damn Glassers, what they're like. What did you think was gonna happen?

Them cops were in on it too . . . you know that.

You fucking know that. You can't trust any of 'em.

What about that whore of a wife of his? You question her?

What about that goddamn baby on the way?

What the fuck are you going to do now?

How the fuck do you sleep at night?

Until Casey finally had enough and wondered out loud to Janelle Dix if she was asking those same goddamn questions of her brother's wife or, better yet, those fucking Glassers he'd always worked for, leaving the furious woman to tell Casey to go fuck herself before finally hanging up.

But she'd already gotten deep under Casey's skin. She'd made her goddamn point. They both knew her brother wasn't hiding out in some holler; he hadn't run. He'd hated the Glassers and, on some days. hell, maybe *most* days, hated his wife too, but he'd been legitimately infatuated with that impending baby, his or not. He was all wrapped up in the idea of being a daddy, since his had been so shitty.

He might have even tried to be a decent one, if he'd ever had the chance.

Frustrated and furious and fed up too, Casey had wanted to pull Renfro and Little Paris in right then and push on them. Push fucking *hard*. If Dix was already dead, whatever those two suspected about him didn't matter anymore.

Fuck them both.

She needed to look them in the eye and make them tell her they didn't have anything to do with his disappearance. And although Van Dorn mostly agreed with the sentiment, he told her you don't just *push* on the Glassers. They're implacable, immovable, like a fucking rock.

You'll break yourself long before you ever break one of them.

And by then Holly Dix was moving on anyway. Word was, she and the baby she was carrying had headed to family she had over in Sutton, West Virginia.

Janelle's midnight calls had mercifully stopped, too.

So it really was done.

Over.

No one was ever going to talk about Jerry Dix again, and *especially* not one of the Glassers.

But Casey kept at it anyway, finally wearing Van Dorn down—the same way she'd worn down the prosecutor and ASAC Dubois—convincing him that if the opportunity ever did present itself, they had to at least try.

She had to try.

And that was still her thinking two months after Dix's disappearance, when she and Van Dorn finally rolled up on Renfro alone, gassing his pearl-white Escalade at a Marathon in Tomahawk.

They flashed their badges and Renfro shrugged, unconcerned, showing teeth nearly as white as the Escalade.

He told them to fuck themselves, or fuck each other, didn't matter so much to him which, before he went back to gassing that ugly SUV and smoking a Swisher Sweet.

Until Van Dorn, *now* the frustrated one, pulled that big old S&W from his shoulder holster and aimed it at Renfro's grin and told him to get the fuck in the fucking Explorer.

22

It was hot, the sun red and swollen and low in the sky, as Jamie Renfro slouched against the passenger-side door, most of his six-foot-three frame folded up like a switchblade, hiding his face in late-afternoon shadows.

Up close, he wasn't bad-looking, in a sharp-edged way.

Bright, broken glass . . . That's what Casey thought at the time. Dark hair too long, slicked back and curled at the base of his neck. A white T-shirt and black jeans and motorcycle boots. Exposed arms long and veined. Powerful. He had hints of that distinct Glasser profile and a weathered face, like he'd spent too much time working out in the fields under a burning sun, although Casey knew Renfro hadn't spent a day of hard or honest work anywhere in his life.

He reminded her of the coal miners she'd seen around Angel and the other nearby towns. That careful, languid way he moved, like he knew there were a thousand tons of black rock balanced above him, just waiting to fall. And since he knew it all had to fall someday, the only question was if today was the day.

She guessed that when you're already standing in your own grave, it gives you a certain freedom to live your life however you goddamn please.

He had interesting green eyes. River green, flecked with sandy brown. If he weren't drifting around the ass end of Kentucky, someone might pick him out to model jeans or cowboy boots, make a beer or whiskey commercial.

If he wasn't a liar, a drug dealer, a thief, and more than likely a murderer, he might have really been something or someone. Instead, he was somehow nothing at all.

That's what she felt sitting next him—*nothing*—even with Van Dorn close by in the backseat, his revolver still out, resting in his lap. Renfro was an absence of light. He was fucking *vacant*, a hole in the world, and if you weren't careful, you could fall right into him and disappear forever.

Just like Jerry Dix.

But he didn't have any tattoos like Dix or Little Paris, no ink running up his neck or arms. No necklaces or earrings or even a gold tooth. He was unadorned, smooth, featureless.

Nothing . . . except for that one big silver ring on his right hand. A finely wrought laughing skull that probably cost several hundred dollars, sporting rubies or garnets for eyes, jewels that glowed with their own captured light.

Bloody light.

Casey knew if he struck you with it, that ring would leave more than just a bruise, but instead a deep, penetrating scar.

A ring like that would cut you all the way down to the bone, a lasting reminder of the moment you crossed him. A hurt you'd be forced to wear like some sort of scarlet letter.

And from the moment Renfro got in the Explorer at gunpoint, he sat there tapping his hand casually against the dashboard, that skull ring beating like a heart.

Casey didn't bother with a long prologue or windup. She asked Renfro where the fuck Jerry Dix had gotten off to, and after some silent thought on it, he told her he thought Dix had some family on the West Virginia side of the Big Sandy.

Maybe Hurricane, maybe Nitro, maybe somewhere else.

Or . . . maybe Renfro just couldn't fucking remember and didn't really care, since he and Dix weren't so close anymore.

See, Renfro went on, *I don't give a good goddamn for rats.*

Then he flashed more of that feral-dog smile from the pumps and said whenever they had vermin like that loose down at the Big House, they flushed them out right away. It was easy enough to drown the babies, the pups. *They weren't no problem at all.* After that, you just had to bait and poison the mamas and daddies.

There was nothing to it if you had the right help and caught 'em early enough. But if you didn't, then no telling how many you might end up with. They could keep you up all night with their squeaking and carrying on.

And he said it all without blinking, without concern, without even breaking a sweat in that hot SUV . . . and with that goddamn ring still tapping away the whole time.

Nothing.

His green eyes, which Casey hated imagining were probably beautiful in the right light, as empty and unalive as a flatlined heart.

She knew then—

Jerry Dix had been dead the moment they first sat down with him, the moment he first imagined he could ever trade his freedom for one of the Glassers.

Just another rat trying to get out of a trap.

She wondered, though, if they ever did find his body, if they'd also be able to tell where Renfro had struck him.

A scar across the face.

Blood in the eyes.

A crack in a bone that couldn't be from anything else other than that goddamn ring.

23

They pull on dust masks as they carefully move into the trailer, and when Casey steps over the body, sees the motorcycle boots, she knows for certain it's Renfro.

Green eyes and all.

Wide open and not so interesting or beautiful anymore, but just as vacant.

Casey works the math in her head, imagining her desk calendar and the months flipping by since Dix disappeared. Is it possible the woman in the house is the wife, Holly? The bloody baby girl theirs?

Casey can't be sure.

There's a second body deeper in the Lance, sprawled against a low-slung set of counters.

Empty glassine stamp bags lay scattered on the Formica countertops, along with boxes of Bob's Red Mill baking soda and Argo cornstarch. The air is still thick with the stuff, floating like fine snow in the heavy beams of their flashlights.

They were cutting heroin here, stepping on it hard.

Renfro and Little Paris could turn a pound of heroin into thousands of stamp bags, about a tenth of a gram each, depending on the cutting agent and the raw purity of the heroin itself. The Glassers were allegedly selling individual bags at anywhere from five to ten dollars, sometimes cheaper than a pack of cigarettes, though the bags were usually pulled together into ten-bag bundles and sold at a bit of a discount or wholesaled at bricks of five or more bundles each. Price and amount always varied like that, state to state, dealer to dealer, even street to street, but corner dealers pushing Glasser dope in Catlettsburg and Charleston were recently moving as much as one or two bricks *a day.*

Van Dorn wide-eyes the scene over his mask, making a wrap-it-up motion to Casey. The dusty trailer is no safer than the meth lab on the other side of the property, and probably much, much worse. For the past year they've been finding more and more Mexican heroin laced with acetyl fentanyl, a synthetic opiate analgesic eighty to a hundred times more potent than morphine, the resultant heroin mix easily fifty times stronger, a thousand times deadlier. That powerful high *is* the allure for those in the know, the truly snake-bitten, but newer and casual users often don't have any idea what they're taking, no way of even suspecting, and accidental overdoses were already becoming alarmingly all too common.

But now, that *pure* fentanyl was being cut with just a touch of Mira-Lax or caffeine powder, or being pilled and passed off as real oxys (still the drug of choice for the suburban set who haven't convinced themselves they're real addicts . . . not yet, anyway), and accidental ODs were really *exploding.*

Fatally.

The numbers were staggering, more people dying from overdoses in the past year than the number of Americans killed in Vietnam.

And all this loose powder in the air in Renfro's trailer is just as deadly to cops and first responders. A small bit of fentanyl-mixed heroin, even if it's cut with starch or baking soda, is deadly. A few grains of pure, raw, inhaled fentanyl will put a grown man down for good.

It's foolish for them to be in here, and it's going to be hard to get these bodies out anytime soon.

But before Casey retreats, she plays her beam over the counter. One of those glassine bags winks back at her, a tiny image of a dancing skeleton. She sweeps the light down near the corpse below it, wondering if it's possibly Little Paris. But his face is turned away from her, like he's looking back over his shoulder, staring at something chasing him down. His shadow. A ghost. She follows that lifeless gaze and discovers the Lance is puckered with holes.

A real gun battle between the two dead men.

Renfro didn't go down without a fight.

There's a gun near the dead man by the counter, something black and square like a MAC-10, a bloody extended grip and a long silencer or flash-suppressor that makes the gun look larger than it really is.

The shooter's in jeans, brand-new Adidas.

A nondescript blue shirt, like something a gardener might wear, is messily hiked up, revealing his torso and chest.

Unlike Renfro's, the shooter's skin crawls with tattoos.

She takes a step closer to get a better look and Van Dorn follows now too, close at her shoulder, breathing hard behind his mask. He finally sees the same thing she does. The same understanding.

A huge *M* and *S* mar the dead man's stomach, each thickly inked letter filled in with a hundred tiny skulls. The letters are bisected by a wide cross adorning a grave. The number *13* is on one arm of the cross, the word *mara* on the other.

There are more Spanish words etched into the gravestone itself, none of which Casey knows, even though she took a couple of years of Spanish when she was working out west.

She gets even closer now, nearly bending over him. He looks young. Real young. No more than seventeen or eighteen, hair razored right down to the scalp, like the deputy waiting for them outside. A few deeper lines cut into the temples. Ugly acne across his cheeks, pitted scars, but no tattoos on his face and neck. He no doubt already earned them, but whoever sent him wanted him low-key, able to blend in, at least with his shirt buttoned up.

He reminds Casey of Arizona . . . of young Ramón Álvarez.

This dead man isn't Glasser kin. He's not from Kentucky or West Virginia.

Whoever he is, he's a long way from home.

Those Mexicans always made Dix nervous too, the way they stared at him with their dark eyes as they counted the money they all knew wasn't enough, the way they casually kept their shirts high enough for him to see the guns in their chinos and talked around one another in a language he didn't understand.

The way the threats they never quite made were somehow still clear enough.

He understood those just fine.

He's Mara Salvatrucha. MS-13. A marero.

A sicario.

An assassin.

24

Casey's always been good at observing things.

A sixth sense, kind of a roving radar that's always on, that she wouldn't turn off even if she could.

Things just catch her eye, like the tattoos beneath the shirt of the dead marero.

Her daddy used to say she had the attention span of a magpie and the chattering to match, but it wasn't that. It's not that she can't focus, it's that she focuses too fast.

She takes everything in.

Like in Arizona, sitting with Devon, watching that house out in Surprise. They'd been at it for three days, staking out an alleged Sinaloa stash pad holding at least two hundred kilos of coke destined for Detroit. The house had been given up by a snitch, but with no timetable, no probable cause for a warrant, no names to run, and really nothing to go on other than the uncorroborated say-so of said snitch, there was nothing much to do but watch it for a few days. See what happened. Hope to get lucky.

Luck . . . hope . . . These aren't investigative tools, but sometimes it's all they have.

They'd submitted a request for a pole camera so they could

remotely record the house and street, but the tech guys claimed it would take them at least another week to get the cherry picker out there to install it, and they hadn't wanted to wait.

Fortunately, she didn't mind spending the time alone with Devon, who didn't mind spending it with her. He carefully avoided talking about his wife and two kids, and Casey carefully avoided mentioning them, but it wasn't like she couldn't see the titanium wedding band on his pale skin. It was a constant reminder to them both, so he just chose not to look at it and so did she.

It was a bad situation, and of course she knew better—her daddy would've said he raised her better—but it was what it was.

She liked the secret thrill of it. Sitting a little too close, staring a little too long, talking a little too openly.

It would have to end before it ever really got started and they both knew it. The Phoenix office was too small, their task force group too tight-knit. People would talk, if they weren't already, and neither of them needed that.

But for three days that summer, it was all right.

25

Finding the marero shooter changes everything.

His gang ties and the powdered heroin in Renfro's trailer all but confirm the drug-related motive both Casey and Van Dorn already suspected but assumed would take a backseat to the more immediate homicide case.

But the very real possibility his cold corpse can give up hot leads to an ongoing, active DEA MS-13 case means Casey and Van Dorn still have a role to play, which means they aren't going anywhere anytime soon.

It also means they need to get the bullet-riddled bodies out of the trailer ASAP, even with the obvious chemical hazards. They'll want as many good photos as they can get of their dead marero, and get into his pockets to find out if he's carrying any sort of license or ID.

They need to run his fingerprints too, or hope to get clear prints off the MAC-10, the only weapon so far recovered from Lower Wolf they can reasonably tie to someone *other* than a Glasser.

There are more shooters out there, somewhere. But if they can ID this one, he might lead them to the others.

So Van Dorn makes the calls. First, on moving the two dead men from the makeshift heroin lab before hazmat or a clandestine lab team arrives; second, to several local hospitals, in case the other shooters were exposed and start dropping too; and finally, to ASAC Dubois, letting him know that he and Casey are going to need some help.

Van Dorn finds more bottles of water and a pack of beef jerky shoved down between the Explorer's front seats.

They use the water to wash off their arms and faces, scrub clean the snowy dust from the trailer. Casey ruins a second T-shirt in the process but is stuck wearing it anyway.

The jerky is already opened and half eaten.

It's going to be a long night.

They don't strike real gold, not at first. No convenient ID in the marero's pockets, just three dollars in wadded cash and some change. *But . . .* there is a bloodstained note written mostly in Spanish they can get translated.

Fortunately, the two English words are clear enough—

Angel. Tomahawk.

A rough hand-drawn map too . . . along with a single 606-area-code phone number.

Eastern Kentucky, Martin County.

As Van Dorn expedites a subpoena on the unknown number, she pulls out her laptop, praying for a good Wi-Fi signal, hoping she can log directly on to the office system and run the number against every DEA investigation nationwide, as well as pull up everything they have about MS-13 affiliates or crews or cliques in Charleston and every other nearby city of any decent size.

Louisville. Columbus, Ohio. Virginia. Washington, D.C., or Pittsburgh.

Charlotte.

Dozens and dozens of cases. Thousands of intel hits. A massive web. All the gang's code words and terminology—*palabrero, paro, chequo.*

Their tats and the symbology. The number 13, the devil's horns.

MS-13 has always been a notoriously poor drug-trafficking syndicate. They've tried again and again to break into the big leagues, but the loose nature of the organization and the insular and violent nature of local cliques—far more loyal to one another than to anyone or anything else—always undermine their efforts. They're better suited to work as muscle or assassins or low-level runners for real narcos, like La Familia or the Sinaloa cartel.

The sources for the Glassers' heroin.

So while the KSP crime-scene techs work on inking and printing the dead marero—rigor hasn't quite set in yet—she keeps working to link him to something, someone.

Anyone.

A name, a face.

Anything.

She's still falling down that rabbit hole when a local ambulance finally arrives.

26

Casey's been watching the kid for the better part of an hour now.

That old sixth sense.

She doesn't fully trust that feeling so much anymore. Knows now, after Arizona and Devon and Ramón Álvarez, that even knowing what's coming doesn't help you do a goddamn thing about it.

Sometimes it only makes it worse.

But the kid's been pinging her radar ever since she saw him hovering near the bodies.

Jamie Renfro.

The young marero.

They're part of his job, she gets that. He arrived in that homemade ambulance with the other paramedic, the heavyset guy in the weird black tactical outfit. It looks homemade too, like something his mom or someone sewed together for him. They're here to clear the dead from the Lower Wolf crime scene, but the kid's been studying the two bodies she and Van Dorn first moved out of Renfro's trailer.

He's not horrified. Not really moved one way or another. But he sure is fucking observant, taking everything in. Calculating. Weighing. Almost like he's waiting for his chance.

His opportunity.

For what?

Casey doesn't yet know.

He's about medium height and build. Nondescript in about every way possible, like a thousand kids walking across college campuses everywhere. But not him. Right now he's surrounded by the dead, the sort of scene that leaves even a seasoned homicide detective with nightmares. But the kid's either damn good at hiding his feelings or it truly doesn't bother him at all.

Bloodless.

That's the word for it. Even with all this bloody carnage around him, the spray and spatter and the yellow piss and voided bowels, the kid is untouched, unfazed.

He'd be a damned good poker player.

It's possible he did a stint in the military and saw some action in Afghanistan or more likely Iraq. He could be just old enough, barely. His hair is long, not fashionable, the shaggy, unkempt look of someone who finally got tired of a constant buzz cut or just doesn't care anymore. There are long earbuds draped around his neck running to a phone in his pocket. His heavier companion is clearly the boss, and the kid does what he's told, without question, without complaint. It's obvious they've worked together for a while, sharing their own second-hand, silent language. It's in the way they move, the way they delegate and defer without saying a thing.

Like agents, like cops.

The heavy guy is totally focused on the task at hand.

But the kid . . . not so much.

He's probably just waiting to snap a picture or shoot some video, maybe steal something from the crime scene. She's heard about stuff like that—morbid curiosity, murder junkies—and if that's his angle, it's not her concern. She has plenty of other problems. Way too fucking many.

In fact, she's just about to turn her attention away from him alto-gether and walk over to Van Dorn when she finally spies the moment she and the kid were probably both waiting for all along—

As he's loading Renfro's body onto a gurney, the kid slips his hand into the dead man's pocket.

27

Van Dorn's tied up now talking to Sheriff Dunn and one of the FBI agents.

Gesturing emphatically and seriously at both.

She's sure she just saw that kid slide a furtive hand into Renfro's pocket.

She knows he didn't find anything, because there was nothing to find. She'd checked Renfro herself when she dragged his dead ass out of the trailer.

But the kid was searching, too.

She closes the laptop and walks over to him anyway.

28

Up close, he doesn't look much different from Casey's first impression. If anything, only younger, but the light is so weird anyway—a kaleidoscope swirl of headlights, the light stands the evidence techs set up, and the interior lights of the house itself—that everyone looks unnatural, unreal.

Cartoons or caricatures of who they really are; smooth and polished and pale, all carrying shadows under their eyes. It makes Casey think of smeared makeup.

Most of the Lower Wolf compound is on the local electric grid, but the mareros cut the lines before or during the attack. One of the deputies found a backup diesel generator and got it up and running, so the Big House still blazes in the night, every window bright. Each one roseate.

Almost looks pretty from here, hiding all the horrors inside.

She approaches the kid just after he loads Renfro's gurney onto the ambulance. He steps back from her as if there's somewhere to go, as if she's going to let him go.

"I saw what you did," she says and knows she sounds like a teacher catching a kid passing a note, but all the while holding up the badge on the chain around her neck.

She can tell by counting eye blinks he's trying to read it, figure out who she is.

Calculating just how much trouble he's in.

Her back is to his heavyset partner, so she has a few seconds with him alone.

"There's nothing there. I mean, nothing in his pocket, right?" she offers, gesturing at Renfro with her badge. "Look, I'm not interested in getting you in trouble. I'm just curious what you were so curious about."

He starts, "Nothing . . . I . . . was . . . just . . . nothing . . ." before trailing off, staring ahead as if he's been slapped. Trying not to throw up or run or both.

Still badge-pointing at Renfro, she says, "Do you know who that is . . . *was?*"

He shrugs, a barely-there gesture. Hard to decipher, but she goes with it anyway.

"Look around you. Look at this fucking mess I'm dealing with. You really, really don't want to make my night any harder. So I want you to think very carefully about the questions I ask you and the next fucking thing you say."

He finally finds his voice. "Dobie doesn't have anything to do with it."

"*It?* What's that mean? And who the hell is *Dobie?*"

The kid points to his partner, now watching them and waiting awkwardly a respectful distance away. He's circling, coming and going at the same time. He wants to be included but knows he isn't invited.

Clearly worried, but also completely unsure what he's supposed to be doing.

"Is that his real name? *Dobie?*"

The kid's eyes flash. "What the hell is your name?"

And she almost laughs out loud, admiring the fact that his first thought is to protect, defend, his partner. Whatever trouble he's into, he doesn't want to take this Dobie character down with him, and that's a point in his favor.

"Fair enough. I'm Special Agent Alexander."

She raises the badge up to his eye level for emphasis. Wants to make sure he really looks at it.

"DEA."

"Oh," he says.

"*Oh* is right. But you know what? That's a good place for us to start over, to get it right this time. Get to the truth. So what's your name?"

The kid puts his hands in his pockets, the sort of gesture that most cops and agents would see as a certain threat, but Casey doesn't.

She sees it as a sign of acceptance.

Of starting over.

He looks at her.

"I'm Jon. But everyone just calls me Trey."

29

Dobie . . . Dobie Timmons . . . finally screws up his courage and approaches, but she sends him scurrying back just as fast with her badge.

She explains to him there's no problem, she just needs a few minutes of Trey's time. Dobie is respectful but still worried.

Casey suspects worrying is his natural metabolic state and tells him to go find a cup of coffee or something, that she'll bring Trey back over to him when they're done.

She then guides Trey over to the Explorer, where he tells her about Angelcare Rescue Service. How he's worked for Dobie Timmons for about a year and half and that he's twenty years old.

She asks for his license and he gives it up without complaint. He lives in Angel and looks even younger in the old license photo; hair different and acne on his face. She holds on to it as they talk.

"Do you know who that was you were frisking?"

"*Frisking?*" he repeats awkwardly, half-assed pretending he doesn't know what she means.

"Yeah, you know, like when a cop pats someone down for weapons, for contraband. Needles. Money. Drugs." She underlines the last.

"He's one of the Glassers. I mean, not a real Glasser. I've seen him around some. A cousin, maybe? Jamison. Jamie."

"That's the one," she says. "What about the Mexican, the gang-banger?"

"No," he says, quicker this time, with certainty. "Not him."

"How about all this?" She waves his license at the house and all the assembled cars.

"Nothing, I don't know anything about it. Why would I?"

"Because everyone around here knows something about the Glass-ers," she says.

He looks at her, taking in her *Martin County Deputy* T-shirt, and the DEA badge over it.

"You're not from here?"

"Yes and no," she says. "I'm based over the river in Charleston, part of the federal drug task force there. We work this part of eastern Kentucky because we're closest. So, yeah, I guess I know a lot about the Glassers, too."

Over Trey's shoulder, Van Dorn's done with Sheriff Dunn and the Feeb and now he's eyeballing Casey and the kid standing together. Like Timmons, he hesitates, unsure whether to walk over or hang back. In the weird light, all the shadows and off-color glare, he's trying to read her body language, and wants to give her space and time if she's work-ing something he might ruin by accidentally stepping all over it.

"Then you know what a shithole this place is," Trey says.

She smiles. "Well, I know how shitty the Glassers and others like them are making it. I'm not convinced there's anything wrong with the place itself."

"You don't live here. And you can get the hell out whenever you want."

She's about to tell him he can get the hell out whenever he wants too but realizes she doesn't really know a damn thing about young Jon Dorado, aka Trey, other than he had his hand down a dead man's pocket and is loyal to his friends.

Maybe he can't leave, either. Or *won't*, for a hundred reasons of his own.

Either way, right now, he's *not* free to leave until he answers a few more of her questions.

But Van Dorn's finally made up his mind and is now walking toward them, head down.

"Stick around, don't go anywhere," she says, before adding, "I was born and raised in Kentucky, too." She flips him the license, a show of goodwill. "I did leave, for a while. Then I came back home."

Trey shakes his head, catching the license cleanly and slipping it away.

"Why the fuck would you do that?"

30

The house sat in a bedroom community on the western side of Surprise, Arizona. North of White Tank Regional Mountain Park, almost near Wickenburg.

Lots of desert sky and low mountains. Feathered clouds and hanging dust turning each sunset into a kaleidoscope, scarlet and mauve and tangerine and gold.

All the houses nearly identical, taupe boxes surrounded by rocky xeriscape. Beds of agave and barrel cacti, yucca, Mexican bird-of-paradise and blue fan palms. Stunted orange trees and mesquite struggling beneath the weight of the heavy Arizona sun. The occasional bright blue pool with a small waterfall.

Mostly two-car garages.

Just like the one she and Devon were staring at.

They were parked with a long eye about four houses down, where they could see residential traffic east and west, most of the front of the house, both garage doors, a side door leading into the garage itself, and part of the fence that marked off the backyard.

A backyard of unimproved dirt dotted with weeds.

Not much had moved for three days—

Hot, dusty air.

The occasional bird way up high.

The mail.

Their first day on surveillance, an APS bill and circulars in the name of Elena Cruz had been dropped off at the row of mailboxes at the end of the street, but no one had yet walked down to retrieve them. She and Devon just kept running the plates on all the cars roving up and down Tonto Place, then wants and warrants on all the drivers, with no luck.

Kept staring hard at the windows blackened by sunshades at 1311 Tonto when they weren't sneaking looks at each other.

Despite the deep tint on the windows of Devon's Dodge Durango, they did draw some attention. On day two, a curious neighbor called in the complaint about the parked SUV, and they had to badge the Surprise PD marked unit that showed up to check them out.

They moved to the other side of the street.

Kept right on running plates and taking pictures of 1311 Tonto that probably meant nothing.

Their long looks, the shared secrets. It was silly, high school stuff. But given how she and AJ had crashed and burned, she'd needed the distraction, wanted the new attention and the interest, for at least a little while. All her relationships ended up wrecked and discarded and unrepairable. She drove them off the road yet kept getting behind the wheel, some sort of crazy death wish, although she was the one who always seemed to walk away unhurt. *Seemed to*, anyway. AJ wasn't really her fault, not this time, but there was Finn before him. And Carter. Miles. Jonah before that.

Jonah—decent, nice, a tenured professor at ASU—even asked her what the hell she thought she was looking for. She told him *Not you* and that was that.

Special Agent Devon Kim Jeon would eventually be another *not you*, but not yet.

———

It was late on day three when she saw the car.

Devon was talking about his life before DEA, when he worked at the San Antonio Police Department. Telling a funny story about a stint on vice, doing undercover at Asian massage parlors, when the green Sentra rolled past them a little too slow.

She was laughing at Devon's story, feigning interest since she'd heard it before, but she glanced down long enough to check the Sentra against her log and notes. The car was new, the first new thing in days.

Still laughing, she kept one eye on the Sentra as it continued east up Tonto, past 1307, 1309, then 1311, before nosing down the street and out of view again.

As it cruised past 1311, she half expected it to hit its brakes, but it didn't.

But it sure *felt* to her as if the unseen driver had nearly stopped. Had really wanted to.

That sixth sense of hers working overtime.

Now there was something off about the house, too. Nothing dramatic, something subtle. But definitely something *new*, like the car itself. Something she should have been able to pick out because she'd been staring at it for three straight days.

She put out a hand to quiet Devon. She grabbed his hand and he grabbed hers back, twining his fingers up with hers, misreading the moment and the gesture itself.

She'll always remember this—

Holding hands for two, maybe three heartbeats, but no longer than that.

The brief, cool, metallic touch of his wedding band against her skin . . . even though she would later leave that out in the after-action report to the Office of Professional Responsibility investigators.

Instead, she would simply say she got Special Agent Jeon's attention.

Made him aware.

And the investigators would nod and never follow up.

She couldn't admit how she'd touched him in that moment, how they'd touched each other like that.

Only later, when he lay dying.

She cataloged the house, checking it against her memory, even telling Devon to pull up all those pictures they'd taken, only to figure it out before he had the chance.

The side garage door was still closed, the way it had been since day one. But the small security light next to the door was a bright mote. With the sun at their backs, burning away the roof shadows that might have otherwise made it stand out and making the whole world white in the way only the desert sun can, it was nearly impossible to see. But she was sure now that security light was glowing.

On.

A signal to the passing Sentra that had first grabbed her attention, caught her eye.

Then it went off.

31

Casey heads Van Dorn off before he can get to the Explorer. He's irritated, throwing looks back behind him at the two men still standing there. It's like they finished a conversation he wasn't quite done with yet or was sent away before he'd decided they were through.

"What's going on?" she asks.

"Was about to ask you the same thing," he answers, nodding a heavy chin in Trey's direction.

"Okay, let's trade. You first."

He crosses his arms. "This is a fucking mess. No one's in charge and everyone is. Even though KSP and the FBI are working the evidence for him, our friend Sheriff Dunn still wants to first-chair the investigation. Says it's a routine murder, his county."

"There's nothing routine about this," Casey says, although Dunn is otherwise right. Murders generally are state investigations, with only a dozen exceptions that kick them into federal orbit.

A murder-for-hire, crossing state lines, is one of them. A drug-related homicide is another.

"Exactly. I explained as slowly as I could that finding that dead Mexican cholo changes the math. That FBI agent, Feur, explained it to him too, but trust me, he isn't on our side, either. It'll be a pissing match between us and Feur eventually, but we'll worry about that then. Oh, and not to mention your ATF buddy, what's his name, Bell? He also wants his piece of the action because of that fucking MAC-10. Everybody's calling everyone else's boss, except for Dunn, who still thinks he *is* the goddamn boss. He's giving this up one way or another even if he doesn't know it yet."

"Speaking of calls, what about the subpoena on the number we pulled off the marero?"

Van Dorn scratches at a bare arm. The mosquitoes have started to work on all of them, Van Dorn most of all. "I'm working on it. It's coming." Scratches again, angrier. "I bet Feur can get it faster. Feebs get everything faster. Hell, he may already have it." He glares in Feur's direction, as if the agent really is holding out on them. Then he flashes a wolfish, unhappy grin. "You still want to call it, see what happens?"

"I do and so do you." Before they're done, every phone they find will be important, a necessary evil of modern high-tech law enforcement investigations. By checking call records and cell site date, dumping and pinging phones, they'll probably ID most of the victims and the remaining shooters as well, possibly even track them, if all the stars align. But that's a long, complicated process, so Casey already suggested a more low-tech, old-school approach to the one phone number they do have—cold-call the mysterious number from the marero's pocket and see if someone answers. She was willing to bet a thousand dollars no one would, but it's a classic agent trick that's worked before. Van Dorn originally shut the idea down in deference to Dunn and his deputies and the other federal agents working in the dark and heat and blood and flies . . . the mosquitoes . . . but he's just irritated enough now it seems she might be able to tempt him with it again.

He definitely has his moments, like when he put that gun in Renfro's face.

"Yeah," he says, lost for a moment in the Big House in front of them, ablaze with lights. Through the windows, shadows move across the bloodstained walls inside. "Thing is, even though I'm over there fighting for this case, I really, really don't want it."

"I know. But you're fighting for it because it's the right thing to do. Dunn and his deputies can't handle this, even if he thinks they want to. And they shouldn't handle it."

It's a fear she's had since she debriefed Dix and he disappeared— that one or more of the local deputies are working for the Glassers.

They have eyes and ears everywhere.

"Okay, I'm done dicking around," he says. "I'll give Dubois another call, let him throw his weight around for us, for a change. And then we'll dial up the number that cholo was holding, although I have a feeling we're kicking a fucking hornet's nest, for sure." And Van Dorn's suddenly pensive, fixing Casey with a long look. "I hope to hell Sheriff Dunn's *own* cell doesn't start chirping."

She can't tell whether he's joking or not.

"Now you," he says, raising his eyebrows in Trey's direction.

Casey runs down the situation, but only the highlights, as Trey watches them talk about him. When she gets to the part where she caught his hands riffling through Renfro's pockets, Van Dorn stops her—

"Have you gone through *his* pockets?"

"I'm working on it."

"What a fucking mess," he says again.

"Yeah, but it's gonna be *our* mess."

He laughs angrily. "Lucky us. Remember you feel that way a month from now." He stares at Trey, really taking him in, and Casey has no idea what he's thinking. What either of them are thinking.

"EMT, huh?"

"Well, in training," she says.

He shakes his head, dismissing Trey for the moment.

"Okay, then . . . phone or pockets?" he asks.

"Definitely phone," she answers, trying not to smile, not to look too victorious. "Our young trainee over there isn't going anywhere for a while."

32

It reminds Casey of those days she and her daddy spent searching that wooded run behind her home, looking for Royal, her missing dog.

All the things they found there.

And the one thing they didn't.

In their few hours in Lower Wolf, they've discovered twenty-five guns, everything from hunting rifles and handguns to an AR-15, a SIG SG 550, and the MAC-10.

Six women's purses with the contents dumped out and scattered around like fallen leaves. Wedding photos and credit cards and lipstick and tampons and orphaned earrings with missing studs.

Innumerable knives. Bucks and Spydercos and everything in between, including two switchblades.

Brass knuckles.

An athletic sock filled with buckshot.

Decent quantities of meth and heroin and coke and plenty of marijuana in various stages of processing and packaging.

Nine bodies, including two teenagers and the marero.

Seven cars and trucks, some up on axles, and that rusted-out Coupe de Ville. There are dozens of rotting roses inside it, that never-ending memorial to Danny Glasser.

Two dead dogs.

One live baby.

About twelve thousand in loose cash and two locked safes that still need to be drilled.

A handful of troy-ounce gold bars in a crawl space.

A Civil War–era bayonet and musket balls.

A Confederate flag.

A plastic toy six-gun.

A random assortment of wallets, many of which were searched and dumped out contemporaneous with the attack.

More fallen leaves.

Driver's licenses, which they hope will be matched to some of the bodies.

Three fragmentation grenades.

Four sets of SWAT-style body armor.

And eighteen cellphones.

33

All the recovered phones are spread out in plastic bags on a blanket behind the KSP evidence collection van.

They were photographed where they were found, then moved here. They've already been logged, and the bags numbered and labeled corresponding to a map of locations across the Lower Wolf crime scene.

Of the eighteen phones, twelve are juiced and working. Three, from visual inspection alone, look to be broken, either before or as a result of the attack. A Samsung Galaxy was even shattered by a bullet. The others were found discarded beneath beds and couches.

Black and dead, charges long ago expired.

Once they really comb through the house, they'll probably find another twenty or more cheap burners in drawers or still in Walmart bags.

The most promising ones will be data-dumped, their text messages and call logs and saved photos downloaded and searched.

Maybe one of the killers had a photo snapped sometime in the past.

It was Van Dorn's idea to make the 606 call within eyesight and earshot of all these recovered phones, just in case it's the one. Many of them are still silently twinkling, like tiny stars spread out on the ground, as dozens of text messages go unread and lost calls go forever unanswered.

It's like that old saying—

If a tree falls in the forest and no one is there to hear it, does it make it a sound?

They're about to find out.

34

Van Dorn uses his own cell—his number will be blocked—and ATF agent Roderick Bell agrees to help them.

He and Casey will eyeball all the seized phones, try to catch one of them winking or blinking, or even firing off a ringtone.

Some of the crime-scene techs and a few of the deputies have now circled in to watch what they're doing. One or two have figured out what's up, and Casey half expects them to reach down and silence the phones on their belts.

"We good?" Van Dorn asks, his own iPhone held up like it's a starting gun.

"Yep," Casey says, as Van Dorn punches digits.

He has the number written in his notebook in his other hand but doesn't bother to look at it. He's good that way. Always remembers the important things.

He puts the phone to his ear, then gives her and Bell a thumbs-up. Somewhere in the world, a phone is ringing.

She and Bell have the twelve working recovered phones in a line on the blanket in front of them.

They remain still, stubborn. Soldiers at attention.

"Nothing," Bell says, shaking his head.

Van Dorn keeps his thumb up. It's still ringing, but no one's answering.

Casey's eyes scan back and forth, back and forth. But it's her ears that pick it out first.

A hint of a song.

A goddamn ringtone.

One of the bags glows blue, insistent.

She grabs it, pulls it toward her. The phone inside is another Samsung like the one punched by a bullet, at least a year out of date. Its big LED screen is cracked, a jagged line right down the middle, but it's still readable.

Unknown caller.

There's a picture on the lock screen. It looks like flowers. Real flowers, taken up close, a photo the owner once snapped and saved, sometime long ago.

The phone has a whole song for a ringtone. But it's turned down, muffled by the thick, sealed evidence bag, a distant radio in a room far away.

Or a car driving by on a mostly empty road, headlights pushing back the night.

"Hell, I know that song," Bell says, taking the bag from her to look at the phone up close. "'She's Country,'" he adds, and when he senses Casey's confusion, as they both remember that during their one awkward date they never listened to the radio or even discussed what music they liked, he tries to clarify.

"It's a popular country song by Jason Aldean."

35

The evidence bag with the phone has a number.

A-12-6WF.

A is the main house where the Samsung phone was found.

12 designates a room in that house.

6WF identifies the victim the phone was found closest to. The suspected owner, a white female.

But Casey doesn't need to know all that to know who the phone belonged to.

It was recovered near the woman with the tattooed flowers on her back.

The Jason Aldean fan.

The bloody boot print.

"'She's Country.'"

Shot dead crawling toward her baby.

36

She'll always remember this too—

Devon turning away from her to look at the house.

His short, dark hair, and the fine hairs on the nape of his neck. The slightly sunburned skin. His left hand rubbing at that delicate spot there, the sort of gesture she already knows he does whenever he's lost in thought, thinking hard.

Both watching the garage door go up, waiting for another vehicle to pull out, another vehicle to pull in.

She hasn't forgotten about the Sentra, not really. Is still expecting any moment for it to reappear from the direction it disappeared, even as her sixth sense goes off a second time.

Catching a ghost of the Sentra in the passenger sideview mirror, coming east up Tonto. Faster now than before. It must have squared the block, getting behind them again. Fifty, twenty, ten feet away, eating up the distance.

Objects are closer than they appear.

But this is way too close, way too fast, almost brushing Devon's side of the Durango. Metal on metal.

The security light, the open garage door. All the usual signals for a load car pickup or drop. But this goddamn car has another agenda. It's a living thing with dark thoughts all its own and all the passenger windows are down.

There's bloody muzzle flare before she ever sees the guns themselves.

Then she's reaching for her own gun in the small of her back.

Reaching then for Devon, grabbing at his neck, trying to pull him down and toward her.

Safety glass in her hair. Blood all over her.

Devon's breath in her face, each of them trying to save the other.

Someone screaming—her—and the Durango rattling and rolling and coming apart as the Sentra rockets past.

Blood all over her. Her blood.

Devon's breath in her face. Someone screaming.

Dying.

That's the only time she ever admitted touching Special Agent Devon Kim Jeon.

Holding his hands, holding his head in her own bloody hands, holding him upright, trying to help him breathe and keep him alive, after he'd been hit three times at close range by automatic-weapons fire.

37

Casey walks Trey out to the Lance.

Van Dorn walks behind them.

As they make their way through the woods this time, they don't need their flashlights. Orange Cyalume sticks sprout all along the path, and portable light stands are now set up around the trailer.

Casey and Van Dorn had already moved the bodies before Trey and Dobie arrived, so Trey hasn't seen the trailer itself. Casey's not sure why she's showing it to him now, but she's working on instinct here, feeling her way in the Cyalume-lit night.

Van Dorn is giving her a little latitude. She was right about the phone and has earned it. But he'll start insisting soon they need to cut the kid loose.

Casey described the tattoos on the dead woman to Trey. *Country Girl.* But she couldn't bring herself to show him the actual body, to expose it in that way. *The flowers. The bloody boot print.* But he claimed he didn't know anyone with tattoos like that.

He couldn't or wouldn't hazard a guess at who the baby girl might be.

Still claims he doesn't know who the marero is.

So far, she still wants to believe him.

————

When they get to the trailer, she stops him by the front door, opens it, and takes out her flashlight. She works the beam around inside . . . *all that falling snow* . . . where it swirls and twirls like it'll fall forever. No one will enter the trailer again until the cleanup crew arrives.

Trey takes it all in.

The bullet holes. Dark splattered bloodstains like Rorschach tests.

That snowy heroin and cut floating in the air. The bags and bricks still spread out on the counter.

His eyes stop on the bags, like he's counting them, before looking away.

It's quick, but Casey catches it anyway. He'd rather stare at the blood than at the bags.

"You ever see that much H before?" Casey asks.

"H? You mean heroin? No, never," Trey says, shaking his head.

"But you've seen it around plenty, right? All around Martin and Lawrence Counties, up in Angel? All the time."

"Yeah," he says. "Too much. It's everywhere."

She flashes the light quick and close in his eyes and they're wide and dark. Pretty, like Renfro's, but otherwise different in every possible way.

He pulls back, startled.

"Are you using, Trey? Is that what all this is about? Is that why you were grabbing through Renfro's pockets, looking for your next fix?"

He backs down the Lance's steps. Van Dorn is ten or twelve paces behind, arms crossed.

"Fuck no, not me. I'm not using."

She follows him down, shutting the door behind her. "Look, after this shitty day, I don't even care. Go in and grab all you want. There's enough to kill everyone in this entire county, maybe two counties. All of Kentucky. That's a death sentence in there, but you already know that, don't you? You're too smart not to know it. You've been watching people you know die for the last year now, you and your buddy Dobie driving around in that hearse, picking up the dead."

"It's not like that. Not everyone. We save plenty of people, too," Trey counters, angrily. "Well, not me, but Dobie does."

He's breathing faster, scared now and uncertain and trying not to show it.

"We're usually not even interested in users, you know?" she says. "DEA, I mean. We only go after the biggest and baddest, right at the top. And around here, the Glassers are the top, I guess.

"But this epidemic, this crisis . . . whatever you want to call these people dying everywhere . . . has turned everything upside down. Not just here, but all over. Now we're paying attention to that very first OD death, right down on the street corner, working our way back to whatever piece of shit sold it. Now that piece of shit can be staring down a homicide charge for selling that lethal dose."

"What do you want from me?" Trey says. "I didn't have anything to do with this. I don't know anything. I didn't kill anyone. I'm not a god-damn Glasser."

She clicks off her light and sits down on the trailer's step.

"I know. But my partner over there wants me to turn out your pockets anyway and search that ambulance. He thinks you've been pinching dope from your callouts, either using or selling it yourself, and either way, that makes you one more problem we got to deal with. You're right, you're not a Glasser." She points the darkened flash-light at him. "But you have lived here your whole life and you know your way around. You know these people, which means you know *something*. So I have to ask myself, are you willing to help me make sense of all this? Because I sure could use some goddamn help right now. And right now everyone is either part of the solution . . . or another fucking problem."

She looks up at him, makes sure she has his attention. "Some animals showed up here today and killed all these people. Your friends, your neighbors. They shotgunned them to death and blew their fucking faces off so we'd have to sit around, like we are right now, trying to figure out who is who, trying to put all their pieces back together. But for some reason I still can't guess at, they left that one baby girl alive, maybe because even evil fuckers who'd do something like this *still* have some sort of conscience, somewhere. I don't know. I just really don't know anymore. The one we pulled out of this trailer looked young, not much older than you."

She pauses. The dead marero is even younger than Trey.

A real kid . . . like Ramón Álvarez.

"But that still didn't stop him from putting his boot in the back of a woman and shooting her inches away from her baby. *Inches.* There was blood all over that baby girl when we found her. So what about you, Trey? Do you still have any sort of conscience?"

Casey's tired now, and it hits her all at once. It takes out her knees, so it's a good thing she's already sitting down. Her damaged leg, the one that's half-dead and will never be quite right again, hums with high voltage, so many nerve endings gone, but still she feels pain anyway. The loss of it. Her whole body now shaking in the heat.

She still doesn't know where the baby went to, and it haunts her, not knowing.

She points back at the trailer behind her. "All these people died here tonight because of what's in there, no different than if they'd shot it all up or smoked it or snorted it or whatever. No different than if you'd sold it to them. That's the harsh truth. This shit doesn't just kill the user, the addict, although no one likes that word anymore, and it doesn't even matter. User, seller, supplier. Family and friends. It's all terminal, all fucking fatal. The dope business kills *everyone*, eventually."

The pain in her leg subsides. She can stand again, but she's not ready to.

"That's not fair," Trey says. "You can't put all this on me like that."

She knows it isn't fair. He's not Little Paris or Renfro or the dead marero or even Jerry Dix. *He's not Ramón.* But she's rolling the dice and hoping he's better than all of them. "Life's not fucking fair, but you know that already, too."

"No shit," he agrees, slumping to sit on the step next to her. "There really was a baby here?"

"Yeah," she says. "No shit, there was."

"Are you going to search me? Mess with Dobie, too?"

"Are you going to make me?"

"No," he relents. "No." He reaches into his pocket and takes out a tiny stamp bag and hands it to her. She holds it up, flicking on her flashlight again to get a really good look at it.

There's a dancing skeleton on it. The letters *DOA.*

No shit.

Exactly like the ones in the trailer.

"Are you going to tell me where you got this?"

"Yeah," Trey says, "I will. But there's another thing. I'm not sure, not completely, but I think you're missing one."

"What do you mean?" she asks.

"*A Glasser.* The bodies, I mean. I know you haven't ID'd everyone yet, or maybe even found them all, but when Dobie and I were moving Jamie Renfro, I heard some of the Martin deputies talking about it, and I think they're right."

She waits, gives him a moment.

"Right about what, Trey?"

"I didn't see Little Paris Glasser among the dead."

38

Two months after Special Agent Jeon was shot and buried, Casey's daddy died.

She was still on administrative leave, dealing with her own injuries, when she got word from her mom. It was a terse, tense message—delivered ice-cold, if such a thing was possible—but no different than most of their conversations both before and after she left home. Her dad's dying wish was that the frosty relationship between them might thaw, but Casey and her mom knew it never would, not even for the man they both loved.

The call was not unexpected, but still too soon. For two years, Simon Alexander had been succumbing to late-stage Alzheimer's, a particularly cruel punishment for a man who'd made a life of learning and knowing and studying and remembering the past. It was never clear if he really understood the true extent of her injuries, but he clung on long enough to see her through to the other side of recovery. He couldn't really travel, and early on after her shooting, neither could she, but in the months leading up to his death, they FaceTimed often. His face was so thin, so tiny, in the screen in her hand. When he could still remember something of what they'd both said the day before, they both went to the trouble to lie—he about the lesson plans he was preparing for a next year he'd never teach or that book about Lost River he was finally going to finish, and that she was doing fine, getting stronger, getting better.

It was good the screen was so small, the image so distant. Neither of them could see the other cry. But it did nothing to hide the shaking in both their hands.

He'd suffered and struggled with depression too, handing down to her those same black moods and storms, although his emotional tempests weren't as violent or as long, his fugues not quite as impenetrable. But he understood her in a way no one else ever could. He was patient with her because he knew what it was like to wait out those rains, living for the eye of the storm.

Both depression and Alzheimer's *could* be inherited; at least, some studies and scientists had suggested as much.

She'd never know which one had really killed him in the end.

During their last talk, he told her he was *sorry . . . so sorry.*

Her daddy hanged himself with a belt in the bathroom at home.

She grabbed an early flight out of Phoenix and got to Louisville in the late afternoon. It was still another hour-and-a-half drive out to Bowling Green and she took it slow, keeping the rental below the speed limit, windows down, warm air in her face. She booked a room at a Best Western a couple of miles from the Western Kentucky University campus where her daddy had taught for twenty years.

She didn't call or text her mom when she arrived. Just sat in her hotel room, drinking the Bulleit bourbon she'd picked up at the liquor store in Louisville. She opened those chintzy plastic-wrapped cups in the room and filled up one after another with a handful of ice and three fingers of bourbon and the warm Diet Coke she'd been sipping on the drive. She set them in a row on the table in front of her like she was serving drinks (an old college job) and turned up the AC and turned down the lights and opened the thick hotel curtains and watched Bowling Green under cover of dark. Streetlights and stars were all she had to drink by, her only company.

It was like sitting alone in a cold cave of her own making, reminding her of summers with her father.

Lost River Cave had been his passion, a seven-mile stretch of tunnels and warrens sixty feet below U.S. Highway 31W. It dated as far back as 8500 B.C., when prehistoric Indians hunted in the surrounding woods and sheltered in its cool passageways and buried their dead there, leaving behind bits of tools and spear tips and cracked arrowheads. It was Shawnee and Cherokee territory, then later, during the Civil War, both Confederate and Union soldiers quartered in the caves, where the river running beneath the city was one of the only local sources of water for the troops.

Those long-dead soldiers searched the cave, scrawling their names and ranks onto the rock.

There was a legend that Jesse James himself hid out in Lost River after robbing a bank in Russellville, but her daddy told her there was never any proof of that. The caves were used to house a flour and wool mill, even a sawmill, and bootleggers allegedly hid booze in the cave's shadows.

Ghosts haunted the place.

In the thirties, the cave was turned into the Cavern Nite Club, a novelty because the cool temperatures in the cave kept the club air-conditioned. Electricity was generated by waterwheel. *Billboard* magazine profiled the club, and there was a bar and a stage and an entire dance floor, and famous acts like Dinah Shore and others played there. Visitors and tourists rolling down the Dixie Highway made it famous for a while.

There was a photo that used to hang by her daddy's desk, a black-and-white taken in the forties, that showed the club filled with dancing couples. Groups sitting casually at tables strewn with bottles and glasses. A band playing, a man at a piano. The women all in dresses and heels and the men in coats and ties. A few of the couples were caught staring right up at the camera, and Casey used to imagine what they were thinking right at that moment—that quick flash in the electric-lit cave, the heat of the bodies against each other, the music echoing off the stone walls.

What did they do later that night? The day after? Who were they? Where did they go? Were they in love? When and how did they die?

Eventually travel on the Dixie Highway slowed down and the nightclub itself died out—just like all those who'd danced in it—and the cave fell into disrepair. It was used as a dumping ground and nearly forgotten except by the Friends of Lost River, a nonprofit trying to protect and restore this unusual piece of history and geology. In the eighties, the owners donated the cave entrance and twenty-acre valley surrounding it to Western Kentucky University, and in the nineties, the underground river was dammed, the cave reopening as part of the Lost River cave boat tour, the only one of its kind in the country. The whole valley became a protected sanctuary with walking trails and a butterfly habitat.

Casey's daddy taught history and classics at WKU but spent almost as much time in the university's Center for Cave and Karst Studies. He had hundreds of pages of notes and planned to write not one but two books—a nonfiction history of Lost River Cave, and a novel about a Union soldier who camped there. *A ghost story.* He was an active Friend of Lost River and convinced Casey to spend her teenage summers working at the cave with him, helping turn it into the sanctuary it later became. It was a gentle way to keep an eye on her, to keep her out of the sort of trouble she was already prone to get into and the increasingly frequent fights with her mom.

It was their time, their place. And although much of her adolescence was defined by a certain darkness, that darkened cave with all its ghosts was somehow safe, a shelter from her storms.

Her mom didn't care for any of it. She didn't share their passion for the history and secrets and stories it held. Originally from St. Louis, she hated Bowling Green and Kentucky, and never made much of a secret of it. Never hid her resentment over the closeness between her daughter and her husband.

And Casey didn't make it easy. The nights out, the running around and running away. Cops bringing her home. The threats and the anger and her storms, that depression like a heavy chain around her heart that she couldn't lift off, couldn't break. No matter how her daddy tried to explain it for them both, her mom couldn't or wouldn't understand it and expected Casey always—always—just to get over it.

Her daddy once told her Civil War soldiers suffered from something called the *melancholia*. It was diagnosed as *nostalgia* at a time when homesickness was still considered a disease that could be cured by leeching and beatings and public shaming. For soldiers, it was often worse in the fall and winter, as falling leaves and barren trees and shorter days reminded those who had faced Death's specter of life's short season; the ephemeral nature of breath and heartbeat.

It was like that for Casey too, whose blackest moods blew in with cold weather.

She used to tell herself she moved west to Arizona chasing both sunlight and sanity.

Following the sun.

———

She didn't sleep that night at the hotel. When the Diet Coke gave out, she drank the bourbon straight, right until dawn. Bottle empty, plastic cups crushed and tossed on the floor.

She showed up drunk at the cemetery with her hair messily pulled back and big sunglasses on, wearing the same black dress she'd worn to Devon's funeral, although then she was still so badly wounded it took three nurses to help her get into it and two dry-cleanings later to get her blood out of it. She stood opposite from her mom on the other side of the grave and looked straight down at the mahogany casket and the wind moved the flowers on all the wreaths and her hair and she grabbed the arm of the man next to her to keep from swaying and falling.

There were more than two hundred people there, friends and family and faculty, and Casey was alone.

Afterward, her mom hosted at the house, and Casey mumbled through a few conversations with people she sort of recognized or who remembered her, and then sat alone nursing a glass of garnet Ceretto Barolo 2013 in the room that used to be hers that her mom had converted completely to a guest room with glossy fake flowers and an even glossier pearl-white bedspread. She couldn't remember—or was too drunk to recall—when her mom threw out all her things.

Later, her mom stepped in to smoke one of the cigarettes and said only one thing.

"I guess I should have buried him in that damn cave, Cassandra."

Then left her behind in a trail of hot smoke to thank those who had stopped by to give their condolences.

Casey took the Barolo she'd been sipping and poured it out all over the bedspread and went down to her daddy's office and took all his notes and unfinished pages and stories and that single picture of the Cavern Nite Club.

She headed to Louisville without saying another word to anyone and took a red-eye back to Phoenix.

But her mom was right, she too wished they could have buried her daddy down in the cool shadows of Lost River, with all the ghosts he'd come to know, instead of alone.

The dead still there in the cave, all those spectral dancers and soldiers, would have welcomed him with open arms.

39

think you're missing one.

  A Glasser.

I didn't see Little Paris Glasser among the dead.

No . . . No.

Not just Little Paris.

There really was a baby here?

Casey remembers those long, smoke-filled debriefings a summer ago with Jerry Dix—

He said Little Paris even had a bastard boy by one of them, then a couple of years ago, that he was already calling his little outlaw . . . real name Harmon Glasser, although everyone just called him Hardy.

Hardy would strut around in a little cowboy hat pulled low over his blond hair and a toy six-gun in his hand and he was more like a mascot, cooed over and looked after by all those girls.

The list of items recovered from the Big House included a plastic toy six-gun.

That old sixth sense.

And now Casey's running back through those nebulous woods, toward the Big House, with Trey and Van Dorn trailing after her in the damp, misty night.

Van Dorn's calling her name, telling her to wait, to stop, to *just slow the fuck down.*

But she can't, just like she can't stop thinking about the bodies inside and the bloodstained layout of the hallways and rooms.

A-12-6WF.

Where Country Girl and her phone and her baby girl were found.

The room next to that one . . . either A-11 or A-13 . . . although it really doesn't matter which.

It reminds Casey of those days she and her daddy spent searching that wooded run behind her home, looking for Royal, her missing dog.

All the things they found there.

And the one thing they didn't.

A tiny cowboy hat on a badly painted dresser.

A trundle bed with twisted-up sheets . . . and hanging over the one bedpost, a little tooled leather belt with twin holsters.

But only one toy six-gun.

40

Y ou're out of your fucking mind," Van Dorn says politely, delicately, without much heat behind it.

He knows it's a reasonable plan, probably even a necessary one if she's right about Hardy Glasser, but still feels the need to officially object anyway, to spar with her over it, so if it goes sideways, he's preserved the right to say *I told you so.*

Casey punches him in a bare arm, right where he was scratching earlier. He winces and runs his big hands through his red hair. She can tell he's tired by the slow, deliberate way he's moving, even for him, but he'll catch his second wind.

He always does.

If they're going to run with Casey's plan they don't have much time.

Because she has no idea how much time Little Paris's son has left.

They're standing together near their Explorer and it's getting later, darker, despite all the emergency and evidence lights.

The moon hangs above the trees, a pale cut in the otherwise blackest blanket of night.

She's been making the practical arguments first, because she knows he's still reluctant to buy the Hardy Glasser theory.

"Look, the phones are a dead end right now. We have subpoenas out, but this time, on a Friday night? It's not happening. Not fast enough. You know it, I know it. We're not getting into Country Girl's password-locked phone either, not without some special equipment that'll take hours, if not days, to work, and so far, everyone around here pretends they don't have any clue who she is anyway. Now, I happen to think that's total bullshit. I think instead these deputy dawgs don't *want* to know who she is . . . or they sure in the fuck don't want *us* to know."

"Casey—"

"Don't defend the total lack of help we're getting here. Just don't."

"Fine," Van Dorn says, shrugging. "But my money is on Holly Dix."

He's already said it three times.

"Maybe. But remember, right after Jerry went up in smoke, she and that baby were long gone, so I'm not willing to make that bet. And you can't afford to, not with all those ex-wives you still support. If it's Holly Dix, when did she come back? Who's the other man in the room with her? Obviously not Renfro. But more important, why does our shooter lying next to Renfro out in the trailer have *her* number?"

"I don't know, Casey. No more than you do. You're guessing. We all are. But it is fucking weird," Van Dorn concedes. More hands through his hair.

It *is* weird. The whole scene, the way the mareros were both very efficient and curiously sloppy at the same time. They cut power to the main house but didn't put a bullet in the diesel generator. They took plenty of phones and IDs, blasted away most of the victims' faces, and even gunned down the one person who might be able to finger them right away (presumably an ally), but didn't think to completely wipe out that link by taking that note and phone number off their dead companion.

Worse, they left him behind . . . although as Van Dorn pointed out, that fuckup can be explained by the deadly powder floating in the trailer. Even their careless shooters were probably smart and otherwise careful enough not to go in there after him.

The attack was brutal but haphazard, the calling card of killers who were eager but maybe not very seasoned. Or maybe high on crank. Or just young, like the one they found. It's unclear how many there were or how they even got onto Lower Wolf property, although it's increasingly likely that their Country Girl helped with that too, somehow.

Too many questions and not enough answers.

And then there's the matter of Little Paris.

"We all know Little Paris Glasser is short, right? No more than five-five, if that. Trey says he used to wear these high-heeled cowboy boots to make himself look taller."

"Yeah," Van Dorn says. "Expensive ones."

"Not one of our dead adult vics matches that description. No one's wearing cowboy boots."

"That's damn thin, Casey."

"Probably," she agrees. "Paper thin. But it's not just that. It's the *car*. Do you remember what Little Paris drives?"

Van Dorn looks skyward. "Renfro had that Escalade. I want to say Little Paris had some sort of black sports car."

"Bingo. A late-model black Mustang. I just checked our case file. We've got seven vehicles here, including that creepy, rusted-out Caddy, but no Mustang."

"Huh," Van Dorn says. They've already run plates on all those vehicles to match registered owners to victims, like a real game of bingo, but the Glassers often swapped plates all around and paid others to use theirs. They can't run what isn't here.

You can't hide what's already missing.

"Trey picked up on the Mustang, too," Casey says. "No Little Paris, no car. He's not here. He was probably never here."

"And the locals?" Van Dorn asks. "The deputies?"

Casey waves off the question, letting him know she hasn't discussed it with them. It's not worth discussing with anyone here. "Well, *you* talked to Sheriff Dunn, what did he say?"

Van Dorn shakes his head. "He won't speculate one way or another about *any* of the vics. He wants positive IDs from the county coroner. Right now, he's trying to throw all of us out of here. Says he's going to call the governor."

"Sure. Right . . ." She holds on to the word longer than she has to and leans in to him. "You know what's going on here, Dunn's running interference, buying time. Look, for all the bogeyman talk about the mighty, terrible Glassers, they're one of the biggest economic boons in this whole county. It's only coal and the Glassers, and right now, coal is a whole lot less popular. Jesus, they're like fucking Google or Amazon around here. Their dope, their money, keeps everyone and everything afloat. There's probably not a sheriff's office or city PD for three counties they didn't invest in. I bet they donated more to Dunn's last three reelection campaigns than everyone else combined."

She leans back again, folding her arms. "On the border, over in Nogales, in Ciudad Juárez, the cartels did the same thing. They bought whole police departments. They bought the fucking military."

"This isn't the border, Casey," Van Dorn says. "And we're a long fucking way from Mexico."

Van Dorn gets tired of hearing about her work back west but knows firsthand how rural law enforcement and the people and communities they serve are entwined, coiled together sometimes like a knot of snakes.

"Don't pretend it's all that much different," she fires back. "There's plenty of folks standing around here that don't want us getting into those phones. They're afraid if we start dialing numbers, their cells are going to start ringing. And they definitely don't want us finding Little Paris. They're probably hiding him."

"And your bright idea is to use this kid from the ambulance?"

"Yes, Trey. That dope he showed me is bagged up just like in the trailer. Exact same. Same markings. Little dancing skeleton. DOA. He picked it up earlier from an overdose call. He's been running similar calls all evening. The same bad batch. His boss, Dobie Timmons, confirmed it. You saw how they were still cutting and bagging in the Lance? Renfro and Little Paris must have got that load in recently. Trey's ODs bought recently too . . . maybe yesterday or today. Maybe even a few fucking hours ago, right before all hell broke loose. They could have been right here, reupping, and that means maybe they saw something. They might know something . . . like where the fuck Little Paris is or how to find him."

"That's a lot of *maybes*, Casey, and I've got one certainty. Little Paris doesn't move his own stuff. Glassers stay arm's length away."

"Trey says otherwise. Little Paris did hand-to-hands all the time when it was to help a young woman he'd taken a shine to. Dix said the same thing."

"*Trey says?*"

"At least someone's talking. You've been over there jawing with Dunn all afternoon, and what do you have to show for it?"

Van Dorn shakes his head but concedes her point.

"We heard those stories," Casey says. "Little Paris trading dope for sex. Dix said Little Paris was practically a walking hard-on." And they've seen it in plenty of other cases, even so-called respectable and professional doctors all over Kentucky and West Virginia trading scrips for blowjobs. "Trey and Dobie's ODs from earlier fit the bill. Young, local, female. So let me take Trey up to Angel, have him help me run down these women from earlier. Find out what they know.

Working from the street *up*. If it's nothing, then I'm on the hook for all the paperwork we're going to be doing on this."

"Trust me, as the junior partner, you're on the hook anyway." Van Dorn stares over her shoulder in Trey's direction. "You really think you can find Little Paris that way? And the shooters are supposed to be the priority here, not Little Paris."

"One leads to the other. At least it's a real *lead*. Our best one. If he's alive, he knows who they are."

"*If* he's alive."

"Yes, *if* . . . and if he's still drawing breath, he might be in a position to finally *deal*. Like Jerry Dix, he might not have a fucking choice. Most of his family is dead, his empire is gone. His friends, even all these cops and deputies, won't hide him or help him forever, not with us and the FBI looking under every rock, and definitely not with those fucking sicarios breathing down his neck. We hold all the cards. We're going to make that sonofabitch trade his life and freedom for his Mexican sources and the cops he's always kept in his pocket."

"He'll never do that."

Now it's Casey turn to shrug, her chance to turn his earlier arguments against him—

"What, you're not willing to make *that* bet? Given everything at stake, how can we afford not to?"

He knows exactly what she's talking about when she says "everything." "Little Paris's son," he says unhappily.

"Right. Hardy Glasser. If Little Paris is alive, he's got that little boy with him."

Van Dorn looks uncomfortable. None of the local badges have been willing to admit or even concede the little boy exists—or if he does, that he was recently at Lower Wolf.

But Van Dorn saw the little gun belt just like she did.

That missing toy six-gun.

The shooters left one baby girl alive, so it's possible if Hardy Glasser was also here, they left him alive too and he's now somehow with Little Paris.

Or, worse, they took him.

Given how awful that is to imagine, Casey's actually praying he's with Little Paris. Either way, he's in incredible danger.

Danger that's *impossible* to imagine . . . or ignore.

Van Dorn can argue the merits of tracking down Little Paris but won't long turn his back on the risk to that little boy.

"We're not Child Protective Services, Casey. We have no support here."

"Who cares? Let Dunn bitch and complain and muddy up his *murder* investigation all he wants," she says. "You said yourself the math's now changed, and that math includes multiple OD fatalities from Glasser dope tonight. Dunn can call the governor, call the fucking president, but he can't stop us from chasing down the drug half of this. He can't take the dope from us. We can pursue that and don't need his permission and don't need to be here running all around his crime scene to do it."

Van Dorn chews his lip, still thinking.

"Little Paris is alive," Casey says. "I know he is. He's desperate and on the run and probably dragging this poor little kid with him, and we need to find them both before anyone else does. Not these local cops, definitely not the Mexicans gunning for him. We lose him now, we probably lose him forever." She pauses, letting that sink in. "Just a couple of interviews, that's all. If it's nothing, it's nothing. But if it's something, it's everything."

Van Dorn stares at Trey again. "No one else will give us the time of day. Why is *he* being so damn helpful all the sudden?"

"Trying to save his ass, and frankly, the much bigger ass of his part-ner. If it comes out he was stealing from their callouts, they're both fucked. Hard."

"And that was your sales pitch?"

"Not a pitch. Not even a threat. Just an observation."

"He's using, Casey. Has to be."

"No, I don't think so," she says. "Selling, maybe. But he's not using. Not tonight, and tonight is all I need."

"*Tonight,*" Van Dorn echoes. "I'm not winning this argument, am I?"

"You lost it before we walked over here. I was just being polite, go-ing through the motions, respecting my senior partner and all his vast experience."

Van Dorn rolls his eyes. "I don't want you going alone." And when those eyes settle, they're serious, concerned. In the best light, they're a piercing sky blue. In these faltering shadows, they're black.

"I know, I know. But it's getting late, and I need to at least get a run-ning head start. Sykes is already on his way out here, right? Let him take point on this, then join me."

Sykes is another task force agent. Dull but competent, and ASAC Dubois has him en route to Lower Wolf to lend a hand, at least until Dunn makes good on his threats and throws everyone back across the river.

Van Dorn settles against the Explorer, sighs out loud. "You're so worried about Little Paris's kid, but you got this one right here over a barrel, Casey." He makes a gesture toward Trey. "A big fucking barrel. And you know who that reminds me of? Jerry Dix."

"Not the same."

"Yes, it is. This kid lives *here*. When we're done, we get to walk away. He doesn't. At best, he'll have to answer to all his friends and family and all these deputies you don't trust why he was joyriding around with a federal agent. Or worse, if Little Paris *is* alive, and we don't find him fast enough, then the kid probably ends up answering to *him*."

She's got Van Dorn convinced, or at least cornered, so she doesn't argue. But he knows as well as she does that this is what they do, the risks they're forced to take, and the sort of risks they get others to take right along with them.

Like Jerry Dix.

"You're taking the Explorer, aren't you?" Van Dorn asks.

She smiles, thin. "Well, I'm sure in the hell not riding around in an ambulance with a bunch of dead people."

41

She waits while Trey talks with Dobie Timmons, explaining to him that he's leaving with her.

He doesn't even finish before Timmons starts walking toward her, alone. Trey retreats to the ambulance and retrieves a backpack.

Timmons is a big man, but her impression is there's something small, meek, about him. Unfortunately, now that Dix is on her mind (thanks to Van Dorn), she sees the missing snitch everywhere, even trapped inside the paramedic's skin. It's that same nervousness, same uncertainty. The world probably never treated either of them fairly. When Timmons gets to her, he's sweating badly in his black jumpsuit, his face shiny. He reflects the lights.

"Agent Alexander," he says, voice soft, matching her probably unfair opinion of him. He doesn't seem to have a clue what to do with his hands. "For the record, I strongly object to what you're doing here."

"*Strongly object?*" she echoes, and not kindly. "Okay, well, that's noted." She doesn't know what Trey said to him, but she doesn't want to reveal the baggie Trey showed her if he hasn't admitted it himself. "Unfortunately, Mr. Timmons, this isn't a democracy, so you don't get a vote." She tries to soften the blow. "Look, I understand this isn't convenient, but I need his help for a few hours, that's all."

"Is he in danger?" But he doesn't ask if Trey is in *trouble*.

"No, I hope not. But others are."

Timmons wipes his forehead with a sleeved arm. At least he was willing to admit he'd heard about Little Paris's son, even if he couldn't speculate who the mother was or where the boy might be if he's not with his daddy. "You need to understand that Trey is a good kid. Really good. But he's had a hard time of it. His family situation is difficult. His father isn't in the picture anymore, and his mother's not well. He takes care of her. It's all he does. It's just the two of them, no one else. Don't use that against him. Don't use that to make him do this."

She's not sure what Timmons is suggesting; she hasn't had the chance to quiz Trey about his home life. And it's not relevant, not for this one night. Trey *isn't* Dix, he's just providing some info, filling in some blanks. A little local color. That's what she can tell herself. "I'm not making him do anything, Mr. Timmons."

"Are you sure about that?" He stares at her, almost startled by his own question. It's clear he doesn't question other people often. "I'll help you. Whatever you need."

He's dead serious, even though he has no idea what he's offering or what he might be agreeing to. She can't help but respect him for it, and suddenly suspects he's known all along—or at least suspected himself—that Trey's been stealing from the very people they were supposed to help. For reasons of his own, he's chosen to look the other way, risking his own job and reputation. But he'll never be the one to get those women to talk to her. It's just not how he's wired, no matter how serious he is about trying. Trey might not be able to convince them either, but right now, her money is on him.

"I appreciate that. I really do. But Trey will be fine, I promise."

Timmons shakes his head. "You can't do that. Make a promise like that, I mean. And he isn't. Not even close."

"Isn't what?"

"Trey's not fine, Agent Alexander, and the fact you can't see that scares the hell out of me." Timmons stares at his hands, as if he's holding something in them. "He's broken, and I mean that in the nicest way possible."

Trey is now slowly walking to them, his backpack slung over his shoulder.

Earbuds in, listening to music. He can't hear them.

"I don't think there is a nice way to put that," she says, as she fobs open the Explorer's door, signaling that their little talk is over. "But if you truly want to help me, help *him*, there is something you can do. Something I think I might need from you."

Without hesitation, Timmons nods. "Anything."

"Okay," she says. "But just for the record, I think we're all a little broken."

And Timmons doesn't even try to argue with that, as she tells him what she needs.

42

Before she lets him in the Explorer, she finally does turn out his pockets.

Searches the backpack.

Wintergreen mints in his jeans. A wallet with two dollars. Not much else.

The wallet also holds a picture of Trey with his mom and dad.

She can't get a great look at it in the lost light, but Trey looks to be about fifteen or sixteen. His mom is dark-haired, pretty. The dad tall and good-looking too, one arm draped around his son. *A perfect family.* They're on a beach somewhere, bright sunlight threatening to wash both Trey and his dad out of the picture altogether.

She holds it up to him.

"Outer Banks a few years ago," Trey says, answering the implied question.

"So how's the family, Trey? Dobie tells me there's some issues. Anything I need to know about? Something you want to tell me?"

"No, we're all good."

She knows he's lying but lets it go.

She just needs tonight, that's all.

She slips the picture back into the wallet.

In the backpack there's a spare T-shirt, a phone charger, a paperback book from an author she doesn't recognize, a bottle of Bacardi Dragon Berry . . . and a loaded SIG Sauer 320.

"My dad's," Trey says. "A guy tried to rob the ambulance, looking for drugs."

"And your dad gave it to you for protection?" More likely, Trey slipped it out of the house, unnoticed.

"Yeah, something like that."

Casey can't imagine Timmons or Trey pulling a trigger. She drops the mag and clears the chamber and slides the gun into her jeans.

"I'll hold on to this for a little while," she says, "for both our sakes."

Then flashes the Bacardi at him. "Now, *this*? This I can get behind. I could use a goddamn drink, too."

But she holds the bottle down low, out of sight, as she pours it out on the ground anyway.

43

The idea of a drink sounds even better when thirty minutes later she and Trey pass a dump called the Crow Bar out on U.S. 23.

Front door open, watery light spilling out.

People mill inside, framed by the brighter, pulsing glow of TVs. Bodies and the shadows they throw are all in motion, indistinguishable. Are the patrons sitting on their bar stools just now learning about Lower Wolf? How much of what's happened has gotten out?

Is Little Paris Glasser hearing about himself and his family on the news, seeing the first pictures smuggled out?

Did the killers stop in for a cold one before or after they slaughtered all those people?

Hiding bloody shoes, hands still reeking of gun flash.

As they leave the bar behind, Trey tells her a story about a woman dying in the snow in the parking lot last winter. He does it again a few moments later when they roll past a vape shop, lit up brighter than the bar. Then it was a young couple who died there inside their car in the heat of summer, windows shut up tight. Sat putrefying for three days before anyone even bothered to call it in, their bodies swelling with methane, hydrogen sulfide, and ammonia. Sulfhemoglobin marbling them like mossy stones in a river, distorting their faces and features, turning them horror-movie black and green.

The woman's abdomen had exploded all over the dashboard, all over her husband, by the time Trey and Timmons got to them.

Now it's a gas station backed by tall maples, where a daddy of three was found in the shit-stained bathroom, needle still in his arm. A raccoon had gotten in at him.

As they draw closer to Angel, Trey continues to point out such places, one after another; house after house, trailers and parking lots. Mini-marts and gas stations. An old motel. A Baptist church. Gravel ditches on roadsides that would be all but indistinguishable from one another, if not for the fact someone had overdosed . . . had died there. Like a former teacher and track coach at Lawrence County High, still sitting in his Toyota, engine running. Trey knows them all. And although Casey's known the opioid epidemic was bad, her concept of it has been intellectual, statistical, framed by reports and investigations and arrests. Purely professional. For Trey, it's personal. All these people he knows and has grown up with. Maybe his own family.

Van Dorn was right, Trey can't walk away from this. Not tonight. Not tomorrow. Not the day after.

It's Angel.

He lives with an entire roll call of the dead and dying.

Including the two names he's already given her—

Anna Bishop.

Kara Grace.

44

They start with Kara.

The other one, Anna Bishop, isn't going anywhere. Van Dorn already checked, she's still in Angel PD lockup. Trey found one of Little Paris's stamp bags on Kara anyway: in her hand, holding on tight.

Kara's a single mother who lives in a trailer park that takes Trey a couple of false starts to find.

Angel's circled by a lot of trailer parks.

They've left the main road and they're driving through one now. Not really a *park*, nothing like ordered homes with manicured lawns in gridded lines and well-maintained streets, but more like a collection of child's blocks scattered all over the wild, rustic ground. Tucked on hillsides beneath oak and maple, all ready to fall over. Last year's Christmas lights silhouette a lot of them. Red, green, white. Fake icicles, a toppled Santa. A pack of deflated reindeer holding stale rainwater. The trailers wander and ramble and rust just like so many of the lives they hold.

It's not a charitable thought and Casey's in no position to judge. You do what you do to get through.

Cars park in zigzags at impossible angles; Fords and Chevys sit on blocks.

In the dark they hang weightless above the ground, held up by magic.

Trey searches for a sign, something recognizable. Casey has no idea what that might be, how he can tell one trailer from another, before realizing he's probably looking for whatever car or truck Kara drives around town.

That's how he's seen her most. Behind the wheel. Coming and going.

Given some time, Casey can pull up all of Kara's registered vehicles, but whatever she's driving now might not be in her name. Might not even be her car.

Trey's turned away, staring out his open window. He's rolled it down, the tinted glass interfering with what he needs to see.

The night's like heated metal. TVs grumble in the passing trailers. Dogs bark. A stereo is turned up loud and a man sings along with it, voice strong and clear, and Casey almost wants to park and listen for a while, try and make out the words.

"You grew up in Kentucky?" Trey asks.

She slows the Explorer down to a crawl, her window down, too. She likes the night on her face, even if it's only hot breath.

"Not here. Bowling Green, mostly, western Kentucky." She makes it sound like it's a whole other state.

"I've never been there."

"Not so different. I went away to college and then lived out west for a while. I wanted to get away for so long, but then my dad got real sick, and then somewhere along the way, I guess I did too . . . homesick." She laughs, bitter. "Silly, right? A stupid joke. Anyway, there weren't any openings in Louisville or Lexington or London. And DEA doesn't have an office in Bowling Green, so Charleston was as close to home as I could get."

"Did your dad get better?"

"No, no, he didn't." Christmas lights wink at her. "He was very sick, suffering a lot, and when he died . . . well, maybe it *was* for the better. That's what I tell myself, anyway. That's what other people tell you. Some sort of final peace and all that."

"I guess," Trey says, still looking out the window. Given all the death he's seen, how close he's been to ravaged bodies and decay and suffering and fleeing spirits or souls, she wonders what *peace* even means to him.

"My dad got sick, too," he says.

His father isn't in the picture anymore, and his mother's not well. He takes care of her.

"So your dad died, too?"

"No," Trey says, and then raises his hand, motioning for her to stop. "Sometimes I wish he had, though."

He points at a trailer no different from all the others, at a beat-up Ford Fiesta parked in front of it.

"I think this is it."

45

asey runs the plates. The Ford is registered to a Kara Jewel Grace. A pretty name.

"There's another car I've seen her driving around, though, like an older Camaro, something like that? It's this ugly-ass green, really hard to miss. That must be Ronnie's or Duane's, the guy she was found with earlier tonight at the baseball park." Trey shifts in his seat, angling for a better look. Craning his neck. "But I don't see it. Nothing else."

Casey doesn't, either. The trailer's mostly dark, with only one window shining. Imagining the layout, counting possible rooms in her head, Casey guesses it's a bedroom. That pale nimbus of light suggests a TV.

After cutting the engine, she and Trey sit silent in the dark, listening, but the trailer remains still and quiet, too.

A kid's bike lies in the grass out front, a rusty heap with a banana seat. Trey mentioned Kara's boy, but thought he'd been left with a family friend.

There's a wind chime of old glass bottles near the front door, tinkling gently like random piano keys. A big rubber trash can sits close to the trailer's side, overflowing, and behind that, a rising spread of trees and darkness, threatening to overtake everything like a wave.

She opens her door, and when Trey does the same, she points him back into the Explorer. "No way. You stay here, let me go up there first."

He pauses, half in, half out of the car. "Is this how it's done?"

And she almost laughs. It's a strange question, *strangely perceptive.* Even young Trey Dorado understands there are rules and procedures to follow, and that driving around alone with him like this, chasing people down, and knocking on their dark trailer doors in the night probably doesn't fall within any of them.

But there was a baby, covered in blood.

Bodies everywhere.

A toy six-gun.

Sometimes there just aren't rules.

She hands him her small flashlight. "In case you see anything." Then pulls her Glock from the holster at her waist.

"Just wait here."

46

It was her senior year in college when Casey decided she wanted to be a cop.

Mostly because she was already dating a cop—Eric Royce. She was working at a bar off campus when she met him, and although he was about five years older than she was, they hit it off. It could be argued that she was already hitting it off with a lot of men like Eric Royce back then, but she was twenty-two, six months shy of graduation, and she'd finally learned how to illuminate the darkness that had plagued her since high school. Or at least cope with it. She spoke with her Student Health Services therapist once a week (who'd found a combination of meds that seemed to keep the worst of it at bay) and had learned to heed the warning signs forecasting her deepest bouts of blackness. That figurative, sometimes literal, change in her emotional weather: one of those sudden, sweeping storms that could send her raging or keep her curled in the fetal position in her bed for two days.

That chain around her neck, weighing her down.

But she *was* managing.

No, better than that, she was *overcoming*.

And Eric didn't know any of that. He didn't take himself too seriously, given his job (she'd learn later most cops took themselves way too seriously) and she was an up-for-anything redhead (she was red then too) majoring in history at Brafferton.

Brafferton College was great for history. It was in the heart of the Blue Ridge Mountains, just outside Shenandoah National Park, and with all the redbrick buildings and ancient ivy, the place breathed history, and Casey had fallen in love with it the first time she saw it. There were also three major cave systems nearby: the Shenandoah Caverns, Grand Caverns, and Luray Caverns. During those college years, she and her daddy visited all three.

Eric was with the Virginia State Police, a trooper for a couple of years, but by the time she met him, he had just transitioned over to their Bureau of Criminal Investigation. He was off the road and out of that starched uniform, his trooper buzz cut already starting to grow out, but not quite long, as it would be a few years later, when she saw his picture in the paper because he was part of a joint FBI/VSP task force struggling with a string of high-profile murders across Virginia. It was hard to reconcile *that* serious-faced man, worn and weathered, with the one she once knew.

Harder still to say if it was that horrible case or the job itself that had aged him. All those the intervening years, the inexorable passage of time itself. She'd wanted to call him but wasn't sure what to say or where to begin. *Thank him, maybe.* By then she'd already passed DEA's Basic Agent school and had two years under her belt at the Washington District Office and her transfer out west was pending.

She never did reach out to him. As grateful as she was for how he'd unknowingly set her on a path, he was the past. *Her history.* If she'd learned anything from her daddy's fascination with Lost River and her own Brafferton studies, time passed, and everyone became someone else's old photographs and letters and regrets and memories. Everything became history, eventually.

It's no use going back to yesterday, because I was a different person then.

That was from *Alice's Adventures in Wonderland*. Her daddy used to call her *my Alice*, but for someone who'd always revered history as much as he did, who'd searched it for secrets, he knew the past mattered only because without those years gone by, there was no present, no *here and now*. The past was your path forward.

Like a brief fling with a man named Eric Royce, who'd unwittingly shown her the way.

And she thought she'd understood that. Until Arizona and Devon Jeon's death.

Until Ramón Álvarez.

Until, with nowhere else to go and no one left to turn to, she'd tried to come home again, only to find both home and she had changed.

It's no use going back to yesterday, because I was a different person then.

If he had to do it again, Casey's daddy might have named her Alice . . . *my Alice* . . . but he'd been really into Greek mythology when she was born, so he'd named her Cassandra instead, who'd been blessed by the gods with the ability to see the future yet cursed to have no one believe her.

If nothing else, Casey's daddy had a wicked sense of humor. A scholar's idea of a joke.

He used to say *You can't predict the future, Cassandra, no one can.*

But she knows . . . *Even knowing what's coming doesn't help you do a goddamn thing about it.*

Those memories of Eric Royce—

He liked Moosehead beer. Enjoyed basketball. Didn't read much. Had a scar from an old fishing trip on the inside of his thigh, a soft place she once kissed again and again.

His hands on her.

Spending a weekend at his parents' old farm in Roanoke and his arms around her as he showed her how to steady and aim his duty gun, the first gun she'd ever held, since her daddy never believed in them and never owned one.

He abhorred violence, too many Civil War stories and photos.

Shooting at targets set up against hay bales in a field behind the barn.

The weight of that gun in her hand.

Eric telling her she had a natural aptitude for it, while tracing the tight grouping of holes she'd made. Amazed. He rolled up the target sheet and gave it to her and she held on to it for years.

Holding on to Eric's badge too, feeling that weight in her hand.

His offhand comment while taking the badge back from her and slipping it into his pocket . . . Damn, girl, you should think about being a cop. We're always looking for tough women like you.

That smile of his, a thousand kilowatts. That suggestion and the hidden compliment within it, forgotten as soon as it was uttered, as soon as he ran his hand beneath her T-shirt and over her breasts.

Tracing her skin there, with the same fingers that had traced her first shots just a few minutes before.

I think I will.

Whispering it again underneath her breath, as he kissed the words away.

47

Before she makes her way to the front door, she takes a quick look around the back, the dark turning everything muddy, indistinct. Odd shapes that, if she stares at them too long, shift and move on their own. There's a small back porch, a concrete slab, an even smaller Weber grill, and a door. No porch lights, no fencing. If someone runs, they have free access to the deep woods and whatever lies beyond. And she won't follow. Not into those trees, not alone.

Swinging back around, she uses her cellphone to briefly light up the trash can. Empty cans of SpaghettiOs. Two liters of soda. Go-Gurts. Pop-Tarts. A box of Lucky Charms. Kid food.

A bottle of Crown Royal and two *Hustlers*.

She pauses beneath the lighted window, puts her ear to the trailer. Listening. She was right, it's a TV turned down way low. No other sounds, no movement.

When she gets to the door, Glock held low by her side, she glances back at Trey. His window is still down, his face a pale thumbprint.

She pulls open the battered screen and knocks, shielding her eyes in case a porch light pops on. Instead, that TV glow halfway down the length of the trailer disappears.

Shit.

"Kara?" She knocks again, raises her voice. "Kara Grace? This is the police and I need to talk to you. *Now.*" There's a low whistle, Trey from the Explorer, and when she turns back he's pointing at the trailer, at something she can't see.

There's shuffling, stumbling, someone running inside.

Running toward the back door.

48

She tries the knob once, finds it loose but locked, and sprints away, circling back past the Huffy on its side and the choked trash can.

She won't follow into the trees.

Out of the corner of her eye she catches Trey sliding out of the Explorer and yells at him to get back, stay way the fuck back.

As she turns the trailer's corner, the porch door flies open, someone bailing out. The runner's back is to her and she drops to one knee, a braced stance, putting her Glock center mass, the Trijicon sight glowing green.

Aims small and tight between hunched shoulder blades. A shadow lost in other shadows.

She calls out *Stop* as fucking loud as she can and, amazingly, the shadowy figure does, turning back toward her.

There's something wrong about the runner's size, shape.

Odd shapes that, if she stares at them too long, shift and move on their own.

But there's something gripped tight in the runner's hands, her whole world narrowing down to it. Despite the ocean-thick dark, it's like there's one lone spotlight shining down from high above, illuminating the runner's hands.

A fucking gun there, metallic and bright.

Then, just like that, she's back in Arizona. But then she never saw the guns themselves, just the muzzles flashing.

Just the blood and broken glass.

Dropitdropitdropit, she's screaming.

She should be putting the goddamn threat down, protecting her partner. But there is no partner, no Van Dorn. No Devon anymore. Just her.

No.

Trey.

It takes roughly five pounds of pressure to pull a standard trigger. A human heart weighs far less than that, about eleven ounces. After Arizona and Ramón Álvarez, she never wants to shoot anyone again. Never, ever wants to stop another person's heart. Not if she can fucking help it.

She'll take the bullet herself first.

Then the runner drops the gun and cries out.

Lucky Charms and Pop-Tarts and Great Value soda pop.

A little kid's cry.

Trey is at her shoulder and has no idea what he's run into, what just nearly happened, but he calls out, "It's Dillon." Then again, louder, either because he's not sure she heard him or because he's scared, too.

"Just Dillon Mackey."

He's shining her flashlight into the dark in front of them both, so she can finally see it for herself.

Not Hardy Glasser.

But a boy all the same, eleven or twelve years old. Down on his knees, covering his face, crying.

Wearing a grass-stained Little League jersey.

A gun at his feet.

49

After the heavy shadows at Kara's trailer, the overhead lights in Angel's small, antiquated police department are way too harsh, way too bright. Like a goddamn hospital room.

But Officer Davis Andrews isn't half that bright or is trying awful hard to play dumb. Either way, he's not being helpful. Not at all.

Trey and the boy, Dillon Mackey, are waiting outside in the Explorer as Casey tries one more time to get through to Officer Andrews.

"I'm looking for Kara Grace, a local resident who OD'd earlier tonight. I went out to her trailer to speak with her, and she's gone missing. She left her minor son, Dillon, alone. I need Child Protective Services to take the boy, and I need you to put out a lookout for Ms. Grace. It's possible she's in an older-model Camaro, possibly registered to a Duane Scheel or her husband, Ronnie Mackey."

Andrews is thick through the neck, through the middle, too. His uniform is a half-size too small and his forehead shines as he lets slip a smile, really enjoying his hick routine. Hamming it up. He spits into a Dairy Queen cup on the counter in front of him. "Kara Grace isn't *missing*. She's run off again to get herself a little taste of that shit she likes so much and left that boy on his own like she always does. She'll turn up soon enough."

"I don't want her to *turn up*, Officer Andrews, I want her fucking *found*. Now." Casey flashes her own zippered smile. "There is a god-damn difference."

Andrews crosses his arms. "Now, ma'am, there's no need—"

"No, not ma'am. That's *agent*. *Special Agent* Alexander—"

"Okay, *Agent* Alexander." Andrews grins again, too sharp, too un-natural, like it doesn't go with the rest of his round head. A jack-o'-lantern smile razor-cut into a ripe pumpkin. "I saw *Ms.* Grace earlier tonight, along with that boyfriend of hers, Scheel. They both dropped out in front of half of Angel at her boy's Little League game. Embar-rassing is what it was. Scheel's on a slab right now and I honestly have no idea where that crazy woman is. But last time I checked, there's no crime in leaving her boy alone at home."

"She left him with a *gun*."

"No crime in that, either. Boy's gotta be able to defend himself." Now there's a nasty gleam in his smile, and he turns his attention back to the papers in front of him and continues without looking up. "And there's damn sure no law says you can't be a shitty mama. Call the woman if you care to. Raise all sorts of hell. I'm sure there's family, relatives, someone around who'll take him in if you're all that concerned."

Casey takes a breath and collects herself, wondering how much of Andrews's attitude is because she's a federal agent, or a woman, or if he's just a run-of-the-mill prick. Probably a healthy mixture of all three. Van Dorn tells her all the time she has a real way with people, and that way is neither pleasant nor patient—kind of like nails on a chalkboard—but she *really* doesn't have time for this shit now. She can't even pretend to play nice. She and Trey talked with the boy, who was scared, angry, and uncooperative. He had no idea where his mom ran off to, and although he could recite her cellphone number by heart, he didn't have a landline or a cell of his own to call her, which makes leaving him at home alone all that much worse.

Kara didn't answer when Casey tried her from her own phone, and her most likely illegal search of the dingy trailer didn't turn up anything.

All the while, Dillon kept asking them to take him to his daddy, who she already knew was locked up at Big Sandy RDC.

Her batting average so far isn't good. She's held a bloody baby, drawn down on a small boy, and basically forced a teenager into playing local tour guide. She's got zero patience left for a man like Andrews, even if he is wearing a badge.

She reaches behind her, pulls out the old Colt revolver Dillon Mackey was running with, and drops it on the papers in front of him.

It's not a toy six-gun. It's the real fucking thing. Heavy and impossible to ignore.

"I figure that's unregistered or stolen. Either one is a fucking crime."

"There's no need for language like that." He stares at her, spits slow into his cup again. He clearly noticed her T-shirt earlier but hasn't commented on it until now. "You down at Lower Wolf, looking into the Glassers?"

"I'm not at liberty to discuss that with you."

"Sure," he says, then shrugs, like he's not at liberty to help her, either.

She gets up close to the counter between them and nearly leans over it. "Call your fucking chief."

Andrews glances at the old-style clock on the wall. Big round face, black numbers, slow-moving hands. The kind that don't seem to move at all if you're looking at them. "*Ma'am,* it's almost eleven o'clock. I already rustled him up once tonight, and I'm not getting him up again for this."

She pulls the badge on the chain from around her neck and starts tapping it on the counter, to make sure she has his attention.

"Look, if you don't make that call, I will. I want a BOLO put out on Kara Grace, I want some help dealing with her minor son, and I want to speak with Anna Bishop, who I believe you're holding here in lockup."

"There's no visiting hours tonight . . ."

She taps the gold badge again, louder. "And I want all that *now*, Officer Andrews. Right the fuck now. Or come tomorrow morning, I'm going to ram roughly one hundred DOJ attorneys up your ass for interfering with a federal investigation. *My* investigation." She points out the window behind her. "See, your jurisdiction, whatever pissant authority you think you have behind *your* badge, ends about three streets over from here, right at the city line." She holds up hers, swinging it in front of his narrowed eyes. "*My* authority is the whole goddamn US of A. I don't like doing this, but you're not giving me much of a choice. And make no mistake, when all is said and done, you're not going to have much of a fucking choice, either."

She drops the badge back around her neck. "So which call do you want your chief to get? One from you, one from me, or one from some amped-up DOJ lawyers? They live for shit like this, I promise you, and so do I."

Andrews works his dip, staring at her hard. He's breathing hard now too, like he's just run around the building.

"Or," she offers, "no calls get made, and we just work this out between us, right here, right now. Good old professional courtesy. Agent to officer, cop to cop."

Andrews blinks. Slow. Then reaches for the Colt between them.

"Be careful with that," she says. "It's loaded."

50

Casey and Trey stand outside the Explorer. Dillon's still inside, playing a video game on Trey's phone.

Trey's been good with him, quiet and patient. Better than Casey could ever be. She's picked up on the fact that Trey's really into music, and on the way over, he let Dillon listen to different songs on his phone, anything to take the boy's mind off what happened in the dark behind the trailer.

She wishes she could.

Despite the heat, Dillon brought along an old jacket. It's far too big for him, but he's held on to it tight since they left the trailer, like a little kid's security blanket.

He is just a little kid, Casey reminds herself.

But where Trey somehow seems too old for his age, Dillon Mackey seems way too young. Impossibly young. He'll never grow up right, not like this.

"I went around it a couple of different ways," Trey says, "but he really doesn't know where his mom is. Says she goes off all the time, so he's used to it. When I saw him earlier tonight out at the baseball fields, he was with Tanya Heck, so I just assumed that's where he still was.

But after we left, Kara must have brought him back home with her and then . . ." He pauses. "I'm sorry. I didn't know he'd be there alone."

"It's okay," she says, even though it isn't. She was shaking for ten minutes after she reholstered her gun, the first time she's drawn it and aimed at another human being since Arizona.

A goddamn child.

A part of her is still shaking.

Everyone talks about the trauma of a shooting, but you just can't know until you've been in one.

You have no way of knowing how deeply it's affected you until your next one.

Trey continues. "Tanya is a friend of Kara's, someone who could still take him in tonight, if she doesn't show." Trey shrugs. A lost gesture, as lost as Kara.

"Let me get this straight. You just left her? There was no follow-up? When someone ODs like that, you don't have to take them to the hospital or something?"

"Sometimes . . . It depends. In her case, she was conscious, responsive, and didn't want to go. She's an adult."

More or less, Casey thinks. But like Officer Duck Andrews made clear, there's no law that says you can't be a shitty mother . . . or an addicted one.

After Casey told Trey about her run-in with Andrews, he copped to a few of his own encounters with the infamous "Duck." At least she didn't feel she had to take her run-in with him personally anymore.

"Our friendly local officer is pulling Anna Bishop out of the tank now. What do I need to know? Anything I can use to leverage her help?"

Trey tells her about a former local basketball star, Mark Crosby. About a young girl who may or may not be named Ruby. Admits he once dated Anna, when they were both still in high school, but can't imagine how that would be any help. Neither can she.

Too little to go on. Too many dead ends.

He didn't find any of Little Paris's skeleton bags on any of the three of them but is still convinced they had some. Or were trying hard to get their hands on it.

"Duck said something about his chief getting called out earlier tonight? What was that about? Lower Wolf or one of these ODs?" she asks.

Now Trey's suddenly uncomfortable, clearly something he doesn't want to get into. "Chief Floyd? We ran another call earlier . . . the wife of the *former* chief. She was found in the Big Sandy." Trey points past Casey's shoulder, in the direction of the tri-bridge, where the unseen river flows. "Another possible OD. She was a big-time user, like Kara and Anna. But they're ruling it a suicide. Chief Floyd came out to see it firsthand. I was there."

"Jesus," Casey says. "The former chief?"

"Yeah," Trey says. "Paul Mayfield. His wife, Marissa."

There's a brittleness when Trey says it, as if he doesn't want their names in his mouth. He didn't even sound like that talking about Duck Andrews.

There's something fragile there.

"You didn't mention any of this earlier."

Trey doesn't look at her, focusing instead on Dillon in the Explorer, on the little lighted screen in the boy's hands, where tiny men and monsters run around one another, locked in eternal battle. Never-ending, no one ever winning, the score only going higher and higher. Casey doesn't play those games and has never even seen the point in them.

"I didn't think it was important. Look, I don't know what *is* important. I'm not the cop here, you are."

"Yeah, I know," Casey agrees. "And I'm doing a bang-up job so far, right?" She needs to call Van Dorn, let him know where she's at and what she's found. He's worked this area long enough that he probably knows this former chief, Mayfield. Probably has spent time with him at all sorts of law enforcement breakfasts and memorials. The name's even vaguely familiar to her.

"Trey, I need you to sit here with Dillon while I talk to Anna. I want to see how far I can get with her, then I'll cut you loose."

"I never thought I was under arrest."

"Well, I didn't cuff you," she says, offering a smile. "And I do appreciate the help. I didn't mention your name to this Duck character, and I won't to Anna, either. Once I'm done with her and we get Dillon settled, you can leave it to me and the rest of Angel's finest to track down Kara."

"If you're relying on Duck to help you crack the case, you'd be better off deputizing me, or Dillon in there," Trey says, with a hint of a smile of his own, before it soon disappears. "I talked to him some, you know, about Harmon . . . Hardy. Figuring maybe he saw him whenever Kara was visiting with Little Paris or whatever."

"What did he say?"

"He said he did see another kid, once. A little kid, younger than him, sitting in the back of Little Paris's car. Said his mama made a fuss all over him, but it was all pretend, all for show. She told him later she didn't like that boy much at all. That he was already mean, too much like his daddy."

He is just a little kid.

He'll never grow up right, not like this.

"Like father, like son," Casey says.

"Yeah, I guess." And Trey looks uncomfortable, unsettled with that thought. "But, listen, he's hungry, and so am I. I got all of two dollars on me. How about you give me a few more bucks and I'll walk over to that Marathon across the street and get the two of us something to eat."

"Fair enough," Casey says, as she fishes out a twenty and hands it over. "No booze, though. Nothing like that."

"I got it, chips and soda only. I'll bring you the receipt and the change."

She remembers the half-eaten bag of jerky in the Explorer and suddenly realizes she's starving, too. Can't even guess at when she last ate.

"Make that the three of us. Grab me one of those nuclear hot dogs and a Gatorade. Also, I need a pack of Marlboro Reds and a lighter."

"Jesus, you and Dobie both. That stuff will kill you," Trey says, as he folds the twenty into his hand.

"I know," she answers, "but what doesn't kill us makes us stronger, right?"

Then she dials Van Dorn as Dillon Mackey slays another monster.

51

Anna Bishop sits cuffed in the tiny room in front of Casey, a small desk between them.

The desk is scuffed and scratched and stained, marked by a thousand pencils and pens. Penknives and fingernails. It reminds Casey of one you'd find in a high school, where the people waiting behind it were once called up to the principal's office.

Trey dated Anna then. Maybe one or both sat here before.

There's also a folder on the desk, containing the arrest report and whatever other information Angel PD has on Anna. Andrews unceremoniously dropped it when he dumped Anna here, just as unceremoniously.

It was clear he couldn't get away from the two women fast enough.

Casey opens the folder, pretending to read the papers there, but is really studying Anna Bishop instead. How she keeps her handcuffed wrists high on the edge of the table, so her hands won't shake. The way she turns her head side to side: a facial tic, as if scanning a large crowd of strangers for one smiling face she might know. A friend. She smells funky, sweat and cigarettes and old perfume, and no doubt also the stale interior of the Firebird she was found in and the miasma of the two dead bodies found with her.

There's a black smear on her hand, as if something was written there in marker but has since been wiped off.

Her fingernails are chewed down to bloody crescents. The forefinger on each hand picks at the corner of the thumb next to it, steady as a ticking clock. She's dope sick, already deep in withdrawal. Casey can almost hear the woman's teeth chattering in her head.

Her eyes are glassy, unfocused. When she looks up, really takes Casey in for the first time, Casey finds they're a startling, wonderful gray. The color of smoke or the sky after a good long rain.

Kentucky rain keeps pourin' down . . . just like that old Elvis Presley song. Casey was twelve or thirteen and can remember singing that song with her daddy in the car on their way to Lost River.

Anna's mascara is smudged all around her hollowed eyes, just dark thunderclouds now.

Maybe she's not just looking for a friendly face in a crowd only she can see, but also searching an invisible sky for her next storm.

There's not a goddamn thing Casey can do about the weather. She learned that long ago, but . . .

I sure can be your friend, she thinks, as she closes the folder.

52

I wish Officer Andrews had uncuffed you. But, you know, his department, his rules." Casey shrugs, showing Anna it's out of her hands, a cruel decision she wouldn't have made if it was in hers.

Instead, Casey pulls out the lighter and the Marlboro Reds Trey got for her. She slides both over to Anna.

"Want one?"

Anna hesitates, then grabs the soft pack and fires one up. She hands the pack and lighter back to Casey, who shakes one free for herself. "I'll join you. I need one, too." Casey hasn't smoked since high school, since college, really, and even then it was only when she was out drinking with Eric Royce. And she hasn't done much of that since Devon was killed, just a few nights here and there. Bad nights. That first night she was released from the hospital and then in the hotel after her daddy passed.

But thankfully, muscle memory takes over, the same muscle memory she's strengthened at the range by firing her duty weapon, again and again and again. She lights the Marlboro as if it's her third one already.

She can take small drags here and there and fumble along with it. A prop for her hands.

She puts her empty Gatorade bottle up on the table for the two of them to use as a makeshift ashtray. She had only a couple of sips before pouring the rest into the street.

"You Martin PD?" Anna asks, gesturing at Casey's T-shirt. She probably means Martin *Sheriff's* Office but doesn't know the difference.

"No, I'm not." Casey's gold DEA badge has been hiding beneath her T-shirt, but now she pulls it out on its chain, letting it hang free. Anna leans forward to look at it, but it doesn't mean anything, either. It's all the same to her.

"I already asked for my lawyer," Anna says. At least she's watched some TV.

"I know," Casey answers, blowing smoke at the ceiling.

"They're going to try and put Mark and that girl, Ruby, on me. Like I did something wrong, but I didn't. I'm no . . ." She searches for a word someone once taught her. "Accessory." Then blows a mouthful of smoke of her own. "I'm sick. Too sick to talk."

Casey opens the folder again and holds up one of the papers inside, like she's reading it, but keeps it out of Anna's sightline. "That girl . . . Ruby . . . well, her real name is Monica Dupuy. She was barely sixteen. From Catlettsburg." Casey drops the paper. "*Sixteen.* Someone is going to that girl's home tonight to tell her mama and daddy that she's dead. They're going to tell them their little girl died sitting in a car with a couple of drugged-up strangers who were so desperate to score again they wouldn't do a damn thing for her."

Anna shakes her head, either disbelieving what she's hearing or refusing to accept Casey's version of it.

Casey slides the folder aside, settles her elbows on the table. "I don't want to be here talking to you like this, Anna. I don't want to say these things to you. I'm guessing you didn't mean to hurt that little girl, but

I'm not even going to ask about that. I only want to know about Little Paris Glasser."

"But my lawyer—"

"It's late, Anna. Way too late. Your court-appointed lawyer isn't showing up tonight, and even if he was to walk through that door right now, he'd only tell you exactly what I'm trying to tell you. I'm not asking about your role in the deaths of Mark Crosby and Monica Dupuy, so invoking doesn't help. There's no protection there. True, you still don't have to answer my questions, but you can't hide behind a lawyer if you don't. Not forever. I'm trying to help you. I really am, and I hope you can see that. Do you know what happened today at Lower Wolf?"

Casey waits, judging Anna's reaction. The way she looks off at the wall to her left, the flutter in her hands just before she turns to hide her eyes, signaling nerves beyond the dope shakes.

She's been there. Maybe not today, but recently. Very recently.

Sill looking away, Anna says, "I don't know what you're talking about."

"Anna, some men showed up there and killed everyone. Butchered them. A bloodbath. More kids, like Monica . . . *Ruby*." The girl's name gets Anna's attention again the way Casey wants it to.

"Well, Mark and I . . . We weren't down there. I mean, I never really went down there much. I don't know anything about that. Sure, I guess we saw LP earlier, running around, but later, after that . . ." Anna now realizes what she's said and closes her mouth like she's trying to hold the rest of the words back. Chew them and swallow them all.

"LP? Little Paris. Tell me about that."

Anna picks at her nails, at the ragged, bloody skin. She shakes her head, angry with herself. "Goddamn."

"This is easy, Anna. Nothing to it. Just tell me about Little Paris. I think he's still alive, and I need to find him. He's a dead man if I don't."

Anna laughs, bitter. "Now, why the fuck you trying to save Little Paris Glasser?" There are hot sparks in her eyes, brighter red than the cherry at the end of her cigarette. She laughs again, an angry, ugly sound that turns into an angrier, uglier cough. "Trying to save *him*? How's that make any goddamn sense? After all the miserable shit he's done? How is that even fair? *Look at me.* Why the fuck isn't anyone trying to save me?"

Casey pushes the cigarette pack to Anna. The lighter, too. She settles back in her chair.

"Tell that to Monica Dupuy. Tell that to her parents. Tell that to little Harmon Glasser and his mama, whoever she is." Something subtle moves across Anna's face when Casey says the little boy's name: recognition, or a memory. "This whole fucking world doesn't make any goddamn sense, Anna. None of it."

Casey leans in close, softens her tone. She's got to make this work. She's got one chance to pull Anna close.

I sure can be your friend.

"We both want Little Paris to pay for what he's done, and I happen to think that means spending the rest of his worthless life in a tiny cell. I don't want him to have the luxury of riding a bullet out of this town, like his brother, Danny, or any of the rest of them. He's got to pay every fucking cent of what he owes. So you're still here, and I'm still sitting here, ready to listen. You want saving? This is where it starts. Right here, right now. Or this is where we end it. Your choice."

Anna collapses in her chair, almost folding herself in half. She's fetal, but still sitting, held off the floor by invisible strings. The pain grips her, clenched like a fist. It won't let her go.

Her body is wracked, twisted. Bones and blood demanding another fix.

Her soul, Casey thinks, *if you believe in one.*

"I'm so goddamn sick."

"I know. I do. So let's see what we can do about that," Casey says, reaching over to steady her.

53

Casey's glad the old station doesn't have cameras in its interview rooms.

She pulls the Narcan out of her pocket. It's not the DOA that Anna *really* wants, or even the buprenorphine that could help ease or step down her symptoms, a process called precipitated withdrawal. But it's *something*. Right now Anna's body and brain are so desperate for the opioids she's become dependent on, she can't concentrate, can barely think. Hardly even knows who she is anymore. She craves that fix like air. Her bones ache and warp and freeze like water pipes in cold weather, even though she's sweating through her shirt.

Her eyes are blown so wide only the rims of those pretty irises are visible. It's like staring into twin eclipses or the dark eye of the storm.

The same Narcan that Trey and Dobie Timmons used to bring Kara back to life can jump-start Anna, buy Casey a few minutes to talk to the woman when she's not doubled over or throwing up or shitting herself.

Casey got the Narcan from Timmons and was left with the distinct impression she's not the only person he's shared some with.

It took him fifteen seconds to show her how to administer it.

She holds Anna close and fires a dose up each nostril, feeling the naloxone start working its way through Anna's system. Shoulders sagging, the slow steadying of her breath, her body unclenching. Bones and muscles warming up to room temperature.

Anna holding her too as subtle strength returns to her hands.

It's not the drug she really wants, but it's all Casey's got and all she's willing to give.

Casey thinks Anna's crying.

What she's doing isn't illegal and doesn't even really violate any DEA policies, but Casey's still glad there aren't any cameras.

There's no need for anyone to see Anna Bishop like this.

No need for anyone to see the two women hold each other until the shaking stops.

54

Jamie Renfro is a piece of shit," Anna says, working on a fresh cigarette. She's still hunched over, but at least she's coherent now. Held
together with duct tape and baling wire. Her tears are dry, and smoke
and hot breath circle her. "But he's got nothing on LP."

"Renfro's dead," Casey says. "We found him shot to hell."

"What about Old Man Glasser? Ricky?"

"Let's focus on Little Paris."

Anna shrugs, unconcerned. "The Old Man's been out of it for a while,
and Ricky's just a big fucking retard. None of the others ever trusted
him with anything. Jamie and LP were the real brains, and that ain't saying much, given there's hardly a lick of sense between the two of them.
But somehow they've been running it all since Danny died."

Anna scoots forward, eyeing the corners for the cameras that aren't
there and seeing the room clearly for the first time.

"Jamie was mean but acted like he was a real businessman. Tried to
be like Danny. Everything was always about the money, about the
business. Mostly. You never shorted Jamie and he never gave out anything on layaway, never fronted. LP's different and always has been.
He doesn't seem to give a damn about the money or the business. He's
something else altogether." She blows more smoke. "The devil."

"How's that?"

Anna drops her voice to a whisper. "Girls. LP has a thing for us girls in the worst way. He's sick too, got a disease, like me, but different, if you know what I mean. You can work a deal with LP. He'll take care of things personally, help you out if you're short. If things are light or tight . . ."

"But only if you're a girl," Casey finishes, and Anna looks away, not wanting to face what she's already said. She watches her cigarette smoke drift.

"When's the last time you saw him?"

Anna rubs at both eyes with the heel of her hands. "Yesterday, maybe? Day before? Just running around, though, like I said. Mark usually copped for us and dealt with all that, 'cause most times he didn't want *me* dealing with LP. But Mark had it bad all day and was already looking ahead, knew we were going to be light tonight. We barely had enough gas money to pick up Ruby, so he had me call LP direct, trying to meet up later. He knew LP might be more flexible if it was me on the line." Anna pauses a beat too long. "But he never answered."

"Do you have his number, the one you were calling?"

"It's in my phone." She waves at the room beyond the door, at some mysterious place where only phones exist.

"When you saw him yesterday, just running around, did you cop some of his new stuff? A bag stamped with a skeleton?"

Anna blinks through her smoke but doesn't answer.

"Who else would he meet like that? Like you?"

"All us girls know LP."

"What about Kara Grace?"

"Sure, yeah. She and LP were even a thing for a spell."

Casey thinks on this, how all roads seem to endlessly circle back to Lower Wolf and Little Paris and how they all still go nowhere.

She doesn't think it's possible that Kara is Hardy's mother but has no idea who else it might be.

Then remembers what Trey told her out by the Explorer, about the former chief and *his* wife. "What about this Marissa Merrifield?"

Anna smiles. "You mean Marissa *Mayfield*? Miss High and Mighty? The chief's trophy wife? Sure, her, too. All the time. But you didn't hear that from me." Anna drops her cigarette into the Gatorade bottle, then shakes the bottle around like she's trapped a firefly. It sparks, tossing tiny embers that die quick for lack of air. "LP liked her best of all. She was somehow better than the rest of us. Still young, still pretty. At least she looked young, and that was his thing, right? The younger, the better. Hell, he thought I was too old. Doesn't matter that he helped make me this way. He once told me I was like a song he'd heard too many times, one of those shitty tunes that get stuck in your head, where you know all the words but fucking hate it all the same. Never stopped him from coming back for more or doing the things he did."

Anna lights a fresh cigarette. "Like I said, the goddamn devil."

Casey thinks about "Country Girl" . . . a song she doesn't know at all. "Did he hurt you? You and these other girls?"

"Now, what do you think?" Anna answers, but before she can elaborate, Casey has a sudden realization; a truth so horrible she wants to stand and walk out or run out and strip off her clothes and burn them and then cold-shower off this woman she was holding only moments before.

The younger, the better.

Ruby . . . Monica Dupuy. That's why Mark and Anna were driving around with the young girl from Catlettsburg.

They were going to barter her for their next hit.

She was a present . . . a gift . . . *a fucking offering* . . . to Little Paris Glasser.

The goddamn devil.

55

ut Anna's already moved on, talking about something else.

Someone else.

Trey.

"I saw this old boyfriend tonight. His name's Trey," she says. "Well, we went out once. One of those high school things."

Casey tries to follow Anna's ping-ponging thoughts, why she's suddenly mentioning Trey, and wonders if she knows he's just outside.

Music.

Anna was talking about songs and Little Paris Glasser and that must have made her remember Trey from earlier tonight. She saw him wearing his seemingly ever-present earbuds and maybe they got to talking about music, about the past.

Lights are flickering off and on in Anna's head; she's seeing shadows on walls. Ghosts. Making connections.

"Does this old flame know Little Paris? Where he might be?" Casey asks.

"Flame? Not hardly. No, Trey was always . . . cold. No other way to say it than that." Anna twists her hair around her fingers, tighter and tighter. "He was super-serious, a real straight arrow in high school. Played in the band. I thought he was sweet but boring. Safe. That sure seems nice now, though. Safe, I mean. But we always pick the ones who fucking burn us up." Anna nods at her, like they're sharing a secret, an understanding.

She curls back into the chair.

Casey's losing her again, but she's not going to bring her back a second time.

"Be careful what you wish for, right?" Anna continues. "Anyway, tonight, I think he really was trying to be nice. We were standing there, and it was like I was looking through his eyes, right back at me, seeing me the way he sees me now. And that was so fucking weird, because when I look at myself in the mirror, I don't see anything at all. A big fucking blank, well, except for these." Anna holds up her arms, track marks visible. "And no matter how hard he tried, I guess that's all he could see, too."

Anna tosses her cigarette away, not bothering with the bottle. "He was embarrassed for both of us. Disgusted. It made him sick to look at me and be standing there next to me . . . kinda the way you're looking at me right now, though you're trying harder to hide it."

Casey watches her own cigarette burn.

"And you know what? I didn't even blame him, and don't much blame you. Both of you think you're better than me, I know that. I get it. But I gotta wonder if he looks at his own mama the same way he stared at me. Does he see her the way she used to be? Or all that's left of her now."

"Come again?" Casey asks, still trying to follow Anna's scattered thoughts, like the ashes on the floor.

"His mama. She's spent some time with LP, too. Got it bad just like the rest of us, just like this whole damn town." Anna fixes Casey with a long look, eerily steady. Prescient. "I gotta wonder if you've taken a hard look in the mirror lately. What do you see there? Who the fuck do *you* see?"

Anna smiles. "I think I'm done talking now. I don't care what you say about it, I don't want you saving LP. I hope some fucker kills him like the rest of them in Lower Wolf. Fuck all of them. They already done murdered most of this town anyway. I don't need him to rot in jail. Dead is good enough for me."

"It's not that simple," Casey says, crushing out her cigarette and pushing out of her chair. "I wish it was, but it isn't."

"Funny. A minute ago, you said it all couldn't be any easier." Anna wraps her arms around herself. She's small, faded, like old, balled-up paper. "If he's not dead today, he'll kill me tomorrow, because I'm gonna crawl right back to him like I always do. I told you I'm sick, so goddamn sick. And that's what happens when you're sick like me. Eventually, you just up and die."

"I get that, but there's also this issue of Little Paris's boy, Hardy. I think he's still alive, probably with his daddy. You seem to know about everyone else's mama, how about his?"

"I don't know nothing about him," she says. "Don't know anything about *her.*"

"Could be anyone, right? Could be anywhere. That's how things work around here. But that's not going to fucking cut it, Anna. Not tonight. You already have Monica Dupuy to answer for, you want to add that little boy, too? No matter what his daddy's done, he doesn't deserve that."

Anna looks away.

"Okay, fine," Casey says, "but I'm still going to need your phone."

"There's nothing there."

"LP's *number*, Anna. I know he changes it all the time, but he always makes sure you and Kara, all his other *girls*, have the new one, right? You called him, texted him, tonight."

Anna closes her eyes tight, like fists. "I don't think I remember it. I don't think I can help you with that. That's not safe, not smart."

If he's not dead today, he'll kill me tomorrow . . .

"Just slip me the password, then. I won't even keep the phone; that way you're not giving me anything, I'm taking it. No one will know. And you'll have it in the morning when you get out of here."

"When I get out," Anna echoes. "Don't you understand? No one gets out, ever."

"I'll get it one way or another, Anna. I'll subpoena a year's worth of your phone records and what do you think I'm going to find? *Who* have you been talking to? Everyone you've ever shared a needle or some dope with? I'm going to bang on all their doors and pick them up on every outstanding pissant warrant and fucking jaywalking ticket. You may not care about Monica Dupuy or Hardy Glasser, but do you have any kids of your own, Anna? What about them? Because if you make this hard on me, everyone's going to know about it. They're all going to know *why* . . . and they're all going to know it was you."

"Fuck you."

"Fine, fuck me. But one way or another, you're going to help me first."

"Miss High and Mighty, too," Anna says, nearly spitting the words. "Don't fucking pretend like you really care about any of them kids, either." She shakes her head, but when she finally opens her eyes, she knows she's beat. She says—

"My birthday. Ten, twelve, ninety-two."

"Got it." Casey grabs the cigarettes and lighter, eager to get away from Anna Bishop, desperate to get outside to fresh air.

But still can't stop turning over what Anna said about Trey and his mom. About all of Little Paris's girls and all the kids that circle them—

Monica Dupuy. Dillon Mackey. Hardy Glasser.

The bloody baby girl at Lower Wolf.

Country Girl.

Don't fucking pretend like you really care about any of them kids, either.

"One more thing," Casey says. "You know a girl who runs around with the Glassers who has a big tattoo all over her back? Pretty. Flowers. Like a garden."

"Dix?" Anna says.

"Right, exactly. Jerry Dix . . . his wife, Holly."

"Sure, I know them," Anna says. "Jerry got sideways with LP and Jamie and supposedly ran out last summer." Anna makes a vague, disappearing gesture with her left hand, like Jerry Dix just vanished into a cloud of her cigarette smoke. She starts chewing her bloody nails. "But that girl you're asking about, the one with all them tattoos? That's not Holly. That bitch didn't want any part of her own baby or anyone who had anything to do with it."

Casey knows before Anna can say it—

All those angry phone calls with a woman she never met.

A face she never saw.

"That's Jerry's twin *sister*."

Oh, fuck me.

"Janelle?" Casey asks.

Anna touches her own nose, leaves a spot of blood there.

Bingo.

"Yeah."

"Big Jason Aldean fan?"

"The biggest. How the hell you know all that?"

Casey doesn't have to answer, as it suddenly dawns on Anna, too.

Those ghost lights flickering behind her eyes. More shadows danc-ing on walls. Even she knows exactly what it means if Casey is asking about Janelle Dix.

"Oh, shit, she was there, too? Down there at Lower Wolf? Oh . . . oh . . ."

"The baby?" Casey asks.

Anna nods. "A little girl. Jerry's daughter. *Lucy* . . . "

56

When Casey walks out of the interview room, she nearly runs into Van Dorn.

He's standing with Duck Andrews and another man she can only assume is Angel's current chief, Oscar Floyd. Floyd looks disheveled, hair askew, like someone just got him out of bed. Maybe it's a hair-piece. He must not live far away, but in a place like Angel, nothing and no one is that far away.

She can tell by the way they're all looking at her they were talking about her.

Van Dorn's arms are crossed.

She ignores the other two, turns only to Van Dorn. There are framed pictures on the wall over his shoulder, photos of Angel officers who've won past department awards. Commendations for valor, that sort of thing. Earlier she was so focused on sparring with Duck Andrews and getting to Anna, she didn't really pay attention to them. Now she does.

Third down from the left, she recognizes the face.

Fuck me again.

She stares at Van Dorn, then nods back at the closed door behind her.

"We're going to need that woman's phone."

Then leaves the station to find Trey.

57

Casey shot Ramón Álvarez three times.

The first was moments after the windows of Devon's Durango exploded, frantic seconds after she and Devon tried to protect each other.

Special Agent Devon Jeon took three rounds himself, one through the throat.

He probably saved Casey's life. That's what everyone said afterward, even if most didn't say it to her face. Although some did.

Casey caught one herself then. The two-two-three round that passed through Devon's shoulder, shattering both his scapula and clavicle, tumbled and slowed down just enough that it didn't blow out Casey's heart. It felt like someone had punched her really, really hard, though, like a great fucking hand had reached inside her chest and *squeezed*, taking her breath away. But with glass in her hair and eyes and Devon's blood all over her, she was still able to push backward out of the Durango and onto the driveway of the house they were parked in front of.

Bright sunlight burning her eyes.

Rusty Arizona heat in her mouth . . . or Devon's blood.

The green Sentra, containing Ramón and two others who were never identified, had clipped the side of the Durango and spun nearly sideways to a stop in the street in front of her. The shooters must have been surprised by the sound and fury of their AR-15s going off in the small car's interior, the spiking adrenaline making them crazy or careless or both, and as the driver fought the wheel, trying to get the Sentra true again, Casey finally got her Glock free and fired wildly at it. It went against all her training; she didn't account for the "background," as they call it, the other cars or houses or people who might be running to their windows to see what the noise was about. Kids playing. Truth was, she didn't care. Locked and loaded, her Glock could hold seventeen Federal Hydra-Shok hollow-points, and she dumped an entire fucking mag of them into that Nissan, stumbling toward it as she did so. Her rounds kicked up sparks off the bent metal and blew out two tires.

Bounced and danced off the pavement.

She'd learn later that she'd already struck Álvarez once in the chest during that opening fusillade, but it took the shooting-scene investigators six days to find the trajectory of all her other rounds. They were picking them out of the walls of nearby houses and wounded mesquite trees.

She shattered two second-story windows.

One was found in the bottom of a backyard pool, fifty yards away.

As she fought her way toward the Sentra, one of the other men was still shooting at her, trying to put her down for good, even as he and his companion were abandoning the car, running away from her deeper into the neighborhood.

One of the two-two-three rounds passed by her face.

It felt like Devon's fingers, brushing back her hair.

Another kicked off the pavement in front of her, sparking memories of her and her daddy camping out by Lost River, kicking at a cooking fire, counting the embers flying skyward. She took the ricochet in the thigh, where it grazed the femur, barely missing the femoral artery running parallel to it.

One of the doctors would later tell her how lucky she was.

She heard that a lot during the months she recovered.

You're lucky. So goddamn lucky.

That lucky round didn't bleed her out, but it knocked her back down hard, right on her ass, all but guaranteeing she couldn't give chase.

But she could still stumble, struggle, *fucking crawl* if she had to, to the stalled Sentra, and so she did.

It sat at the end of blackened tire streaks where it had slid to a stop. She focused on those blood-black lines, following them forward.

She reloaded before approaching the open doors, hands slick with Devon's blood and her own. Nearly dropped her fresh mag twice, the Glock itself once.

Felt herself blacking out but held on.

Ramón was still sitting behind the wheel, holding on to it for dear life, like he was still driving on down the road, trying to escape. He was gasping for air.

They'd tell her later he was seventeen years old. Had turned seventeen only two days before.

So for all intents and purposes, he was sixteen.

He was only the driver, and of the three men in the car, the only one who never fired a shot.

And he had looked so much younger than seventeen or sixteen. Wispy mustache. Head shaved down to pale skin and his white T-shirt almost all red, stained with his blood and clinging to his thin chest.

Rising and falling and slowing with each weakening heartbeat.

When she finally crawled up to him, he was talking to himself, eyes rolled upward.

Praying.

He saw her out of the corner of his eye and raised his hands. More praying. Begging.

She couldn't hear him, though. She didn't want to hear him.

She leaned in through the open passenger door, put her Glock within a hair's breadth of his face.

His short, dark hair, and the fine hairs on the nape of his neck. The slightly sunburned skin. His left hand rubbing at that delicate spot there, the sort of gesture she already knows he does whenever he's lost in thought, thinking hard.

And pulled the trigger twice.

Then she tossed the gun onto Ramón Álvarez's body and crawled back down those same black lines to where Devon lay dying.

Holding his hands, holding his head in her own bloody hands, holding him upright, trying to help him breathe and keep him alive . . .

58

Trey's still leaning against the Explorer, earbuds in.

Dillon is in the backseat, asleep.

Trey straightens when he sees her. Expectant. "What did she say?" he asks, casting a glance over Casey's shoulder at the station behind her.

She ignores him, points instead at the phone hidden in his pocket. "You listening to your music?"

He must have caught something dark in Casey's expression, a look she's too tired to disguise, because he hesitates, now wary.

He chews his lip, still staring at the Angel Police Department.

She's tired enough to crawl up in the backseat with the small boy and go to sleep next to him.

"Your partner is here. He showed up. I think he's pissed," Trey says.

"Yeah, I saw him. And he is pissed. But I don't want to talk about that. I want to talk about you. About your music. Anna mentioned it. Said how much you were into music, even in high school."

"I was in the band. Played clarinet and other instruments." He knows she's not going to let this go, so he takes out his earbuds. "I listen to a lot of different stuff now. I'm sure nothing you'd like. There's this band out of Texas, American Vampires . . ."

"*American Vampires*," she repeats.

"Yeah, I know, it's just a name. A dumb one, I guess." He reluctantly holds out the earbuds. "Like I said, you're not going to like it."

"You have no idea what I like. But I want to hear *your* music."

"Oh."

She takes the earbuds from him and slips them in her ears and waits for him to cue up a song. Even a week ago, she would've had to push back her hair to do that, but not now, not since she cut it all off.

"Okay," Trey says. He sounds far away. The earbuds distance his voice, even though he's standing close to her, only the length of the cord between them.

"This is something I've been working on."

59

It starts slow and low first.

A needle-drop on vinyl. A hum. The wind. A sound that might be thunder.

A watch ticking.

Then stanzas of a song she's heard before, an old song like "Kentucky Rain" her daddy might have once sung to her in the car, driving out to Lost River. The voice has been sampled or stolen, but she knows it all the same. She can sing the words, too. A memory so deep, a muscle memory all its own.

A gently rising chorus, a whole church choir, subtly expanded because there's *another* voice rising above it all. Doubled, tripled, echoing in beautiful harmony. It's Trey singing about the moon and the darkened land, a subtle turn on the original lyrics. It's plaintive, sad, ethereal.

A prayer.

Like young Ramón Álvarez praying before she shot him in the head.

There's a drumbeat now, like a heartbeat. Finger taps on glass or falling rain. The promised thunder from the opening verse.

That watch ticking, marking off forever.

Casey's eyes are closed but she can see that land, that place.

A rolling sea. Salt on her face.

The mountains won't crumble, they won't fall. There's a moon high above it all.

The lyrics go on and on about not crying, not shedding tears, although part of Casey desperately wants to. It's not just the exhaustion but something deeper than that, bone deep, and if those tears fall now she wouldn't even be ashamed of them. Wouldn't even bother to hide them.

But she stopped crying after Devon's funeral. She barely even cried for her own daddy. She just doesn't have that many tears left.

She wipes at her dry eyes and takes out the earbuds and hands them back to Trey.

"Okay, now really tell me about your mom and dad."

60

Trey hops up on the Explorer's hood, where Casey's chart and laptop once were.

That feels like days ago now.

But he does it gently, so as not to wake the boy sleeping in the back.

"Dobie's coming around to pick me up," he says. "Your partner told me he had to. If there's no one else to do it, we'll take Dillon over to Tanya Heck's."

Casey doesn't like the idea of the boy riding in the ambulance, where all those dead were before, but is it really any worse than all those hours alone in his empty trailer? She can't answer that.

Trey folds his earbuds away, puts them in his pocket with his phone. "His mom isn't coming home, is she?"

"I don't know. I don't think so." Even through the tinted windows, they can see Dillon's sleeping chest rise and fall. "What about your mom, Trey? Is she coming home tonight?"

Trey makes a face, shakes his head. "She's home. She's always home." He looks at his hands. "But you know that, right? Anna said something, didn't she?"

"Yes, she did."

"I do everything I can to keep her there."

"Anything to keep her off the streets, right? Like Kara. Like Anna."

"Yeah," he says, clasping his hands in front of him. "You know, she's always been an artist. Loved painting. I tell myself it's all because of her tendonitis, and when the pain got too bad, she got a prescription for it, like you're supposed to do. Like everyone does." He holds up one of his hands, curls it into a claw. "Her hand would swell up and hurt so much she couldn't even hold a brush. I tried to hold it for her, help with the strokes . . . but . . . it just didn't work."

He drops his hand back to his lap. "And it always starts with *some* kind of pain, right? But with my mom, it wasn't just the pain in her hand. It was more than that. It was *her*. Marissa Mayfield."

"Your dad's a cop here, isn't he, Trey?" Casey asks. And Trey stares back at her, either surprised or relieved. But he shakes his head again.

"Was," he says. "Anna tell you that, too?"

"No, not really. I saw a picture inside. The man in the picture in his uniform matched the one of you and your family in your wallet."

Trey nods. "I forgot about that. I haven't been in there in a while. I mean, I don't go in there now, ever." He pauses. "It was some sort of award, right? He was always winning awards, getting his picture in the paper and stuff. My mom always wanted to paint him, a picture of her own, but he never let her. Said it made him feel weird, uncomfortable." Trey glances back at the sleeping boy. "Did he look happy?"

"Your dad? In that photo? No, not particularly." Casey slides up on the hood next to him. "But, hey, it's just a silly picture. Who can really say? I think most everyone's faking it when they're smiling in photographs."

"True," Trey agrees.

"So tell me," she says. "About your family . . . and Marissa Mayfield."

And then he tells her everything.

61

My dad was a cop here in Angel for like, forever."

Trey leans back and looks up at the few stars.

"Worked for Paul Mayfield, when he was still *Chief* Mayfield. Marissa was his second wife. His first passed away and he met Marissa somewhere not long after that and brought her here. My dad was close with the chief and got close with Marissa, too. I figured it out before my mom did, but after she did, they started fighting about it all the time. She was already taking those pills for her tendonitis, just one every now and then, just like was prescribed, so she could paint, but when my dad started running around with his best friend's wife, she started taking more."

"How did your mom find out?"

"I didn't tell her," Trey insists, "but maybe I did leave hints around. My dad knew I knew. We were fighting, and we never used to. Look, I'm not going to say we were ever super-close or anything like that. That's just not how he was, and he was always so focused on his job, on his work. But I wanted us all back the way we were, the way it used to be, like that picture you saw in my wallet. I was about to graduate and then all this shit gets dumped on me."

"Did the chief know?"

Trey shrugs. *"Really* know? Maybe. I don't know how he couldn't. This town kind of knows everything, and my dad worked for him. Marissa had something of a reputation, too. There were all kinds of rumors. There are always rumors around here."

"Rumors about Marissa and Little Paris?"

"Yeah, that, I guess. Marissa was using, and that was no secret at all. Not for long. The chief tried like hell to hide it for a while, until he couldn't anymore." Trey ends with another shrug. "I mean, look, I don't *know*. My dad never admitted anything to my mom or me, he never came right out and said it. Maybe he loved her or thought he did, and maybe he wanted to run away and start this whole new life with her, like he didn't have a whole fucking life already, right here with us."

The hurt, the rage, radiates off him like an open flame. Anna said Trey was *cold*, but Casey can feel that he's angry enough now to set the night on fire. "It happens, Trey. It's shitty, but it does. People get caught up, they fuck up, royally. They don't mean to, but they do."

Like sitting with Devon, watching him laugh.

The heat in the car, the heat between them.

All those moments before that when they knew where things were headed and knew it was wrong. All those moments after.

"Even parents fuck up. But that's not your fault," she says. "You know you didn't have anything to do with it."

"Sure, easy to say. That's what you're supposed to say, right? But you want to know what's really fucked up? Sometimes I wish they had run off together. At least someone might have been happy out of all this."

"So what did happen?"

"What always happens," Trey says. "Things got worse until it all blew up. It was this big scandal that everyone talked about but *no one* talked about. The police chief's new wife is this total addict, running around with one of the biggest fucking drug dealers in three counties. And in the middle of it all is my dad, the hero cop, who loved her and hated the Glassers . . . every single one of them. He'd been gunning for them forever, particularly after that young girl was found dead up at that old motel we drove by, the Tamarack. My dad knew Little Paris killed her or had something to do with it. He felt guilty about it, like he and the chief hadn't ever done enough to stop him. They'd never done enough when it came to the Glassers." Trey shakes his head. "Some people say my dad is the one who shot Danny, did you know that?"

"No." She wonders what Van Dorn would say about that theory. "Did he?"

Trey shrugs. "I don't know anything about that. I really don't. But I know he couldn't let it go. And he couldn't let Marissa Mayfield go, either. Neither of them could . . . not my dad, not the chief."

Trey looks up at the night sky again. The same stars, unmoving.

"The chief supposedly sent her up to rehab a couple of times. But I think he was so busy trying to keep her out of his own jail, out of the local papers, he couldn't really worry about her and my dad, even if he did know about them. And then it was over anyway. After that I thought for sure things might get better between my mom and him, but you know what was worse than all their fighting? The silence that followed. All that fucking silence."

Casey can imagine that, and how that silent house drove Trey back to his music. Anything to fill the quiet.

"The whole mess . . . the Glassers, the chief, Marissa . . . drove my dad crazy, so he up and left. Left me, left my mom. He moved away from Angel altogether. No, I take that back. He didn't leave *us*, he was running from *her*. He and the chief both loved her, both wanted to save her, but she was always going to love the drugs more. My dad didn't save that girl behind the motel, couldn't save Marissa, and then couldn't stay here anymore with either of their memories. Every time he looked out at Angel all he saw were his failures, and that makes me ask myself what he saw when he looked at me."

Casey knows what it's like running from memories you don't think you can live with anymore. All your mistakes and all your wrongs. But she wants to believe that when Jon Dorado Sr. looked at his sensitive, perceptive son, he saw one of the few fucking things he got right.

She wants Trey to believe that, too.

"Where is he now?" she asks.

Trey pulls out his phone, checks the time or his messages before putting it away again. "Doesn't matter. It really doesn't. He still sends some money and calls every now and then. But someone had to stay here and take care of my mom, so I did. I do."

"Where is he?" Casey asks again. And it matters to her. Suddenly, finding Jon Dorado almost matters as much as finding Little Paris Glasser.

"Texas," Trey says. "Austin, I think."

She gets it then. Trey's favorite band. American Vampires.

"Does he know how bad things have gotten with your mom? Everything that's going on here?"

"He knew her pills were a problem before he left, but he wasn't going to sit around and watch her fall apart. Not like Marissa, not again. He left that to me."

"And that's why you've been stealing from your callouts. Not for you. For *her*."

"Yes . . . and no," Trey admits. "At first it was just the pills, but when those really started drying up around here, I had to do whatever I could. Whatever I could get my hands on, just like everyone else. But at least she wasn't running around, getting it on the street or getting it from Little Paris herself.

"I've been dealing too, here and there, mainly over in some clubs in

Charleston. I needed the money. There's a rehab clinic near the lake called Karen's Place. It's supposed to be nice. I've been over there to see it. Got the brochure and everything. I was hoping to save up enough to send her there, if I can convince her to go."

"If Little Paris found out you were stealing and then reselling his dope," Casey says, "he would've killed you." But even as Casey says it, she knows that's probably the least of Trey's problems.

"Sure, it's fucking stupid." He turns to check on Dillon. "But at least I'm not the one sitting around wondering if she's ever coming home again." His eyes settle back on Casey. "This way, it's almost like she doesn't even have a problem. We can both lie to ourselves that it's all okay."

"That DOA that's out there now, the stuff you got from Kara, the stuff in that trailer in Lower Wolf. That's straight-up killing these people, you know that, right?"

But of course he does. Trey understands that better than anyone.

So he looks away again, won't meet her eyes, searching the night sky for one last time.

Staring at the stars.

Trying to find answers up there, something that makes sense in their bright, clockwork order and imperceptible movements.

"On those days when I can't lie to myself anymore," he says, "it almost feels like she's dead already. Like, I see her curled up there in the bed she used to share with my dad, and I *know* she wishes she was dead. And I wish it, too. And that's a horrible fucking thing to say, but at least *I'm* not dealing with it all anymore. Those are the days I'd rather she was gone like my dad and I was all alone if that meant none of us were living like this. She's killing both of us anyway."

Anna Bishop said almost the same thing—

I told you I'm sick, so goddamn sick. And that's what happens when you're sick like me. Eventually, you just up and die.

"We'll get you some help," Casey offers, and she knows how simple and trite and hollow that sounds.

Trey does, too. "Sure," he laughs. "Sure. Like the way you've already helped me tonight? You're not here to *help*, Agent Alexander. You've used me, and that's okay. It is. You have this big thing you're trying to figure out and deal with and I'm just a small part of it. Tomorrow you'll go on and do whatever you have to do and tell yourself you're making some sort of difference, but what you don't see, what you don't know, is that you can't really help anyone here. This place, this town. It's fucking cursed."

Casey doesn't believe that places are cursed. Not anymore. She tried running away too, like Jon Dorado Sr. Even tried running back home again. But everything that happened—Devon Jeon and Ramón Álvarez in Arizona; all her mistakes both before and after—followed her anyway. Ghosts that still haunt her now. It was never the fault of any particular *place*.

I gotta wonder if you've taken a hard look in the mirror lately. What do you see there?

Who the fuck do you see?

But she can't blame Trey for desperately wanting to outrun his choices and his hurts and all the things he's done. To leave it all behind.

Like father, like son.

Just like her.

"Your partner's heading back out," Trey says, as he slides off the Explorer's hood. "And he still looks pissed."

62

At least Van Dorn grabbed Anna's phone like she asked.

Casey meets him before he gets to the Explorer, where Trey waits for them both.

They're standing in the empty street and the next block over a lonely traffic light flicks red to green, but no cars pass through.

Casey reaches for the phone. "I think I can get Little Paris's most recent number out of that. I told Anna if she cooperated we'd get it back to her."

But Van Dorn won't relinquish it, not yet. "All you were supposed to do was ask some questions. Nice and easy. I'd be fucking furious right now if I didn't have a hand in it. But I agreed, so I have to own it."

"Own *what?*" Casey shoots back. "What are you so pissed about *now?* I yanked the chain of some local keystone cops. Fuck them. That cartoon character Duck wasn't being cooperative, at all."

"This is their town, Casey. Their home. I try not to win a few battles only to lose the whole goddamn war." It's one of his favorite sayings, one he trots out all the time and applies to all sorts of situations, both personal and professional. Given his brigade of ex-wives, Casey thinks he's just gotten in the habit of losing . . . a lot. "We'll be back here tomorrow or the next day or the day after that, and we'll still need their help. You know that."

She does. Just like she knows his ties here run deeper than hers. He's worked with these local cops a lot longer than she has, but still—

"I needed their help tonight. *Now*. I don't give a fuck about tomorrow and neither should you. Tomorrow is too late."

"Yeah, yeah, I know," he says. "I get it. And now they most definitely get it, too. But I smoothed it over."

Casey doesn't like that Van Dorn feels the need to smooth anything over for her, that he has to apologize for her.

"You know what? You go fight your own fucking battles," she says, "and let me fight mine."

But he glares right through her, still holding Anna's phone tight. "Don't act like we're not in this together. I'm on your side here. But, Jesus, you can't fight everyone. You just can't, Casey." He pauses, wiping sweat off his forehead with the back of his free hand. "And when were you going to tell me that your *Trey* over there is Jon Dorado's son."

"I only just figured it out. I saw a picture inside. He didn't tell me his dad was a cop here. How the fuck was I supposed to know that? And how did you find out? Did you say anything about him to those two inside?"

Van Dorn raises his hands for peace, some sort of calm. Looking for a way forward that doesn't leave them shouting at each other in the street. "It came up, Casey, like it was bound to, sooner or later. Just like I fucking warned you that it would. You're driving around with this kid, banging on doors and shouting questions and demands, and someone was always going to figure it out. Even these local hicks you don't think much of and don't trust."

She knows he's right . . . *again*. Just like she knows now how much of a mistake it was to make a big deal about Anna's phone in front of Duck Andrews. But she needed to get her hands on it one way or another, and in the heat of the moment—

She's doing a fine fucking job of losing a lot of battles all on her own.

"Did you know his dad?" she asks.

"Jon Senior? Some, not much. He was the assistant chief here. A hot-shit cop for many years. A decent man as far as I know, but hard to really get to know, if that makes sense."

It does, but Casey's not going to waste breath now telling Van Dorn about Jon Dorado's less-than-secret affair with the ex-chief's young wife; his boss's wife.

Instead, she tells him about Country Girl and Kara and Anna, and the very real possibility that Little Paris's latest number is saved in the phone in his hand.

"Let's get a ping order and track his ass down," she says. Before she left Lower Wolf, they issued a BOLO for both Little Paris and his missing Mustang, but a lookout relies on someone actually putting eyes on your target and then being willing to call it in. A *ping* is shorthand for using cell-tower data to follow and triangulate an active phone; all those invisible roaming cellular signals bouncing off different repeaters as the phone itself and the person you're trying to find with it move around. It's never perfect, but it's almost real time, as long as the phone is on. She's used the technique to track high-value cartel targets on both sides of the border, where they had even better equipment—an IMSI-Catcher mobile platform, a powerful cell site simulator that can force a phone to bounce to it—but it was always going to take too long to get a similar setup and crew out of D.C. to run it tonight.

Eventually, they'll use similar pings and cell tracking to zero in on their remaining Lower Wolf shooters. All they'll need is one of the marero's numbers, and odds are they already have one, locked away in Country Girl's phone.

Just like Little Paris's number is hidden now somewhere in Anna's.

But Van Dorn's still clearly bothered about Janelle Dix, a Jason

Alden fan who liked flowers and tattoos and furiously loved her brother and that's probably all they'll ever know about her.

Why was her number scrawled on a scrap of paper in that marero's pocket?

Did they talk to each other before that slaughter?

Did she somehow have a hand in it?

There's also the question of the baby girl, Lucy. Maybe it was never going to be clear who her true biological daddy was, but once she was on this earth, Jerry was ready to raise her as his own. Talked about it all the time. Has Janelle been raising her for him?

Did she furiously love that little girl too, only to end up dying while protecting her?

She knows Van Dorn feels they should have puzzled some of this out sooner, even though too many of the pieces still don't quite fit; all these questions that still don't have answers and may never have any. They start every case looking for the answers, seeking some sort of justice. You never figure it all out, because their investigations are like life itself, messy and incomplete and full of contradictions.

Like people.

And sometimes there are no answers. But sometimes you can still find justice.

"Sure, we'll just whip that order up. We haven't been able to get a quick turnaround on anything, Casey," Van Dorn says. "Not quick enough for you. I know it feels like we're standing in mud here, but Sykes is still down at Lower Wolf, holding point, working on the emergency orders and warrants, making progress. I commandeered his car to catch up to you. He bitched when I took his keys." Van Dorn points over to an older gray Impala parked across the street in the Marathon lot.

He probably was already on the way to Angel when she called him before meeting with Anna.

"Anna gave me her passcode and her consent," she says. "I can run through her phone right now, take a shot at one of the more recent numbers. One of them *has* to be Little Paris. Then we can get Sykes spun up on *that* ping order and warrant."

But Van Dorn's unconvinced. "Little Paris was a decent lead, Casey, but the shooters are still more important. They have to be. We've been working on that original 606 number since you left. If this Anna Bishop was telling you the truth about Janelle Dix, if she really is Country Girl, that helps us, too. That's confirmation, a new lead to run down. Little Paris or not, you've already done a hell of a job."

She shakes her head, trying not to get angry again. "It doesn't help much. And it doesn't help little Harmon Glasser at all."

"I know. I talked to Andrews and Chief Floyd about that. They think the boy is with his supposed mother in Danville . . . or maybe Nicholasville or Somerset. They'll work with Martin County SO and check on that."

"At least someone's finally willing to acknowledge he exists."

Van Dorn's look is uncertain and unhappy. "Well, just barely. They said there's a lot of young girls around here who could claim they've been knocked up by one of the Glassers. Who might find a good reason to say they were."

"Right, because having a Glasser baby is better than having to work down at the Dollar General?"

"Something like that."

"I'm never having kids," she says, and although Van Dorn looks like he's going to respond to that, he doesn't. "Look, even if we're right about Janelle Dix, and I think we are, we still have to exploit her phone, which we can't because it's password-locked; or get her phone records, which you're telling me we still don't have. And either way, we're likely left cross-checking number after unknown number or connecting the dots to every cell tower around Lower Wolf, matching cell-site hits around the approximate time of the shooting to damn near *every* phone in the state."

"Yes, and that's what we do. In fact, that's what Sykes and I *have* been doing, while you've been running around up here."

"But it's not like we can't keep doing both," she says. "Let Sykes go ahead and do his thing. But Anna texted Little Paris *today*, trying to meet him. His latest number is right there in that phone in your hand and I have the password to get to it. That's as close as we've been to him all night. And I still think finding him is our fastest option."

Van Dorn looks at the phone he's holding. "Fastest for *who*? And for what? We're all making assumptions here, Casey. About Janelle Dix, about the shooters, about Little Paris and his boy."

"Like you're assuming he's not a worthwhile lead anymore, and I think you're wrong," she says. "Little Paris knows enough. He knows the men he was dealing with, all his dope sources. He knows the corrupt cops here. He's got numbers and connections for everyone." She crosses her arms as Van Dorn continues to stare at Anna's phone. "And if you didn't think I was right, you never would have asked for that phone for me."

Van Dorn shakes his head, but they both know she's right.

"He survived, and no else did. That has to mean something," she says. "And speaking of leads, here's one more . . . but you're *really* not going to like it."

63

arissa Mayfield, the former chief's wife. She died earlier tonight, probably another overdose. Anna suggested she was very tight with Little Paris, too."

"I know. I was talking to Chief Floyd about it," Van Dorn says, motioning back to the police station. "I met her once at a dinner party. Pretty lady. But troubled."

"Yeah, so I've heard."

"And she didn't OD, Casey. Apparently, she killed herself."

"I don't think Trey believes that. He was there. And Anna said Marissa was copping from Little Paris. So we get her phone too, cross-check it with the best number in Anna's. It's possible they were both talking to him as recently as this afternoon, as late as tonight. We pin him down that way. There could be more text messages . . ." Casey hesitates. "And maybe we really need to talk to the former chief anyway. He and Trey's dad worked the Glassers long as anyone, even longer than you. He knows them and might have an idea where Little Paris is lying low. He's going to know something about Hardy and might even have some idea what the hell happened down there today." She doesn't want to suggest he might also be in Little Paris's pocket, too. "He can help us make sense of Janelle Dix and this whole fucking mess."

"We're taking direction now from a kid . . . and an addict? C'mon, we're better than that."

"Fuck you," Casey says. "A moment ago, you were congratulating me for doing a hell of a job, and part of that job has been listening to that kid and that addict. You keep wanting to talk about leads? The only ones we have are because of those two and me."

"Marissa Mayfield died tonight, Casey, practically in Paul Mayfield's arms, at least according to Chief Floyd. For Christ's sake, he'll be burying her in a couple of days. We're not doing that." Van Dorn looks down again at the phone in his hand. "Listen to me, please. You're as good an investigator as I've ever met. One of the absolute best. But you cannot bulldoze your way through every fucking wall, and not everything or everyone is a wall. You have to open a few goddamn doors now and then."

"Okay," she says, "then *you* be that door . . . be my fucking key if you want. You know Mayfield, so talk to him. Once a cop, always a cop. He'll understand what we're up against. He'll hear you out."

"Sure, just long enough to tell me to go fuck myself. He won't mind hearing the world is short a few Glassers. Trust me, that's going to be one very brief conversation."

Casey laughs, angry. "Right, right. Half these people around here don't want to know what happened and the other half don't care."

Van Dorn points Anna's phone at her, jabbing it for emphasis. "Don't suggest I'm one of them."

"That's not it, and you know it. But not everyone down at Lower Wolf was a Renfro or a Ricky Glasser. Not everyone deserved to have their fucking faces blown off."

She doesn't have to say Janelle Dix's name again. Or even Hardy Glasser's. She knows they want the same things . . . answers, closure, *justice* . . . and they always have, even if those things look different to each of them.

"Goddamn it," Van Dorn says.

"Goddamn it is right," she says.

But now a van or SUV stops briefly at the light, heading their way. When the light drops green and the vehicle slow rolls through, its headlights feathering them, they start walking out of the street to get out of its way.

It's Dobie's Angelcare Rescue Service.

Van Dorn finally hands over Anna's phone.

"You already called Mayfield, didn't you?" she asks. "When you were inside the station."

"No," he says, "but I knew you'd want me to. I knew you'd harass me until I did it, worse than one of my ex-wives. And if I didn't come around, you'd just pick another fight with the cops here, or drive out to him anyway."

They meet Trey at the Explorer as Dobie pulls up next to them. Casey wonders if he still has dead bodies in the back of the ambulance.

"Are you going to make the call?"

"Yeah," Van Dorn replies, "I will. Even after what happened tonight. No matter what you think, there are still plenty of people who care about what happens around here. I'll see what he says. We'll probably still need to go out to his place at the Point . . . and then we're both going to burn in hell after that."

But even in victory, she can't find a smile.

I gotta wonder if you've taken a hard look in the mirror lately. What do you see there?

Who the fuck do you see?

She hopes she hasn't just won a battle only to lose the war.

Van Dorn checks his watch, then bitterly shakes his head, staring now at Trey. At the gently sleeping little boy in the back of their Explorer.

"Let's see if we can at least un-fuck all this before I make the call and we head out there."

64

Van Dorn gives Trey and Casey a few moments alone while he goes over to call Mayfield and talk with Timmons.

"We're going to try and see Paul Mayfield," she tells Trey. "But I won't mention you. Your name is out of it."

Trey thinks on this. "I don't have anything against him. I really don't. It's just hard, seeing him, knowing everything that happened. It was hard seeing her tonight, like that. I want to feel bad for him, I really do, but I'm not sure I can. I'm not sure I ever will. Is that a shitty thing or what?"

"It's the truth. And sometimes the truth is shitty. Most times it's fucking hard, too. Lying is a lot easier."

She watches Van Dorn on his phone, wondering what he's saying to Mayfield. "Give me your phone," she says. And when Trey hesitates, she pushes. "We're square, Trey, I promise."

"Yeah, promises are easy to make, too," Trey says, but hands it over, and she punches in her number for him.

"Text me after you get over to Tanya Heck's. Text me again when you're home."

"You really don't need my help anymore?"

"No, like I said, we're square. You're done. Free and clear."

Trey hesitates again, turning the phone over and over in his hands the way Van Dorn was clutching Anna's a few minutes ago.

The way you hold on to almost anything sometimes, just so you know there's one thing real to hold on to.

"Dobie cares for you, Trey. I get the feeling he's a good man, one of the real good ones. When this is done, we'll talk again. Really talk. I'll see about getting you help with your mom. I'm serious about that. I can help with Karen's Place."

"Thanks, I'm sure you were. It's just . . ."

"Just what?"

She knows what Trey's *really* holding on to right now—

This four-way stop he's stared at his whole life.

The police station on one corner, the run-down Marathon on the other.

The vacant lot filled with weeds and bowed trees and the night over his shoulder, giving way to the woods and hills, and somewhere beyond that, the blasted land punctured with coal mines. *The land is dark.* He's a young man lost here at his own crossroads, who could take the road he's standing on anywhere and never once look back, even though there's every chance or possibility he never will. That he'll stay here.

That he'll die here.

He's got more than four or even a thousand choices, but he can't quite let go of *this* place, because he's afraid nearly all those choices will bring him right back here anyway.

That's the fear is in his eyes, as scared and lonely as young Dillon Mackey. Terrified he's going to grow old here, like Dobie Timmons. He doesn't want to spend the rest of his life driving that goddamn ambulance around and doesn't want to end up carried off in the back of it.

He doesn't want Angel to drive him crazy, like his daddy.

Like father, like son.

This place, this town. It's fucking cursed.

He doesn't know how to leave but doesn't know how to let go.

Casey reaches out and stills his hands. Wraps his in hers.

"I suffered from depression. I mean, I still do, but I really struggled with it when I was growing up. I couldn't understand why I hated my life, so I blamed my parents, my home, everyone and everything else, and told myself if I could just escape, get away from it all, it would all be okay. But home wasn't the problem, Trey. Not really. And running didn't fix a goddamn thing, because I couldn't outrun myself. No one can. Your dad will figure that out, too."

Trey stares down at the road beneath his feet, the cracked gravel and dust.

"It's going to take time to heal no matter where or how far away you go. Time and effort and a willingness to accept you're either part of the problem . . ."

"Or part of the solution," he finishes for her.

"Exactly. I tried it twice before finally figuring it out. My partner over there says I'm fucking stubborn, maybe it's I'm just a slow learner. I'm willing to bet you're a hell of a lot smarter than me."

"Sure," he says, unconvinced.

"It's okay to hate this town and everything it's become. I don't see how you couldn't. Give yourself that. But it's also okay to love it too, to be scared to leave it all behind. You might even miss it one day. It'll surprise you, sneak up on you, when you least expect it. It did for me. It's *home*, Trey, and always will be. You're always going to carry it around with you, wherever you go. Friends like Dobie, memories of your family. All the good and bad. It's part of who you are, and you can't leave it behind. Not completely."

"Because you can't outrun yourself."

"No matter how far or fast you go," she says.

He smiles, bittersweet. It's the closest thing to a real smile she's seen from him all night, and it makes him look even younger. So goddamn young.

"You really think I'll miss this place?" he asks.

"I do. I really do. When you're older. Long after you're gone." She lets go of his hands.

And he seems to accept that.

"Hey, are you going to give me back my gun? It really was my dad's."

She hesitates for a long time, then pulls the empty SIG Sauer from the back of her jeans, as well as its lone mag, and carefully hands both to him. He slips the unloaded gun beneath his sweatshirt.

"Be smart with that. No more riding around with it. And promise me you'll keep up with your music." Then she adds, "It was good. Really good. I liked it."

He laughs. Another real sound. A perfect sound that breaks her heart. "I figured you only liked country music. Everyone else around here does."

"No, I never did."

"Me either," he says. "My dad did, though." A beat. "I guess he still does."

They stand together, silent, until Casey sees that Van Dorn is done with his call. He's done with Timmons and it's time for them to go.

"I'll wake Dillon," Trey says. "Kid's okay. I'll look after him."

"I know you will. I appreciate it."

As they walk back to the Explorer together, Trey asks, "You have any kids?"

"No, none. Never felt that maternal instinct. Not yet, anyway, and I don't think I ever will. Never been married, either."

"Huh," Trey says, as if that surprises him, or maybe it doesn't. Before they get to Timmons and Van Dorn, he reaches out and touches her arm.

A quick gesture, fleeting.

He was smiling before, but he's serious now.

"I'm sorry about what I said about you not helping. All that angry bullshit. You're doing what you can. But be careful. Whatever happens now. Please."

"Sure," she says, surprised at his urgency, at his genuine concern. "It's going to be fine."

"Really?"

Lying is easy . . . too easy.

"Really. This is just my job, Trey. It's what I have to do."

"Yeah, sure. That's what I'm afraid of," Trey says, and as they walk past the Angelcare van, he nods toward it—

"Because *that's* my job, and I really don't want to do it anymore."

65

Casey and Van Dorn drive in silence over the tri-bridge, the Big Sandy dark and nearly invisible below them. Most of the large houses down on the Point are dark too, so soon after midnight.

He's behind the wheel and she's searching through Anna's phone but stealing glances below them.

She's rolled over this span countless times and never thought it looked quite real, this weird bridge hanging impossibly out over the broad river. It's like an illusion, someone playing a trick on her eyes. She passed over it once during a heavy storm, the bridge swept by thick mist and sideways rain, and the turnoff faded into a watery wall of gray, going nowhere.

She's never been out to the Point itself, the genteel neighborhood that sits in the bridge's shadows, that splits Tug Fork on the West Virginia side, Levisa Fork in Kentucky.

Levisa Fork runs right by Lower Wolf, but the river goes by another name down there.

It leaves her wondering if the Big Sandy somehow flows all the way to Lost River, too. If it's all the same or connected in some way that's impossible to see, to ever truly understand.

Her daddy would have been fascinated by the Big Sandy's history,

all the daguerreotypes and ancient stone roadside markers. Indian arti-
facts and myths.

Van Dorn told her about the Hatfields and McCoys, whose legend
took root here.

He makes the turn and they start to descend to the neighborhood
below.

"Please let me do the talking," he says. "At least at the start."

She nods, but in the dark, his eyes forward, he can't see the gesture.

66

Paul Mayfield has already made them coffee, which is a nice gesture, given the hour.

Given that his wife passed away only hours earlier.

They sit in his dimly lit study, shadowed like the rest of the house, as if he doesn't want to wake it or disturb any of its ghosts. Van Dorn told her there are no children from either marriage. Mayfield's buried two wives, women that he loved and probably still does, which is two too many.

That's enough for a lifetime of ghosts.

As he led them here, Casey guessed the rambling house was re-modeled not long ago. Not exactly a showroom like her mom's, but close. It's more welcoming, comfortable, lived in. Books and maga-zines lay open, chapters and stories unfinished, and unopened mail leans precariously on a heavy wooden end table. A coffee mug sits for-gotten on a bookshelf. Photographs hang expertly in the halls, too hard to see clearly in passing, in the dark. But here and there are other subtle touches only a woman might make. A vase of flowers, a throw pillow, a brightly colored afghan folded neatly on a loveseat near the fireplace.

They're like rumors, hints. Like fingerprints on glass.

Reminders of the woman who made them.

For once, Casey is glad Van Dorn is going to do most of the talking.

She doesn't know what to say.

67

Mayfield is in his late fifties, early sixties, but doesn't look it. He's tall even sitting down, wearing a collared shirt and jeans. They can't be the same clothes he had on when they pulled his wife from the Big Sandy, but his hair is still wet from the fresh shower he took before they arrived, and the study is filled with the smell of black coffee and mint and evergreen shampoo.

Casey can't take her eyes off that wet hair, those damp stains collecting on his collar.

She *knows* it's not the Big Sandy, can't be, but she can't shake that awful thought all the same.

When they were introduced, she shook his hand and his grasp was hard, cold, smooth.

Like river water.

He gets up and retrieves a bottle of Johnny Drum from the bookshelf, pouring a shot into his mug before offering it to them. In the half-light, the amber whiskey glows with fire all its own, shines like a star trapped in the glass. Casey says no, but Van Dorn nods the go-ahead, holding out his own mug until Mayfield really tops it off. Van Dorn shouldn't, but also knows she won't say anything about it. He's doing the polite thing, the right thing, sharing a drink with a grieving man.

Opening a door.

Mayfield settles into his leather chair, bringing the bottle with him, and Van Dorn says, "I'm sorry, Paul. About Marissa. About everything. Mostly about us showing up here like this."

"I know, but it's fine. You have a duty. It wasn't like I was sleeping anyway. I understand."

He has the voice of a much larger man, deep, with a definite drawl: tobacco and amber whiskey like the bottle in his hand. It's not hard to imagine that voice singing the sort of sad country music neither she nor Trey Dorado like.

"I only know a little about what happened at Lower Wolf," he says, "just what some of the men said in passing. I gather it's bad, though."

"That's an understatement. One of the worst I've ever seen."

Mayfield arches his gray, serious eyebrows. "We've both seen too goddamn much."

Then they both raise their mugs, a silent toast. A silent acceptance.

"Do you miss it? The job," Van Dorn asks.

Mayfield takes another sip of his coffee and whiskey. "On a night like this, I don't. Not really. Not when I know what you're about to tell me." He lifts the mug again, higher, using it to point at Van Dorn. "But you will, Terry, if you don't have something to replace it with when you finally hang up the spurs."

Terry. Mayfield calls Van Dorn by his first name and almost no one does that. Not even Casey. Most people don't even know it.

"One day you're important, needed, vital," Mayfield says, "and the next, you're not. Not at all. So don't *rust*, Terry. Don't waste away. Don't walk away empty-handed."

Mayfield didn't. He left on his own terms to take care of his young wife. In the end, she'd been more important than the badge, even the job itself. But now that she's gone, Casey wonders what will become of him.

He looks at her. "So why don't you and Agent Alexander here tell me how you think I can help."

68

Van Dorn walks Mayfield through everything they know and all the things they don't.

The whole bloody scene at Lower Wolf and the unidentified marero they found. The phone number in his pocket. Casey's attempts to find Kara Grace and her interview with Anna Bishop, two women who OD'd from the latest batch of tainted heroin recovered at Lower Wolf.

Possibly the last two to see either Renfro or Little Paris Glasser alive.

He avoids mentioning Marissa might be the third.

He tells Mayfield they think Little Paris is still alive, on the run somewhere, but have no idea where he might be, and reveals that Jerry Dix was a snitch for them last summer. He's been missing for some time too and presumed murdered by the Glassers.

His sister, Janelle, lies dead at Lower Wolf.

But there's a baby, alive, and possibly another young child, Hardy Glasser. Mayfield winces at that before retreating to his mug again. It's the only expression he makes.

Throughout it all, Casey stays silent, only nodding where appropriate, whenever her name is mentioned or when Van Dorn includes her with a gesture or subtle nod of the head.

The room only grows darker with the things he says.

When he's done, Van Dorn takes a long drink of his own coffee and whiskey, which by now has probably gone cold.

He waits to give Mayfield a chance to take it in and sort through it all, to decide when and if he wants to begin.

Mayfield has finished his first mug and now doesn't even bother with the coffee. He pours three fingers of straight Johnny Drum and sits silent for what feels like a very long time, reluctantly nursing the drink.

He has the look of a once hard drinker who's practiced twice as hard at holding back and pacing himself.

Finally. "Are you here to talk to me about Little Paris . . . or Marissa, my wife?"

Van Dorn doesn't answer fast enough, so Casey does—

"Both."

69

Mayfield surprises Casey.

"A little while back I nearly shot Little Paris Glasser myself," he says. "As close as I've ever come to killing another man, and I've carried a gun for a long time." Mayfield rolls the whiskey around inside his mug. "You ever take a man's life?"

Van Dorn shakes his head, finishing off the last of his own drink.

Casey hesitates before nodding hers.

If it's Mayfield's turn to be surprised, he doesn't show it.

"It's impolite to ask the circumstances, so I won't. But I'll assume the other deserved his reckoning and leave it at that. Little Paris *deserved* his, if any man ever did. Most would say he had it coming for a long time.

"I think about that sometimes and wonder how things would be different if I had pulled that trigger. I ask myself if one bullet could have saved all these people. This town."

He takes another drink, steadily working his way toward drunk.

"You're seeing Angel at its worst. Don't get me wrong, we've always had our problems. All these old Irish and Scottish clans like the Glassers that settled here three hundred years ago, still carrying on their blood feuds and whatnot. Burying their family secrets. It's easy to bury things way up in these hills, deep down in the hollers and mines. Mining is hard living and always has been. Men go down a hole and sometimes they never come up again. Back in '85, we lost six at Crown Hill, all of them leaving behind wives, kids. We lost another four in '92. Three more last year. Even those we don't lose below suffer. I once had some university researchers tell me we've got one of the highest rates of cancer in the whole damn state, and now there are these pills and the heroin and whatever the hell else it is out there. Like I said, we bury too many things here."

Mayfield pours more Johnny Drum into his mug and then stands and puts the bottle back on the shelf. He pulls down a framed photo and hands it over to Casey.

"That's my daddy," he says. "Temple Mayfield. He didn't work the mines because he had rabbit blood, least that's what he used to call it. He couldn't stand the dark. The loud noises. The dynamite. Said it scared him, made him jumpy. He used to joke about it, but deep down, deeper than the shafts he couldn't bear, it bothered him. I know it did. But he ended up delivering mail instead and everyone round these parts knew and loved him for it. He could tell you every road, every holler, every family, across three counties. They'd invite him in for lunch. Give him cakes, pies. Strawberry jelly in canning jars in the summer and peach moonshine in those same jars in the fall. Just a little something to push back the cold, keep him warm on his route. He read letters for those who couldn't and helped deliver more than a few babies. He was friends with Paris Senior, the Old Man, and that was a feat, considering the Old Man's never taken to anyone, other than that oldest boy of his, I guess.

"My daddy would drive around, windows down no matter the weather or the season, and he loved this place in a way he didn't even have words for. Angel was in his blood too, all of it. He said he got more fresh air, saw more sky, than any man in a coal town ever had a right to."

The picture shows a man standing beside a Ford truck, gold over green, radio aerial sitting up high. He's good-looking, tall like Mayfield, in jeans and a T-shirt with the sleeves rolled up, revealing thin, taut arms. He has a mess of thick, blond hair, and his head is cocked toward the camera, eyes smiling, a cigarette with curling, wind-blown smoke obscuring half his face.

He's got one arm over the hood of the truck, caught laughing at something or someone off-camera.

Casey hands the framed photo back and Mayfield places it carefully on the shelf.

"He was so afraid of dying down in one of those holes, but in the end, it was all that open sky and fresh air that killed him. See, he was smoking a cigarette every damn country mile, at least a two-pack-a-day habit. Eight years back he started having pulmonary problems and then lung cancer finally got him. He was a fighter. He was angry about it. It wasn't quick."

Mayfield returns to his seat, clasping his veined hands in front of him.

"Cancer got Donna, too. My first wife. We grew up here in Angel together. We bought this house in the Point and made it our own, and we were going to have kids but that never quite worked out. It just doesn't sometimes for some folks. She never smoked a cigarette a day in her life. Barely drank. Yet for reasons I'll never understand, that same blackness took her, and I think it's fair to ask how that makes any goddamn sense." Mayfield unclasps his hands, rubs them on his jeans, like he's wiping away a bad memory. "She was gentle, couldn't get angry about anything. She didn't fight at all and was gone way too soon."

Mayfield studies Casey, Van Dorn. "I was always proud to wear that badge and always believed I was doing right by this town . . . keeping it safe . . . but when I had my chance to shoot Little Paris, I couldn't do it. I got scared and I guess that means I got my daddy's rabbit blood in my veins, too."

"That's not how it works, Paul, you know that," Van Dorn says.

"I'm not sure I know how anything works anymore," Mayfield says, "other than Little Paris and his kin have been a cancer on this town, as black and sure and final as what took my daddy and my wife. So if someone had the nerve to do what I couldn't, I'm not going to pretend I'm sorry about that." Mayfield shakes his head. "I know that's not what you're asking me, and probably not what you want to hear, but I wanted you to know it all the same. I wanted to get it right out in the open."

"That's fair," Van Dorn says. "We understand."

"Good," Mayfield answers. "Now I'll tell you what I know about that sonofabitch."

70

'll ask someone down at the department to pull the files, but honestly, you're not going to find much there. Lower Wolf wasn't technically our jurisdiction, more Sheriff Dunn's cross to bear, but those lines are easily blurred around here, and truth is, they were everyone's problem."

"You knew what they were up to," Casey says. Not much of a question, but she tries hard not to make it sound like an accusation.

"Sure, of course I did. Dogfighting and stolen property. Arson. Assault. Prostitution. You name it. They were growing weed when most were still planting tobacco, when we still thought *that* had a future. They were nothing if not forward in their thinking. That was mostly Daniel. He always had vision, I guess."

Mayfield looks back up at the shelf where his daddy's picture sits. "A few folks will always want to romanticize them, pretend they're modern-day Robin Hoods. Like they've earned some sort of nobility out of being outlaws. It's the way of these hills. My daddy used to talk about the Old Man as if he was a real gentleman, almost respectable. Used to tell me you could share a whiskey or Popsicle with him over a game of Saturday-afternoon checkers, and if you told him you had a problem, well, then maybe he'd take care of it for you with just a phone call or visit from one of his own. I guess that really was how things *used* to be, but not anymore. Not with those sons of his. Especially not after Daniel was killed.

"Everyone liked that boy . . ." Mayfield pauses. "Although he was just as bad as any of them. And when he died, the Old Man all but died, too. Little Paris never recovered, either. He never quite got over the fact he wasn't beloved like his brother. Or that his daddy saw fit to remind him of that every damn day. I'm not making excuses, I'm just telling you the way of it. They all went far past colorful local legends a long time ago."

Mayfield sits back. "It was Daniel who moved the family first into meth, then cocaine, and now all that heroin you're seeing. A bloody, bloody business."

"We think that business finally caught up to them at Lower Wolf this afternoon," Van Dorn says. "You ever hear of any Mexicans meeting with the Glassers?"

"Here? No. And not the sort you're talking about. Not any that would gun a Glasser down in broad daylight. None that would have the *nerve* to do it."

Silence settles as Mayfield lets the words hang there. Until Casey finally breaks it.

"What would Jon Dorado say? He was your assistant chief and investigated the Glassers extensively, right?"

Mayfield considers her closely, probably wondering where she's going with the question. She's not sure yet either, but there's *something* about Mayfield that bothers her . . . that fires up that sixth sense of hers. It's the big house on a small-town police chief's salary, the quaint old tales about Angel and his beloved mailman daddy and the Glassers and summer Popsicles.

It's more than all that, yet somehow *less*, too.

He's drunk and grieving but there's just something empty, hollow, and a little too pat about Mayfield and the stories he wants them to believe.

"Yes, Jon took an interest in the Glassers, but he's no longer with the department," he says.

"But those files you dismissed earlier, they're still here, right? They'll include his investigative reports, his notes. Everything? There might be more there than you know."

Mayfield smiles wearily and looks toward Van Dorn. "I think you're going to be very disappointed, Agent Alexander. Your definition of *everything* is far different than ours here in our small, rural department. Even for a good cop like Jon, and he was very good."

Casey presses. "And he *hated* the Glassers. He was looking hard at Little Paris for the murder of a young girl, right? Jon dealt with *all* of them at one point or another." She tries to ignore Van Dorn's tense, steady gaze. "Who did he think killed Danny?"

"That was outside our jurisdiction. We didn't investigate that."

"But I'm sure you talked about it? I mean, just in passing . . . over coffee . . . over a drink." Casey gestures toward the Johnny Drum. "How about a Popsicle? And that girl *was* your jurisdiction. She was killed right here in Angel. Like you said, they were everyone's problem. Seems to me someone tried to solve at least one of those Glasser problems back then with a bullet."

"If it were that simple, maybe I should have put that one in Little Paris, too. But I didn't, and it isn't." He leans forward. "Or maybe the only thing we're going to learn from what happened today is you just got to kill them all to finally be rid of them."

"Is that how you feel about Hardy Glasser, too? Little Paris's son?" Mayfield doesn't answer.

"Did you know Jerry Dix? His sister, Janelle?" Casey asks.

"He was a Glasser runner. A mule, a nobody. Jon picked him up a half-dozen times on misdemeanors. There was bad blood between Jerry and Jamie Renfro over Jerry's wife, but everyone knows that."

Now Van Dorn steps in, making sure things don't heat up further between Casey and Mayfield. He already sees the sparks.

"Well, everyone but us," he says, motioning to Casey. "When did Janelle start shacking up down at Lower Wolf? Why was she there after what happened to her brother?"

"I talked to Janelle," Casey adds, before Mayfield can answer. "Trust me, she was no bigger fan of the Glassers than your assistant chief."

"I can't say. She was in and out of Angel. As I heard it, she was raising up that baby mostly on her own. Of course, it was never clear if it was Jerry's or Jamie's or even Little Paris's. But she would have needed the money, for sure . . . and if one of them had decided to call that baby a true Glasser, well, family was big for them, even if they had a narrow view of what that meant. Blood only . . . and blood is thicker than water. Even bad blood."

"Somehow it always comes back to that, doesn't it? *Blood*," Casey says. Again, not quite a question, but a hell of a lot closer to an accusation.

Van Dorn warns her to back down with a stare of his own.

"Do you know anything about Hardy's mama?"

"No," Mayfield says, unblinking. "Not enough to be helpful. Little Paris could be as fickle with his women as he was serious about family."

"What about the business, then?" Van Dorn asks. "Our guess is that Little Paris finally got on the wrong side of his Mexican suppliers and business went bad. He was either bringing too much heat down on everyone by pushing out that spiked heroin so fast, or he ended up owing too much for it."

"Dix told us Renfro and Little Paris were always holding back," Casey suggests. "Skimming from the till."

"No surprise they were cheating these Mexicans. They cheated everyone. And they felt invulnerable here."

"Until today, they were," Casey points out. "It was probably no coincidence Danny was killed across the river . . . outside your jurisdiction."

But Mayfield isn't willing to let that go. "I know what you're suggesting, Agent Alexander, and I would love to say you're wrong. But you're not. Right now, there's a Glasser cousin, second or third removed, who works for the Martin Sheriff's Office. And over the years, we've had more than our share of other Glasser acquaintances and associates wear an Angel PD badge, men who no doubt put a few extra Christmas dollars in their pockets by keeping an eye out for them and letting them know when folks like you were asking about them or getting too close. It happened long before me, long as I led the department, and probably long after I was gone."

"You haven't been gone all that long," Casey says.

Mayfield smiles and nods. "I guess you're right. Both Jon and I knew there was very little either of us could do to stop it, and I never pretended otherwise. Blood *is* thick, and real or imagined, sometimes that's all that matters in a small town."

"Okay," Van Dorn interjects, "we understand." He says it as much to Casey as he does to Mayfield, still staring at her to back the fuck off.

His eyes say *Paul Mayfield is doing us a favor. He doesn't have to put up with this. And I don't have to, either.*

"So," he continues, "if you're Little Paris and you're now on the run, and you've got all these extended family and friends, where the hell do you go first?"

"Not far," Mayfield answers. "He's got people in Catlettsburg. Bowmansville. Martha. Not necessarily blood, but longtime friends who'll take him in anyway." Mayfield thinks, eyeing the darkness pooled on the ceiling. "There are plenty of others like Dix or Ray Ray Sitton or Duane Scheel. I'll talk to Chief Floyd, and it's possible even our less-than-thorough files will have the last-known addresses on most of them, if you don't have them already."

At the last name Casey sits up. "Duane Scheel? He died today, too. Another overdose. At the baseball park."

Mayfield's look suggests he's neither shocked by the news nor moved by it.

"He was with Kara Grace," Casey says. "One of those women I was trying to talk to tonight. First Kara, then Anna Bishop. I believe they both saw Little Paris at some point today."

Van Dorn's now a live wire, anxious current running through him. He knows what she's going to say next, but instead of throwing her out the front door before Mayfield does, he throws himself in the line of fire.

"And that does raise a question we have about Marissa." Van Dorn still tries to be delicate, gentle with her name. "The other reason we're here. I'm sorry, I truly am, but we think it's possible she saw him today too, Paul."

"I'm sorry as well," Mayfield says. "I know you're just doing what you need to do, what you think is right. I appreciate that. So we'll talk a few more moments about Marissa, the woman I'll bury the day after tomorrow, and then I'll politely ask you to get the hell out of our house."

71

Casey met Devon Jeon's wife for the second time at his funeral, only a few days after he was shot to death and died in her arms.

But the first time had been in passing at a group barbecue at his house a couple of months earlier. She was with AJ then, and AJ was already drunk by the time they got there, knocking back a few Coronas while she drove.

When he was drinking, AJ was funny, the life of the party, but he got ugly quick whenever the party was over.

Lynn Jeon, with her long, dark hair, was standing beneath an orange tree in their backyard, where Devon or someone had strung red and white lights just for the occasion. They glowed hot in the early dusk, coloring a sky already turning pink and purple.

The small house was elegant. Very modern and mostly white, or a color that was probably described somewhere as *cream* or *winter mint* or *sand pearl*. Kids' toys were discreetly tucked away in IKEA bins, and French doors opened wide to the yard. Kitchen light pouring through the green glass made beautiful viridescent patterns on the pavers, on a closely tended heart-shaped patch of grass. Wooden bench tables were draped in luminous tablecloths and decked with old bottles filled with flowers that looked handpicked but were likely delivered earlier that day.

It seemed fussy, too manicured. Way too much and over the top on an agent's salary. But Devon's wife had successfully sold homes in Scottsdale for years and knew plenty about staging and probably made more than her husband.

And she was very attractive, as stunning and perfect as her house. Asian, slim. She'd barely touched the Kirin in her hand (more staging, like the flowers) when she and Casey said their few words—Casey complimenting her on the house and her powder-blue sundress; Lynn going on and on about how much Devon enjoyed working with her.

Both were gracious and reserved and removed. Saying the sort of thing you say to someone you don't know well and never imagine you'll ever really have to know at all.

That night was important less because of Lynn Jeon or that barbecue or that beautiful home, and more because of what happened *after*.

When AJ, back at his place and well past drunk and fun and deep into ugly, smacked her for the first and only time. It caught them both by surprise, but not so much she didn't pull her gun and put it to his temple and tell him if he ever put a hand on her like that again, she'd shoot him right the fuck where he stood.

Of course, he never did hit her again. And after he sobered up, he cried, apologetic, but things were never the same again, either. They weren't married, so she wasn't going to make a DV claim, the sort that had cost so many other agents and cops their badges, but it was a serious fuckup all the same, and he knew it. He was a homicide detective with the Phoenix Police Department and had been working with DEA's elite drug-homicide REDRUM unit for more than a year. All she had to do was make one call, file a battery report, and at a minimum he'd be on light desk duty until he completed counseling. He'd be kicked off the task force either way.

She didn't want that, so instead, as quietly and quickly as possible, she wound things down with him. It was still messy, pulling two lives apart that were coiled together both professionally and personally, and that's also when she started spending more time with Devon, doubling down on a series of bad decisions.

By then she'd nearly forgotten about his wife, Lynn, and the things they said when they first met.

The house and the red and white lights and the trees.

The colored glass bottles and the flowers.

That second time they met was at the funeral and memorial service.

Casey was in no condition to be there and her attending physician had refused to sign off on letting her leave the hospital, but she went anyway.

Six agents showed up to help get her out of there, to drive her to the service. To carry her, if necessary.

AJ, too.

No one blamed her yet for what had happened with Devon, and most never would. She was still weeks away from the full shooting investigation and reconstruction, months away from the more difficult questions put to her by DEA's OPR after a review of their sketchy surveillance plan for Tonto Place and her and Devon's text messages during the days prior. It was clear to anyone who reviewed them they'd had some sort of personal relationship, that they were more than close, and it was fair enough to ask if they might have been distracted during the hours leading up to the attack.

His short, dark hair, and the fine hairs on the nape of his neck. The slightly sunburned skin. His left hand rubbing at that delicate spot there, the sort of gesture she already knows he does whenever he's lost in thought, thinking hard.

Both watching the garage door go up, waiting for another vehicle to pull out, another vehicle to pull in.

It was also fair to ask about the execution-style shooting of Ramón Álvarez. She had to answer a lot of difficult questions about that, both on and off the record, with counsel and without. Those who didn't blame her for surviving the attack also painted her as a hero for punching his ticket, no matter the cost. But that was easy, none of them were paying it.

She claimed she shot Álvarez to *stop the threat*, the legal language everyone expected to hear and that she'd always been trained to say. It made sense too, because even a kid behind the wheel of a three-thousand-pound missile is a threat. But she also made it perfectly clear she would've shot Ramón Álvarez *no matter what the cost*, because it was the right fucking thing to do. Despite his age, despite the fact he'd never fired a weapon.

They turned off the recorder when she said those things, letting her curse and get angry without the specter of a transcript.

OPR and DOJ at least had to go through the motions that they cared about Álvarez any more than she did.

But later, when the sleepless nights started to pile up and all she could ever seem to dream about was Ramón *praying*, his wispy childish mustache and the thin contours of his young face, the way he reached out a hand for her help even as she put the gun to his temple, she was forced to admit to herself that she might have been wrong.

That there was a cost that was just too goddamn high.

But all that was months and months away, as was Casey's transfer back east, and on that Sunday four days after Devon's murder she sat there still bleeding from her stitched-up wounds in a wheelchair beneath skies that were way too blue and too hot and scoured almost completely and infinitely clean and told Lynn Jeon how sorry she was.

I'm so fucking sorry.

Snapping flags at half-mast.

A line of dark cars stretching around the cemetery.

More flowers that had been delivered earlier in the day.

Casey was dreading this one moment but refused to allow herself to avoid it and so she grasped Lynn's hand, afraid but accepting if the woman somehow *knew*, but Lynn seemed only gracious and devastated and the moment passed almost as quickly as it had begun.

But not before she leaned forward and whispered *Thank you* and Casey had no idea what she was being thanked for.

Lynn was crying, delicate tears that framed her face.

Casey was crying too, the last time she would.

And although she wanted to pull away, to run or get away and not look into the woman's eyes anymore or count the tears streaming down her face, Devon's widow still held on tight, their fingers almost entwined, and Casey was afraid she'd never let go.

72

arissa had her problems before I married her, before she came to Angel," Mayfield says. "Of course, I didn't know that then.

"Or it's possible I did," he adds. "That a part of me suspected all along." Mayfield looks at Van Dorn, raises his hands as if he's been asked a question he doesn't have an answer to. "Older, grieving man falls for a younger woman. Marries her too fast. Moves her out to the sticks where she soon grows bored, realizing what the rest of her life is going to look like day after day after day. It's a horrible cliché and I understand that.

"But with Marissa, it wasn't just boredom or the age difference, although that all played a part in it. She wanted children too, and after Donna, I didn't. Not anymore, not after we couldn't. I never saw marrying Marissa as sullying the memories of my first wife, but I did see having children with her as the closest thing to it. I couldn't quite *erase* Donna like that."

Mayfield retreats to the bottle again. He stands and pours more into his mug, hands shaking. "Things were dark after Donna passed, and my daddy so soon before that. Things were so goddamn dark and then I met Marissa and she was like this . . . *light*. This warm, incredible, guiding light. And I needed that. I can't explain it any better than that. I won't justify it more than that."

"You don't have to," Van Dorn says. "Not to us, not to anyone."

But Mayfield's sour look suggests otherwise. "Now, with the benefit of hindsight, the warning signs probably were there, everywhere, but she shined bright enough to blind me to them. I wanted her to. There was a doctor I met when I took her to her first rehab, a young man named Farris. He told me not to blame myself and not to blame her. But I think there was more than enough blame to go around.

"I can't tell you exactly when it really got bad, but I do know when the lies started. When the money started disappearing. All those times she wasn't home when she was supposed to be. I know when the rumors started up."

"About Little Paris?" Casey asks. But she doesn't mention Jon Dorado and Marissa. Not yet.

"Well, it was obvious where she was getting it. Where everyone was getting it. And Little Paris did have a thing for a pretty woman. Before Marissa, there was an old motel on the other side of Angel where he used to hold these little parties. He ran drugs and young girls out of the place for a while. Out there, he wasn't under the Old Man's thumb. We checked into it a few times, but not much came of it. No one ever wanted to talk, no one ever saw anything. The motel's shut down now, but rumors persisted. All those rumors about Little Paris still do. Most are true."

"That motel, that's where that girl died?" Casey asks. "The one Jon Dorado investigated?"

"Yes, but she wasn't local." Mayfield shrugs, as if again that somehow makes a difference. His gesture is meant to seem casual and it's anything but. "She was over from Catlettsburg. It was a particularly ugly crime and she was so young. Jon wanted to hang Little Paris for it, but just could never come up with enough rope."

Mayfield takes another long drink, steadying himself. "It truly bothered him, though. Hell, it bothered all of us. Still does. The way Little Paris dirties everything he touches."

"Is it possible Marissa saw him yesterday, today, even tonight?" Casey asks.

"No, not at all."

"How can you be so sure?"

"I'm sure because I've been living with *it*, Agent Alexander. Not just yesterday, or today, or tonight. Because living with it has meant letting it define what living even *means*. If Marissa's every thought, every waking moment, was struggling to stay sober, then *my* every thought, my every waking moment, was consumed with making sure she did. You could say neither of us slept much anymore."

More whiskey. Mayfield's bottle is finally empty.

"Have you ever dealt with someone struggling with a substance-abuse disorder?" he suddenly asks.

"No," Casey concedes, shaking her head. But Van Dorn doesn't join her.

"That's the preferred term, by the way, at least according to the good Dr. Farris. All these doctors and mental-health experts can't agree among themselves when a set of behaviors *becomes* a disorder, but I know, and I don't even have a degree.

"I know what it's like, all those weeks in and out of rehab. The days after spent following her around and checking up on her, confirming what she's doing and the places she's lied that she's going to be. The shopping she never does and the friends she doesn't visit. The appointments that were promised but were never made or kept. Every hour spent worrying and wondering and expecting the worst, while desperately, futilely, hoping for the best. Right down to the minutes spent searching through her phone, reading all the messages for clues or signs. It's the trust that goes first but none of the love, and I don't know how to explain that if you haven't experienced it. It'd be easier if you could just hate her and everything she's doing to your life, but you can't. Or you do, and then hate yourself for what you're doing to her. It's exhausting and endless and it's like falling down a hole and you keep waiting to hit bottom, only to find there is no bottom. It just goes on and on, and you're holding on to each other because there's nothing and no one else to hold on to. Falling together."

Mayfield puts his empty mug next to his empty bottle. "So, I ask you, who was really suffering from a goddamn *disorder*?"

He shakes his head. "Jon once went to talk to the grandmother of one of the locals around here, a young kid named Desmond Beamon. Desi was probably barely older than the girl from the Tamarack, and Desi's mama was already dead by then from her own drug issues. Desi ran around with the Glassers and did little errands for them. He was a habitual user, too. And when Jon knocked on his grandmama's door, Velda, who was about in her seventies then but still spry, asked him if he was there to finally tell her that her grandbaby was dead. See, she'd been expecting that knock for months, figuring the way that boy was living, dying had to be just around the corner. She'd already watched his mama, her daughter, die and knew Desi wasn't long for this world, either. She cried in Jon's arms and said she just didn't know what to think of such a world anymore. It didn't make any sense to her. And then Desi did die, about three months later, with a Glasser needle still in his arm, and Velda passed away shortly after that. A real broken heart."

Casey tries to imagine Dillon Mackey's fate, his prospects or future no better. And Harmon Glasser too, wherever he might be.

"So what happened with Marissa tonight?" Casey pushes, but trying hard to be gentle too, the way Van Dorn was earlier.

"Marissa was struggling again. She was always struggling. When she was sober, the world just didn't make any sense to her, either. It took so little to set her back. A bad day. A good cry. A goddamn rainy day."

And Casey does understand that. How little it used to take for her own darkness to overtake her. Nothing more than a change in the weather.

"She was tired of failing," Mayfield says. "Of falling."

"You believe she killed herself?"

"A couple of triazolam and two glasses of wine. Both perfectly legal. The triazolam was *my* Halcion prescription, Agent Alexander, just plain old sleeping pills. Like I said, we weren't sleeping much. And the wine was a bottle of Three Horses Chambourcin we bought together in Stamping Ground last year."

Casey knows a full tox screen will reveal if there is any heroin or fentanyl, Little Paris's DOA, in Marissa's system. But Trey told Casey that Mayfield was adamant he didn't want one. He already knows his wife's cause of death.

And Van Dorn agrees, nodding along with Mayfield's words. But his phone is buzzing as well, although he doesn't want to break the moment and look at it.

"She was afraid of the Big Sandy," Mayfield says. "It scared the hell out of her. She knew how dangerous it could be. She didn't accidentally overdose and end up there. She went into the water tonight because she *wanted* to. There's no other way she walks into that river otherwise."

"You mentioned Marissa's phone," Casey says. "Is it possible we can see that? We have Anna's and we're still trying to track down Little Paris's latest number."

"No," Mayfield says, and looks to Van Dorn. "You cannot have my wife's phone. Little Paris knew well enough to stay away from her. He knew I would not have lost my nerve a second time."

He's talking about the time he almost shot Little Paris, and Casey is left wondering too how things would have been different if he had.

"She was struggling," he continues, "but she was sober. I know that."

He looks back and forth between Casey and Van Dorn. His eyes are bleary, red. The drinking has finally caught up to him. "But you can write down the number you're looking for, and I'll check it tomorrow, or the day after, just to be sure."

"Tomorrow is too late . . . and—"

Mayfield stops her, leaning forward, closing the space between them. He's talking only to her now and there's that mint shampoo again, the hot whiskey on his breath. "Her phone is just evidence to you, Agent Alexander. Another clue, one more link in some chain you're following. But to me, that phone *is* part of her. You might as well be asking me to give up her body. It's got pictures of us together, moments in our lives and messages we shared. I'm not ready to let go of her."

You're holding on to each other because there's nothing and no one else to hold on to.

Falling together . . .

But it was Marissa alone who landed in the Big Sandy River.

"It's too soon," Mayfield concludes. "Far too soon to trade those memories for Little Paris Glasser."

"Or even his son, right?" Casey says.

"We're so sorry," Van Dorn interjects, standing and signaling to Casey that it really was time for them to go. His patience has worn thin too, and he's also pointing subtly to his phone.

But still she hesitates. There's a lot more she wants to ask Mayfield, more about Jon Dorado and the Glassers and Jon and Marissa. But she doesn't want to anger Van Dorn any further after he got her this far.

They're done here.

"No, *I'm* sorry," Mayfield says. "Sorry if I wasted your time. I will call over to the department and get all those things for you. Names, addresses, Jon's files. I'm not the chief, but they'll help you out all the same, for my sake. Chief Floyd will get you some men too, if you need them." He stands, the third point of their triangle, and first shakes Van Dorn's hand, then Casey's as well.

"If there's anything we can do, Paul, just let us know. And thank you for everything tonight," Van Dorn says, as he finally leads Casey to the front door.

But like that moment with Lynn Jeon, Casey's not sure what they're thanking Paul Mayfield for at all.

73

When they get into the Explorer, Van Dorn finally returns the call that had distracted him in Mayfield's study.

He nods along with a voice she can't hear, and when he finally hangs up, he starts the engine.

"That was Sykes. It looks like Little Paris's missing Mustang was finally found. Torched down to the rims, out near Yatesville Lake."

"Who found it?" Casey asks.

"One of Sheriff Dunn's deputies."

"Bullshit."

Van Dorn shrugs, defeated. Maybe even relieved.

"Was it empty?" she asks.

Van Dorn shakes his head. "No, there was at least one body inside." He looks at her. "Only one body, an adult."

"No," she says, still unwilling to accept it.

"But it's going to take a while before they'll know who it is," Van Dorn says. "About the only thing the fire left behind are teeth."

74

They drive back over the tri-bridge as silently as they first drove over it.

There's no need to discuss the call from Sykes.

There's no need to replay the conversation with Mayfield and neither of them are ready to get into it anyway.

If Van Dorn's still angry about the things she said, the tone she used with the former police chief, he's too tired or over it to spar. She's too tired as well.

It's almost 1:30 in the morning and they've run into their last wall. They've been at this for almost twelve hours now.

She also got a message while they were talking to Mayfield. Trey texted her to say he was finally home and Dillon Mackey's safe with Tanya Heck.

He asked how it was going, if there was anything he could do.

She didn't answer then. Doesn't answer now. She leaves his questions unanswered like so many others.

Instead she idly scrolls through Anna's cell, checking the woman's messages and jotting down recent numbers. She finally has that one strong possibility for Little Paris she'd wanted all night—a West Virginia area code, although there's no name associated with the contact.

The text messages back and forth are equally cryptic, barely more than a handful of emojis, but the timing sure feels right.

Anna texted and called it a half-dozen times in the hour before she was arrested.

Not that it matters now that they have all the time in the world.

If she could've cross-checked that number against Marissa's recent calls, or Kara's, or even Mark Crosby's (Van Dorn found out that Crosby's phone was both battery-dead and password-protected), then she would've had a straight line to Little Paris. But the number is a dead end now, like Little Paris himself.

Still, she calls Sykes and asks him to start working on a subpoena for the subscriber and tolls on the West Virginia number anyway.

Start prepping a warrant.

It's still evidence.

One of the emojis that Anna tapped out again and again was a tiny skull with crossbones.

75

She and Van Dorn need to get back over to Angel PD to return Anna's phone and pick up Sykes's Impala and then wait for him to get the orders and warrants done.

They'll keep trying to draw new lines to the shooters on the loose.

Tomorrow, maybe, she'll check out the burned-out Mustang herself and wait for the ID on Little Paris's body.

But ex-chief Paul Mayfield is still on her mind. His hollowness has left her feeling incomplete and unfinished too, just like this whole fucking night. He talked a lot but revealed nothing, both more *and* less.

All she heard were all the things he wouldn't or couldn't or didn't say. He went on and on how Marissa blinded him, but there's no way he never saw what was going on all around him.

"Mayfield's lying about his wife," she says.

"I don't know that," Van Dorn replies. "And neither do you."

"Yes, we do. All that bullshit about the sleeping pills and about her not seeing Little Paris? He doesn't want to admit to us—"

Van Dorn stops her. "Maybe he doesn't want to admit it to himself."

"Now? After everything he's been through with her? What's that, some half-assed sense of honor? Does he think he's protecting her memory, her reputation? Or is it his own he's worried about? Don't tell me you weren't thinking the same thing."

"I am not crucifying that man, Casey. I'm not doing that. Not tonight. You wanted to see him, so we did. He agreed to help us, which is more than we had any right to ask for, and a hell of a lot more than we had any goddamn right to expect."

"But—"

"But *nothing*. We're done here. Tonight, right now, we're done."

She tries to start again, but this time Van Dorn wheels on her—

"Goddamn it, Casey, you just push and push and push. Is this what happened in Arizona? Is this how things played out?"

This is the first time Van Dorn's ever hinted at the shooting there. He's never asked about Devon Jeon or Tonto Place or Ramón Álvarez. But the agency's so goddamn small. *He knows* all the same. He knew all about it even before she arrived in West Virginia; everyone's warned him again and again about his new partner and her history.

How she walked away, when her old partner didn't.

But it also took her two months to walk a straight fucking line without a cane.

"Fuck you," she says.

Van Dorn pulls over and slams the Explorer in neutral. It's so late it's now early. The road's empty, black and barren in both directions, except for the bridge lights behind them and a few buildings and signs in Angel ahead.

The imminent sunrise.

He turns in his seat, faces her.

"Fuck me, I guess. You're right, that's unfair. A cheap shot. I know that. I'm tired, frustrated too, but that's no excuse. Look, Arizona . . .

here . . . one place has nothing to do with another. But if Paul Mayfield wants to find peace in a lie, I'm not going to take that from him."

"My dad killed himself," Casey says. "There was no fucking peace for me when he was gone."

"I'm sorry, I didn't know that."

Casey knows he doesn't know. She talks less about her prior life in Kentucky than she does about her time in Arizona.

"He was sick. Very sick," he says.

They sit together, both staring out their respective darkened windows. If they sit here long enough, that sun will inevitably come up over Van Dorn's left shoulder. It'll turn the sky gray, then pearl, then bronze. It'll burn and blaze. The world will rise and brighten around them and Casey will still feel like they're sitting in the dark.

"You're making excuses for him," she says.

"I understand him. Don't judge him by tonight and the things he said. The things you *wanted* to hear."

"It's more than that," she says. And she can't help but remember Van Dorn's studied silence when Mayfield asked them if they'd ever dealt with someone struggling with addiction.

That look on his face.

"You *know*, don't you? What he's been going through."

Van Dorn looks away, then nods. "My own son, Casey. He's starting his first semester at GW, but it was touch and go for many years. And just like Paul said, it still is. It always will be. He's a twenty-four-year-old fucking *freshman*.

"But when I look at him, I *still* see him at sixteen, seventeen. I can't shake that fear and anger and hurt and all those sleepless nights, everything Paul Mayfield talked about. His mother and I didn't see eye to eye on how to deal with him, or if we even should. She refused to abandon him, and I refused to enable him, and who even knows where that line is? I didn't want to blame my own son for that marriage falling apart, but a part of me did then, and still does today. I kicked him out a dozen times, but with your kids, you can't kick them out of your fucking heart. You hate yourself for not loving them enough. Or loving them far too fucking much."

"You never told me."

"I didn't really tell anyone. Mitchell knew a little about it, but never how truly bad it got. How does it look, the son of a DEA agent, an addict? What answers do I have for someone else, when I don't have any of my own?"

"No one expects us to have all the answers."

"Maybe not," Van Dorn agrees. "But that's why I understand Paul Mayfield. He doesn't have any answers, either. Not as a cop, not as a husband, and not as someone struggling to break the grip of addiction on his family and his life. I get the shame and the lying to himself and others. I do."

Casey leans her head back, closes her eyes. "I wish you had said something . . . just told me all this. Just so I knew. Before we came over here, before we got into it with Mayfield."

But she was the only one who got into it with Mayfield. Not Van Dorn. And although it's going to sound small, somehow petty, she still needs to know—

"You trusted him, Mitchell?"

Van Dorn smiles at her, thin and sad and tired. "Not half as much as I trust you." He slips the Explorer back into gear. "But we both know you don't even like kids." He grips the wheel. "He reminds me so much of you. Not Mitchell, but my son. Both of you stubborn as hell."

"I'd like to meet him," she says. And she means it.

He laughs a little, not much. "You may find this hard to believe, but I was once just like you, too. I've broken skulls, busted balls. I've knocked down plenty of walls. Then I grew up."

"No, you just got fucking old," she says. And she smiles, tossing a little laughter back.

Letting him know it's okay.

They're going to be okay.

"Let's get the hell out of here," Van Dorn says, and they both know he's talking about Angel and a whole lot more.

76

Casey wants them to grab a couple of rooms and stick around for the night, or what's left of it.

They can get a few hours of sleep under them, then start up again in the morning. That way they're already in place, if something breaks.

Once they ID Little Paris.

She's glad Hardy's body wasn't found with his daddy's but worries now that he really was kidnapped by their shooters, a horrible idea she was all too willing or desperate to dismiss earlier. Maybe Mayfield and the others are right, and he's safe instead with his mama, somewhere.

Like Dillon was safe with Kara?

Or maybe he doesn't exist and never really did.

Van Dorn tells her a hotel is fine, and she remembers spotting a Fairfield or Days Inn just outside of Angel when she was riding with Trey. Remembers asking herself how they even stay in business.

Who passes through Angel?

Where do they come from and where are they going?

That was after they passed that old motel where Jon Dorado found the body of a young girl that sent him on a collision course with the Glassers.

Not far from the bar where his own son found a dead girl lying in the snow.

All these kids . . . these children . . . someone's son or daughter . . . passing through Angel.

Come and gone.

As Van Dorn fiddles with the radio, searching for a decent station, Casey has a thought—

"Remember Mayfield saying something about a motel?"

Van Dorn pauses, thinks back. "Yeah."

"That place where Little Paris used to party and do deals. Used to run girls? Well, Trey mentioned that place, too. He pointed it out to me when we were driving up from Lower Wolf. The same place his dad investigated that girl's death, the girl from Catlettsburg."

"Fine, but so what? Paul said the place was shut down, abandoned."

"Shut down, maybe. But he also said there was still talk about it. The exact word he used was *rumors*."

"Right, rumors. We've been running them down all night, Casey. Chasing shadows."

"Sure. And it's one hundred percent a coincidence they *both* had the place in mind. It was called the Tamarack, I think"

"Like that travel plaza on I-64?" Van Dorn asks, slowly circling the idea with her.

"Yeah," Casey says. He's talking about the big Beckley Travel Plaza on the other side of Charleston, and the artisan showplace and conference center nearby—*Tamarack, the Best of West Virginia*. They've both passed the signs heading to Virginia or D.C. Casey's never stopped there and can't imagine Van Dorn ever has, either. He's never struck her as the artisanal type.

"The one thing we *all* agree on is we don't see Little Paris running far," she says. "So it'd take nothing for us to just run by there, maybe eyeball the place. I didn't pay much attention to it when Trey and I passed it the first go-around, but a second look now can't hurt."

"It certainly doesn't help. We're both exhausted. And Little Paris is dead."

"No, a body and his car were found. That's it. *Burned up*, not shot up like Lower Wolf. Our shooters didn't torch the others, and they would have had the time. More than enough time. They could have burned that whole fucking house down. Torching that car is a lot of trouble to keep us from finding out what we were always going to find out anyway . . . that it's Little Paris Glasser. Unless . . . it isn't."

Van Dorn doesn't say anything for a long time. "Shadows, Casey." But he turns off the radio. He never found a station. "Did Dix ever say anything about this place when we debriefed him?"

"I don't know. I've got my laptop, I can go back and check the old sixes." A DEA-6 is their basic Report of Investigation, an ROI. She knows if she digs though them she will find buried in one or more of them that Dix *did* mention the Tamarack. It just didn't matter to them then. They didn't know it would matter.

You can't predict the future, Cassandra, no one can.

"I can text Trey too, ask him more about it. He's still awake." She goes for her phone, but Van Dorn shakes his head.

He reaches out and takes it from her and gently puts it up on the dashboard.

"Don't bother the kid. We've done enough of that tonight. I want to believe someone's finally getting some rest in this fucking town."

"I'll even make it easy," she says. "Drop me at Sykes's ride and I'll take a spin by the motel myself. Just one look. It probably *is* a waste of time, so I'll make it quick, I promise. You can go ahead and get those rooms for us."

He shakes his head. He wants to argue, but he won't, for all the reasons he let her leave with Trey and got Anna's phone for her and agreed to talk to Mayfield and then let her press the ex-chief even after he warned her to let him take the lead.

Because they're partners.

Because he believes in her.

Because he trusts her.

"We're going?" she asks.

He stares down the road, the direction they were already traveling, opposite the dawn that will eventually brighten the sky at their backs. Maybe Lower Wolf and Angel and the whole world will look different in that liminal light, a brand-new day.

Maybe there'll be revelations, then . . . *answers.*

Or there won't.

They are racing the sun, *chasing shadows,* as Van Dorn's called it, and he won't let her chase them alone.

"Yeah, I guess we are," he answers, and then guns the Explorer down the dark, empty road.

77

It's called the Tamarack Inn.

A "tamarack" is a type of tree.

The old motel backs up to a thick, knotted stand of trees, tall and black and vertigo-inducing in the night. Casey has no idea if they're even the namesake tamaracks or not, but they remind her of those sable woods behind Kara Grace's trailer, that same impenetrable, endless dark she was unwilling to run into.

They might as well go on forever, too.

It slumps along the side of U.S. 23, two long rows of low-slung roofs and stained wooden doors, eighteen in all, joined at the northern corner. It's shaped like a huge letter *L*, fronted by an empty parking lot, the deserted pavement probably cracked by weeds, but Casey can't tell from where she and Van Dorn sit by the side of the road, headlights off.

Some of the windows are glassless. It's easy to imagine storm-punched holes in the roof, long-empty rooms full of trash and leaves and decay. Fetid, ankle-deep water speckled with faint and fading starlight from above.

Run-down, abandoned, unused. Just like Mayfield told them.

"Doesn't look like much," Van Dorn says. "Doesn't look like anyone's been home a long time."

"Yeah," she agrees, disappointed, and not even sure what she was really expecting. Or hoping for.

"But," Van Dorn says, pointing to the side of the motel that looks like it was once the main office, "there's another little road that runs behind the place. A path." He studies the motel. "Fuck it, since you dragged us out here, I'll get out and take a quick look."

He reaches up and slides the dome light to "off," so it won't shine when he gets out. And before she can stop him, he cracks the door.

"Hey, let me go," she says, grabbing at his arm. "I know I talked you into this, but I can still run faster than you, even on my gimped leg. I'll be there and back before you get your fat ass across the road. If you drop dead from a heart attack, I'll have to call Trey and Dobie to come get you."

He smiles wide in the dark. "This fat ass needs the exercise. Besides, I never want to miss a chance to tell you I told you so."

She shakes her head. "It's a wonder you got all those women to marry you."

"It's more amazing any of them stayed around long as they did."

He winks at her and shuts the door, jogging slowly across the road to the motel.

78

She loses him in the dark.

Seconds pass. Her eyes strain, searching, waiting for him to come back. She should have gone but didn't want to embarrass him. He was just trying to be decent, to do his part, although he's never been one to coddle or patronize her. They carry the same badge, have been through the same training (Casey a lot more recently), and he knows she can handle herself, but he wasn't going to sit in the Explorer and wait this one out. Not this time.

It's a little old-fashioned, but given what she's put him through to-night, she figures she owes him.

He doesn't know what happened to her at Kara's trailer, but can guess she's still on edge from pulling a screaming Lucy Dix out of that bloodstained horror show at Lower Wolf.

Time ticks by.

And she grows nervous by the second, wondering if he really did have a goddamn heart attack behind the motel. Or ran into a fucking bear back there? *Do they even have bears here?* A heart attack or a bear or maybe he fell down a hole . . . Those things aren't off the table.

Despite Van Dorn's admonishments, she texts Trey anyway, just a short message that she and Van Dorn are out checking the Tamarack. Their last stop for the night.

She wants someone to know they're here.

She wants to know how Trey's doing.

Then she waits some more.

She's finally about to open her own door and follow him into that darkness when she spies his bulky shadow moving back across the road.

Jogging twice as fast as when he left her . . . and that makes her sit up straight.

Makes her draw her gun.

She scans the veil of night behind him but there's nothing but the motel ruins.

Those damn endless trees.

When he reaches the Explorer, he slides in, breathing hard. Wipes at his forehead with his hand. He's broken out into a thick sweat.

"What the fuck?" she asks.

He looks at her.

"Well, I guess I can't say I told you so after all."

79

He found an old Camaro backed in and tucked up close behind the motel on a strip of quartz and gravel, partially hidden by sumac.

An ugly color of green, almost as much primer and rust as anything else.

He decided against trying to get around behind it to cop the plate.

"Doesn't matter. That's either Ronnie Mackey's or Duane Scheel's," Casey says. "And Kara Grace's gotta be driving it. Trey said he saw her in a green car before."

"All right," Van Dorn answers. "All right."

"There's only one reason she's here." Casey pauses, not sure she's ready to believe it herself.

Not sure if saying it out loud makes it more believable. "She's with Little Paris."

Van Dorn nods, working his way through the possibilities. "Okay, let's say she called him tonight looking for a hit. He recognizes her number and trades whatever dope he has left for a lift, for a way out of Lower Wolf or wherever the hell he's been hiding. He dumps his own car, then torches it."

"Or someone torches it for him," Casey adds.

He now draws his own gun from his shoulder holster, that big S&W

revolver, the same one he put in Renfro's face and that Casey would have trouble holding with both hands. He also carries a little thirty-eight snubnose on his ankle.

"He's too afraid to drive it around much or smart enough not to," Casey continues, following his line. "Anna said Kara and he were a thing for a while, so he trusts her, more or less. Makes her bring him here. This way he's close, but not too close, to the action."

Van Dorn stares at the hotel, lost in thought. "He could have killed her, Casey. That could be her torched body in the Mustang."

"Or that," Casey reluctantly concedes. But she also remembers what Trey told her about Dillon—

He said he did see another kid, once. A little kid, younger than him, sitting in the back of Little Paris's car. Said his mama made a fuss all over him, but it was all pretend, all for show. She told him later she didn't like that boy much at all. That he was already mean, too much like his daddy.

"Little Paris wants her help with Hardy," she says. "Maybe that's her boy. She could be the mother."

Van Dorn's still lost in thought, but she knows he heard her. She's not sure she believes Hardy is Kara's son, and is even less sure he does, but he finally turns to her—

"Toss me that phone from the woman in lockup."

"Anna," she reminds him, fishing around in her bag until she finds it. She unlocks it, hands it over.

Van Dorn puts his S&W in his lap, then thumbs through the phone. He scrolls the call log back and forth, eyeing the numbers. "Which of these do you think is Little Paris?" He holds it low, shielding it with one hand, but still high enough she can see.

"Best guess?" She points at the West Virginia area code. "That one."

He raises Anna's phone a little higher. "Then he'll know *this* phone, this number. He'll recognize it, like he did Kara's."

"Yeah," she says, and knows now where he's going with all this, a new spin on calling the number in the marero's pocket like they did earlier tonight.

"Watch the motel. Watch it close," Van Dorn says.

"He didn't answer Anna earlier," she says. "And you figure his phone's gotta be off by now or he's finally dumped it. Or he burned it up right along with his fucking car."

"Probably," Van Dorn says. "That's my guess. But think about it, he really hasn't had a whole lot of time to plan this out. He's been running for his life all night, making it up as he goes, just like we are. So maybe he needs a lifeline. He needs help. You've been making that argument all night."

But when he dials the number, the tension doesn't last long. It goes straight to a generic voice mail, like every other burner phone in the world.

"Goddamn," Van Dorn says. But now he's given Casey another idea. Another spin—

He needs a lifeline.

He needs help.

"Here, let me do it," she says, and takes Anna's phone back. She still has Kara's number jotted down from Dillon earlier, so now she reaches out to *her*.

She doesn't make a voice call, she simply *texts* her.

All us girls know LP.

Which means they all probably know one another.

Casey taps out a single emoji, again and again and again—

Skull and crossbones.

80

They wait.

As Casey decides she doesn't like the decaying motel anymore.

Doesn't like them sitting here in the dark like this . . . *waiting*.

It's too much like Tonto Place.

Like Arizona.

That fear she felt outside Kara's trailer is back now too, gripping her.

But she stares at the front of the motel, daring something to happen.

Staring, staring.

Until . . . *There it is*.

A gleam, a reflection, a fleeting ghost in the glass window of one of the rooms.

A cellphone lighting up. And the one in her hand, also brightening. A response.

A single, solitary question mark.

"Fuck me," she says.

"There's someone by the window, looking out," Van Dorn says. "That's got to be Little Paris Glasser."

And he retrieves his S&W from his lap.

81

D id he see us?" Casey asks, mentally marking the now-dark room.

It still has glass in the windows, a set of ragged draperies. It's not quite midway down the second arm of the L.

Hiding in plain sight.

Counting down from the office, or what she thinks of as the office, it looks to be number seven.

Lucky Number Seven.

"I don't think so," Van Dorn says, "but we sure fucking saw him."

Hopefully, Little Paris wasn't able to pick out Anna's phone reflected in their windshield, the way Kara's phone lit up the glass window for them, but it's impossible to know.

"Did we spook him?" she asks.

"I'd say he was fucking plenty spooked already."

"But does he know *who* we are?"

Van Dorn checks the cylinder on his S&W. An unnecessary gesture. A nervous gesture. "Does it matter?"

It matters to Little Paris and what he does next.

"Now what?"

Van Dorn reaches past her into the glove compartment and retrieves his own tiny SureFire flashlight, like the one buzz-cut Deputy

Buechel used when he walked them out to Renfro's trailer. It's even smaller in his big hands. "We go get that sonofabitch."

She's got her light too, in her bag, but doesn't reach for it. She reaches for Van Dorn instead, pulling at his arm, the way she did only a few moments before when he got out of the Explorer.

"Look, maybe it's time we call Sykes and Sheriff Dunn. Or the FBI. Fuck it, let's call Angel PD and have them get us some men, like Mayfield offered. A whole lot of men."

Even she can't believe she's saying these things, and neither can Van Dorn.

"Casey, you pushed this all night. Drove us both fucking crazy over it. Now, call it luck or fate or instinct or whatever, but that fucker's *here*, and we're sitting here too because of you. And maybe he has already killed this Kara woman and just took her car and phone, but it's possible she's alive and still helping him out, willingly or not. And since you've been right on everything else, I guess that means you could be right about that little boy being in there, too. But if we wait for a full crew to roll up, set up a perimeter and all that, I guarantee they'll both be dead or actual hostages before dawn."

Van Dorn pulls his snubnose off his ankle and slides it behind his belt where he can grab it easier. "Exigent circumstances, Casey. Let's get them both out of there and end this."

And there's not enough time to finally tell him about Tonto Place and security lights. About Devon Jeon's blood all over her or Ramón Álvarez begging her not to kill him.

Why her sixth sense is spinning wildly and how this wrecked motel two thousand miles from there is setting off all those warning bells again in a way even that Nissan Sentra didn't.

Not before it was too late.

She can't explain how knowing what's coming doesn't help you do a goddamn thing about it.

Can't put into words that unexpected shaking after Kara's trailer, a fear that gripped her and wouldn't let go.

She doesn't know how to tell him she's not ready for this and how she's afraid she'll never be ready again.

"Another thing," Van Dorn continues, "as far as we know, our shooters are still looking for Little Paris. If we found him, they might, too." He stares right at her, making all her same arguments from only an hour ago. "Just one question, and it's the only one that matters. Do you really think that little boy is in there?" He puts a hand on her shoulder—

"Are you willing to bet your life on it?"

"How can we afford not to, right?" she says. The only answer she can give.

"Right. Your words, partner. And I believe you. I always have. We've come all this way for him, for you, and I don't know how we stop now."

The Explorer is hot with his adrenaline, Van Dorn's heart beating fast. He's the one who's always so slow to act, but she's got to own the fact she pushed and pushed and pushed him into this and shouldn't be surprised when she can't hold him back now.

Speed kills, he once told her, when she was complaining about his glacial driving. And even though the Explorer isn't moving at all, it feels like they're hurtling down the darkened highway, headlights off, the dividing lines and guardrails merely blurs. Too fast for the naked eye.

Did he ever sit outside another motel like this one, waiting and wanting to save his own son?

"All right, you win. But, Jesus, can you even fit in your vest anymore?" she asks, trying to keep it lighthearted. But this thing he's put in her hands is too heavy for her.

Too heavy for either of them alone.

Their armored vests are stowed in the back of the Explorer.

"Tell me how you want it to go down."

82

They make their way across the main road, about twenty feet apart.
They have the night for cover, although it now feels flimsy. Useless. Neither dark nor deep enough.

They're going to take up flanking positions by room seven and eight when Casey redials Kara's number from Anna's phone a second time, hopefully distracting Little Paris for a few seconds longer, Van Dorn, bigger and heavier, will call out *Police, police* and blast the flimsy door apart with the handheld ram.

She'll drop the phone and he'll drop the ram and then they'll both go in and save Little Paris from himself. Most important, Kara too, if she's there to save.

It's not a great plan, but it's the best they've got.

There are a hundred ways it can go wrong and Casey knows all the difficult questions people will ultimately ask. With the benefit of time and reflection and introspection and the perfect science of knowing what really happened, those people will have all the answers she and Van Dorn don't.

You can't predict the future, Cassandra, no one can.

Good or bad, reports and findings and informed opinions will reflect how this turned out and all the things they should have done differently. All the different choices they could have made.

Call Little Paris out.

Set a perimeter.

Call SWAT.

Wait for backup.

But all those people and all those possible futures aren't here running across this road in the night and heat and they're not making this choice *now.*

Are you willing to bet your life on it?

They're not the ones who'll live or die with it.

83

Once they hit the parking lot itself, they slow down, move at a tandem, as if they've practiced all day for this.

The lot is mostly gravel and weeds and broken bottles. Used condoms and other junk. An old tire and rim. They step carefully.

Van Dorn looks big even hunched over. A big target.

Casey takes in the Tamarack's other rooms, all the glassless windows. They stare back at her, defiant. Curtains in one of them move with the slight breeze that followed them over the road. Everything stinks of wood and rust and long-standing water. Cat-piss reek.

This is worse than Tonto Place.

She thought they had the same door in mind as they left the Explorer and crossed the road, but now as they approach, they all start to look the same. Glass or no glass, up close, in the shadows, they're identical, all the numbers pried off or lost. The way the windows and doors are situated, they're close together but oddly spaced. She heads toward what she thinks of as room seven, but Van Dorn moves toward room eight.

Goddamn.

She hesitates. She wants to whistle or signal at him, but he's already set up to the left of the door, in front of one of the adjacent rooms, which, by her count, is the one they should be hitting.

She takes up her position, she's kneeling beneath a window. The glass is broken, shattered.

This can't be right.

Different choices.

But Van Dorn's already hefting the ram, aiming it at a spot just above the lock and knob. He's got his S&W tucked in the front of his pants and his SureFire and the snubbie next to it. After he gets through the door, he's got to drop the ram and retrieve some combination of them in one clean motion.

She's got to do the same with Anna's phone and her own gun, but she'll be faster.

She should be the one going first, and even made that argument twice back at the Explorer, but he insisted he can get the door punched fast enough and get them inside.

Different choices.

She'll be right on his six, right on his goddamn shoulder.

But kneeling beneath her window, unsure of herself, she wants to back them both out of here and start all over again. Better, she wants to go back to the moment she walked into the house in Lower Wolf and saw the bloody baby, Lucy. She wants to pick her up a second time and walk her out of the house and just keep on walking until they're both safe.

Different choices.

He believes in her. She could stop him. *He trusts her.* She needs to stop him.

But Van Dorn isn't looking at her. Too focused on the door.

The wrong door.

Already hefting the ram.

She redials Kara's number on Anna's phone and tosses it aside and draws her Glock as a sudden bright light shines and spins in the window.

84

*N*o . . . not the window above her. The one *behind* Van Dorn.

Not the right one because they are one room off.

As Van Dorn hits the wrong door, as it loudly splinters and gives way and he struggles to get one of his guns and his SureFire up, Casey calls out.

Calls his name, not caring who hears. Fucking screams it and warns him to get down.

He's busting into an empty room yelling *Policepolicepolice*.

She's rising, gun almost at eye level, as the door next to Van Dorn flies open.

Lucky Number Seven.

And now, over his shoulder, there are other lights, bright as the sun, although it's still too early for dawn.

It has to be.

Headlights.

She has no idea who it is and no more time to worry about it because there's a darker shadow standing in that blackened hole of a door and that gaping hollow reminds her of Lost River cave or maybe one of Mayfield's coal mines and Van Dorn told her they've been chasing shadows all night and that's all she's been doing her whole life.

Just a shadow of herself or who she wants to be, and then that shadow opens fire with the heart-stopping chatter of an automatic weapon.

She didn't beat the sun after all.

Just like the dawn the whole world blazes, burns, catches fire.

So bright it hurts.

PAUL

85

He watches her turn in the water.

Watches her turn and turn, and she looks like a flower floating on the surface. Like she's sleeping, and in a way, she is.

Good night.

Sleep well.

Sweet dreams.

She turns and turns.

And as she does, he turns to head back to the house to change his clothes and make the call.

86

He sits with her in the back of Dobie Timmons's van, holding her cold hand.

A few hours from now, DEA Special Agent Casey Alexander will shake *his* hand, and think about how hard, smooth, and *cold* it is too, but Paul Mayfield doesn't know that now.

If someone expects him to cry, he's past crying. There have already been plenty of tears, a million of them, but he's sanded flat on the inside now, right down to his very bones, way past the point of pain or regret or remorse. She took everything and left him hollowed out.

He *gave* her everything.

Everything he was and everything he'd ever been, but if there had been more to give after that, he would have done that, too. He loved her that much, without sense or reason. She was his *light*, and he followed her right out of the dark place he was lost in after Donna's death. Even when people told him he was foolish and whispered how unseemly it was and even after he became the butt of their jokes and their sly, hidden smiles, even when things got bad and then worse and then whatever you call the place beyond that.

This place he is now.

He will never forget how she brought her light to him. Shining, brilliant, almost unearthly. So when she was suffering and lost in her own dark place, how could he do any less for her? She gave all her light to him, shined so bright she burned out. And that's what people with their jokes and opinions will never understand, all those who've had the grace or good luck never to be in this black place he's found himself in not once but twice.

Hell.

A place where no compass needle points true north. Where right and wrong get turned inside out and upside down.

Where there are no constellations to follow or stars to guide you.

Nothing to light your way home anymore.

87

Marvin Watkins isn't at Sacred Rest, nor is his son, Marvin Junior. They're both still down at Lower Wolf, where the Glassers were attacked and killed. Paul assumes that means Little Paris too, but didn't ask Floyd or Duck by the Big Sandy, and doesn't ask Cal Schulz either, who greets him when they arrive at Sacred Rest.

Cal isn't technically a funeral director, not even Watkins family, just an assistant. But he's hastily thrown on a sports coat and collared shirt over what are clearly pajama bottoms and says all the right things and holds open the doors as Dobie and Jon Dorado's boy roll Marissa out of the ambulance and into the funeral home.

They take her into one of the embalming rooms and gently move her onto the big metal table.

Paul tries not to look at the drains at the end. At the curved troughs running alongside his wife's body that collect blood.

How many times have I stood here? Not like this, not for himself, but on behalf of others. Facing another body on this steel slab and someone else's lifeless eyes staring at him.

All the crushed bodies they pulled out of the Crown Hill mine. Out of Conleith hole.

That Greer boy they fished out of the shallows of Rice Branch and Levisa Fork. Marv determined he was strangled, then tossed in the rain-swollen water. He was all of seven, eight years old. Bruised, battered. A hard life that had ended badly, like so many. It was Jon who got the father, Edgar Greer, to confess, who made him cry tears over the dead boy he'd never cried a single day over while alive.

Greer sits on death row in the state penitentiary in Eddyville.

The girl from Catlettsburg, Carolina Arsenault. Found behind the Tamarack, loosely buried in soil and leaves. It was the dead heat of summer, and animals and bugs and nature itself had already gone to work on her, something like fine, dusky webs stretching over the bones of her ribs. Flowers growing right up through her hair, vines twisting across marbled skin. *He'll never forget that.* She was like a moss-covered statue, broken and left on the ground, given back to the earth. This was, what, two, three years ago now?

Desi Beamon and the needle in his arm and a crushed skull to boot, broken up like a goddamn egg. Either would have been enough to kill him. They all figured either Ricky or Little Paris for it but could never quite prove it. Jon handled that one, and they went around and around over it. That was Jon's last case, if you could even call it that, before he gave up the badge. Before he gave up on Paul and Angel altogether.

They were going around and around about a lot of things by then.

Betsy Joyce, all cut to hell by her boyfriend. The last one before Paul himself gave up the badge.

So many, for so long.

A river's worth of blood has rolled down those drains.

Dobie and Jon's boy leave him alone with Schulz, who stands aside, just out of the corner of Paul's eye. Maybe he's expecting Paul to cry or to kneel and grasp her hand. To talk to her or say a silent prayer.

He's already done all those things. He's already said goodbye.

He bends over and kisses her gently on her forehead.

Then, as he walks outside, he tells Schulz that if anyone touches his wife's body, he'll come back and shoot them in the heart.

88

When he walks outside into the muggy night, Dobie is waiting for him, leaning beside his ugly van.

He's smoking a cigarette but throws it away when he sees Paul.

Jon's boy, Trey, is in the van itself. He's a shadow, motionless.

Paul's ten, fifteen years older than Dobie and was barely an Angel PD sergeant when Dobie's parents were murdered. There's that photo of Dobie that's still famous in these parts—pale and shell-shocked, sitting in the back of a police car after the bodies were found. Few people know or remember that it was Paul who put him in the car and drove him back to the station.

It was Paul who gently talked to him, brought him to his senses, and then bought him an RC Cola without ice and a moon pie.

In some strange way, the clock has now turned, history repeating itself, although now the two have changed places. One has become the other.

Paul rode in the back this time.

Dobie wrings his hands. Every time Paul sees him, he's a little bigger. It's like he swallowed all the hurt and anger of that night and washed it down with another RC or moon pie. And over the following years, he's kept right on swallowing it, all the whispers and the jokes and the taunts. He's swallowed whole that little boy in the backseat, but he's still there.

He peeks out through Dobie's adult eyes, like he once stared through the window of Paul's squad car.

"You need us to give you a lift back to the Point?" Dobie asks.

"No, it's fine," Paul says. "I'll call Duck. He'll bring me home. I still need a minute before I face that house, and you need to get on to Lower Wolf. I know they called you to go down there."

"Yeah," Dobie says, wringing his hands more. He looks over at Trey. "So, you hear anything from Jon?"

"No," Paul says. And he hasn't. "He headed out to Texas, got on with a department out there. They called, and of course I recommended him. Always one of the best, and I miss him." And that's true, too. He was angry when Jon up and left Angel, but not surprised.

Betrayed is too strong a word, though it's not far off, either. Paul had asked too much of him, until Jon felt betrayed, too.

Since he's been gone, Paul's been so focused completely on Marissa, he hasn't given much thought to Jon's wife or his boy. He can't remember the last time he's spoken to him.

He looks so much like Jon.

"His boy doing okay for you?" he asks, gesturing toward the shadow in the ambulance.

"He's . . . He's getting by. That's why I was hoping maybe if you talked to his daddy, you could . . . I don't know . . . say something to him."

"And what, exactly, would that be, Dobie?"

"I don't know . . . just . . . I thought. Hell, this isn't the time, I guess . . ."

"Not so much, no," Paul says, but adds, "Jon didn't leave me a number, a way to get a hold of him. When he left, he didn't want anything to do with Angel anymore." *Or me.* "But give me a week or so and then bring Trey and Renée around. We'll see if they think it's worth me talking to him then."

Dobie brightens. "Well, now, that'd be good. Real good. I'd appreciate it. Trey will, too."

Paul doesn't believe that for a moment, but lets it pass. "You're a good man, Dobie."

And Dobie looks away, embarrassed. "Most people would just tell me to mind my own business."

Paul claps him on the shoulder. "Thankfully, you're not most people, and a few of us are glad for that."

"I can't tell you how sorry I am. Is there anything I can do? Anything you need? Want me to come around later and check on you?"

And there are probably a hundred questions Dobie really wants to ask . . . most of them about Marissa and the river . . . but he won't do it here or now. And Paul won't let him come by the house later where they'll be alone, and Dobie might just work up the nerve.

"I'm okay," Paul says. "I just need that time to myself."

Time to myself . . . That's all that stretches out in front of him. Far too much time alone. But better alone than trapped with Dobie, fending off his questions. "I'm going to walk a bit, and then have Duck pick me up."

"If you change your mind, let me know."

"I will." And he won't.

Dobie wants to say more but just shakes his head instead. For a man who's spent so much time around the dead, he doesn't do as well with the grieving and those left behind.

"How bad is it at Lower Wolf?" Paul asks.

"Bad. Sheriff Dunn will be sorting it out for a while. Marvin says it's going to give him nightmares."

"Couldn't have happened to a better group of folks, though," Paul says, and when he catches Dobie's wide-eyed expression, he realizes he's revealed too much of that hateful streak toward the Glassers he's always worked hard to hide.

That Jon never tried to hide at all.

"And Little Paris?" Paul can only pray now Little Paris isn't still drawing breath, but Paul won't push Dobie to find out. If he is alive, Little Paris might even reach out for him, although that won't be smart for either of them. Paul will probably hear something from Sheriff Dunn himself anyway before the night is through.

"I don't know. Marvin said most of the bodies were . . . *defaced*. That's not the word he used, but you know what I mean. It's going to be tough to identify them. It won't be quick."

"I know I'm not the chief anymore, Dobie, but I still feel like this is my town, my people. My responsibility." He adds, "Even the Glassers."

Dobie nods. "Well, Oscar Floyd is fine, but he's not you. You're still the chief around here as far as most of us are concerned, and always will be. You could probably have it all back tomorrow, if you wanted it."

Paul puts his hands in his pockets and gets ready to walk on down the road. He eyes the dark oaks lining the road like mourners at a funeral, soon to be his only companions. "I don't want it. I gave all that up. I'm just not that man anymore."

He walks away from Dobie, toward the trees.

Wondering, now, if he ever really was.

89

Paul never liked Duck Andrews and never wanted to hire him, but he was Donna's cousin, so that's how it happened.

A few hours from now, he'll tell Agents Alexander and Van Dorn how blood is thicker than water, how to most folks in a small town, blood is often all that matters.

He won't tell them that sometimes there are things even thicker than blood.

Some men are born to carry a badge and gun and others grow into it, no different than learning to shoot straight. But there are those who forever struggle with all that responsibility. It weighs heavy on them, and since they don't have that God-given steady hand, they're always overcompensating, the same way a nervous shooter will grip the gun too tight, afraid of the recoil.

Those men tend to be bullies, quick to remind you of just who and what they are and what you aren't.

That's Duck. The worst kind of man and an even worse cop.

Jon hated him and never accepted that Paul hired him. And before Paul retired, he did try to find ways to sideline Duck, to keep him off the street and away from the public. But Oscar's since seen fit to put him back in a cruiser. In fact, the current chief has given even him more authority, and to a man like Duck, that's like adding gas to fire.

Like giving good whiskey to a bad drunk, and Paul knows more than a little about that.

Duck's driving Paul home from Sacred Rest, one hand on the wheel, another holding his dip cup.

Tapping his thick fingers on the wheel.

He said the right things out beside the Big Sandy and then again when Paul got in the cruiser, but Duck doesn't know jack shit about much of anything *right*. He's practiced at the art of faking it, though. It's a slick façade, as if the man keeps a stack of mental cue cards hidden around to remind him what a truly decent or thoughtful man might do.

If he ever lost those cards, somehow found himself exposed, Paul can't imagine that'd be good for anyone.

Paul has no idea if Duck knows just how much he dislikes him, but Paul also has no idea how much Duck may or may not despise *him*, either. He's damn good at hiding his real thoughts and motivations behind his small, dark eyes.

So they both just pretend.

Duck shifts his bulk in the seat and Paul feels those black eyes on him, considering. Duck's probably scanning those internal cue cards of his right now, checking to see the appropriate topics—if there are any—you can raise with someone whose wife just died an hour before. Duck *wants* to talk. He needs to. He can't help himself, because he avoids silence like it's a disease.

He probably talks to himself when he's on patrol, circling Angel in his cruiser. But for once it's okay, because Paul needs some answers.

"Tell me about Lower Wolf."

Duck holds his cup close and spits into it. He almost sighs, he's so relieved Paul finally broke their silence. "A goddamn slaughter down there, Chief. A massacre. I talked to one of them Martin deputies I know. Remember Buechel?"

Paul knows Buechel well . . . a lot better than Duck. Buechel's a young kid, but both his daddy, Vernon, and his boss, Sheriff Dunn, have been on the Glasser teat for years. Young Buechel will be too, if he's not already.

Duck continues, "He tells me they're saying some crazy-ass wetbacks came in there and shot up everyone. Carved up their faces, took dicks for trophies. Killed a baby. Maybe even raped some of them women before or after." Duck pauses for Paul's reaction. "Anyway, the state boys and them Feds are all over the place now, throwing their weight around. Sheriff Dunn's about to blow a gasket, head about to pop right off. They're pushing him right out of it, or so Buechel says."

"How do they know it was some Mexicans?"

Duck rolls his eyes. "No one else crazy enough to do it. Besides, Buechel said it was just like something he's seen at the movies, like that one where—"

Paul cuts him off. "When did this happen?"

Duck spits again. "Sometime this morning or afternoon. No one knows for sure."

Paul turns this over . . . *the Feds*. Could be FBI, DEA, anyone really, since everyone's put a target on the Glassers at one time or another. If Dunn and his men aren't driving the investigation, if the sheriff can't steer it where they all need it to go, then something might truly get done, no matter who's behind the wheel, and that's a problem for everyone.

"What about Ricky? Little Paris? Renfro?"

Duck's head bobs. "Seems both the Old Man and Ricky bought the farm for sure, so to speak, but Buechel don't know about them others.

Not yet." Duck skips a beat. "Bodies all over the place, Chief, so they're still sorting out who's who."

But Paul figures that's not exactly the whole truth. Duck's good at pretending about most things but damn bad at lying about others. Although he's not officially on the Glasser payroll, at least not yet anyway, he wants everyone to think he's in good and deep with Little Paris.

His badge isn't enough. He craves the authority and respect and fear and infamy that come with associating with the Glassers.

So Duck may not know where Little Paris is *now* but doesn't believe for a moment he's lying dead at Lower Wolf. Paul doesn't believe it, either. That means he's loose, running around, and if Little Paris Glasser is dangerous anytime, he'll only be more so now, on the run.

Worst of all if he gets cornered.

Paul doesn't want to accept that meeting Little Paris earlier today might have saved the man's goddamn worthless life, but that's the way it looks right now.

No matter what he does, it's always the wrong thing, at the wrong time.

He should have killed that sonofabitch months ago. Or let Jon kill him long before that.

And that makes Paul desperately wish Jon were here now, the only man he trusted to talk it over and work it all through. But Jon's gone, leaving him with men like Buechel and Dunn . . . and Duck.

The last man in the whole world he trusts and the last man he wants to talk to.

He lapses into silence and pointedly turns to stare out the window, hoping Duck gets the goddamn hint.

They're done talking now.

He's got nothing more to say.

90

When they found Carolina Arsenault's body out behind the Tamarack Inn with what looked like flowers growing in her blond hair, Jon told Paul right away that it was Little Paris.

Little Paris had been running girls out of the Tamarack for a while, renting a couple of rooms for a few days and partying the time away, selling it by the hour, by the minute. It was a goddamn affront that Jon had angrily called *one-stop shopping*. You could buy meth, weed, coke—the avalanche of pills and heroin was still a few months away—along with a young girl to party with. Jon swore Little Paris was filming low-grade sex films out there too, horrible stuff Little Paris was putting up on the Internet or whatever. Paul couldn't understand how he could talk these girls into doing those things for him, for friends and even strangers driving in from West Virginia and Ohio. But maybe they didn't know they were being filmed . . . maybe they did and were too far past the point of caring.

At one time or another, Jon got sideways with all Glassers, but Little Paris most of all.

Paul used to tell Jon it was going to be that sort of anger, that hatred, that was going to get him killed. Jon used to tell him he didn't give a damn.

Seeing what Little Paris was doing to those girls, to the whole god-damn town, he was way past the point of caring, too.

It was raining when they found her, and little Carolina hardly looked real.

Maybe it was only the waxy light or the rain. Or the way it was hard to tell where she ended or began, covered up like that in leaves and loose dirt and all those pretty flowers with their pretty names. Green adder's-mouth. Thimbleberry. Golden Glows.

The bugs crawling on her.

Gauzy webs spun between her ribs.

Duck Andrews had to walk away. He threw up his sausage and grits and corned beef hash in the motel's gravel lot. He couldn't get away fast enough. Couldn't get far enough away.

But Jon was different. He knelt next to the body, leaned in close, pulled in closer by her impossible gravity. It wasn't morbid curiosity, just a curious kind of sadness.

He didn't want her to be alone. He wanted her to know that he was there.

That someone was there.

Rain on his face, tapping on the leaves over his head. The warm water from the thunderstorm pooling in the hollows of the dead girl's eyes.

Jon was tall, trim. Dark-haired. A good-looking man who looked twice as good in his uniform. He looked every inch a cop, like he should have been on a glossy poster, and if Angel had been a big city where they did that sort of thing, he probably would have been. Others in the department said he was something of a poon hound, but Paul never put much stock in that. *Not then.* Cops always talk and joke and bullshit one another. Not that a man couldn't stray, because it happened all the time, and often for reasons that didn't make much sense.

But for Paul, the question wasn't whether a man strayed, it was how far he wandered, and if he eventually made his way back home.

That's what Paul thought even when folks eventually started up about Jon and Marissa. And it was a lot more complicated than anyone else had a right to know.

Jon knelt by the Arsenault girl for a long time. They didn't know her name then, and she didn't have any ID on her. They had no idea how truly young she was or what had been done to her or what she'd given up. All there was of her was naked, exposed, raw. Incomplete. They wouldn't know anything about her for another twenty-four hours, but when it finally broke in the local news and it came time to call on the family, Jon did it himself.

Alone.

At least they never had to put her picture in the paper or on a poster to find out who she'd been and who had loved her, for a time.

And after Jon called on the family, after he told him how they found their little girl and how things had ended for her, he went to call on Little Paris.

91

Little Paris was never going to say a damn thing about the dead girl.

And he didn't, not even when Jon hit him in the face.

The shot sent Little Paris sprawling out of the chair in the department's interview room. He tumbled and fell against the back wall but didn't stay down long, rolling to his feet faster than Paul would have imagined, even in those damn high-heel boots of his. *Snake quick.* That was Paul's thought as he grabbed Jon and held him back from going after Little Paris again, as he caught out of the corner of his eye Little Paris feinting for the knife he had hidden beneath the scallop of his right boot.

Those boots gave him another inch or so and he needed every bit of it.

But at the last second, Little Paris smartened up and didn't go for the knife, backing as far away as the small, hot room would allow. Hands up and a shit-eating grin on his face.

He knew they didn't have a goddamn thing on him, but even he couldn't slip out of stabbing a police officer during a consensual interview.

And he was right, they didn't have a thing on him. Nothing like real evidence. He'd rented rooms out at the Tamarack in the days preceding her discovery, but he did that all the time, and there wasn't a single pair of eyes that had seen the Arsenault girl out there. Ever. Just like there was no one who would admit that they were there, either. And no cameras at the motel or out in the parking lot. The time of death, even the cause of death, was going to be tough if not impossible to pin down due to the condition of her body, exposed to the elements the way it was. Marv Watkins had done a preliminary autopsy and then she'd been shipped off to the KSP central crime lab in Frankfort, further results pending, but that could take a while. Weeks, at least. In life, Carolina had been a troubled young girl who fought with her family all the time and was prone to running away afterward. They hadn't seen her regularly in *months* by the time Jon sat down with them and explained where she'd been found.

They hadn't even bothered to look for her.

The three of them standing in the Angel interview room knew all that, and Little Paris most of all.

That's why he couldn't keep that grin off his face even as he wiped blood from his mouth.

"I'm gonna have your badge," he said, staring at the crimson stains on the tips of his fingers, holding them up for both Jon and Paul to see. "You can't hit me like that, you sonofabitch. No one alive hits me like that."

"Shut the fuck up and sit down or I'll call your daddy or Danny and one or the other will give you this same whipping, only twice as bad, for raising your voice to me." Paul pointed at the seat. "Plus, I'll just say you took a swipe at him first."

"You gonna lie like that, Chief? Just like that?" Paris asked, but he sat back down, still grinning, still rubbing at his mouth. "A man of the law and all?"

They all knew Paul wasn't beyond lying.

"I won't think twice about it, so don't test me." Paul then pushed against Jon, forcing him to sit too, and he could feel the other man's heart banging inside his chest like a caged dog hitting its bars again and again. He got close to him and looked him in the eye. "And don't you test me either, son."

Jon raised his hands, indicating he was going to be calm, and sat down.

Letting Jon get Little Paris in the same room with him had been a bad mistake, but not allowing it would have been worse, since it would have meant Jon was out there riding around on his own, getting angrier and angrier by the moment. This way, at least, there was a chance Paul could keep it from blowing all to hell in Angel's streets, could keep Jon from rolling into Lower Wolf spoiling for a fight he'd never win. Not there, not then, not ever. Confrontation wasn't how you dealt with the Glassers, but sometimes a confrontation, a goddamn fight, was all Jon Dorado ever wanted.

Now he'd finally gotten his licks in. Drawn some blood. And no doubt left a bruise Little Paris would feel for a week and remember a hell of a lot longer than that.

Paul hoped it'd be enough.

Little Paris rubbed his chin, the pale skin flecked red, just starting to blue like the edges of a raw steak. His long hair was swept way back on his head, a whole mess of it, and his brown eyes were brackish in the harsh, flat lights of the interview room. He was delicate, small, but had a coiled intensity that was tough to sit close to. His jawline was triangular, defiant, which, along with his size and that menacing glower, always made Paul think of a baby copperhead. His granddaddy used to say that a snakelet was even *more* dangerous than one thick as your arm because those little ones didn't know how to control their venom, but that was mostly nonsense. Still, Little Paris looked the part. Poisonous, downright venomous.

Snake quick.

He had a thick, fancy cross tattooed up one side of his neck (although Paul had never known him to darken the door of a church), and there were all kinds of others scrawled up and down his arms, across the back of his hands and his knuckles, over his heart. A pair of dice. A skull with crossed bones. A thirty-eight revolver. A naked female silhouette with angel wings on one shoulder, one with devil horns and a tail on the other. There were sayings and images that meant nothing to a man like Paul, and Old Man Paris probably didn't understand any of it, either. He surely hated all that ink, no doubt telling his boys such shit was for convicts and West Virginia niggers. Danny understood that, too. But no one told his youngest what to do, not ever.

"Goddamn it, Chief, I said I don't know shit about that pretty girl," Little Paris drawled, still smiling. "But you tell Daddy I done cooperated anyway. I answered your questions."

Little Paris had funny notions about what cooperating meant, but before Paul or Jon could point that out, the interview room door opened and Danny Glasser himself walked in. He'd evidently caught just enough of his little brother's last words to now put a hard hand on his shoulder and stop him from saying anything more.

"You're done here, LP, unless these old boys want to address their questions to Elton."

Elton Charles was the family attorney out of London they kept on permanent retainer. He was a drunk who'd nearly been disbarred twice for malpractice but was sober enough most days, and knew just enough of the law, when he wasn't in the bottle, to run interference for the Glassers when called upon.

He and Paul had shared a few tumblers of Four Roses now and again.

"Daniel, you're not to be in here," Paul warned.

But Danny Glasser just shrugged, nodding over his shoulder at Duck Andrews, who'd let him past the door and was fast disappearing behind it. "Guess you should have made that clear to your man Duck, who didn't seem to think you'd mind at all if I slipped in to check up on my brother. I can't have y'all in here berating him." Danny leaned in and took a good look at the blood and the darkening, soon-to-sour bruise on Little Paris's face. "Or beating on him, neither."

"He fell," Jon said, looking up at the ceiling, as if Little Paris had dropped from the lights above. "Tripped on those shit-kicker boots of his."

"You're about to find yourself on the business end of these here boots," Little Paris shot back, eyes narrowing.

Jon leaned into him. "They'll never make you tall enough to see over the pile of shit you've gotten yourself into. You're neck-deep in it now, and I'm going to bury you before I'm done. Just try and keep that weak chin up."

"That's enough," Paul said, trying to gain control.

"You're right, that is enough," Danny agreed, as if his saying it was the final word. He pulled Little Paris up, yanking him toward the closed door and nearly pushing him straight through it. He called out to the other side.

"Duck, open that up and get him on out of here. Get him a cold cola or something, so us adults here can talk."

Just like he owned the place.

Then he sat down in Paris's seat and lit up a Marlboro.

92

Danny Glasser was clear and smooth as high-dollar window glass. Just like his family name. It was like you could see right through him.

But it was all an act. Oscar-winning. He was just as dirty as the rest of his kin, though he had done a year at the University of Kentucky and even lived outside Lower Wolf for a spell. He'd traveled to Detroit, Washington, D.C., New York, and rumor had it down to Arizona and California and Texas. He was damn near worldly, by Glasser standards. By the standards of most anyone raised up in Angel or anywhere in Martin or Lawrence County. Jon believed he was the one who'd brokered the face-to-face agreements with the Mexicans or whoever it was who kept the family supplied, and Danny could put on a suit and tie or Bermuda shorts or a pearl-button shirt and jeans and would look natural in any of it, not like you'd dressed up a feral dog.

No one ever imagined Danny would be the first to die.

He sat there wearing a pressed shirt, calmly smoking a cigarette. Paul had watched him grow up and remembered him cruising around town in his daddy's fire-engine-red Cadillac. He could have bought anything, probably rented much nicer and newer vehicles whenever he left town, but always stuck with that Cadillac when driving through Angel. He understood its symbolic value and was smart enough to know that some things were even more powerful left unsaid. Folks had been staring at the Coupe de Ville forever, all polished and smooth and red as a drop of fresh blood. *Blood is thicker than water.* There were all sorts of stories about men being wrapped up in plastic and tossed in its trunk, never to be seen again. Tall tales about Old Man Paris, when he wasn't all that old, outracing the law hell to leather over county backroads, a gun in one hand and a bottle of 'shine in the other. More than a few girls swore they'd lost their virginity in the backseat and even more wanted to. In eastern Kentucky, it was as famous as Hank Williams's '52 Cadillac—the Death Car—and the mere sight of it idling in a gravel driveway made some men piss themselves. It was just a rolling hunk of old metal, shined up mirror-bright, but over time had proven as effective as holding a gun to a man's temple.

It was probably sitting out in front of the department right at that moment, drawing stares and pictures.

Danny blew hazy smoke and tapped a thin, ringless finger on the desk. "Now, Chief, I know you got to look into this thing, and it is a serious matter, no doubt. But there's no sense bringing in my brother like that. Humiliating him." He said it sympathetically, as if he understood the idea could never have been Paul's alone. In fact, he looked straight at Jon, letting them all know exactly where he thought such a crazy idea had come from.

"If he doesn't run around making a fool of himself, Daniel, then no one has to get humiliated," Paul said. "It's that business up at the Tamarack. The carrying on all hours of the day and night. Even if you take that poor girl we found out of it, it's gotten out of hand. Way out of hand."

He wasn't even sure exactly how you did that—*take that poor girl out of it*—and if it was impossible for Jon, it wasn't much easier for him. But it *was* easier. It had to be. He needed something worthwhile to come out of the whole mess and had long ago made peace with the idea that that sometimes meant looking the other way, cutting small deals with the devil.

It was all part of keeping the peace in a small, tight-knit town. An understanding that Angel would forever be dealing with the Glassers or someone just like them.

But he had the age and wisdom and perspective to see that. Jon didn't. And, if he kept pushing, might not live long enough to gain it.

"I see your point," Danny said, nodding, sagelike. "I will have that talk with him. He's young, likes to sow his wild oats. Hell, we were all young once." He circled an arm, including the three of them like they were co-conspirators. "Can't say I blame him. He likes all the pretty girls and they do like him back." He waved his own smoke away. "My brother isn't the only one who shines like a diamond for that good pussy." He threw a look at Jon, who started to say something but thought better of it. For once. "You might even be surprised, Chief, by who swings through those parties of his. You lie down with dogs and all that . . . and all that fun on Saturday gives good folks something to repent on Sunday. Gives Preacher Pauley something to breathe fire and brimstone over."

"You're a public fucking service now?" Jon said.

"Well, let's be honest, gentlemen," Danny said, "there just ain't been much to do around here since the drive-in shut down."

He crushed out his cigarette on the tabletop. "Anyway, you've made your point here, all loud and clear and official. For your trouble, I'll knock some sense into that thick skull of LP's, and things will quiet down out at that shitbag motel for a while, I can promise you that. But if you want to talk to him again about that young lady, you'll have to do that through Elton. You know that, Chief. You know that's how it's got to be."

"Should we bring a bottle of high-dollar?" Jon asked, showing teeth. "Something to ease the man's shakes?"

"Probably, Officer Dorado. As expensive as you can afford or whatever you think you're worth. And be sure to make that *two* glasses, one for our good chief here, too." Danny smiled at Paul. "We all know *you* like top-shelf. I hope you still appreciate the bottle Daddy sends you every Christmas, wrapped up with a nice bow, along with the usual thank-yous."

Paul started to raise his hands in protest, but Jon jumped in too quick.

"Fuck you. And that's *Detective* Dorado."

Danny laughed, getting to his feet. "Really? A *detective*? I didn't know we had one of those around here." He rapped on the door to let Duck know he was ready to leave. "You call it whatever you want and go right on ahead and do as much *detecting* as you damn well please, but it doesn't mean shit to me. *You* don't mean shit, no matter what the chief here lets you believe. You're just a little dog on a leash. If you ever get loose and bite the wrong person, you might just have to get put down." Danny aimed a finger gun at Jon and pulled the trigger. "Either way, you dare hit my brother again? Then you'll have to go through me."

"Count on it," Jon said as the door opened, and Danny nodded goodbye to Paul.

"Daddy does send his regrets about Temple. He didn't get a chance to talk to you at the funeral or the wake, but your daddy was a good man and put up the good fight. He told me to tell you that if you ever need anything, anything at all, just ask."

But Jon still wasn't done. Not satisfied.

"Tell me about the baby, Danny. Tell us about the fucking *baby*," Jon said. "We know about the baby."

Danny ignored him. Instead, as a final courtesy, he nodded and mouthed *Chief,* but the silent word didn't have any weight, any meaning.

Not to Danny Glasser.

Not to Jon.

Not to Paul.

93

Danny Glasser was shot dead less than one month after he walked out of that interview room.

The Glassers had the bloodstained Caddy he was killed in pulled down to Lower Wolf and set up as some sort of shrine.

Even the devil grieves.

Paul went to Danny's funeral, along with three hundred other people. But Jon Dorado wasn't one of them.

Things went to hell around the counties for a few weeks, with the surviving Glassers and their allies turning everything upside down over Danny's killing. But with Danny dead and gone, and the Old Man broken in two by his grief, Little Paris had to grow up fast, leaving no time for his little pussy parties at the Tamarack. Soon enough the place was sold, abandoned, and in a way none of them could have predicted, Danny ended up keeping his promise, and things quieted down.

For a while.

Carolina Arsenault was forgotten.

Marv Watkins's initial autopsy findings were buried, as were the later KSP lab results.

It was done to protect the sensitivities of the same family that hadn't cared enough to really look for her.

But a few months later, Jon came by the house and showed Paul a video.

He'd downloaded it, or it had been given to him. He never said where he got it or even how long he'd been holding on to it. He just let it play, sound off, because the sound made it so much worse, if that was possible.

It was blond-haired Carolina and two men with their faces out of frame, out of focus. In that awful little movie—grainy and ugly and jittery—the thirteen-year-old girl had looked so much younger than that, so impossibly helpless and small.

One of the men doing all those things to her didn't look much bigger, even with his boots on.

It didn't matter, because all Paul could see were the tattoos—

A pair of dice.

A skull with crossed bones.

A thirty-eight revolver.

A naked female silhouette with angel wings on one shoulder . . .

. . . and one with devil horns and a tail on the other.

And then there was the other man. He wasn't doing nearly as much, mainly watching, working the camera.

Smoking a cigarette.

Wearing a pressed shirt.

It was always going to be impossible to tell whether the video was shot before Carolina Arsenault gave birth or just after.

Or who the daddy might have been.

94

Duck's dropped him off and he's alone and the house still smells like Marissa.

The candles she liked so much.

Her expensive perfume, her skin.

Donna had always wanted to keep the windows open, let as much fresh air as possible blow through the rooms. While Donna was growing up, her mama still hung laundry on the line, so she got used to the sound of clothes snapping taut in the breeze, the touch of windblown fabric against her skin. The raw smell of sap or pine or water or rock in her dresses.

In winter, Donna would even leave the windows cracked so they could smell the smoke of other chimneys. That smell—the faint scrim of burning wood, far away—always made Paul feel like Angel itself didn't exist. That nothing existed, and beyond the river and trees there was only an endless, silent stillness. On and on forever.

Marissa never left the windows open in winter or any other time.

She liked to be closed in, held close. She wanted things maintained and manicured and polished. Wanted her world as glossy as a magazine, decorated like a stage play or a store display. Artifice made to appear natural, like faux-wood tiles, even when there was nothing natural about it.

She tried so hard to keep the outside at bay and the chaos that came with it right where it belonged, far away.

But despite her best efforts, her big coming-out dinner party right after they were married had sprawled out into the backyard anyway, and she'd been forced to set out so many citronella candles and torches to fend off the mosquitoes and chiggers that circled in off the river, the entire yard had *glowed*.

Just like her.

Don MacGruder, a controller from the Big Sandy Power Plant, joked that you could fire up the old coal plant with her tiki torches alone, and probably see the house from orbit.

It was late July, still eighty degrees and humid at dusk, and all those torch flames only raised the temperature around the yard even more. Every fifteen or twenty minutes, Marissa slipped into the downstairs bathroom just to towel herself off, so her skin would stay cool and smooth and unblemished by sweat.

The appearance of cool, even though she was anything but.

It was her first real introduction to the people Paul had known his whole life, and she'd been nervous, preparing for weeks, picking out the food and insisting on professional catering even though no one catered anything in Angel, unless you counted placing an order for baby back ribs or pulled pork from Gunny's Smokehouse.

Paul would have been fine with that.

But the only barbecue she served that night was a barbecue, bacon, and blue cheese potato salad. And the rest of the menu was just as extravagant. Shrimp-boil kebabs. Smoked Gouda and bacon burgers. Rosemary and garlic butter steak. Chili-lime chicken.

French goat cheese and radicchio salad with figs. Grilled watermelon and brown sugar–cinnamon pineapple.

Lemon bars and cinnamon almond cookies and heavily frosted cupcakes.

Blueberry mojitos.

For two days prior to the party, Marissa had scrubbed the kitchen floor and back porch on her hands and knees, polishing everything until it shined, until you could see your face in the silverware. She'd folded the cloth napkins again and again and picked out and discarded a dozen different dresses.

Contemplated cutting her hair before deciding to just keep it as it was. Then had her nails done twice.

She'd been too nervous, overly anxious about making a good impression, and he should have realized that and understood exactly what she was feeling and going through. He should have known, too, just how much it would hurt her when he commented on all those who had refused to come, those who were *never* going to accept or celebrate a new woman living in Donna Mayfield's home.

No amount of extravagance or perfection or chili-lime chicken was ever going to overcome that.

Donna . . . Marissa . . . neither better nor worse than the other, despite what some wanted to believe.

Just different.

So, so different.

95

He walks through the empty house now and still finds that constant push and pull between him and Marissa everywhere.

Her insistence on design and order and sharp, squared corners. His willingness to let a little dust accumulate, let the upholstery fray, accept a few curves to round things out.

He always knew when Marissa was using because she'd let such things go for a day or a week, before ferociously imposing her will on their world again for however long she could stay clean and sober.

He wanders the dark halls until he finds himself in their kitchen, where he pours himself three fingers of Eagle Rare, the first drink he's allowed himself in two days. *He's* been sober long enough.

He clutches the whiskey tumbler tight, throws back one shot and then another.

When did Marissa last hold this glass? What was she doing and where was he?

Had they argued recently?

Had she just gone off again to see Little Paris . . . or only just returned?

This glass has a history all its own and he holds it up now like it's some sort of crystal ball, staring hard and deep into it, as if he can will it to show him his future.

Donna never held this glass. Marissa made him buy a new bed and sheets and all new silver and glassware right after they were married.

He thinks back again to that first dinner party, the same one Special Agent Terry Van Dorn attended and will, soon enough, recall himself. *She was beautiful that night.* And although she'd been frantic at playing the perfect hostess—slipping off into the bathroom to towel herself off from that summer heat, secretly dry-chewing another of the oxys she'd hidden in the folded linens beneath the sink—she always made a point afterward of standing close to him, touching his hand, lightly kissing his cheek. Laughing again at the stories she and everyone else had heard a thousand times.

Still playing the perfect wife.

Picture-perfect as a magazine.

Wanting to show them all how much she loved him. Fiercely, passionately, without reservation.

Even now he wants to believe she truly did love him that way, at least for a little while.

Just the way he loved her and still does.

And always will.

96

It started with her forgetting things.

That's too simple, but that's how it looked to him then.

A month or two after their dinner party, standing in the kitchen late one afternoon with sunlight pooling on the floor at their feet, asking her about a bill that hadn't been paid.

Light, maybe? The electric or trash bill?

He can't remember anymore. But he'll forever remember her reaction.

A quick glance up to the ceiling fan as if she really was thinking, trying hard to recall. Then the shrug of a bare shoulder, a suggestion of defeat.

Remorse.

That gentle smile, disarming him like it always did.

She said she would take care of it and did straightaway, even though Paul had never paid *anything* late his whole life, and certainly not a bill. Donna would never have allowed it.

The week after that, though, it was something else. She didn't pick up his uniforms from dry-cleaning. Forgot to grab those thick-cut steaks he'd asked her to get from Bahr's.

After that she started outright losing things. His wallet, her keys. Even a favorite tennis bracelet that he'd bought her as a surprise engagement present (although he'd later learn she'd simply sold it for pennies on the dollar). Until she started losing *time* itself.

She couldn't account for a few hours or even a whole afternoon. She stopped answering his calls. She was always coming and going from somewhere else and was never where she claimed or pretended to be or where he could find her.

Friends she'd been supposedly meeting in Lexington or Louisville would call and say they hadn't seen her in weeks.

How's our Marissa doing, Paul? We miss her back here . . .

That's when Paul truly realized he was losing her altogether.

His first thought, even then, was that it was another man, and that was only natural.

They'd barely been married a year, time that had passed in an eye blink for Paul, but to Marissa, so many years his junior, it probably felt like an eternity. They'd always sworn to each other their age difference would never make any difference to them, but to those few friends who had the nerve to raise it to his face, there was no way it couldn't.

It had to. It was inevitable, like time itself. She was so goddamn young. So goddamn beautiful and wild and fierce. *Everyone* told him that.

That's when he started having Jon follow her, find her and drag her back home, whether she wanted to come or not. He somehow convinced himself it was unseemly for her own husband, the chief of police, to chase her down, but wasn't above having his best friend and assistant chief do it for him.

In the end, it was Jon who told him about Little Paris.

It was another man.

Just not the way he'd first feared.

Once Jon told him what to really look for—the fake scrips and empty pill bottles shoved down in the trash, later the tiny bags and bindles and balloons folded into her clothes or hidden beneath the seat of the new car he'd bought her—he also had to face the hard truth that he was dealing with more than just boredom or acting out or unhappiness or infidelity or their age difference. Not even the loss of the child he refused to give her.

Jon even warned him again and again—

You've got a real problem on your hands, Paul. And I can't keep dragging her back here. And you can't do this on your own and I don't know that I can keep doing it for you.

This is going to kill you or her.

It's going to kill me.

Or one of us is going to have to kill Little Paris.

As far as Jon was concerned, the Glassers were the root of *every* problem in Angel. After Carolina Arsenault, even after Danny's death and reckoning, he couldn't just leave them be, and it only made it worse that Paul was asking him to pull Marissa out of that same damn motel where they'd found the girl, still sick and strung-out and stinking of Little Paris and his dope.

Paul should have realized it was like rubbing it all in Jon's face: that in doing so, Jon would hold them *both* accountable for all those years Paul had looked the other away for the Glassers and ordered Jon to turn away, too.

Keeping the peace came with a price . . . and maybe Marissa and Little Paris together was part of that price. Some sort of cosmic joke or karma. Payback. Jon would never come out and say Paul deserved it, but he wouldn't say he didn't, either.

But Marissa didn't.

And it was possible Jon had even fallen a little bit in love with her by then. It wouldn't have surprised Paul and he wouldn't have blamed him.

She was so goddamn young. So goddamn beautiful and wild and fierce.

Still beautiful that first morning he found her passed out on their couch. After that initial OD, he made Dobie give him multiple Narcan injectors and show him how to use them.

Still beautiful the second he found her, this time on the kitchen floor, eyes rolled up, skin clammy, and the remains of that silly, stupid, unbaked cake spread around her.

A needle next to one of their new spoons.

A tiny stamp bag still clutched in her fist.

The same kitchen where only a few months before she'd first looked up at the ceiling fan, trying to recall.

That gentle smile, disarming him like it always did.

It was Paul, not Jon, who saved her life that morning in their kitchen with Dobie's Narcan. And it was Paul, not Jon, who took her to Keystone, to Dr. Farris, for the first and last time.

97

H e's lying on their bed, fully clothed, staring at the darkened ceiling. He doesn't sleep so much anymore, and when he does, his sleep is fevered, troubled.

Dreams . . . mostly of Donna, his dead first wife.

Her last days.

Occasionally even tiny, pregnant Carolina Arsenault.

Now that Marissa's dead, will all his dreams finally be of her instead?

But Paul doesn't want to think that, can't let himself believe that. He can't even begin to face what it means if he can only dream of dead women, other than he'll be hard pressed to ever sleep again.

It hurts too goddamn much to dream.

He's still lying there awake when his phone rings.

He's already gotten multiple messages from Sheriff Dunn, updating him from Little Wolf, seeking Paul's advice. The man's worried, but there's little Paul can do to help him. Not tonight.

And if most of the Glassers truly are dead, there's nothing either of them can do, except wait to see how it plays out.

Other than Dunn, there's only one *other* person who might try to call him at this hour, who might demand his help and have a reason to expect it, but when Paul sees it's actually only Duck, he forces himself to answer anyway, because whatever he wants, it can't be good.

That's when Duck tells him about the two DEA agents, Terry Van Dorn and the girl.

Paul's known Van Dorn forever, enough to know he's a damn good investigator. According to Duck, Van Dorn and his partner have taken up a serious interest in Lower Wolf and got it in their heads that both Little Paris and his boy survived. Now they're trying to track them both down.

Duck says the female agent is a real bitch and already put the full-court press on Anna Bishop, who was locked up from an earlier OD. Just a few moments ago, Floyd even let them take her goddamn phone.

Floyd also told Van Dorn about Marissa's suicide tonight and her body in the river.

Duck has no idea where they're going next or what they're doing, but it's clear they're not done. They're just getting started.

Paul stays silent, buying himself a moment of his own to think. Dunn didn't say anything about the DEA agents, so he probably doesn't even know they're running around, but why is Duck telling him? What does he know or *think* he knows?

Paul tries to convince himself Duck doesn't really *know* anything at all—but what could he *suspect*?

Did he somehow guess that Paul saw Little Paris earlier today?

Has he figured out why?

Is he also talking with Little Paris right now, warning him about the agents hot on his trail? Or does he think Paul's already hiding him or helping him?

Paul spins the possibilities around like the cylinder of his old Colt Python revolver and comes up empty.

And if Duck expects some sort of response, an answer . . . *a goddamn thank-you* . . . Paul doesn't give him one.

Instead, he hangs up, then sits up in their bed, a little unsteady from all the whiskey. Those first serious drinks in a few days still burning in his chest, his throat.

His daddy used to say drinking was always serious business.

Van Dorn and his partner know about Marissa's death. Maybe they'll accept it was a suicide or maybe they won't, but they've spoken with the Bishop woman now, and the only thing to connect the two is Little Paris, so it's not hard to see where that might lead them next.

Tonight, tomorrow, Van Dorn and his partner will decide they have to talk to him—if it was Jon, he would—and although avoiding them is probably the smartest thing, it's the one thing he won't do.

He needs to know what they know—what they suspect and whether they're going to try to tie Marissa's death tonight to the Lower Wolf attack earlier today.

He needs to know if Little Paris is still alive and if that little boy is alive and still with him.

He's already expecting the second call from Terry Van Dorn a few minutes later.

98

Dr. Farris was young, much closer to Marissa's age than Paul was.

He had this habit of steepling his fingers in front of his face and wore wire-frame glasses and tended to unconsciously move the papers around on his desk, arranging them in some order that made sense only to a him. A weird, distracting tic.

One of those thick papers was the medical release Marissa had reluctantly, angrily, signed, allowing Farris to talk with him about her after her intake interview.

It was raining and the window behind Farris was blurry, indistinct. They were two floors up in his office at Keystone Recovery, one of the best treatment facilities in Kentucky.

"We're glad you brought Marissa here," Farris said, arranging his papers again. "But I can't help but wonder why? Karen's Place is right there by you in Lawrence County, out by Yatesville Lake. It's really a wonderful program. Different than what we do here, but very nice. It's beautiful out there. And frankly, Paul, a lot closer."

Paul knew all about Karen's Place. It *was* beautiful, a big-windowed stone and wood home backed by trees. Warm and inviting, one of several similar Christian treatment centers across Appalachia, with names like Beth's Blessing and Lydia's House. They offered clinical drug treatment and faith-based recovery, and it was the *faith* part that had turned Paul off, since Marissa wasn't much of a churchgoer and neither was he. He'd always accompanied Donna to services, she'd been the one with real faith, but after she was gone, he wouldn't have attended at all if he hadn't felt the eyes of the town on him.

But the Bible-thumping at Karen's Place wasn't the only reason he'd brought Marissa all the way to Louisville. The distance itself—all those miles—mattered. They meant Marissa was that much farther from Little Paris.

"I thought it best to get her out of Lawrence County for a while. I'm fine staying here or driving back and forth to see her, whatever you think I should do. And my wife has family in Louisville."

His voice still caught when he said "my wife," that unnecessary explanation always on the edge of his lips.

You see, Marissa isn't my first wife.

There'd been another and now she was gone.

"Yes, I understand," Farris said. "But it's unlikely Marissa will want to see anyone for a while. In fact, we discourage it. It's important that she spend her time here focusing on her recovery."

Paul hated how Farris said "recovery" like it was some sort of tangible object, something that could be put down and easily picked up again, like the papers on his desk, or the silly little coins or tokens or medallions Keystone handed out to mark a day or week of sobriety.

Recovery, it seemed, could be purchased with enough goddamn coins, and Keystone was not cheap.

But Paul knew his biases were born out of his age, growing up in a different era. He'd worked alongside plenty of men who'd silently struggled with the bottle because that's just the way it had always been. You kept such problems private, behind closed doors. Only Donna ever knew how hard it was for him to put down a tumbler of whiskey once he got started, each one after that first always going down that much easier (his fondness for whiskey was something he came by naturally, from his own daddy), but Dr. Farris had already gone to great lengths to explain that opioid addiction was nothing like the whiskey or other vices Paul had seen take their toll on Angel.

So Paul held his tongue as Farris went on to describe the center's thirty-day residential plan, including medical detox and counseling sessions and their patented SMART Recovery 4-Point Program. Something called neurofeedback. Art therapy and group therapy. Guided meditation.

Twelve-step meetings and yoga.

But as he talked, Paul couldn't help but glance through the glossy brochures Farris had first carefully put in front of him, full of pictures of smiling and happy families. Those who'd apparently found their *recovery*, once and for all.

What had been the final tally or price for all that happiness and success?

What had been the cost and who'd paid it?

How many goddamn coins?

99

When Farris finally stopped for questions, Paul slid the brochures back to him.

He had only one.

"Does all this work? I mean really work?"

Farris smiled faintly, as he rearranged more papers into invisible patterns.

"It's not that simple, Paul."

"No, I think it is." Paul didn't like the way the man had already taken to calling him Paul, a level of familiarity he didn't expect or feel or want.

"No, I think you *want* it to be," Farris countered. "And we all do. But how are you willing to define *work*, Paul? No periodic relapse? Unfortunately, statistically, that's not how it works at all. People can and do make significant progress here, but the only person who can say for sure if she will is Marissa. Her recovery is going to be a daily question for the rest of her life. She has to want it to work, just like you do, and she has to work the program."

"*Your* program?"

"A program, yes." Dr. Farris stopped with his papers. "The issues that drove Marissa here didn't appear overnight, and they won't disappear tomorrow."

"Issues?"

Farris hesitated. "Look, I understand your struggle, Paul." And for emphasis, Farris held up the brochures Paul had discarded. "You want answers, guarantees. You want to know *why* your wife is doing these things she's doing. You want to lay blame and assess guilt. You want her simply to *stop* and can't understand why she doesn't. Why, if she loves you and the life you're trying to build together so much, she *won't*.

"And I can explain the science of it, at least as it relates to the opioids Marissa's been abusing. How they create powerful artificial dopamine endorphins in the brain, that with repeated use, her brain has stopped producing naturally at all, starting the cycle of abuse and addiction and withdrawal you're living with now. I could read you testimonials of those who've described that opioid high she's chasing as a whole-body orgasm, like being held in the arms of an angel. Like—"

"I don't need to hear that."

"No," Farris agreed, "I'm sure you don't. Just like you probably don't need to hear about the various childhood traumas and perceived slights and mistakes and accidents and incidents that can drive someone like Marissa to such substances in the first place. But remember, there is *no someone just like Marissa*. We have fifty clients here and they're all different, all facing unique issues and singular paths. There is no one *why* and no single guarantee I can give you. Frankly, you're never going to find my explanations or answers satisfactory."

"You don't have a very high opinion of me."

Farris laughed. "Actually, I do, Paul. I do. Because you're here, right now, trying your best to help her, even though you're frustrated and angry and hurt. Because you've realized you don't know what to do and you can't do it alone. That takes a lot of strength. And Marissa is going to need you to be strong, for the both of you."

But Paul didn't feel strong. Not at all. Instead, he felt like he was losing another wife all over again. *Frustrated and angry and hurt.* He felt helpless, even worse than when he'd watched Donna's cancer waste her away in front of him. She'd begged him again and again to make that pain stop, to take it all away, but he hadn't been strong enough then. And despite Farris's assurances, he didn't believe he was any stronger now.

"And because you're strong, Paul, I can be very real and honest with you. I have no idea if Marissa *will* succeed here, but I know she *can*. I'm proof of that."

That caught Paul's attention, forcing him to look at Farris more closely, searching for a stack of those coins or tokens on his desk, marking the time and the tiny successes and all the innumerable set-backs he was already warning Paul about.

How many goddamn coins?

Paul feared the answer, even though he already knew it in his gut—

A lifetime's worth.

Farris took off his glasses, revealing lines at the corners of his eyes. Hard-won scars.

"However, that doesn't mean she will," he said. "One pretty good predictor of success, though, is *unconditional* love and support, which is harder than it sounds. Are you strong enough to stand by her and help pick her up when she falls again, since she most likely will? But also, are you strong enough to stand on your *own*, if she won't? There are no guarantees, no promises. Just another chance, another oppor-tunity to stand up and start over. That's why it's important for you to accept you might do all the right things and still lose her."

Farris replaced his glasses. "It's that acceptance that will make *whatever* happens next easier. This isn't just about healing Marissa, Paul, it's about healing *you*." He held up the brochures that had con-sumed Paul. "Despite what these suggest."

"That's a hell of a sales pitch."

"I'm not trying to sell you anything. Trust me, I'd be happily unemployed."

Paul stood, and Farris did as well.

"My father told me how he watched me die right before his eyes. Now, he wasn't referring to a specific overdose, although he'd suffered through several of mine up close. Rather, he was talking about how he'd been watching me slowly kill myself for years and accepting that I was dead *already* relieved him of so much. My failures weren't about *his* failures anymore. There was no more blame or guilt or shame. He could make peace with the fact that I was lost to him, so every time he dragged me to the next rehab, the next detox, all he had left was the possibility of a miracle. And although miracles don't happen often, he was a devout Southern Baptist, a deacon in the church, and never gave up hope or faith that one might occur. Are you a religious man?"

"No, not much," Paul admitted.

"Well, faith isn't a bad thing. My father's faith gave him the strength he needed to save us both. There's nothing wrong with that."

"That's what happened? A miracle?"

Farris smiled. "Well, not hardly, no. But I did heal. I did recover, although we were never truly close again. There was no way we could be, not after everything we'd lost and all the things I'd taken from him. But at least I was alive and healthy, and that was a trade he was willing to make."

"Are you suggesting that's what will happen to me and my wife? That she'll somehow get better, but it'll all be different between us?"

Farris crossed his arms. "Isn't it already different, Paul? Hasn't your relationship already changed? Do either of you even know what your relationship is without her drug use . . . or without your grief?"

"She said that?"

Farris paused, letting the short silence speak for them both. Finally—

"Marissa knows you're still grieving for your first wife. She feels like she's a significant presence in both your lives."

"That's got nothing to do with anything. Not this."

"Maybe. But there's a very real possibility the young woman you leave here today *won't* be the same one you see again thirty or sixty days from now. That's neither good nor bad, just a necessary part of her recovery as she owns *all* the choices she's made, before and after you. Hopefully, you'll continue to love and grow with each other. Hopefully, you'll heal too, and I'm happy to help you with that. But we're only doctors and clinicians, Paul. We don't work miracles. But it never hurts to believe in them."

Paul knew what Farris was really driving at, how they could save Marissa only for Paul to still lose her in the end. They'd both already lost so much to her addictions, to Little Paris, maybe even to Jon. On her own, she might never be strong enough to break free from any of it.

Not strong enough to break free from him, either.

He'd brought her back to life on their kitchen floor to get her this far, this last resort to hold on to her, but that meant facing the hard truth that she might be the one to let go.

"And Marissa wants this?" he asked.

"Today, yes. She does. And we want to take advantage of that."

Paul extended his hand. "Okay, well, let's see what happens tomorrow."

It wasn't tomorrow, or even the day after that, but twelve days later that Paul finally got a call from her.

She'd left Keystone Recovery on foot.

She wanted him to bring her home. She didn't like the program or the counselors or the therapy sessions. And the other women in group were hassling her, calling her names.

She wasn't even like those women, not really. She wasn't an *addict*.

All she'd needed was a chance to get the dope out of her system, to get some rest and clear her head a little. But now she was ready to come home. *Their home.*

She needed him.

He didn't ask her about the yoga or the meditation or the art therapy.

He remembered everything Farris had warned him about and knew exactly what he was *supposed* to say, but he was long used to cutting deals with the devil.

He'd been making deals like that his whole life.

I need you, Paul.

That's what he'd desperately been waiting to hear almost from the moment he'd left her at Keystone, and when he finally did, he wasn't strong enough to say no.

Not for either of them.

100

It's been a while, but Terry Van Dorn looks the same. Like rough-hewn rock, like the cracked overburden from a blasted mountain top, revealing the coal seam beneath.

He also looks unbelievably tired, constantly rubbing at his eyes.

Those eyes send signals that are easy enough to read—he's sorry that he and his partner are here so late, on this night of all nights. He says without saying it they won't bother Paul for long and then they'll be on their way.

But his partner's eyes tell a whole different story.

Agent Casey Alexander takes in the house, the study. She even stares intently at the coffee he's made them, which now feels like a touch too much. It's hard to guess her age, but the younger agent's eyes are the oldest part of her. They've already seen plenty.

She reminds Paul of Jon. She's shorter than his former assistant chief, compact and tightly put together, tightly wound. Her reddish hair is cut short, all spiky and messed up, either by design or from a long day—now night—of running frustrated hands through it. She's probably always running, on to the next case, the next big thing, the next new place. She doesn't look like someone who ever stands still.

Agent Alexander is tomboyish, to be sure, but it wouldn't be fair to say she's unfeminine or even unattractive.

Just *tough*. Tough to deal with, tough to avoid. Impossible to back down or deter.

The way she's scanning everything, inventorying everything, means coming here tonight was most likely *her* idea. But now that they're here, Van Dorn won't hesitate to back her up.

She's wearing a Martin County deputy's T-shirt that's a size too big, but she has it tucked in behind her duty weapon, which rides high on her hip so it's easy to draw.

Paul grabs some Johnny Drum almost without thinking and pours it into his mug with his coffee, then offers it to them. Agent Alexander says no without hesitation, but Van Dorn pauses, before nodding the go-ahead.

After all those shots of that Eagle Rare earlier, he doesn't need to risk getting further good and lit in front of these agents now, but he swallows the whiskey anyway, feeling that familiar blaze again in the back of his throat. Marissa bought him this bottle last Christmas and he remembers unwrapping it, the careful, beautiful weight of it in his hand.

Van Dorn says, "I'm sorry, Paul. About Marissa. About everything. Mostly about us showing up here like this."

"I know, but it's fine," Paul answers. "You have a duty. It wasn't like I was sleeping anyway. I understand."

He debates whether to raise it first, then plows ahead.

"I only know a little bit about what happened at Lower Wolf, just what some of the men said in passing. I gather it's bad, though."

"That's an understatement," Van Dorn replies. "One of the worst I've ever seen."

"We've both seen too goddamn much," Paul says, and he means that.

"Do you miss it? The job," Van Dorn asks him.

"On a night like this, I don't." And he means that, too. "Not really. Not when I know what you're about to tell me." He goes on to say something to Van Dorn about hanging up the spurs and not walking away empty-handed, but he's just buying time, paying attention to the silent Agent Alexander.

Her eyes are still searching, roaming, carefully cataloging the room. She's looking for Marissa, trying to pull together some sense of his wife and, more important, some sense of the sort of man he might be.

Her eyes finally settle on him and his shower-damp hair and the third set of clothes he's put on tonight. He has no idea what she's thinking, but he's going to have to watch this one close.

He returns the stare and takes another sip of the Johnny Drum to steady himself.

"So why don't you and Agent Alexander here tell me how you think I can help."

101

Van Dorn tells him all about the horror show at Lower Wolf and the spate of ODs across Angel over the last few days—a spiked batch of Glasser heroin making its rounds—and how he and Agent Alexander have followed the bloodshed by tracking down Little Paris's surviving customers, Kara Grace and Anna Bishop.

Possibly the last people to see Little Paris alive, the only ones who might know where he is now.

Paul doesn't admit that he *already* knows all about those little stamp bags and that dancing skeleton.

DOA.

Van Dorn goes on to tell him about their run-in with Jerry Dix from last summer, and his twin sister, Janelle, and the baby they found covered in blood.

The other child too, Harmon "Hardy" Glasser, still missing.

And although the Johnny Drum now and the Eagle Rare from earlier are rolling through Paul's veins, setting his heart on fire and his thoughts racing, he follows the winding path of their investigation right to his doorstep, even if Van Dorn seems to reluctant to say it.

So he does it for him, getting it out in the open—

"Are you here to talk to me about Little Paris . . . or Marissa, my wife?"

And when Agent Alexander says "both" a beat too fast—the second thing she's uttered since walking through his door—Paul knows he'll need to give her *something*, because she won't leave here empty-handed otherwise.

"A little while back I nearly shot Little Paris Glasser myself . . ."

102

Marissa was off and running again and things were as bad as they'd ever been.

For a while at least, after her shortened stint at Keystone, things had been good. Nearly great, almost like when they'd first met.

He'd saved her yet again. Until it all started to fall apart twice as fast.

Home for a day, then gone for two. And if she stayed any length of time at all, it was only to get some money or steal something from the house to sell.

But is it really stealing when you'd hand it all over anyway?

When all his demands and threats failed to work, Paul started pleading, bargaining. He gave her all the money she wanted, however much she needed, long as she promised to come home afterward.

Just come home to him.

And sometimes she did, but most times she didn't. And since sometimes was better than never, he gave her the money anyway.

Then, to hold her to those promises he so desperately needed to hear, he started driving her himself.

Even he couldn't ask Jon to do that.

But it didn't matter, by then Jon was already gone.

———

After Carolina Arsenault's murder, the Tamarack had stayed abandoned, left to ruin, but Little Paris kept a hidey-hole there, where he could conduct a little private business and get himself cranked to the gills from time to time, far from the watchful eyes of the Old Man.

Danny, if he'd been alive, would have eventually caught wind of it and beat the dogshit out of him, or beat some sense *into* him, however you wanted to look at it.

After all, the Glassers didn't *use* their fucking poison. They were supposed to be too smart for that, even Little Paris.

But . . . *you lie down with dogs . . .*

Waiting out alone in his truck on those nights as Marissa ran into the Tamarack to meet Little Paris, sitting there as the minutes ticked by with his badge in his hand in case one of his own officers or a county deputy rolled up on him, having to imagine them in there together even (and then having that sonofabitch wave at him with that same-as-always shit-eating grin as he drove away), broke something in him.

And once he started covering for her sporadic disappearances by outright lying about further rehab, he knew it was time to retire. Folks around Angel sympathized that he needed to take full-time care of yet *another* sick wife, even though taking care of Marissa meant doing things like driving her to meet her dealer and then sitting on their bed while she shot up alone in their bathroom or living room.

Holding her head in his lap afterward, as she drifted and faded, murmuring words he didn't understand.

Changing the locks around on some of the doors, so he could lock her inside the house.

But nothing was ever going to be enough or the right thing at the right time or the right thing at all.

Marissa was always going to slip off on her own, forever run back to Little Paris if Paul wasn't there to bar their door.

He was still going to lose her . . . until that Friday when he found her gone yet again and convinced himself Jon had been right all along.

Nothing he did was *ever* going to matter, as long as Little Paris Glasser drew breath.

He was already barely sleeping, plagued by horrible dreams. Dreams of Donna near the end, that day at Three Rivers Hospital.

He was more than exhausted.

He was going crazy.

He was broken.

So he got himself good and drunk and grabbed his old duty weapons, his Colt Python and Remington shotgun, and drove out to the Tamarack for the last time.

103

It was raining when he pulled up, just like that day in Louisville in Farris's office.

Little Paris's Mustang was parked around back, next to a car he didn't recognize and Marissa's Ford Ranger, even though he'd hidden the keys from her days earlier. In fact, he'd locked them away in his otherwise empty home safe, where they used to keep her nice jewelry and a couple of gold coins his daddy had left him and his granddaddy's antique watch: all things he couldn't trust around her anymore or that she'd already sold.

But, of course, she knew where he kept the combination scribbled down in case he forgot it (the sort of thing you did when you got old), so he already knew it was her Ranger partially hidden in the sumac behind the Tamarack.

He'd already found his safe open, the keys gone.

She used to have a blue BMW, a gift he'd gotten her right after they were married, but she wrecked it one night on her way back home, passing out at the wheel, and that was right around the time he started having Jon go get her, so at least she wouldn't kill herself or someone else.

To make sure she got home safe.

But what made it worse was that Jon knew . . . Paul knew . . . that the BMW and the tennis bracelet and all the other new things and even the house itself had all been paid for in one way or another by the Glassers and their blood money.

He'd been bought and paid for little by little for years, selling pretty much everything that had ever mattered to him, all those goddamn little deals with the devil inevitably adding up.

It never should have surprised him he'd end up selling his soul, too.

He sat in his truck for nearly ten minutes, his headlights illuminating the front of the motel, casting all kinds of ugly shadows, until he saw a curtain stir at a window and a pale face peek out.

It wasn't Little Paris or even Marissa, but that girl, Kara Grace. He didn't know her well, other than that she'd started whoring around with Duane Scheel, and her boy's daddy was locked up on six years' worth of drug charges that Jon had hung on him, trying to get at the Glassers, but he would never roll.

Even Paul could admire that.

Paul kept the Remington down low, tilted across his lap, and the Colt shoved into his jeans. He'd expected Marissa to be here but not anyone else and that threw him off, made him unsure what to do next. Thought maybe he should just back out and drive the hell away, but before he could decide one way or the other, the motel room door opened and Kara came running toward him through the rain.

He rolled the window down a crack and she grabbed at it and held on like she was holding on for dear life. Shivering, the rain plastering her hair down. She was no longer pretty and might never be again.

"Little Paris wants me to tell you to get on outta here."

"That's what he said, now?"

"Yeah, just like that."

"Just like that." Paul nodded, as if he was agreeing. "My wife in there?"

Kara glanced back at the closed motel door behind her. Between the rain and the dark and her own shivering distraction, she likely hadn't seen yet the shotgun exposed across his lap, but would, if she stood there long enough.

"You don't want to be here. You really don't. It's not smart. Not safe." Paul didn't know if that was another message from Little Paris, or one from the woman herself.

"Where's that boy of yours? You leave him alone again?"

Kara blanched, face paler, colder, like he'd hit her. Then she got mad. "You can't ask me that. You got no damn right. You're not even the police anymore."

"I reckon you're right," Paul said. "I'm not." He looked at her hard. "But you go on inside now and get out of this rain. You tell my wife I'm here to take her home."

"She's not gonna come."

"You let me worry about that. You just tell her that anyway."

Kara blinked, trying to wipe rain out of her eyes. They were the color of the rain itself, weirdly clear and almost empty. Without another word, she turned toward the Tamarack, started walking, and as she approached the door, her back still to him, Paul got out—leaving his own truck door open so she wouldn't hear it slam—and chased up close behind.

Practically running.

If it had been sunny, and if she hadn't been so thin and wasted, he could have hidden in her shadow.

As the door opened for her, he pushed in too, knocking her out of the way.

Shotgun held high.

104

It was dark inside, a little fractured light thrown by some Coleman lanterns, but hardly enough to see by.

More crazy shadows like those painted outside by his headlights.

Twin beds, dirty and unkempt, and a little nightstand between them and some chairs pushed out around a table, a couple of coolers and a bunch of empty beer and whiskey bottles all around.

The bottles held the light like closed fists. Shined like fire.

There were needles and other sharp things on the table.

Tinfoil.

The dust of crushed pills.

Guns here and there.

The wallpaper had long been peeled away, revealing stained plaster beneath, and whatever cheap paintings had once adorned the walls were torn off, leaving behind empty gray squares.

The Gideons Bible in the nightstand was long gone, too. The pages torn up years ago and burned.

The place stank of piss and unwashed bodies, of foil and burned matches. Of sex.

And all of a sudden there was Little Paris himself standing in the back, shirt off, hands raised, eyes all crazy on that shit he smoked, and Marissa curled up nearby on one of the beds.

She was staring at Paul, her eyes as glassy as the bottles all around her, as unseeing and empty as Kara's.

With a tiny boy curled up next to her, sleeping hard, with messy blond hair, wearing a cartoon T-shirt and striped pajama bottoms.

Hardy Glasser.

There was also a third woman he didn't immediately recognize. Nodded out, chin on her chest.

Naked except for her panties.

"Sonofabitch . . ." Paul started to say, beginning to raise the Remington even higher, when he realized the door had *opened* for Kara, meaning *another* someone he hadn't accounted for was in the room with them—

Someone behind him.

Jon never would have made the mistake, but Paul knew it was already too late as he caught first the faint hammer click, then the gentle touch of a barrel against his temple.

Duane Scheel appeared right next to him, grinning like the devil himself.

"Jesus, drop the pop gun, old man, before you go and hurt yourself." Then Scheel pushed the gun harder into Paul's head just to make his point.

"It's okay, Duane-o, he ain't gonna do nothing," Little Paris said. "Look at him, he's drunk, three sheets to the wind. This is just whiskey courage. He ain't really got it in him."

Little Paris stepped close, right over Kara's prone body, ignoring Marissa and the little boy and the other woman. He came forward with arms outstretched, palms held up, the tattoos Paul had seen on Jon's video of Carolina Arsenault seemingly moving on their own, coiling and rippling across his skin, a trick of the shadows and the fiery flickering light.

Paul could just end it all now, blast Little Paris backward across the bed, spray him all over the walls, but even he wasn't sure he could kill the man in front of the sleeping boy. It would take less than a heartbeat to do and several days to scrape up what remained, and Scheel would no doubt kill him in turn, but least it would be over quick. But what about the boy? *What about Marissa?* She would survive, and for what? And for how much longer? How soon after he was dead and buried would she be back in some other motel room, shacked up with another Little Paris, this time in Louisville or Charleston or Ironton?

He would have saved her a third time, only to still lose her.

Or . . . *or* . . . he could shoot *her* instead. End it all that way, too. Let Scheel kill him anyway and what would any of it matter then?

Marissa. Little Paris. Hardy. Carolina. Jon.

Angel.

That awful, unbidden thought of killing her . . . the cold horror of it . . . nearly stopped his heart even without the help of one of Scheel's bullets. It almost made him drop his own rain-slicked Remington on the floor.

Was it even still aimed at Little Paris anymore . . . or pointed at Marissa instead?

I'm too drunk for this, not thinking straight.

I am broken.

I am crazy.

Then Marissa blinked once, twice, seeing him for the first time. She touched the still sleeping boy's head, patted it, and slid off the bed and said Paul's name.

She held the boy against her as if he was her own, protecting him.

"Oh, Paul. Where's Jon?" She looked around and past him. "You shouldn't be here. You know better. Not like this. And he needs me."

And Paul didn't know if she was talking about Little Paris, the little boy, or Jon. "Go on home, baby, go on to bed. I'll be there soon. You know I always come home."

But she didn't. Not always. Not often enough.

Little Paris was smiling. "I'd do what the little lady says. That's what I'd do, if'n I was you."

And it was all so clear then, like the brightest sun ever shining down, lighting up that whole dark, dank room and his whole life. Illuminating everything.

He'd told anyone who would listen that she was his *light* . . . and couldn't avoid seeing anymore all that she'd revealed about them both.

Are you strong enough to stand by her and help pick her up when she falls again, since she most likely will? But also, are you strong enough to stand on your own, *if she won't? . . . That's why it's important for you to accept you might do all the right things and still lose her.*

It's that acceptance that'll make whatever *happens next easier . . .*

But Farris was wrong. Accepting it didn't make it any goddamn easier at all.

She'd forever be running away, and he'd forever be pulling her back, and she'd forever let him, until one of them put an end to it for good.

End it all that way, too . . .

But he didn't react, couldn't react, even as Little Paris took the Remington out of his hands, cracked it open, and dumped the shells on the floor.

"Like I said, Duane, he ain't got it in him. Not today he don't."

Little Paris guided him back toward the door and he was almost gentle.

He patted Paul's cheek and leaned in. "You're not even half the man that prick Jon Dorado was, and that's saying something. It really is.

"But it's okay, you and I understand each other better, don't we?

We both got that *thing*, right? That thing we need so bad it gets under our skin. Need it so bad we'd damn near kill for it. Or die for it."

Scheel opened the door and Little Paris pushed him through it, out into the rain.

"We can settle up what she owes later. I know you're good for it." But before he closed the door, Little Paris glanced back toward the bed, where Marissa was still holding the boy tight.

"She's good with him, you know that? The boy. She would be a good mama. And he's gonna be an outlaw, that one. Just you wait and see. A real heartbreaker."

Little Paris grinned—

"Just like his daddy."

105

A little while back I nearly shot Little Paris Glasser myself. As close as I've ever come to killing another man, and I've carried a gun for a long time."

That's all Paul says to Van Dorn and Agent Alexander.

That's all he'll ever say about that night at the Tamarack. He'll take it to both his and Marissa's grave.

Like he'll take a lot of things.

Then he swallows back most of his Johnny Drum and tries not to look Agent Alexander in the eyes anymore.

106

A couple of months after that night at the Tamarack Inn, Paul found Marissa out in the backyard, staring at the river.

She'd been home almost nine days straight, the longest stretch in a long time—at least since Jon had left Angel—and there were moments during that spell when they both almost felt normal, like those days right after he got her from Keystone.

That was always the best and worst part of having her home, those few hours or days where they both weren't consumed by their needs.

But it was just a mirage.

Artifice made to appear natural, like faux wood tiles, even when there was nothing natural about it.

Even when she'd curl up next to him and hold his hand and run her own hands through his hair that had steadily, steadfastly, gone gray.

When she'd whisper in his ear and lie about how things were really going to be different this time.

How it all felt different to her, although it always felt the same to him.

But he'd believe her anyway, at least for those hours. He'd talk about their future and let her make plans to go on trips they'd never truly take, and then she'd get out one of her old dresses and he'd light some candles and they might have a candlelit dinner that she would hardly eat and they'd both try to not to cry when they made love afterward.

And for both their sakes, so as not to ruin the illusion they both wanted to believe in, he'd pretend not to hear her when she slipped out of their bed and out the door.

So it was this morning after one of those miragelike nights, when he found her out in the backyard, sitting cross-legged in the grass, watching the river.

She was awake, damp from the dew, still wearing the dress from the night before, watching the sun rise. It was glowing through the trees, the light soft and hazy and gentle and welcoming.

It would be hot later in the day, but right then, the world was still cool to the touch.

He sat down next to her in the wet grass and she leaned into him. She was looking out across the Big Sandy, and although he could barely make out the pale white sunlight on it, he could still feel it out there, the roil and rumble of it. He had lived so close to it for so long, it was as if the river's weight was always pulling on him, the friction of it straining against the banks in his bones.

"I thought I was dreaming," she said, "and then I realized I was awake the whole time."

"Let's go inside," he said, urging her to stand, trying to pull her with him, but she resisted, until he relented and stayed in the grass next to her. It hadn't been cut in a long time, one of those things that didn't seem so important anymore, and it was higher than ankle length. Higher than it had been in years. The long, hot summer would eventually scour it, though, burn it down until it withered and died, but not yet.

During that first dinner party, she'd had one of the local boys cut it down so close it had been only a hint of grass, a memory of it, a green so bright and smooth it was like running your hand over glass. You could see your face in it.

She never would have sat in it even then, never would have let it touch her. But this morning, a hundred long blades clung wetly to her skin, to her slim feet and ankles. They were flecked in her hair and it made him think of Carolina Arsenault with thimbleberry and green adder's-mouth growing all around her.

Perhaps Marissa had slept out here for a time, lying in the grass.

The sun was on her face and it burned away the lines and the ravages, all those centuries that had accumulated in the last few years. She was so young and beautiful and always would be.

Exactly how she'd always want him to remember her.

"I'm not Donna," she said, and he said, "I know," and would later have no idea if that really happened or if it was just one more part of the mirage.

If either of them was awake, or both still dreaming.

She reached out and touched his face, leaving blades of grass there.

She said, "I walked right down to the edge of the river this morning. It's always scared me, all that dark water. I don't know why. When Jon used to bring me home, he'd drive over the bridge and just tell me not to look. He used to grab my hand and knew I was afraid. Not because I was up so high, but because of all that water below."

"We go over that bridge every day."

"I know, Paul. I know."

Lately he'd imagined he was the one drowning, Marissa pulling them both down. But she was the one afraid of the water, forever struggling to stay afloat. He never knew how scared she was of the Big Sandy. But Jon did. Jon always knew.

"But this morning, for some reason, it didn't scare me anymore. All that cold awful water. The river. I thought I could swim out there and just finally let it take me away."

"Don't say that. Don't ever say that. You don't want that."

"But I'm so, so tired."

"Me, too. We both are. But I don't want that."

"Don't you? Because we can't keep doing *this*. We can't, even though a part of me wishes we could."

"I can take you back to Keystone. I'll make the call now."

She shook her head. "Do you know where Jon is, where he went?"

He lied. "No, I don't."

"He used to tell me all the time how much you loved me. He said I could never imagine it. That it would kill me if I knew how much . . . or just how much I was killing you."

He nodded and stared out over the sluggish, dark water. "Did you ever really love me?"

"I wanted to love you," she said. "Isn't that the same thing? Can't it be enough?"

Wanting to show them all how much she loved him. Fiercely, passionately, without reservation.

Even now he wants to believe she truly did love him that way, at least for a little while.

Just the way he loved her and still does.

And always will.

"Can I do this, Paul? Can I really do this anymore? That's what I sit here and ask myself."

She'd been trying so hard this time, but she always tried hard, and it wasn't going to last. It never did, because she was already gone. Because she was never really his.

He could see how she was already trembling, sweating, her skin glistening and delicate and green with grass. She'd be gone again by tonight, by tomorrow afternoon at the latest, leaving another hole in the house and his heart and the world where she'd been.

Leaving him all alone with nothing but lingering memories—

The house still smells like Marissa.

The candles she liked so much.

Her expensive perfume, her skin.

She turned and looked at him, touched his face once more. "I'm so, so sorry, baby." And they both knew she was talking about so much more than whatever remained still between them. And he was just as sorry as she was, for the things they'd done to each other and everything they could never be.

She leaned in close, kissed the corner of his mouth, where it still sent shivers through him. Like always. "Where does the river go, Paul?"

"I don't know. Away. Far away from here, I guess."

She didn't say any more, and when he pulled her up again, she didn't resist. He grabbed her up in his arms and held her tight, too tight, realizing just how little she weighed. If she tried to swim the Big Sandy, it surely would carry her away and take what little was left of his heart right along with it.

"Just stay with me one more day," he said. "Please. It's okay. I'll take care of you. You know I will. I know what to do."

Then he carried her back to the house and texted Little Paris.

107

As the agents' headlights finally recede from the living room window, Paul circles the still, silent house, weighing his remaining options and counting each one with a sip from a fresh bottle of Eagle Rare he keeps tucked behind some books in the study.

His breath is heavy, combustible. A match will set it on fire. He hasn't been this drunk in a while and it feels good.

Maybe not quite like being held in the arms of an angel or whatever it was that Farris had said, but damn fine all the same. In a way, Paul always understood what Farris was talking about.

All that getting up, only to fall all over again.

His thirst has always ebbed and flowed like the Big Sandy, always just below the surface, surging and roiling, threatening to pull him under, although it never did. It was probably the whiskey talking earlier when he'd thrown out those worthless names to Special Agent Alexander—Ray Ray Sitton and stupid, dead Duane Scheel—but they'll barely slow her down.

There was nothing he could have said to dissuade her from continuing her search for Little Paris and Hardy.

She left with more questions than answers about Marissa's death, still trying to square what she could glean of her from her house and her pictures on its walls, with the woman he claimed took a handful of sleeping pills and walked into a river she'd been so afraid of. She pressed for Marissa's phone because even if she eventually talks herself into his version of it, she'll never accept that Little Paris didn't have some hand in it, that he isn't connected in some way she just can't see.

She won't be wrong.

You believe she killed herself?

Is it possible Marissa saw him yesterday, today, even tonight?

He never could have accounted for the attack at Lower Wolf today, or for Van Dorn and Agent Alexander crossing his path tonight. How could he? How the hell could anyone? What were the chances that reckoning would occur today of all days and that Little Paris would somehow miss it and still be running around?

What are the chances Van Dorn or Agent Alexander find him?

What are the chance they end up shooting him dead trying to bring him in?

What happens if they don't?

Paul's not ready for them to have a long, serious conversation with the last remaining Glasser. Not yet. The devil knows what he'll say with his back against the wall and hardly any real family left to protect, no skin but his own still to save, except the boy's too, *maybe*. But despite all the things Paul's already done and all those he thought he was willing to do, he's also not quite ready to let those agents face Little Paris's wrath and paranoia either, not even to cover up his own guilt and shame and crimes.

Just like he couldn't quite put Little Paris down in front of that little boy in the motel.

How long do I have?

How long do I need?

Long enough to bury Marissa? That's all he really wants, all he can expect and more than he deserves after all that's happened, and after that he won't care.

Can I do this, Paul? Can I really do this anymore? That's what I sit here and ask myself.

That's what she asked him only this morning.

That's what he asks himself now.

He goes and gets his guns out of the gun locker in the garage.

The only combination Marissa didn't know and that he's never had to write down.

He pulls out the Remington, then his old Colt Python. Since leaving the department, he keeps both clean, well oiled, just in case.

Every time he touches them they're heavier than he remembers.

He makes sure the Remington is loaded.

It is.

He buckles on his worn Sam Browne belt and holsters the Python so it sits against his leg as comfortable as it always did.

The whole time he was talking to the agents, Marissa's phone—the one Agent Alexander had been so eager to get a hold of—was silently buzzing where he'd left it on the nightstand, next to her side of the bed. His own phone, too. He didn't immediately recognize the incoming number on either of them but knew exactly who it was all the same.

He knew exactly what it meant.

Now he finally texts that number back, and is still waiting for an answer when an Angel PD cruiser pulls into his driveway.

108

Donna's hand weighed little more than paper, and although she cried, begged, he couldn't bring himself to do it.

Just as he couldn't the day before and wouldn't be able to tomorrow.

He'd never be able to.

They were in Three Rivers Hospital and Donna wanted him to take her home. She wanted out of the goddamn end-to-end white room with all its machines and tubes and that rank smell of death that hovered over them both. She begged him again to carry her back to *their* bed and the air-dried sheets that she loved so much and to give her his gun and walk into the next room and say a prayer for her while she pulled the trigger.

He knew she didn't have the strength for that, her hand so tiny and frail on his own, like holding a sparrow with folded wings. Its heartbeat, her pulse, soft against his fingertips. And he knew for damn sure he didn't have the strength, either. He reminded her how it was a sin, but she told him God would forgive her this one thing; he really, really would. She was like a child, unaccountable, just like it said in the Book of Romans, where the Apostle Paul proclaimed sin is not counted when there is no law, where there's so much pain. But she wasn't thinking clearly, the drugs and her bodily torment confusing her, deluding her like the devil himself, and Paul knew all about the devil.

Her mind was misfiring, seeing shadows and stars. She promised him that God would forgive them both.

And though he reckoned he had little to fear for his soul either way, he wasn't going to let her risk hers.

He had to walk out of that white room, stand outside and lean his forehead against the wall.

Every second he stood there, every heartbeat that passed, was one less he was sharing with her, and though he'd come to regret them all later, he needed that time right then.

He'd been far from a perfect husband: far too jagged, too sharp. He'd cut her in a thousand tiny ways as most couples do, and they'd been together long enough for those cuts to add up to something measurable. But he'd never truly failed her, not like this. All she wanted was this one thing and he couldn't, wouldn't, do it. Not just to protect her soul, but because *he* couldn't bear to let her go.

It could all be over any minute or within the next hour. He prayed this burden would be lifted from him.

Prayed for a fucking miracle that might save her.

Two years later, Dr. Farris at Keystone would talk to Paul about strength and acceptance and miracles and faith and Paul still wouldn't understand it.

He'd always believed in the devil more than God.

Hell more than Heaven.

————

He turned and walked back into that room and took up her hand again. Just as weak, just as frail, just as delicate. A bird that would never take flight again.

He stroked it and told her stories as she drifted through pain, floated in and out of consciousness.

He told her how beautiful she looked, even with her hair gone and her bones exposed like a map beneath her skin and her veins blue and purple and gray and running close to the surface.

All those cicatrices, the burn scars, from the radiation.

He traced them all, following them to her heart.

He kissed her closed eyes, but was afraid to kiss her lips, because he didn't want to steal any of her hard-won breath.

He promised her it would be over soon.

She didn't die that day or the next.

Every day after that she asked him to help her end it, but he couldn't say *yes*.

He just couldn't bear to let her go.

She lived in all that pain and torment a whole month longer.

109

P aul loves this place.

This town.

His home.

He drives the darkened streets, a few short hours from dawn. His windows are rolled down, just the way his daddy used to do it, the way Donna always did, and he breathes in the pre-sun chill and glides past quiet houses and stores. He knows them all. There was a time you could ride down Angel's main street just like this, at this hour, and hear roosters crowing.

If you held your breath you could almost hear the Big Sandy rolling by.

He and Jon used to argue all the time about when things really started to change, when Angel became ugly and unrecognizable to them both, like seeing an old friend who after years away no longer looked the same; a man returned from a great and terrible war, carrying scars both inside and out. Paul partly blamed it on the coal, that black rock. When the seams tapped out, so did Angel and the whole way of life it represented, a way he'd fought so hard to hold on to and had made his deals to protect and preserve.

Jon saw it all different. Although change was inevitable and always ongoing, to the river and the rock, to the *world*, most change is insignificant, imperceptible, impossible to measure. It's weighed out in hundreds of thousands of years. Eons. *But people?* A man might change his mind in the blink of an eye. A single choice, both good and bad, might be weighed and discarded a hundred times over a single tumbler of whiskey, between the first cigarette and the next.

Over a heated needle and spoon.

Before or after a trigger is pulled.

And a man can lose *hope* just as fast, too. All it takes is a loss or failure or disappointment, a moment's weakness that often ends up lasting a lifetime.

A birth.

A death.

A broken heart.

Jon used to argue there was always a lot of heartbreak in Angel; the place was just too small to hold so much.

No . . . The land and river running past it doesn't change much, not in any way that matters to most or can be easily measured.

Just the people who live here.

Always the people.

Paul is pointedly ignoring Duck nervously sweating in the seat next to him.

The other man surprised him by showing up at the house when he did, but he's almost glad for it.

Duck brought news that Buechel and another Martin deputy allegedly found Little Paris's Mustang burned out down by Yatesville Lake. They discovered a body too, just as charred, nearly melted into the car's seats, although Paul and Duck already know it isn't Little Paris.

But Paul couldn't risk leaving Duck behind. Duck's been burning up the lines trying to reach Little Paris himself, desperate to curry favor any way he can. Desperate too to find out what Paul might have said about Duck's own dealings with the Glassers.

A lot of folks have a lot to lose with Little Paris angry and alive.

Since Paul couldn't decide which was worse—those agents finding Little Paris or a foolish, fearful Duck stumbling straight into their arms before they do—he's brought him along.

Paul has his guns but feels naked without the badge he wore for so long. Same way he felt that night he went after Little Paris at the Tamarack, then tried to justify to himself later why he didn't pull the trigger.

A moment's weakness . . . a broken heart.

His own reckoning.

I'm fucking broken.

Paul wants to believe he changed for the worse, broke for good, that day in the hospital when he decided to let Donna suffer and then lost her anyway.

Or that night at the Tamarack.

Or this morning, when he found Marissa in the grass, transfixed by the river that had frightened her for so long, and carried her back to their bedroom for the last time and understood once and for all she was never going to stay there.

Or a few hours ago . . . when he met Little Paris.

But an even worse thought is there's never been a *before or after* for him, that he's never been any better than Daniel or Little Paris or Duck or the rest of them. Instead, like the hills and the river, he's been forever unchanging. *Always* broken, *always* selfish. A weak man who turned away when it suited him and made others do likewise, who helped ruin this place and those he loved, even as he convinced himself he was saving them.

The same man who never did a goddamn thing for a girl like Carolina Arsenault and a hundred others like her, until it was too late.

Not even then.

I am the river.

Duck finally can't hold his tongue any longer, their shared silence almost killing him. "Look, Chief, how do you want to play this? Do you think anyone's going to buy that burned-up car and body?"

"Who is it?"

"Who is what?" Duck asks back.

"The *body*, Duck. Who did Dunn and his men put in that goddamn car?"

Duck shakes his head. "Hell, I don't know. I don't. I never thought to ask." For a moment, even Duck falls silent. "Anyway, are we gonna meet up with the sheriff or Buechel? He says he doesn't know where Little Paris is laying his head now, but he's got some ideas. Where do you think—"

Paul cuts him off.

"I know where he is. So just shut the fuck up, Duck. Please, please, just shut the fuck up."

110

As Paul rolls up on the Tamarack, his headlights frame the SUV the agents were driving, now parked alongside the road.

In those twin luminous halos, it sits dark, empty.

He stops and kills his own lights, then takes a deep pull from that last bottle of Eagle Rare propped in his lap.

He realizes now his true mistake was not that he rambled on and on to those agents about nearly killing Little Paris, it was mentioning this goddamn motel at all—

Before Marissa, there was an old motel on the other side of Angel where he used to hold these little parties. He ran drugs and young girls out of the place for a while . . .

Agent Alexander's eyes had clicked with recognition the moment it had escaped his lips, even if she didn't yet understand its importance or what it might mean.

It didn't take her long to figure it out.

"Oh, Jesus, they're here," Duck says, holding out his hand for the bottle. But Paul ignores him and finishes it off alone.

Duck gapes, shaking his head. "You're damn drunk, Chief. God-damn drunk. I hope to hell you know what you're doing."

Paul doesn't. Doesn't have any damn clue.

When he opens the truck door, he's greeted by a sudden gunshot.

Then another . . . and another.

He steps out anyway, crouching and stumbling, nearly falling to his knees.

But the bullets aren't meant for him.

111

There's a body lying on the ground in front of one of the Tamarack's rooms.

A door is open. Muzzle flash flares. Someone's inside the adjacent room, firing wildly into the dark.

A window that's not already broken shatters.

Paul's only moments behind whatever's happened here, and he tries to fast-forward those seconds, to catch up.

He hunkers down again, fearing a bullet that never comes, then flattens his body against the wall next to the Tamarack's old office.

Duck is at his shoulder, crouched down, too.

"What the holy fuck?" Duck asks, breathing hard. He's pulled his duty gun but holds it far away from his body, like he's afraid to touch it.

Paul stares at the body sprawled on the small walkway in front of the rooms. Even in the dark, it looks too big to be Agent Alexander.

Van Dorn.

But he can't be sure.

"Goddamn, Little Paris is holed up in there," Duck says through gritted teeth, eyes wide. "Here all along and you knew it." Duck keeps bobbing his head up and down, up and down. "And those damn agents somehow found him, too. I swear to Christ he's got himself an arsenal in there. Sounds like a goddamn hammer on a tin roof."

And Duck's right, the constant barrage does sound like a swinging hammer, or a coal miner's pick, ringing on stone. When Paul came here that rainy night a few months ago, Little Paris had half a dozen or more guns spread out around that shitty room. There's no way Agent Alexander or Van Dorn could have known that, or even expected it.

Little Paris can hold them off forever.

For every three, four, five rounds Little Paris launches aimlessly into the night, Paul counts one lone answer; sparks flying high off the doorframe, striking like Ohio Blue Tip Matches off whatever little metal remains. Most of Angel's abandoned buildings have long been stripped of their valuable metal or copper wiring, like pulling gold teeth out of the dead.

Agent Alexander is hunkered down, still alive, somewhere off to Paul's right, conserving her ammo. Just enough return fire to keep Little Paris's head down and keep him from rushing right down on top of her.

She's being very careful with her shots and Paul knows why.

Duck's near panic now. "Goddamn, this is a mess. I was just worried, you know, for all of us. And LP, he ain't returned none of my calls or messages . . . and you weren't hardly telling me nothing. Nobody telling me nothing. Here I am tryin' to help that sonofabitch, help all of you, not get myself killed. I didn't want this."

Paul leans his head against the wall, just like he once did at Three Rivers Hospital, letting moments slip away again. Duck's been so damn scared all night about the fallout for himself of Little Paris being found alive, he doesn't even realize that if Agent Alexander survives this, she'll eventually find all those stupid, clumsy calls and texts of his to Little Paris anyway.

Dug his own damn grave and doesn't even know it.

But not Paul, who's already accepted that if Little Paris doesn't kill her first, she'll inevitably find *his* call from Marissa's phone to Little Paris earlier this morning.

She'll also recover all those angry texts and calls that Little Paris made barely an hour ago from Kara Grace's phone—that number Paul didn't immediately recognize—while she and Van Dorn were still sitting in his study.

Little Paris demanding his help.

And finally, that solitary return message Paul sent back only moments after they were gone, telling Little Paris to meet him here at the Tamarack.

To stay here, until Paul arrived.

He knew the minute Agent Alexander walked out of his door she'd expose his worst secrets and shame.

All of it . . . for all of them.

"Did you tell Little Paris about Marissa, Duck? Did you tell him about her?"

Duck shrugs.

"Anyone else know you came out to my place?" Paul asks.

Duck shakes his head, a terse movement almost invisible in the dark.

"No," he breathes. "I didn't tell anyone. Just came out straightaway to you, hoping we could figure this all out. We need to figure this out."

"Okay, Duck, that's good. Real good."

Paul stands and takes a step back. Then another. And there must be something in Paul's voice or his eyes, because Duck suddenly looks up at him, his own eyes wide and white.

So white, they almost glow.

Just like it said in the Book of Romans, where the Apostle Paul proclaimed sin is not counted when there is no law, where there's so much pain.

There has been so much fucking pain—so, so much of it. But all those sins *do* count.

Every single goddamn one of them.

Duck doesn't even think about the gun in his own hand, the one thing he might use to save himself, because nothing else now in the world will. He's always been such a lousy fucking cop—*dug his own damn grave and doesn't even know it*—but Paul blames himself for that, too.

He never tried all that hard to make Duck any better.

"Oh, shit, I'm gonna die, aren't I?"

"Yes," Paul says. "Yes, you are."

He puts the Remington in Duck's startled face and pulls the trigger.

112

He met Little Paris behind the Tamarack. The usual place. It was goddamn hot, the sun high. He knew Little Paris wouldn't send a runner, not even Renfro.

Not for her.

Little Paris was even early, already sitting on the hood of his Mustang when Paul pulled up, and maybe it was that small fact that ended up saving his life.

He'd also been *wasping*, smoking a mixture of meth and CRC Bee Blast Wasp and Hornet Killer. Marissa had warned Paul all about Little Paris's meth use and how it had only been getting worse. How dangerous and paranoid he had gotten. Impossible to predict.

She'd told him to be careful dealing with him, but she hadn't told him not to go.

The crank pipe was still lazily clutched in one hand and he had his shirt off, sunning those tattoos around his heart, smoke drifting around him.

He grinned all lopsided, eyes shining like brightly colored church glass.

"Damn, it ain't no welcome surprise seeing you here like this," he said. The fingers of his free hand did a little tap dance on the hood of the Mustang, next to a Beretta laid out on the hood too, just in case. Weeds and sumac growing up through the dirt brushed the underside of the car, and he had all the windows down, engine still running, listening to music that sounded like a running chainsaw. Back and forth, back and forth. Quiet, then loud, but always angry.

Paul couldn't remember it exactly right, but he thought they'd found Carolina Arsenault about five feet from where they were both parked.

"Mary not up to this herself?" Little Paris said, using a nickname that no one else used, except maybe for Jon. "I was damn excited to see her. She feelin' okay? I know she's been trying to be good this time. But she can't. They never can." He drew deep on his homemade pipe, a sixty-watt GE lightbulb.

"We're not talking, you understand that? We're not having this conversation, you and I."

Little Paris sighed, laughed. "Fine, then. It'll be like you ain't even here, and neither am I. We're all ghosts." He leaned forward. "Boo, motherfucker."

He hopped off the hood, went around to the driver's side and reached in, and came back with a small plastic bag like the one you'd get at a 7-Eleven or a Quik Mart. He dropped it on the hood and fumbled around in it until he produced four smaller bags, setting them out next to the Beretta.

"These three are the usual. But this last one here"—Little Paris picked up a Baggie, bouncing it in his hand—"well, this one is all new, a little something special. Like that corner piece of cake with extra frosting that everyone fights over."

The stamp bag had a footloose skeleton capering on it and looked so small in Little Paris's palm.

"This right here is the end of the world." He laughed, not making any sense, before tossing it over to Paul, who easily caught it. Little

Paris danced in place and clawed at his own skin. Paul had seen meth eat people alive in these mountains, and Little Paris was all chewed up, spit back out.

He had it bad, and Paul had no idea what was holding him together anymore.

"Now, Mary's gotta be damn careful with that one. Maybe half, even a quarter, of what she's used to. You tell her that, you hear me? That's some powerful shit right there, like holding a bomb in your hand. Watch out when it goes off." Little Paris made a soft booming noise, cheeks puffed out, followed by an exaggerated, exploding gesture with his own hand. Dirty fingers splayed above his head.

"This is what's been killing all those people?" Paul asked, studying the bag and the three letters—*DOA*.

Little Paris's eyes narrowed, then he shrugged, unconcerned. "It's got some mule kick, can't deny that. Them crazy wetbacks are goddamn wizards. Hocus-pocus and all that shit. Danny told me he saw one of their labs once, way down in Tijuana. Dozens of little naked wetback girls carryin' stuff to and fro. I'd pay good money to see that, even if I reckon he was bullshitting me. But with old Danny boy, you just never really knew. He had the golden tongue, the gift o' gab, that one."

Little Paris's eyes went funny talking about Danny, like he was seeing him right over Paul's shoulder.

We're all ghosts.

"You give Mary a taste of that, though, and she's gonna love you forever." He laughed again and then reached for the Beretta on the hood and turned it on Paul.

"Now, I'm gonna ask you to take your shirt off."

Paul almost laughed. "You're out of your fucking mind."

Suddenly serious, Little Paris agreed. "Why, yes, Paul. Yes, I am."

His eyes glittered, sparkled, angry things buzzing and circling behind them, and he raised the gun higher, leveling it off at point somewhere between Paul's own eyes. "Serious as a motherfuckin' heart attack, old man. Remember when this was all switched around and you had your gun on me?"

"I do." Paul said as he shrugged out of his shirt, revealing pale skin, the wiry gray hair across his chest and paunch. He'd lost weight right along with Marissa. Not near as much, but enough to notice.

His skin hung on him, old and washed out.

"I don't know who was more scared then. You or me." Little Paris stepped closer so Paul could get a good look at his gun. "You shoulda seen your face, old man. Your hands all shaky, could barely keep a grip on that scatter gun. You was just about quakin' in your boots. About to piss yourself."

Paul stared at Little Paris's tattoos, the pair of dice over his heart, the shark swimming against his rib cage. All his beautiful angels and devils. Now there was a new image etched across his thin, wasted torso—

A snarling wolf's head pierced with arrows.

Paul didn't remember that one from the Carolina Arsenault video, or from that night here at the Tamarack.

"You going to kill me now? Is that what this is about?" Paul asked.

"No, *Paul*." Little Paris said his name like he was spitting it on the ground. He sounded like Marissa, when she was high and about to pick a fight with him. "If I'd ever wanted to kill you, I coulda done that just about any time. You ain't the police no more now anyway and nobody gives two shits about you. You're just a memory, something people talk about like you ain't even around. Dead and gone."

"A ghost?" Paul asked, and Little Paris nodded. In ways neither had words for, they understood each other.

"That's right. The world can't hardly touch us no more." Little

Paris looked again at something over Paul's shoulder, something only he could see. "My hand on the Good Book, these last few months, you and Mary been some of my best customers. But I just had to make sure you wasn't wearin' no wire anyway. Just business. Danny was always goin' on and on about business and wires and some such."

Paul pulled on his shirt again, not bothering to explain to Little Paris that if he'd really been worried about a wire, he would have made Paul undress before he showed his dope like some goddamn jewelry-store display.

Once he had his shirt buttoned, he got out his money and tossed it on the ground, where Little Paris watched the bills catch in the weeds or blow away beneath the Mustang. He kicked at a couple of the twenties with his Luccheses.

"You think I'm gonna stoop to pick that up?" He slipped the Beretta into his waistband, so it looked for all the world like the ink-black wolf on his stomach was holding the gun's grips in its jaws. "You think I even need that? I piss that money when I wake up in the morning. Between us, it ain't even about your money. We both know exactly how I'm gonna get paid next time Mary comes runnin' around. And she will. Don't think you comin' here today for her puts a stop to that. But you be careful with that new shit, you don't want to hurt *our* girl, now, do you?"

"Shut your fucking mouth," Paul said, gripping the small bag in his hand.

"Because it ain't just about the dope between me 'n' her, either. She wanted a little baby, you know that? Talks about it all the time. That's why she's always so good with Hardy. But you're so damn old, she got afraid it'd come out retarded or something . . ."

"I said to shut your goddamn mouth."

Little Paris chewed his lip hard enough to draw blood. Grinned through bloody teeth, then spit in Paul's direction. "Every time you kiss her, that's *me* you're tastin' on her lips. I'm *inside* her, just like I'm all up inside your fuckin' head." Little Paris pulled the gun from his waistband, only to tap the barrel against his own temple. "You can lock her up, play the sugar daddy and run around and do all these fine things for her, but you can't keep her. You can't hold on to her, no matter what you say or do. She was never yours. Now, you just think about that."

Rage rolled through Paul like the Big Sandy after a storm and it swept everything else away. Paul said, "We're not done, you and me."

"No, I reckon not," Little Paris said. "'Cause you *need* me and always have. You hate it, but it's true. My family put that fancy roof over your head, all but made you a rich man. You ain't this town, we are. And you'll be back tomorrow or the day after, lookin' for more. Or Mary damn sure will. They all come back."

Little Paris swayed then, suddenly unsteady on his feet, rocking on his big boots. The multicolored church light in his eyes faded, dimmed, and for a second Little Paris looked as old as Paul, just as gray and faded.

"I hear 'em calling my name, you know that?"

Little Paris tossed the Beretta in the driver's-side window and then reached around for the lightbulb he'd left on the Mustang's hood. He sucked down whatever smoke still swirled inside until his eyes lit up again, incandescent, until whatever momentary weakness and unseen ghosts that had gripped him let him go.

But that's not what drew Paul's attention. It was what he could see through that open window.

Who he could see.

Little Hardy Glasser, sitting in the backseat alone, holding a plastic toy six-gun of his own.

He aimed the gun at Paul and said *Bangbang* with a big smile on his small, delicate face.

"My little outlaw," Little Paris said through a mouthful of smoke. "It'll be all on him, even after you and I truly are dead and gone.

"He's gonna run these mountains one day, you can take my word on that."

113

Even in the dark, Paul knows there's blood on his hands.

Duck's blood.

Blood is thicker than water, even bad blood . . . and a lot hotter than the cold river that ran through his hands earlier tonight.

Drunk or not, shooting the man was a hell of a lot easier than he'd thought.

Now he calls out to the other side of the motel, where the return shots have been echoing from.

How many can she have left?

Not many, not nearly enough, if Little Paris is still loaded for bear.

"Agent Alexander, are you okay?"

He waits, drawing a bead with his Remington down his length of wall to the doorway where Little Paris lurks. It's momentarily quiet. Eerily quiet. Little Paris is either reloading or switching out guns altogether . . . or playing possum. But just like the burned-out Mustang and the body inside it down at Yatesville Lake, it would be foolish to assume he's dead.

A voice calls across the lot—

"Fuck. Is that you, Mayfield?"

Her words roll out fast with barely a breath between them, but if she's hurt, already took a bullet, she won't reveal that. She's too smart and has no idea what his intentions are.

Paul almost smiles. He admires the hell out of Agent Alexander.

"Yes, it's me. It looks like Terry's down."

She doesn't answer, her silence enough.

He peers at Terry Van Dorn. The man might still be moving, might still be crawling, but the darkness hides too much to be sure. Even if he is alive, there can't be much fight left in him, he won't last much longer.

"I want you to listen to me. Listen closely. Duck Andrews drew on me, so I had to finish him. He's been helping Little Paris all along, right from the start. It's just you and me now."

"LP's not alone," Agent Alexander calls out. "I think Kara Grace is in there, too." She pauses. "And the boy."

He knows that . . . just like he knows that's why she's being so careful with Little Paris now, even though her partner is down.

The only reason.

That little boy . . . maybe Kara too . . . is the only thing keeping her from rushing the room, whether Little Paris kills her or not.

It makes their already impossible situation a hell of a lot harder.

"Okay . . . okay . . . but he's got no way out of there that I know of. He's not coming out and we're not going in, right? So we're all stuck. We're all just going to sit here while I call for help."

But Paul's already decided help's not coming. Not for him. Not for Little Paris.

"Oh, I already did that," she says. "You hear that, motherfucker?" She's yelling across the lot at Little Paris, anger boiling in her voice. "I'm dropping the whole world on your fucking head."

It's possible she's bluffing, but Paul has no way to be sure or how much time he has left if she's not.

And now a third voice adds to their weird chorus—

Little Paris, suddenly laughing.

"I got this bitch in here with me. You so much as shine a light this way, I'm poppin' her."

He sounds high, *wasping* again, like he was earlier today. Crazy, screaming to even hear himself, because his ears are nearly blown out from the thunderclaps and lightning of his gun going off again and again in the close confines of that old room.

"You're not going to do that," Paul says. "You hear me? They're all gone. All of them. Jamison. Ricky. Your daddy. The Mexicans you double-crossed killed nearly everyone you ever cared about, and that's on *you*.

"So it's just you now. You and that boy. That's all you got left in this whole world. Isn't that what you said to me? He's going to run these mountains one day? Even if you walk out of here tonight, how far are the two of you going to go? Where are you going to go? You just shot up the only people who were even trying to help you, save you, and that's on you, too. This ends right now."

Silence drifts over the Tamarack.

The only sound wind.

But . . . it's enough to mask Paul's movements as he edges inch by inch down the wall toward Little Paris's room.

Little Paris suddenly screams. "I heard all that. I did. And you know what else I done heard? That Mary's gone too, Paul. Gone. I told you to be careful with that shit with her, but maybe you didn't wanna be so careful? Maybe that's why you're here now? You didn't show up to help me, to save me or the boy, because we both know you don't give two shits about us at all.

"You're here to finish what you started. Bury all your damn dirty secrets."

Paul stops about fifteen feet down from Little Paris's room. He doesn't answer, doesn't want to give away his movement.

Little Paris, high as a kite, might not notice either way, but Agent Alexander most certainly will, if she hasn't already.

Paul can finally see Van Dorn laid out in the gravel and weeds. Not even an hour ago, he was sitting in his home, sharing a tumbler of whiskey, talking about Marissa.

Van Dorn came to her one and only dinner party and he was so gracious to her.

None of this is what Paul wanted.

And unbelievably, the man's not quite done. Somehow, he's still moving, bloody fingers scratching away at the gravel, inching toward Little Paris's hideout, just like Paul.

He's a tough sonofabitch, not ready to give up the ghost yet, but not much longer for this world.

Now there's another change in the darkness across the parking lot, a not-so-subtle shift in the shadows—

Agent Alexander, low-crawling from her corner of the motel, making her way toward Little Paris's hideout, too. She's in the open, exposed, hoping to take advantage of the night and Paul's back and forth with Little Paris to cover her own final attempt to end this.

Despite Kara and Hardy Glasser, she can't play it safe anymore while Van Dorn bleeds out in front of her. Can't let Little Paris use that other woman and little boy as shields.

Won't let Paul hold all their lives in his hands.

Paul wants to call out to her, to wave her the hell back, but now that she's committed, she won't stop. He spent less than an hour with her and already knows that much about her.

So he's sprinting those last few feet too, racing her, giving up all attempts at stealth.

Remington held up high.

He's just about to turn the corner into Little Paris's room and whatever's beyond when someone runs out into his arms.

114

It's Kara Grace, all spinning arms and legs. Just like he saw her the last night he was here, when she was standing in the rain outside his truck window.

You don't want to be here. You really don't. It's not smart. Not safe.

It isn't.

He wants to slow it all down and ask her about Hardy, about her own young boy again.

Who's watching him now?

But everything is going so fast, and now she's screaming, clawing at him, and all he can do is knock her out of his way before they get tangled up in each other. Little Paris is a pale ghost behind her, rising fast . . . *We're all ghosts* . . . using her frail body for cover. He's got a long gun tucked in close to his body, an ugly carbine.

His eyes are bright like earlier today.

Incandescent.

Little Paris opens fire, sending spent shells flipping end over end over his shoulder.

Spinning like all of Dr. Farris's coins.

Heads you win, tails you lose.

Little Paris blasts blindly right through the swinging door, right through the paper-thin motel walls, and right through Kara herself.

But Paul dances with her, gets her behind him, shielding her body with his own.

The Remington is shot clean out of his hands, but he grabs for his Colt in his waistband, still walking forward, right into Little Paris's full fury. He's numb from the neck down, weightless, and nothing below that is working quite right. Nothing's connected like it's supposed to be.

His legs turn on their own, churning forward, and he has no control over them.

Momentum alone carries him into the blasted room.

His Colt goes off, muzzle flash bright as the sun. It knocks Little Paris backward, down to his knees.

It booms and booms and booms in the close quarters and the whole hotel shakes.

Dawn's still an hour away but the Tamarack is suddenly bright as day.

115

Of course, he'd watched her shoot up before. Between her toes, usually. He knew how she did it but had never helped her.

She didn't pay close attention when he gave her one of the bags he bought from Little Paris, just thanked him and curled up on the couch like she normally did.

Weighed out her usual dose. Got her needle and spoon— one from that new set of silverware he bought right after they were married—that they used for the first time at their one and only dinner party.

The spoon blackened at the bottom from her lighter.

She told him not to watch her. She always told him that.

So he got up, went into their bedroom, and lay down on their bed.

Maybe half, even a quarter, of what she's used to.

That's what Little Paris had said.

You tell her that . . .

But Paul didn't tell her anything at all.

That's some powerful shit right there, like holding a bomb in your hand.

He wasn't even there as she gently, carefully, weighed out the powder on her spoon and held it over the bright, flickering flame.

116

Little Paris is still trying to get up even as Paul falls in front of him, rolling to a stop at his knees.

He crawls up Little Paris's body, hands grabbing at Little Paris's throat as the other man bats them away. There's blood all over them both, mingling together.

It's in Paul's face, his eyes.

Little Paris is now talking to Paul, still running his goddamn mouth, but Paul can't hear a thing. He's underwater, floating below the Big Sandy. Every sound is muffled and far away. The only world he knows is muted.

I am the river.

Now, somehow, Little Paris has wrestled Paul's Colt from him. It's there in his hand, and he's cocking back the hammer.

Paul will never know this, but to his own blown-out ears, it's no louder than a lighter flicked beneath a silver spoon.

Little Paris holds Paul's head to his chest as they rock gently together, and he puts the Colt to his temple.

It's cool to the touch and Paul welcomes it.

And then, finally, he sees the boy.

117

He came out of their bedroom room four hours later to find her still curled up on the couch.

Cool to the touch.

He put everything in a bag and carried her down to the river.

He walked her out into the water and five, six yards, from shore, let the bag go first into the slow-moving current. It was weighted down with the needle and the spoon and the lighter and the last of Little Paris's stamp bags and the remaining unused Narcan Dobie had given him and six rocks he'd pulled from the planters by the house.

It sank, disappeared, and was gone.

Then he walked a little farther, waited until the river was almost neck deep, and finally let her go, too.

He watches her turn in the water.

Watches her turn and turn, and she looks like a flower floating on the surface. Like she's sleeping, and in a way, she is.

Good night. Sleep well. Sweet dreams.

She turns and turns.

And as she does, he turns to head back to the house to change his clothes and make the call.

118

Little Paris buckles, then explodes all over him.

And as he tumbles, finally falls, letting Paul go and dropping Paul's Colt, Agent Alexander shoots him again from where she's crouched by the open motel door.

Down on one knee, perfect firing stance.

Even though Paul's eyes are open, still fluttering and watching her watch him, they both know he's too far gone to save.

She doesn't bother to come check on either of them but leaves them both to their dying . . . their final reckoning . . . turning her attention instead to the little boy curled in the corner near the bed.

To the living.

He's got his ears covered, trying to make it all go away. There's a toy six-gun on the floor in front of him, all broken in two, where Little Paris stepped on it with his boots, and he's surround by dozens of spent shells and drifting muzzle smoke.

Agent Alexander holsters her weapon and walks over and scoops him up and he holds her tight as she carries him outside.

But then, somehow, some goddamn way, Little Paris is moving again. Shot a half-dozen times yet still alive, the crank still coursing through his system, still trying to rise to his feet with the gun in his hand again and there's not a damn thing Paul can do about it.

The meth and bug spray lights Little Paris all up from the inside and he's horrible. A dancing, smiling skeleton.

DOA.

Paul wants to call out to her, to warn her, ready to make one more devil's deal to save her, but he has no strength, no voice.

Thank God, it's a miracle anyway—

As Little Paris holds his shot for a moment too long, barely a heart-beat, unwilling to hit his own boy, Jon Dorado suddenly appears out of the darkness in front of him, a gun of his own raised high.

Come home at last.

No, not Jon.

Trey.

His boy, who looks so much like him.

Trey's single shot is wild, unpracticed, but the tumbling bullet strikes Little Paris between his left eye and that awful bloody grin of his and shears the top quarter of his head clean off.

He falls limp one final time and then, mercifully, it truly is done.

A miracle.

Paul rolls over, done as well, and closes his eyes.

Where he dreams about *her.*

Donna.

Marissa.

Kara Grace in the rain and young Carolina Arsenault with flowers in her blond hair.

One woman's laugh, another's smile.

A kiss.

A touch.

A heartbeat.

She's light, and for this final time, he'll follow her out of this dark place.

He waits for the light again.

A new day dawning.

That bright, bright light, to finally take him home.

AFTERMATH

CASEY

Casey remembers lights—

The lights of Trey and Dobie's van, strobing over the parking lot of the Tamarack.

The bright muzzle flash of Trey's gun when he shoots Little Paris Glasser.

She and Trey stand together at Paul Mayfield's funeral.

It's windy, warm. There are six hundred people here, maybe more. All of Angel and Martin County.

Trey told her for all the dead he's seen, he's never been to an actual funeral.

He's uncomfortable in his new suit, eyes straight ahead. Blinking in the sunlight.

The bagpiper starts playing "Amazing Grace" and it's haunting, a sound like no other.

Casey's heard it at every law enforcement funeral and memorial she's ever been to.

It was played for Special Agent Devon Jeon.

She cried then.

She doesn't cry now.

⸙

There's still a lot they don't know, that they may never know.

But that's okay.

They start every case looking for the answers, seeking some sort of justice. You never figure it all out, because their investigations are like life itself, messy and incomplete and full of contradictions.

Like people.

Sometimes there are no answers. But sometimes you can still find justice.

They worked the phones, all the pings and traces. But it was a ballistics match from the spent shells in Lower Wolf that led them to a shooting only two days later in Fairfax County, Virginia, involving an MS-13 clique just outside Washington, D.C.

They still can't directly tie the marero in that case, Noel "Joker" Martinez, to Lower Wolf, but they did link a gun found under his bed to several of the people killed there.

He is seventeen years old.

They also learned of a young, deceased Hispanic male at Three Rivers Hospital.

He was dropped off unattended in the parking lot in the dead of night, only hours after the attack at Lower Wolf.

Already dead from acute fentanyl exposure.

———

Casey and DEA's intel folks spent days running through Janelle Dix's phone, backtracking through all her calls.

Their best guess is that in the months following Jerry's disappearance, she took over for her brother, making those rest stop meets with the Glassers' Mexican suppliers just the way he used to. Maybe she did it only because she needed the money to raise his daughter—she didn't have a choice, either—but Casey believes it was more than that.

Revenge.

In the end, Janelle Dix was a much better snitch than her brother and sold out the Glassers to the Mexicans they'd cheated one too many times.

Wasn't it your goddamn job to protect him?

What the fuck are you going to do now?

Janelle—Country Girl, with all her tattoos—refused to let her twin brother go unavenged, and curiously enough, Paul Mayfield may have said it best—

Blood is thicker than water.

And sometimes blood is all that matters.

Sometimes it's all you have.

Casey started her own tattoo a few days ago—a Mexican bird of paradise on her left shoulder, bright red roses winding around her right, guarded by thorns.

It's going to take a while to finish, and every time the artist works on it, she slips in her earbuds and listens to that damn Jason Aldean song on repeat.

It's kind of even grown on her.

Her tattoo is so fresh, so new, it still bleeds.

Baby Lucy was placed with her real mother, Holly Dix-Mudd, over in Chillicothe, Ohio.

Being raised mostly by Holly's older sister, Margaret, since Holly and her new husband, Turner Mudd, just entered court-ordered rehab for the second time.

It was either that or go to jail, and they both took the fifteen-day inpatient stay for opioid addiction.

Casey anonymously sent over a huge box of new baby clothes and toys and diapers, and since she had no idea what to get, she just got everything.

Casey still thinks about her.

About holding her.

That soft, tiny heartbeat next to hers.

Casey spent hours of her own winding her way through Anna's and Kara's toll records, as well as Duck Andrews's and Marissa and Paul Mayfield's.

Not to mention those of Deputy Arnold Buechel, the buzz-cut kid who took them out to Renfro's trailer.

And Sheriff Malcolm Dunn.

They all told a slightly different version of the same story: all the connections and missed opportunities and the web that bound them all together, with Little Paris Glasser lurking at the heart of it.

While she and Van Dorn were sitting with Mayfield at his home on the Point, Little Paris was using Kara's phone to contact both Mayfield or Marissa, seeking Mayfield's help after years of kickbacks and payoffs.

At the same time, Duck Andrews was also trying to reach Little Paris, and that's when Little Paris learned Marissa was already dead.

But there was also a single text from Marissa's phone to Little Paris *before* the Lower Wolf murders, roughly 9:00 a.m.

The shootings started in earnest at or about 10:30 a.m.

And although she'll never prove it, Casey *knows* that lone text was Mayfield using his wife's phone to arrange a meeting with Little Paris, and that it was probably the ex-chief himself who met him afterward. He was scoring for her the same way Trey had been stealing it for his mother—

Anything to keep them both off the street and away from Little Paris.

Mayfield inadvertently saved Little Paris's life, for at least a few more hours, and probably saved Hardy Glasser's young life then, too.

Casey learned about Marissa's other overdoses and the Narcan supply Dobie gave Mayfield after the first one, so it's reasonable to assume that if Marissa did get a hold of Little Paris's DOA stamp bags, Mayfield had the knowledge and ability to save his wife.

He'd probably done it before. Dobie knew that too, when they found her body in the river.

But Dobie still wants to believe she killed herself with some sleeping pills when she could have just as easily done it with the drugs she favored; that she somehow willingly walked into that water that had always terrified her on her own. That's how he needs to remember her, and, more important, that's how he wants to remember his friend, Paul Mayfield.

Call it murder, call it an act of mercy, but Mayfield let Marissa inject herself with Little Paris's fentanyl-laced heroin and then stood by and let her die.

And you know what else I done heard? That Mary's gone too, Paul. Gone. I told you to be careful with that shit with her, but maybe you didn't wanna be so careful?

But Trey Dorado also knew how just dangerous those little danc-ing skeletons were too, so maybe she can't blame either of them.

Marissa's gone, and Duck Andrews and Little Paris are dead, and Paul Mayfield's being buried as a hero.

Because that's how Angel wants to remember him.

They couldn't positively ID the teeth from the torched Mustang.

Just another Hispanic male, about twenty years old.

No medical examiner, certainly not Angel's Marv Watkins, would say exactly when or how he died.

But FBI Agent Feur, in conjunction with the Kentucky State Police, filed abuse-of-a-corpse charges against Deputy Buechel, who finally admitted putting the body in the car and setting it on fire.

The sun-bloated corpse had been given to him by Little Paris.

Agent Feur also filed federal corruption charges against Martin County sheriff Malcolm Dunn.

And for all the talk of blood and family, there was no one willing to take in Harmon "Hardy" Glasser, the three-year-old son of Carolina Arsenault and Little Paris . . . or possibly Danny Glasser.

He was turned over to the Out of Home Care Branch of the Kentucky Cabinet for Health and Family Services, the same foster system that took in a young Dobie Timmons when his parents were killed.

Casey's heard that Dobie's taken a real interest in helping the boy and may legally foster him.

After all, he knows just how hard it is to grow up without family.

Like she sent to Lucy Dix, Casey sends anonymous care packages: clothes and other things.

But no toy guns.

———

There was just one last issue.

That gun—the SIG Sauer—that Trey shot Little Paris with.

Casey claimed she pulled the trigger. She said she took that gun off Trey earlier in the evening and just never relinquished it. That proved fortunate, since she'd already shot her own Glock dry, and needed that last SIG round to finish Little Paris off.

Obviously, during the post-shooting interviews, she admitted she should've checked his body, just to be sure she'd *stopped the threat*, but she'd been more concerned about saving the little boy and her partner and Kara Grace.

No one blamed her.

Fortunately, no one thought to match the ballistics of that SIG, the same one Jon Dorado Senior bought once upon a time at the Fire Power Gun Show in Charleston, to the gun that killed Danny Glasser.

And just to make sure no one ever did, she asked ATF agent Roderick Bell to shift a few reports around. Maybe even lose them altogether.

And he did.

⁕

As the service winds down, she and Trey walk away on their own.

He's finally cut his hair and it makes him look older, serious.

They stand in the long, cool shade of a tree and she can't help but wonder if it's a tamarack. She still has no fucking idea what one looks like.

The crowd mills around, but she picks out Dobie, walking back to his Angelcare Rescue van alone.

He waves at her and keeps on going. He lied right along with her about who fired that last shot into Little Paris. He agreed that she took Trey's gun from him earlier in the night and never gave it back to him.

That's all she could ever ask of him, so she waves back and then he's gone.

"How is Mr. Van Dorn?" Trey asks.

"A mess," Casey says. "Mostly pissed off he's still in the hospital. But at least he's alive."

She doesn't tell Trey just how bad Van Dorn was really hurt. His armored vest saved him, but barely. But if Dobie and Trey hadn't shown up when they did, if Trey hadn't gotten her text and decided to roll out there, Van Dorn would likely have died anyway.

She might have died too, if Little Paris had got that final shot off.

Trey and Dobie saved both her and her partner's life, keeping Van Dorn alive long enough for a chopper to airlift him out. His recovery is still going to be long and arduous, and she knows a thing or two about long, hard recoveries.

He'll end up retiring before he's ever healthy enough to make another case.

She goes to the hospital every morning and brings him a cup of coffee from that place he likes—black, with no sugar or cream, in the cheap foam cup with the plastic lid—along with both *The Wall Street Journal* and *The New York Times*. Every day she's been there at least one of his ex-wives has been there too, as well as his son—Brandon.

He's smart and funny and incredibly nice and most of the time you wouldn't know from looking at him everything he's gone through and everything he's put his family through.

But every now and then, when you look into his eyes, you can see how they're worn and lined at the corners for someone still so young, like he's carrying these tiny little scars.

Battles he's lost and won.

Van Dorn's been chatting up the day nurse, flirting away, even though Casey keeps telling him he can't afford another ex-wife.

"How about your mom?" Casey asks Trey.

"She's over at Karen's Place. Thank you for that. It's going okay, I guess. We'll see, you know?" Trey shrugs, and like his haircut, the gesture looks older on him now. Casey helped Trey get Renée Dorado admitted to Karen's Place, that clinic by Yatesville Lake, close to where Little Paris's ruined Mustang was found. She's paying for the stay for however long it takes. And none of them—Trey, Casey, nor Renée Dorado herself—have any idea how long that will be.

Trey's smart enough to hold on to hope cautiously, loosely.

"How about school?"

"I got that application in with Berea. I had an interview." Berea College is a small liberal arts school outside of Lexington, nationally known for helping low-income eastern Kentucky students.

"You talk to your dad?"

"Yeah," Trey says. "I did. I'm heading out to Austin next week. I'll spend a couple of days with him, see how it goes. I don't know."

"You don't have to know. Just do it." She looks up through the branches at the sun. "You going to catch that band you like?"

"Oh, American Vampires? I think they broke up. Most bands do." He puts his hands in his suit coat pockets. "Another artist I used to listen to just died. A drug overdose, right on his tour bus, out in Arizona." He knows she lived out west, and now he shakes his head. "I'm still working on my own stuff, but it's all different now. Have you heard of Black Stone Cherry? They're from Kentucky. I like them. My dad said UT Austin has a great music program, but I'm not ready for that, and he knows it. Neither of us are." Trey joins her, looking up through the same branches above them. At the same sun. "I've never heard that version of 'Amazing Grace.' It was beautiful."

"Yes, it is. It always is."

Trey turns back to her. "How about you? What happens next?"

"I don't know," she says.

He smiles. "You don't have to know. Just do it, right?"

"Right." She laughs. "I'm home."

And then she surprises them both by reaching out and hugging him tight.

She does it so he can't see her finally cry.

KARA

Kara knows who the woman is. They're not in group therapy together, but she's always out here on the back deck after dinner, painting.

The pictures are beautiful, like the ones you might see in a fancy store or hanging in a museum, although Kara's only seen a museum in the movies. The woman paints the nearby lake and the surrounding woods. The recovery center itself.

Some look like self-portraits or her family.

A son.

A man who might be her husband.

Kara can't imagine how she does that, making something out of nothing.

It's a kind of magic.

There's so much she doesn't remember or even want to remember. OD'ing on the park bench with Duane. The frantic hours after that.

The shoot-out at the motel.

Hardy Glasser.

That woman cop leaning over her.

They say Paul Mayfield saved her life, but that's not the whole truth.

She's since talked with Dobie and Tanya and they told her all about what happened at the park and how Trey Dorado held her hand and told her everything was going to be fine. How later that night he came to her trailer and helped Dillon after she'd left him there all alone, and then brought him safely back to Tanya's and called him every day afterward. Took him out for burgers and bought him some new shirts and a used iPad for his games and even brought him up to Yatesville Lake right through the trees over there and spent a night camping with him.

Spent time with him in a way that no one's spent time with her boy in a long time.

Trey Dorado didn't have to do any of those things, but if a boy she barely knows can reach out and care about her son that way, then his own mama can get her damn act together and do it, too.

After that mess at the Tamarack, the court gave her a choice—jail or here—and she grabbed *here* with both hands.

She's not silly, not stupid. She knows there's a long uphill road ahead of her. Angel's surrounded by rolling green hills and she's stared at them her whole life and never once imagined what might be on the other side. Never once believed she could get there.

She'll stumble and fall, but, God willing, she'll get up again. Or die trying.

For Dillon's sake. For her own.

This woman knows all about those hills too, and just how high they can be, and maybe they can help each other get to the top.

From up there, you can see the whole world.

Kara approaches, and when the woman sees her, she takes out her earbuds. She was listening to music while painting.

She's older, pretty. Her eyes are clear, focused, and that's the amazing thing about everyone here. Their eyes are clear and bright and alive.

They see.

And now, so do I.

"Hi, I'm really, really sorry to bother you. My name's Kara."

The woman sets aside her brush. The painting is far from finished and it's still too early to tell what it is, what it might become, just some faint lines on the blank paper hinting at so many possible things.

Like promises.

"Nice to meet you, Kara. I'm Renée."

"I know. I've been wanting to talk to you. I wanted to tell you that I think your son, Trey, saved my life. It's all mixed up, kind of hard to explain, but I would probably not be standing here now if it wasn't for him."

Renée smiles and it's bright as the sun.

"Well, Kara, I think that makes two of us."

Renée Dorado picks up her brush and grabs another for Kara Grace.

"Here, let's work on this together for a while."

ACKNOWLEDGMENTS

Thanks to:

My ever patient and wise editor, Sara, and all the amazing folks at Putnam who've continued to support me through four books now.

The Wonder Twins duo of Carlie Webber and Holly Frederick, the best agents any author could ask for.

Delcia . . . although this story wasn't hard to write, the path to get here took a little longer than either of us are used to. *All the stars are yours.*

Madeleine, Lily, and Lucy.

All my far-flung family and friends who put up with this nonsense.

Jesse Donaldson . . . whose wonderful book *On Homesickness* reminded me just how much I missed *my* home.

Chad, Randall, and Boyd . . . for riding the range and keeping The Far Empty alive.

DEA's Phoenix Division HEAT . . . there are far too many agents and analysts to name (I'm likely to forget a few, but you know who you are), but I will single out Phoenix FIM Kim P., who worked as hard as anyone to make our vision of HEAT a reality; as well as SAC Douglas Coleman and the entire Phoenix Division executive staff and all the enforcement group supervisors I was fortunate enough to work so closely with—and learn from—during my tenure there.

And one final note—

This book is a work of fiction, but it does draw more than a little inspiration from very real events and issues surrounding the well-reported opioid crisis. However, I would never claim to be an expert. I'm not a politician or a policy maker or a clinician. I'm merely an agent with a badge and a gun, and this story reflects *my* experiences, having seen the problem up close and personal for far too long.

But mine is just one view.

At the time I was writing this, more than 130 people were dying every day from opioid-related drug overdoses.